# The Queen of Dreams and Dust

## Dreams of Faerie Book Two

Grace Carlisle

Moth & Crown Press

Copyright ©2025 by Grace Carlisle

Published by Moth & Crown Press

Cover designed by Spurwing Creative.



Paperback ISBN: 978-1-971568-02-7

eBook ISBN: 978-1-971568-03-4

# Contents

# Chapter One

"I finally found you," Zach says. He looks the same as when he died—the real him, not the witch's wooden doll—a teenager who'd only just started growing into his frame, face tan and hair bleached almost blond from the sun. His throat is cut open, exposing layers of skin, fat, and muscle, though the blood spilling over his shirt is long dry. He studies me amiably, his smile crooked. He has a zit on his chin.

"Now I'm talking to myself," I say. "Of course I'd start talking to myself." Zach and I stand at the beginning of a hallway, the end of which vanishes into the distance. Doors line both sides, crammed together with hardly any wall in between. All kinds of doors. The door to Grandma's house. The door to the shed. The door to Zach's room.

"You're talking to me." Zach sounds indignant.

"And you're not real, because Zach died seven years ago. I just dreamed you up, like everything else here."

Zach. The hallway. The doors. All of it a decorative finish atop the workshop of my mind trying to reclaim the memories of my human childhood while I sleep. It's how all my dreams have been since I broke the prison that once held Leithe. And part of myself, I guess. Since then, I always know when I'm dreaming, which means I'm never really asleep, never really resting.

"If you say so." He steps past me and pushes open Grandma's front door; beyond is a scene from forever ago. The memory settles back into my brain: Zach and I sit on the floor and categorize our Halloween candy while Grandma and Zach's parents chat, beers in hand. Zach was a skeleton.

Zach wanders off and opens another door. And another. Fragments of memories play out before my eyes: my tenth birthday party where the only kids who came were Zach and a girl named Samantha who told everyone at school she'd been a horse in a past life. We were friends because I was the only one who genuinely believed her.

Beyond the next door, Zach's father teaches us to drive his pickup truck when we were thirteen. Brent Foster found it hilarious that I picked up shifting gears faster than Zach even though I was a girl, and at the time I took it as a compliment.

Each mundane memory of my childhood with Zach is another nail driven into my skin.

"If you made me, I could look like anything you wanted. I could be from any of these moments," Zach says. "So why this?" He gestures to his neck.

That answer is easy. "It's the last time I saw you. The real you."

"That's not a reason." He opens another door. The memory beyond isn't new. It finds its way to me every night. The other side is illuminated only by what moonlight sneaks past the forest canopy. We watch ourselves limp over moss and roots.

"I don't want to see this again," I say.

"Then close the door," he says.

I don't close the door. I watch myself lead Zach to Thistledown. To his death. I watch myself scream, cry, beg. I watch Thistledown slit his throat and leave. And I watch Zach die.

"I'm sorry." The words come out as barely more than a whisper.

"About what?" Zach asks.

"I killed you," I say. "I wanted to save Hunter, or maybe I just wanted to win. Either way, you paid for it."

The hallway dims and shudders. Zach's eyes glint in the gloom. "You wanted to save *Hunter*."

"But I didn't save anyone," I say. If I'd been better. If I'd listened to Hunter. If I'd made it through the prison sooner. If I'd been able to stop Thistledown. If I'd been able to do anything but sit and scream. There are countless ifs.

Pieces of the world flake off, leaving behind gaps where early morning light seeps through. I'm waking up. "No," I say. "I don't want you to go. I want you to stay."

Very gently, he takes my hands in his. "Then you should have chosen me."

The drone of the window AC unit drowns out the remains of the dream—a static, unchanging noise that reminds me that I'm awake, along with my sweat-soaked sheets. My bedroom is cast in gray, predawn light.

Zach is gone. Zach is dead. Has been for years, though he's only been officially missing for a month.

If I roll over and close my eyes, I'll once again be kneeling on that patch of blood-soaked dirt.

So I get up. Force myself to cross the hall to the bathroom, where a face that's supposed to be mine stares back from the mirror. It's framed by hair that falls nearly to my hips. Hair I didn't have a month ago. It's missing the tiny crescent scar that once sat above my eyebrow from when I tripped face-first into the kitchen counter when I was nine.

This body isn't the one I grew up in. It's the one that was trapped within the prison tree. Mab's body. The body I wore for over twenty years vanished where it fell from the kelpie's back when Hunter shot me. A tool meant for me to use and discard, just like the thing the witch made of blood and twigs and magic and left in Zach's place. A *fetch*, Leithe had called it.

It was a well-constructed fake. But the freckles that used to dot my knuckles are gone, as are all other marks, blemishes, and old scars accumulated through the course of a life. This new skin is flawless, marked only by the faintest tracery of the veins beneath.

I want to peel it off.

In a burst of savage energy, I yank open the medicine cabinet, take the scissors, and saw off a fistful of hair before throwing the scissors into the sink and hissing in pain. My fingers are red and raw where they made contact with the metal. The stench of burning hair fills the small room. Where the scissors touched, the strands are blackened and curling at the tips.

Half my face is framed by hair that falls in uneven chunks nearly to my shoulders, while the hair on the other side vanishes past the lower edge of the mirror.

I want it gone. Using a hand towel, I take the scissors again, wrap the rest of my hair around my fist at the back of my head, and hack it off.

It looks terrible. The left side is shorter than the right and the back is far shorter than the front. But at least it's something I did myself.

I throw my hair in the trash and rinse my head under the sink to get rid of the burning smell before I go downstairs.

In the living room, Cheeps is perched on the windowsill, staring intensely outside. He doesn't react when I look out over his head. A lone squirrel sits on a low-hanging branch and screams indignantly at something I can't see, tail lashing. Cheeps hates squirrels. That's all it is.

There's nothing else outside. The movement on the ground in the corner of my eye is just the shadow of a branch swaying in the breeze. No faeries. No monsters. No matter what I think I see in the trees at night. No matter how often I consider sneaking Grandma's rifle up to my bedroom.

I take a breath. Force myself to relax. There's nothing outside.

"What are you looking at?" Grandma asks from her armchair.

I jump at her voice. "Squirrels." She gives me a skeptical look, but doesn't push.

"You're up early," she says, coffee mug clutched in her hands. "There's coffee."

"So are you." I fill a mug from the carafe. The bitter coffee lacks the acrid tang of metal that's present in everything Grandma cooks, every dish she uses being cast iron or stainless steel. The smell permeates the house. It makes my nose burn and skin prickle.

Even with the stench of iron hanging in the air killing my appetite, my stomach growls. It hasn't stopped growling since I got this new body. But nothing I eat dulls the pain.

"Bad dreams," she says.

"What kind of dreams?" I ask before I can stop myself. If Grandma remembers that night in the hospital when I tried to tell her the truth, she's never said so. It's simultaneously a relief and a disappointment.

She purses her lips. "Do you want me to even out your hair?"

"No," I say quickly. Too quickly.

"Hm," she says. Her go-to phrase to indicate she's suspicious but choosing not to ask. She hasn't confronted me for answers, not about how my hair grew three feet or why I only use plastic utensils now. I've run through scenarios in my head of telling her the truth. She usually calls me a monster. A murderer. Accuses me of taking the place of her real grandchild. I imagine the scraps of goodwill we'd just managed to cobble together going up in smoke.

Telling her would also mean whatever protection fae laws provide to humans would no longer apply to her. So I tell myself hiding the truth is for her sake and not my own cowardice.

"They're pausing the search for Zach," Grandma says. The sensation of the town of Shrike Run for the past month. There hasn't been anything this interesting here in years. They'd interviewed all the neighbors at this point. A journalist came by to interview me after a picture the Fosters must have supplied ended up in a human-interest profile on Zach for the local paper. Grandma headed them off, wouldn't let them speak to me.

"Oh." She stares at me. That wasn't the right response. I have to sound interested. Invested, like I think there's a chance they'll find something. "Why?"

"Molly called me late last night." Grandma and Zach's mom have been talking every day since his disappearance. "Do you remember Grant Stanley?"

I think. "He was our elementary school P.E. teacher."

"He got separated from the search party yesterday afternoon. They found his body in the creek a few hours later." The creek.

"What killed him?" A dull roar begins at the base of my skull. I already know what Grandma is going to say.

"An animal. He'd been ..." Grandma's mouth scrunches up in disgust. "He'd been partially eaten." By the creek. "Molly knows the medical examiner's wife, and she says he's confused as hell because the bite marks look more like an *alligator* than anything we've got around here. They're wondering if it ..." She hesitates. "If it might be the same thing that ..."

I press my face into my hands. "Okay, I get it!"

"I'm sorry," Grandma says, to my surprise. "That was morbid. I shouldn't have gone into detail."

"It's not you. I'm sorry." It's me. I might as well have killed that man. I pulled the arrow out of the kelpie's jaw and left him free.

"Molly's coming over for coffee in a bit," Grandma says, frowning. "Brent's been fishing most mornings, looking for an excuse to be out of the house, probably, and I don't think she likes being alone right now. Don't tell her I told you, but she's been having awful nightmares. Not sleeping at all."

"Got it." I understand the warning in her words: *pretend to be normal in front of Zach's mom. She's been through enough.*

"How's your job search going?" she asks.

"Nothing yet." Nothing I can do that won't require regular contact with metal. Iron worked by human hands, Leithe explained, including iron alloys, burns fae. And iron is everywhere. It was already hard enough to get a job with no college degree, and now I need to find one that won't burn me alive. *Alleged Faerie Queen* isn't a fit on most resumes.

I take a breath before I launch into the next subject. "I did find some houses online, though. Have you ever thought about Vermont? Washington State?"

She frowns. "We talked about this."

"Seattle is pretty. Or what about Oregon? There's trees there. You could find a place that's just like here." And they're on the other side of the country.

"I'm not moving, Tamsin," Grandma says. "I've been here for forty years and I plan to die here." I must flinch, because her expression softens. "Not that I plan on dying anytime soon."

"What about just into the city? You know, you might want to move closer to civilization soon, so you won't need to drive as much." Do faeries live in cities? How much iron does a place need to be laced with to keep them away?

"Child, I am not even seventy," Grandma snaps. "What is so wrong with this house?"

When a house is haunted, the smart thing to do is move. When your house is in the middle of a faerie-infested forest, the same concept should apply, not that I can say that. "It's just ... there's a lot of memories here. And with Zach

..." I let the words hang. Grandma sighs, and I feel like a monster.

"I understand, but we can't just up and leave while the Fosters are going through this. It's not right." She contemplates her coffee. "I'm not kicking you out, but you know you don't have to stay here, don't you? I'm doing so much better it's throwing the doctor for a loop. You can go back to Boston, if you want."

I can't go back to Boston. My former roommates hate me for breaking my lease and my meager savings were wiped out on the penalties for doing so. But I could still leave. I could sleep on a couch if I was lucky. A park bench if I wasn't—as long as it's not made of metal. Either one might be better than staying. Would Faerie chase me and leave Grandma alone, or would leaving be getting her killed?

"Do you want me to leave?" My voice is small. Vulnerable. I hate it.

"No," she says quickly. "I just mean that you should be traveling, dating, partying, doing drugs responsibly, things kids should be doing. You should be living your life, Tamsin, not trying to babysit me." Something on my face must concern her, because she sighs. "I will *think* about thinking about moving. But it's not happening anytime soon." Then it might not be soon enough. She sighs again and looks up from her coffee, making purposeful eye contact with me. "I know ... things have been hard for you." By the window, Cheeps starts growling deep in his throat like a cat. I whip my head around to look. "*Tamsin*," Grandma says indignantly. "I am trying to say something important."

"Sorry." I focus on her.

She sighs a third time. "I lost Skye twice." This gets my attention. Grandma hates talking about her daughter. My 'mother.' Skye's son, her real child—Grandma's real grandchild—was taken on the orders of the witch who built Mab's prison. I've seen no sign of the witch after my useless attempt last month to get her to tell me what happened to the baby.

Grandma keeps talking; I force myself to concentrate on what she's saying. "Skye left when she turned eighteen because she didn't get along with her father—and me, I shouldn't downplay my role. She came back after she got pregnant, but you know she wasn't ... she wasn't well." Grandma stares at her coffee, a deep line between her brows. "She was convinced ... she kept going on about ..." She trails off, looking for the words. I see the suspicion working its way through her, the threat that she might start putting things together.

"It's okay," I say quickly. "We don't have to talk about it."

"It's not ..." Grandma sighs and gives up. "I don't know if I will ever see her again. I just don't want that to happen to you."

*It won't*, I want to say. But I can't promise that. I don't know what's going to happen. If they come for me, from Grandma's point of view, I'd simply disappear.

# Chapter Two

"WHAT'S WRONG?" I ASK Cheeps after Grandma finishes her coffee and goes to her room to get dressed before Molly arrives.

"Dead things in the trees, Young Miss. Watching us," he says. "They smell. I don't like them." I crouch to his eye level and follow his gaze. Now that he's pointed them out, I notice several birds sitting stock-still in the trees, staring at the house. One, a crow, has a twisted neck and tattered feathers sticking out at odd angles. I only know of one person who can make dead things move around. And I need to talk to him anyway.

"I'll take care of it," I say. I move to go, but Cheeps grabs a lock of my hair in his tiny hands and tugs on it.

"It's court fae," he says, his round, ink-black eyes wide with fear. "The scent of all the creatures that wait under the dirt to reach up and take the dead. The Crawling Court." He tugs on my hair more insistently. "Young Miss, you have not known your nature for long so it is okay if you do not know these things, but the creature you brought home is court fae. Court fae are very very bad. If you anger him, he will eat us all up." When I brought Leithe here briefly after we left the prison, Cheeps hid the entire time. I only saw him again a week after Leithe left. "When the court fae are here, all we can do is wait for them to get bored and leave."

"I don't think he's going to get bored." I'd hoped he would. I thought if I hid in the house, I could wait him out.

*There is nothing here for you*, I'd told him. *I just want to live my life.* And he'd left, but not without telling me how to find him. Every day for the past month, I've thought about going, thought about the questions I'd ask. But I never go. I don't want to give him an inch.

The birds turn their heads in unison to watch me as I leave the house. They follow as I make my way down the driveway, flapping clumsily from branch to branch. I pause at the edge of the yard. For a moment, I consider turning around and getting the rifle, just in case. But I don't think Grandma would let me leave the house with it.

It's just one step, then another. The only monsters in the woods are the ones I'm expecting.

A shiny black Oldsmobile rumbles up the driveway, pulling to a stop next to me. One of the Foster family project cars. If I had any control over the fae ability to vanish from human perception, I'd use it now, as Molly Foster leans across the passenger seat and smiles at me. There are dark bags under her eyes.

"Looks like I just missed you, huh?" she says. "Maybe you'll be around tomorrow? We haven't gotten the chance to catch up since you moved back."

*Because I run away whenever Grandma says you're coming over.* "Tomorrow could work."

"Tomorrow," she says. "You be careful, honey."

Once Molly's car is out of sight, I lean against a tree and breathe until the nausea fades. Every time I see her or her husband, I want to tell them everything. I can't stand the sympathy in their eyes, as if this is a tragedy that *happened* to all of us equally, instead of something I *did*.

The driveway that leads to the old Randall Place is only identifiable as a cut of younger growth curling around the bits of gravel that remain, hedged in on either side by far older trees. Humans haven't lived there since the Randalls died. After that, Hunter made use of it until he returned to Faerie, his duty to watch the prison no longer needed.

Now, the overgrown yard in front of the decrepit three-story house is covered in dead things. Some are intact skeletons—deer, raccoons, lizards and mice fresh enough to still have connective tissue holding their shapes together—thrown together over piles of loose bones and rotting wood. A tree stump as wide as a tractor tire sits on the ground by the porch, roots as thick as my arm sprawling out from its base like the limbs of an octopus. More dead birds perch on the roof. Numerous partially-finished constructs of bone, wood, and chitin lie thankfully inanimate on the ground or draped over the porch banister.

There's no smell of rot as I approach, just age and dirt. Shadows whisper across the ground and around corners. The entire place is colder and darker than it should be on a June morning. No matter how carefully I step, tiny bones or the bodies of insects crunch beneath my shoes. A vague feeling of wrongness settles over me as I get closer; I wonder if that's what keeps the humans away.

"Did someone attack you, or did you do that to your own head?" Leithe asks. I jump in surprise. Seated in the shade of the porch, he blends into the overlapping shadows almost perfectly. A collection of small bones, twigs, and feathers lies splayed out across the rotted planks before him.

My hand goes to my hair before I can stop myself. "It was too long." I cross my arms, trying not to look self-conscious. "Your zombie birds are scaring Cheeps. Keep them away from my house."

Leithe, even while sitting, somehow manages to stare down his nose at me as if I'm one of the many dead bugs scattered across the ground, his yellow eyes glowing in the dim light. "Who's Cheeps?"

"You know who Cheeps is."

He thinks. "The brownie? Tell him to adjust. The birds are guarding you. Lelit certainly knows where you live, since you insisted on letting her servant go." Lelit, one of Queen Mab's vassals and one of the three who betrayed and trapped her in the prison tree.

"I'm going to start sitting on the porch with a rifle. If I can hit the birds, they're too close," I threaten.

Leithe's lip quirks. "If you can get rid of them, I'll concede they're unnecessary." His eyes are the only thing about him with any color. His skin is pale, almost gray. His black hair falls in a perfect sheet past his chest. His robes are also dark, blending seamlessly into the shadows around him—shadows that move on their own. Those robes are made of glamour, hiding the clothes I'd scrounged for him from Grandma's attic. "Your own power would be more effective than human weapons, but you haven't been practicing, have you?"

I haven't. I've thought about it. Of doing silly little things, just to see if I could, like change the color of my shirt or make a twig crawl like an earthworm in an imitation of a trick Hunter once showed me. But I never made it to trying. I don't know if I'm more scared of failure or success.

"I told you before, you're not going to bully me into marrying you, or whatever it is you're doing. I'm not your wife. Fiancée. Whatever," I say. His eyes narrow. He's attractive in a sharp, almost-alien way; his features come together barely enough to appear human. Because he isn't human. And I shouldn't be antagonizing him. For a moment, despite my feigned bravado, I worry my fear shows through. I don't know how far I can push him. It's why I haven't told him what the witch said about Mab's desire for death. If I did, if he didn't think there was a point in waiting for her memories to return, how quickly would he turn on me? The thought doesn't completely bury the twinge of guilt in my chest from the lie.

He idly examines the bones and feathers scattered about, picking them up and setting them down as if looking for something specific. "I cannot understand why you'd rather sit in that house and play at being a human. You refuse to even learn how to shield yourself from worked iron." He gestures at my singed hair. "It's one of the simplest glamours. The brownie could probably teach it to you." A tiny wraith peels itself away from Leithe's shadow and darts into the collection of bones, twigs, and feathers in his palm. They twitch and pull themselves into a skeleton—something between a mouse and lizard, with a sparrow's wings pressed flat across its back. It flutters off his hand and vanishes into the grass.

"Do you have dead rats watching my house, too?" I ask.

"If I did, you couldn't stop me." He crosses his arms. "Are you not the slightest bit interested in what you could do if you tried?"

"I thought this would be over with by now." I veer away from that subject. "I wanted to know the truth. Now I want things to return to normal, but it just keeps going."

Leithe snorts in disgust. "I would think you'd be grateful to learn you're a queen and betrothed to a fae lord."

"Because you're such a catch?" I snap. His expression turns neutral. He stares at me, unnervingly still. My pulse quickens, but that fear only fuels my venom, as if goading him into violence would somehow be a victory. As if his disdain for me would convince him that there's none of Mab in me. I wait, holding his gaze. Holding my breath.

Leithe sighs, life returning to his face again. "What do you plan to do when the courts come for you, then?"

"What I do is none of your business," I say, because I have no answer to that question.

He rises to his feet. "It is, actually, because I'd like to keep you in one piece until your memories come back, and everyone else wants the opposite. Lelit knows we're free, since you insisted on sparing that knight of hers. And folk talk. Enemies will come looking for you: the queen who can't protect herself. You are the most vulnerable a monarch has ever been. *Everyone* will want to take advantage of that."

He takes a step forward. "Some might gamble on your generosity and offer up their service in the hopes of a reward when you're restored to your rightful place. But most are going to take what they can while they can. They'll take you apart while you can't fight back. Some will try to force you into deals, but others won't bother. They'll just eat you. Your flesh, your blood, your bones—they're power, power that others will want for themselves, and right now, there's nothing stopping anyone from taking it." By the time he's finished speaking, he's approached close enough to tower over me.

"Does the height thing usually intimidate people?" I have to look up to see his face.

He rolls his eyes. "Burn the hair you hacked off your head if you haven't already. It could be used against you." He steps back and leans against the wall. "I'm leaving the birds where they are. If that's all you came for, you're welcome to leave." When I hesitate, he adds, "Though it seems you have something else you're going to ask for."

The real reason I came here, before I let myself pick a fight. "I think the kelpie killed someone. A human."

There's a pause as if he's waiting for me to get to the point. "It's probably killed many humans."

"But he promised me he wouldn't kill any innocent humans."

Leithe laughs. "Innocence is subjective. If someone touches you without your permission, is it forgivable because they didn't think they needed to ask? Why would I care how that creature chooses to interpret transgression?"

"But that's ... that's entrapment."

"Obviously." He gives me a calculating stare. "I assume you brought this up because you're going to ask me something."

I shift on my feet. "Could you make him stop killing humans?"

"Oh?" he says airily. "I thought you wanted me to leave."

"Could you make him stop?" I ask again.

He smiles. "So that's why you finally came. After all that bluster, you *need* something from me. That must rankle."

"What, do you want me to say 'please'?" I say, defensive because he's right. Instead of answering, he waits expectantly. "Will you *please* stop the kelpie from killing people?"

"I serve at your convenience." He bows mockingly. "For a price."

"I'll stop complaining about the zombie bird guards?" I offer.

"The last deal we made had you extort me for a wish," he points out. "It would only be fair." A wish. Anything within my power to give.

"No," I say. "Absolutely not." I don't want to know what he'd demand.

"Then best of luck figuring your powers out before the kelpie gets hungry again. Though they're always hungry, you know. Fascinating creatures, really," he says.

"Oh, well." I take a few steps toward the road. "I guess I'll just go ask it nicely to stop eating people. I really hope it doesn't devour my delicious queen flesh. But maybe this is goodbye forever."

"Do you really think threatening to get yourself killed is going to get you your way?" Leithe asks.

"Is it?" I make it maybe twenty feet down the driveway before the temperature suddenly plummets, and I realize with absolute certainty that Leithe is right behind me. His fingers are cold where they settle on my shoulder; the cold spreads across my skin, into my bones, my lungs. I can't move. Can't breathe. I collapse to my knees, unable to support my own weight. I can't force the smallest noise from my throat.

The spell is broken as soon as he lets go. I gulp down lungfuls of air, shivering uncontrollably. "Asshole." It takes a few tries to get the word out through chattering teeth. Any guilt I felt about keeping the truth from him about Mab is gone.

Leithe stands over me, looking unimpressed. "You have so little leverage right now." I look at the ground. He's right. "If you could use your own powers, you wouldn't need my help, you know."

I push myself shakily to my feet, ignoring his offered hand. "Fine. If you stop the kelpie from hurting people, I'll give you a wish. I swear on my last drop of blood." It's my fault it's killing people. I should be willing to pay anything to fix my own mistake. As I say the words, they form a weight that sinks into my chest and rests just above my heart. Palpable, but not painful. A constant reminder of my promise.

Leithe raises an eyebrow. "I expected you to try a little harder to negotiate down, but very well. Let's get this over with."

# Chapter Three

I SHIVER AS WE walk down the winding road toward the creek, slowly massaging feeling back into my arms. "What did you do to me?"

"Pulled a little of your life out," Leithe says. "Not enough to cause any real damage."

"So you could kill someone like that?" I ask. "Just by touching them?"

"Yes," he says. "The kelpie should be little trouble."

"You're going to kill him?" I ask in alarm.

Leithe stops in his tracks, expression exasperated. "Is that not what you wanted me to do?"

"Couldn't you talk to him? You're court fae, right? Cheeps seems to think that makes you important. Wouldn't the kelpie listen to you? I just want him to stop hurting humans."

"People," Leithe says. "You said 'people' before. Which is it?"

"I—It's not fair for the humans. They don't even know what's happening. They don't know the rules."

"Ah," Leithe says. "So it's about sportsmanship. Interesting."

"That's not—" I recall the screeching of the pixies as the kelpie snatched them out of the air in his jaws. "That's not what I meant." I hadn't thought about the fae at all. "Can you tell him not to hurt fae either?"

Leithe raises an eyebrow. "Then what is it supposed to eat?"

"Animals?"

"And if the kelpie refuses to obey?" he asks. "Then what shall I do?"

I'm saved from answering when a faded red SUV whips around the bend in front of us and disappears back the way we came. I scrabble away from the road, though the car came nowhere close to me.

Leithe watches the car with mild interest, and for a moment I hope he forgot his question. "Well?" he asks expectantly after the noise from the car fades.

"Let's ... let's just see what the kelpie says, first," I say.

Leithe snorts. "If you insist."

When we reach the bridge that spans the creek, an old blue pickup truck is parked on the dirt pull off. I want to vomit.

"That's Zach's dad's truck." I can't force away the image of Brent's body lying on the creek bank, waterlogged and mangled.

I pick my way down to the water and start walking upstream, toward where the creek deepens and widens out—a place people sometimes go to fish. Brent only brought us once. I couldn't sit still long enough to catch anything and Zach cried the first time his father shoved a hook through a worm, which made me cry, too.

Rivulets of something dark twist through the otherwise clear water before branching outward like the roots of a tree, splitting and growing thinner and thinner until the red dissipates completely.

No. I'm too late. he's already killed Brent. I run—as if that would make any difference now—following the trail of blood as it meanders downstream.

I slam into something and scream, waiting for the kelpie's jaws to close around my head."Tamsin?" Brent Foster's large hands grip my shoulders. He looks down at me with concern. His hair is darker than his son's and he has a burgeoning beer belly. A beard obscures most of his face. In a few decades, this could have been Zach. "Are you okay? What are you doing out here?" A tackle box and rod lay on the ground near his feet.

"I ... I'm sorry. I saw your truck, and ... I heard there was maybe a bear or something running around, and ..." I trail off. And what? And I came to save him?

He shows me the shotgun slung over his shoulder. "Molly made me bring bear spray, too. I'm not worried."

I almost let out a sigh of relief, then I see what lies in the water beyond him: the body of a large black horse nearly dams the creek; blood, bits of viscera, and water weeds peel off the corpse and drift away with the current.

Most of the kelpie's head is blown away. Wisps of smoke still waft from where bits of shot are embedded in the flesh, now blackened and cracked from the contact with the iron. The smell is horrendous, not just an uncomfortable mix of gunpowder and cooking meat, but the kelpie's innards reek of scum, rot, and stagnant water.

"Did you kill it?" I whisper. Leithe catches up and glares at the scene. He strides past Brent—who doesn't acknowlededge his presence—and stops in front of the kelpie's remains.

Brent follows my gaze and looks blankly at the water. "You okay, sweetheart?" he asks. "You need a ride home?"

His eyes are bloodshot; the skin around them red and puffy. I've known this man my entire life, and I've never seen him shed a tear. Not the time he broke his arm working in the garage; not during the group searches; not during the news interviews; not when someone else might have been watching.

I must stare for too long, because Brent averts his gaze. "Well." He coughs. "The fish keep stealing my bait. I think I'm going to pack up, anyway."

"Wait." Leithe places his hand on Brent's shoulder.

Brent stiffens and turns. "Who—"

"*Be at ease*," Leithe says. "*And tell the truth.*"

"Okay." Brent immediately calms, his eyes glazing over.

"Did you kill anything today?"

"Worms."

"Do you know who killed the beast in the water?"

"What beast?" Brent asks blandly.

"Did you see anything out of the ordinary today?" I ask.

Brent thinks. "You. And the Subaru."

"Subaru?"

"The red Subaru Outback. 2001, probably. It was parked by the bridge when I pulled up. Had out-of-state plates. Thought it might be a journalist or something, but no one was out here."

"*Forget this happened and go home*," Leithe says, releasing Brent's shoulder and flickering back out of mortal sight. Brent blinks several times, then looks around. He looks as if he wants to ask me a question.

"I don't need a ride, but thank you for offering," I say, as if our conversation was never interrupted.

"Right. Well, tell your grandmother hello." With one final, puzzled look around, he quickly makes his way back toward the bridge, as if trying to outrun the feeling that something unexplainable happened.

"What is a 'Subaru'?" Leithe asks once Brent is gone.

"A car. Probably the same one we saw on the way here." I look back toward the bridge. "You didn't have to mess with his head."

"He'll be fine. A few moments under a glamour won't do permanent damage."

"That seemed to be a lot easier for you than it was before." Fresh out of the prison, he'd struggled to glamour human minds at all.

"I've had time to recover." Leithe returns his attention to the kelpie.

"It looks like he was killed with a shotgun," I say. "Do fae use guns?"

He frowns. "No."

I squat on my haunches and force myself to study the ruin more closely, though I don't know what I'm looking for. One of the kelpie's milk-white eyes threatens to spill from his cracked socket.

He was a monster. He tried to kill me. He probably *did* kill Grant Stanley. He's probably killed countless people over the years. Humans and fae.

My first thought is relief. Not just that the kelpie is dead, but that it wasn't because of me. That thought is quickly followed by a wave of self-disgust. As with Thistledown, someone else took care of it for me. I didn't have to pull a trigger, or even hand someone else the gun. I shouldn't be grateful. I shouldn't be relieved that something has died. But I am. And I hate myself for it.

"I have no idea how to find that car." The only lead.

"Why bother?" he says. "The kelpie's dead. Your problem is solved. And if there's a human that thinks it can hunt us, it will come to us eventually. We have more important matters to focus on."

I gesture at the kelpie's body. "They clearly *can* hunt ... us." Us. I stumble over the word.

"No. They can hunt *that*. I'm not concerned." He kneels next to the body, the hem of his robe bubbling with shadows that seep outward as if someone spilled boiling ink on the ground. "This is convenient, regardless." He touches what remains of the kelpie's neck; a piece of the shadows at his feet breaks off and slithers across the ground toward the body, solidifying into the impression of a four-legged animal—a deer, or perhaps a dog—and finally vanishing into the kelpie's remains.

With a shudder, the kelpie's legs jerk into motion. One by one, its limbs prop themselves up and heave the creature's bulk off the ground, wobbling and finding its balance like some grotesque parody of a newborn foal. The kelpie's neck lolls to the side, head barely attached by strips of skin and muscle. Dark, bloody water spills from the pieces of skull still attached to its body. Teeth and other bits of loose bone fall free as it rises and *plink* into the water.

"A shame the head is in so many pieces," Leithe says. "But I can work with this." When it's standing, I can see that another shot blew away a portion of its chest cavity, exposing splintered ribs and dark organs spilling outward. "Head and heart both destroyed. Not necessary to kill a faerie this weak, but I suppose someone wanted to be sure."

"Oh my god." Reality catches back up to me. I turn and run to a nearby tree, doubling over as my breakfast threatens to come back up.

I groan and rest my forehead against the tree trunk. The smell of rancid mud is overbearing, but it's the image of the kelpie's lifeless, unseeing eye that makes bile rise in my throat. But I fight the feeling back and take several deep breaths. I don't want to puke in front of Leithe. *Almost* puking in front of him is bad enough.

After wiping the tears from my eyes, I turn back to Leithe, then look around, confused. "Where did it go?" The kelpie is nowhere to be seen.

"I ordered it to go back to that hovel. It's not much use in pieces, anyway." He picks up a shard of jaw and drops it back into the water in disgust. "What a waste of time."

"Now you're mad because you didn't have to do anything after all?" I ask. As the realization dawns on me, the weight in my chest—the promise—vanishes like a sigh. "Since a mystery party possibly driving a Subaru dealt with the kelpie before you did, the deal's off. No wish for you."

"This doesn't change your real problem," he says petulantly.

I start back toward the road. "Like you said, that's my problem."

Leithe catches up easily. "You're very quick to dismiss me when there's no longer an immediate monster to deal with. Are you that short-sighted?"

"Don't act like you're not using me, that you're here for my own good," I say. "I have no reason to trust anything that comes out of your mouth."

"I *am* here for your own good," he says.

"You're here for *Mab*'s own good. Not mine. You're not my friend. You're just the person I met first. Maybe you're exaggerating this Lelit-and-the-courts stuff to scare me, because it's been over a month and they're not here. Maybe you're just wrong. Maybe they don't know. Maybe they don't care. Maybe we can talk it out." But a knot of worry still squirms in my stomach.

"They *will* come for you, and if you aren't ready, you'll end up in another tree."

"I'm not going to just *get* strong enough to deal with these people just because I *want* to," I snap. "You're all, what, hundreds of years old? Thousands? Old enough that quantifying it is pointless? I'm twenty-one. Am I just going to make a stick move a few times and suddenly be able to kill people with my mind, or whatever you expect me to be able to do?"

"Wanting to would be a good start," he says.

"It doesn't matter what I want to do. It's not going to change anything."

Leithe sighs. "Give me the time it takes for us to walk back to your home, and I'll have the birds fall back to where they won't bother the brownie."

I look at him suspiciously. "What do you want me to do?"

Leithe picks up a small rock. In his hands it becomes an eyeball with a slit, reptilian pupil that rolls in his palm to focus on me. "Turn it into something else."

"How?" I take the glamoured stone from his offering hand. It's wet, and the surface gives slightly against the pressure from my fingers.

"Can you see the threads?" he asks.

If I let my eyes relax until they're nearly unfocused, tiny, dark threads wrapping around the stone-turned-eye come into view. From one angle, it looks like an eyeball, from another, a rock. If I concentrate, it somehow feels like both at the same time, though that quickly makes my head throb. "Yes," I say with some surprise. I tug on the threads until one snaps and the entire thing unravels. The eye becomes a stone once more. "I did it." Suddenly, I don't want to hold the stone anymore. I offer it back to him.

"You have some ability to undo glamour, at least." Leithe doesn't move to take the stone back. "Now try it yourself. Changing one thing into a like form is one of the simplest glamours. It's easier than making something from nothing. Just order it to be something else."

"Um. Be purple." I imagine a deep, royal purple blooming across the rock's surface like paint in water. Nothing happens, except that I feel extremely silly.

I can feel Leithe's annoyed gaze boring into my skull. "Can you feel your power?" he asks.

"What's it supposed to feel like?" I ask. He pauses, frowning, so I continue. "You have no idea how to teach this, do you?"

"You might as well be asking me what it's like to see with my eyes or hear with my ears."

"And you're asking me to see with my ears and hear with my eyes."

Leithe sighs. "You *are* using glamour, or you wouldn't be visible to humans. What does that feel like?"

"I haven't thought about it since I did it the first time. I haven't needed to. It just feels ... normal."

"Hmm." He taps a finger against his chin as he thinks. "Try to do something with the rock again."

"Fine." I look at the rock. "You are a sapphire." It does not become a sapphire.

"Try harder," Leithe says.

I groan and stare harder, imagining the top layer of rock sloughing off and revealing blue facets beneath. Instead, the rock splits open like an egg and the kelpie's head lunges out toward my face, small at first but growing rapidly to its full size, jaws splitting open like an alligator's.

I scream and throw the rock as hard as I can, coincidentally straight at Leithe. He catches it with an unamused expression.

Once I recover, I ask, "Did I do that?" There's hope in my voice. I hate it. I shouldn't be excited. Shouldn't want this. The rock in Leithe's hands looks once more like a rock.

"No," he says. "I did. I thought you might be able to accomplish something on instinct if you felt threatened. Apparently not."

"I was going to apologize for throwing that rock at you," I say. "Now I'm not."

"Perhaps you weren't in enough peril." He tosses the rock back to me. I let it land on the ground.

"Whatever you're thinking, don't."

He sighs. "You're right. It wouldn't help. You need to return to Faerie. The mortal world is too thin for you to recover properly. You need Faerie food and air."

"I'm not going to Faerie with you." I have no doubts he'd never bring me back. "Go back yourself. What I do doesn't need to be your problem."

"I made a commitment that I intend to honor, whether you remember it or not."

"Well, you can go honor your commitments somewhere else. This is my stop." We've reached Grandma's driveway; her house is just out of sight.

He looks down his nose at me. "There's going to be a point where you wish you paid a single mote of attention to what I'm saying." One of Leithe's birds swoops down and lands on his outstretched hand. It croaks; the sound comes out reedy and broken. Much of its face has been eaten clean away. Leithe frowns at the bird. As I turn to make my way up the driveway, he says, "And perhaps that point is now. There's fae at your grandmother's house."

"Who? How many?" Fear. Immediate, shameful fear. I should run to the house. Grandma's there. Cheeps is there. But my feet stay rooted where I am.

"I don't know." He looks at me slyly. My change in attitude must be apparent. "Are you not going to go talk out your differences?" he asks. "You can go hide in that hovel while I deal with this, but I recommend you come with me, in case there are more waiting to ambush you." I stay where I am out of fear, but he seems to take it as my decision to accompany him. "Remember that right now, your best defense is Mab's reputation. She's a monarch; so long as the vultures *think* you are capable of what she was, you'll be safe. Act as if you believe everyone else is beneath your notice." Leithe thinks for a moment. "Actually, just don't talk." He starts toward the house and I follow, in part because I don't want to be left alone—the normal noises of the woods now sound far more threatening.

With each step down Grandma's driveway, I expect monsters worse than the kelpie to appear and run me down. I clamp my hand down on the fabric of my pants to resist grabbing onto Leithe's sleeve like a toddler.

But we reach Grandma's house without issue. Standing in the yard, arms clasped behind his back and a hound at each heel, is Hunter.

# Chapter Four

"Hunter," I say, speaking against Leithe's advice. Hunter's clothes are different—nicer—with a deep emerald cloak and a leather breastplate tooled with roses and serpents twining together. A uniform. He has a bow across his back and a dagger at his waist.

"Your Grace." Hunter bows at the waist. There's nothing but rigid disdain in his eyes when he looks at me. Anything I might have said perishes under that gaze. His hounds remain stock-still, watching Leithe warily. "My lady is waiting for you inside." His voice is neutral, his face a mask.

Lelit is *here*. I want to run inside, yell for Grandma, but Leithe loops his arm through mine and leads us at an unhurried pace. Hunter opens the front door for us, allowing overlapping peals of laughter from multiple women to escape.

"And the time they gave each other haircuts; do you remember that?" Molly's voice carries from inside. "I had to buzz Zach's head to even it all out. I almost cried. I loved his hair at that age. It was so curly."

"How adorable," says a woman's voice, low and smooth. I recognize it from the prison.

Lelit sits at the dining room table with Grandma and Molly, all three of them holding coffee mugs. Like her appearance in the prison, Lelit looks like she should be on magazine covers: all gleaming olive skin, long copper hair, and vibrant green eyes—airbrushed, unnatural perfection, even in just a simple cream dress and a narrow green scarf. And she's *sitting*. With my grandmother. Lelit watches me, a small, conspiratorial smile on her lips, one inviting me to share in her secret. I want to go in screaming and swinging, but I can't bring myself to move from behind Leithe. It's not until now that I realize I believe every warning he's given me.

"Tamsin!" Grandma says, beaming up at me. "Your friend from school wanted to surprise you." Her eyes are glazed over the same way Brent's were when Leithe glamoured him. Molly's, too. "We were just about to break out the baby pictures." Lelit's in Grandma's house. Lelit's in Grandma's head.

"His hair was so soft," Molly says, oblivious to the rest of us. Tears begin streaming down her face. "I just wanted to ... I just wish ..." Her breath hitches as a sob constricts her throat.

"Shh." Lelit takes Molly's chin in her hand. Immediately, Molly's eyes close and she slumps forward as Lelit gently lowers her head to the table. "Dream of nice things. Be free of those nightmares for a while." Then she turns and takes Grandma's hand. "I saw your garden. You already know that no matter how many flowers you rear from seeds, it will not fill the hole in your heart left by ... not a lover. Him, you don't miss as much as you feel you should." She looks closer, tapping long, manicured nails on the dining table. Her eyes flare. "A child, then? One that's lost to you?"

"Yes," Grandma whispers, tears gathering at the corners of her eyes.

"Leave her alone," I say. But I don't move. She's threatening my grandmother, the only person I have, and I'm watching myself not do anything about it.

Lelit ignores me. "Working with your hands lets you forget the words you said to her that day, though they can never be unspoken."

"No," Grandma whispers. Tears flow freely now.

"Then sleep," Lelit says. "Go to your garden and find what passes for peace." Grandma sinks down onto the table.

"Why hurt her?" I ask. "She didn't do anything to you." I want to sound angry, in control, demanding, like this is *my* house, but the words come out a traitorous, pleading whine.

"I had to give her something as thanks for her hospitality," Lelit says. "Though the truth is a gift few know to appreciate."

"It's poor manners to trespass in someone else's home," Leithe says. "Even a human's."

Lelit takes a sip of coffee. "I was invited. The woman wanted so deeply to believe her ... granddaughter ..." She says the word as if it's foreign, "had friends. She asked me inside before I'd finished introducing myself." Her mouth curls into a smile as she turns back to me. "I've missed you. I thought you'd return to court as soon as you were out of that tree. When you didn't, I had to see what was so interesting in the mortal world." She taps her nails on her mug as she speaks.

"Did it cross your mind that your queen has better things to do than entertain you?" Leithe glances around the room. "Where is Noctiva? I thought you two traitors were inseparable." Lelit's fellow vassal and co-conspirator in Mab's imprisonment.

The corner of Lelit's mouth curves down. "I wasn't speaking to you." The scarf around her neck ripples, and for a moment, I see its true form: an emerald snake with a body thicker than Lelit's arm. "Noctiva is busy with her own affairs."

"Look," I say. "I really don't care that you locked me in a tree. The court's all yours. We're good. I'm going to stay here, and you can stay in Faerie, and we can both live happily ever after." *Please just leave. Please just take it all and go.*

Lelit's eyes glow with sudden rage—*literally* glow—and her skin ripples as if something within wants to escape. My knees buckle as the air gets heavier. Then she stops, closes her eyes, takes a calming breath, and smiles—an expression that says *oopsie, that was almost bad.*

I gasp as breath suddenly crashes back into my lungs. I didn't realize I hadn't been breathing.

Lelit studies me and I fight not to shrink back, afraid of what she'll see. "I've been hard at work planning a celebration in your honor. Will you not return to court with me?"

"I'm not going anywhere with you," I say. This time, I manage to sound more confident than I feel.

Lelit sighs theatrically. "Then I will give you the gifts I brought and depart for now, Your Grace." She crooks a beckoning finger, and Hunter moves to her side. "My knight reported that he struck you with an arrow. I offer you the offending hand."

"No, that isn't—"

Lelit looks at Hunter and speaks a word. Her mouth moves; my ears refuse to process the sound in a way that makes sense, but Hunter goes rigid. Lelit follows it with an order: "Cut off your hand." Without hesitation, Hunter draws his dagger and places his hand on the table.

"Stop!" I scream. But the blade flashes down.

Lelit speaks the word again and orders Hunter to stop. The blade freezes a hair's breadth from his wrist. "Is something wrong, Your Grace?" she asks innocently. But her eyes burn.

"I'm not mad about the shooting thing and I don't want his *hand*," I say. "Don't do this."

"Of course, Your Grace. Silly me. You've been coveting my knight, haven't you?" Hunter still stands stock-still, but his eyes widen. "You don't just want a *hand*."

"I don't—" *I don't care about this. Hurting him won't bother me.* Those would be lies.

Lelit finishes her coffee and gently sets the mug on the table. She stands, checks her nails, adjusts her dress, and before I can hope she's just going to leave, her hand strikes out, graceful and fast as a snake, and vanishes through fabric and flesh into Hunter's chest.

I whimper, mouth opening and closing while producing no coherent words. Hunter doesn't make a sound as Lelit twists her hand and tears free a dark, beating heart from its cavity. Hunter buckles but remains on his feet.

"I think I'll keep this," Lelit says, "since it's mine anyway. Do what you wish with the rest." I stare dumbly, unable to tear my eyes from the blood where it pools on the floor around Hunter's feet. I should do something.

Lelit turns away from Hunter and steps around the table, making her way toward us. She's barefoot; a dollop of blood hits the top of her foot from the messy prize in her hand. I should do something.

Leithe takes a half-step forward, placing himself between her and me.

"Oh?" Lelit looks more amused than worried. "Are we getting violent already? I doubt a century in a tree left you in any position to fight. And in a place where a single accident could render you a rule-breaker? Please, kill one of these humans and wither to a husk." She draws a small scroll from her dress pocket. "I've planned a ball at your palace to celebrate your return, Your Grace, to be held in three days." She holds the scroll out to me.

I stare at the scroll, at her other hand, stained with Hunter's blood. I can't get any words out. Slowly and deliberately, Lelit places the scroll on the table and gives me a sly look. "If you want to save my hunter, you should come before I get bored. Or hungry." She holds the heart up pointedly. "I'd rather my plans not go to waste, Your Grace." With a final dazzling smile, she steps around us and out the door, shutting it behind her with a delicate click.

"That went terribly," Leithe says.

A roaring in my ears jumbles my thoughts. I need to do something. I'm supposed to do something. Hunter grabs the back of a chair for support. The dogs howl and whine outside, scratching at the door. Molly and Grandma sleep, oblivious to everything. "Leithe," I say. "He's ... the ... dying?" My mouth doesn't want to work.

"He's not going to die unless Lelit destroys his heart." Leithe frowns. "You gathered that he's bait, correct?"

Hunter's bleeding. Some distant part of my brain reminds me I should do something about that. "Here." I loop Hunter's arm over my shoulders and lead him to the bathroom. If he couldn't support most of his own weight, I would keel over immediately. Leithe watches, offering no help.

After setting Hunter on the toilet, I scramble for the first-aid kit as if it would have something to treat traumatic heart-removal. I curse when I grab the scissors without thinking and the metal bites into my fingers. "Um." I look at Leithe. "Can you do something?"

"Alas," he says. "I can do him no harm. That was your wish, remember? He's in a delicate state; I wouldn't want to risk hurting him by accident." That *was* my wish, made a month ago in a blind panic to keep Hunter alive—keep him alive for this. Leithe leans against the door frame, watching like I'm a soap opera.

"Fine." I grab a pile of gauze pads. "I'm going to take off your shirt." I peel away the bloody fabric to reveal the shredded flaps of skin beneath. Still-warm blood stains my fingers and I'm back in the glade, staring at the life leaving Zach through the gash in his neck. My throat closes; my hands shake.

"Tamsin," Hunter says. "Just give me the bandages. I'll do it."

"It ... You need stitches." I realize that's an idiotic thing to say. He just had his heart ripped out and he's still alive. I hand over the kit. "I'm sorry."

"You shouldn't be," Leithe says. "Lelit would never have dared coming here and baiting you like this if she wasn't already *certain* you were vulnerable, and the only reason she would know that is if someone told her." He gestures pointedly at Hunter. "And who knew, aside from the three of us?"

Hunter's mouth tightens, though he doesn't look up from his work. "I'm not as stupid as you must think I am, *My Lord*. She didn't ask about my relationship with the queen and I didn't tell her."

"Regardless, she knows." Leithe snorts. "Tamsin, you might as well put him out of his misery now. He's caught between two Gentry. He's dead and he knows it." Hunter doesn't protest.

I get up and shut the bathroom door, locking Leithe outside. "I ..." I'm about to offer some useless platitude, when the truth comes out instead. "I don't know what to do."

"Tamsin," Hunter says, then balks. "Your Grace. I failed to guard the prison as my lady ordered, and she's punished me for it. My lady will return my heart if she sees fit to do so. I don't require further help. There's no use." Further help. I've never helped Hunter. Everything I've ever done has just made things worse for him.

"I'm so sorry," I say.

"Your Grace, the 'innocent human' act can only work on me once." He sounds exhausted.

"It's not an act, Hunter." I watch him dig through the first-aid kit, other hand pressed against his chest. "If I go to Lelit's ball, would she actually give your heart back?"

"She never said she would," Hunter says. "She didn't make a deal with you." He sits up straight, trying to look serious, but has to lean himself against the sink. "The more you show her what you care about, the more she'll use it against you."

"I'm supposed to leave you like this? When she could kill you whenever she wants?"

"She could already do that," he says.

I sit quietly, staring at the far wall. Hunter being hurt is a perverse reversal of circumstances. When I was a child, he seemed so tall, his sullenness I took as quiet confidence. "What are you going to do?"

"My lady left me at your disposal. I'll do whatever you wish." Maybe he doesn't know what to do any more than I do.

"Then rest," I say. "Please."

Hunter gives me a long, tired look. "Yes, Your Grace."

# Chapter Five

ONCE I LEAVE THE bathroom—politely but firmly dismissed by Hunter—I pull the door shut behind me and finally feel myself begin to crumple inward. I need to throw myself on my bed; scream into a pillow.

"I could still hear you," Leithe says petulantly, emerging from whatever corner he'd been lurking in, "through the door. It's not very thick."

I close my eyes and quash the scream; force the tears to stay in. I won't fall apart. Not in front of him. "It was more about sending a message."

"Speaking of messages, I hope you don't need help deciphering Lelit's."

I don't answer, instead pushing past him and into the living room. Grandma and Molly are still asleep at the table. "Grandma?" I approach the sleeping woman and gently place my hand on her shoulder. The moment I touch her, I'm not in the house anymore.

I'm in the front yard, staring down at Grandma and Zach as they dig through a flowerbed. Zach is young—hardly more than a toddler. He cradles several pill bugs in one pudgy hand.

"Look at this one," Grandma says, pointing at a large praying mantis resting on a tomato stalk. "She eats bad bugs. We want to be careful, though. If we try to pet her, we might hurt her." Zach nods somberly.

"Grandma?" I say.

Grandma turns to me, squinting in the sunlight. Tears run freely down her face. "Tamsin? Why are you so old? Did you bring the watering can?"

"You're dreaming, Grandma," I say. But it feels so *real*. The sunlight, the breeze. The fat red roses mewling like infants as Grandma pats soil over their roots.

The front door shudders in its frame, and somehow I'm beyond certain that if I opened it now, the inside of Grandma's house wouldn't be on the other side.

"I'm sorry, but you need to wake up." Tentatively, I poke her shoulder. She shoves my hand away.

"This is a dream," she says. "Zach should be older. No, he's—" Her face twists; she covers her mouth to stifle a sob. "Tamsin, I forgot to water the flowers."

Zach, with Grandma distracted, picks up the praying mantis with clumsy hands. "Let me see that," I say on reflex, guiding the mantis from his hand to mine. I can't remember if they bite. The creature's legs tickle as it walks from my palm to the back of my hand. It feels real.

Then I'm back in Grandma's house. Grandma gasps, jerking awake and wiping wet hair from her face. Leithe holds a partially upended glass over her head. She sputters, looks around, sees me instead of him.

"Did you pour water on me?" she asks in disbelief.

"You ... looked like you were having a bad dream?" I say. She doesn't answer. She only stares at me. Not at me, I realize. At my hand, upon which sits a very real, very alive praying mantis.

"Oh. Um. I found this. In the garden. I should just ..." The mantis flies from my hand and *thunks* audibly against the window. "Are you okay?"

She watches the insect bounce off the floor and start crawling back up the wall, then eyes me with suspicion. "Why wouldn't I be?"

"You fell asleep at the table," I say. Grandma stares at me, gears in her head turning and apparently coming to no solution she likes.

Leithe pours the remainder of the water on Molly, who jerks awake with a gasp. The noise pulls Grandma's attention from me.

"Molly, honey, are you okay?" Grandma asks.

Molly rubs her eyes. "I'm so sorry. I haven't been sleeping well. I can't believe I nodded off." Grandma looks like she can't, either.

"What are you doing here?" Grandma asks Leithe. He hasn't made himself visible to humans. She shouldn't be able to see him.

Molly turns to see who Grandma's talking to, and Leithe makes himself visible, glamouring himself into a T-shirt and jeans in the process. "Oh, hi," Molly says. "Tamsin, is this your, ah, boyfriend?"

"I invited him," I say to Grandma, then to Molly: "And no."

"Okay. Well." Molly looks between the three of us and picks up on the tension. "Mrs. Bellamy, thank you for having me. I should go see if Brent's home yet." We say our goodbyes and Grandma waits, arms crossed, until Molly's car vanishes down the driveway, staring at me, at Leithe, and at the three coffee mugs on the table.

"Tamsin," she says when Molly's car is out of sight. "Would you mind driving me to the store? I want to make another casserole for Brent and Molly, and the doctor still doesn't want me driving; he's not sure if the muscle spasms will start back up." Liar. She's been driving herself around for weeks.

"If you would like me to leave, you may say so," Leithe says with some amusement.

"I would like you to leave," Grandma says without missing a beat.

"As you wish." He inclines his head in a gesture of respect that Grandma clearly takes to be mocking, based on the way her frown deepens.

"I'll walk you out," I say, then turn back to Grandma. "I ... Um ... There's a mess in the bathroom. Don't go in there. I'll clean it up later."

I stop once we're off the porch. "Can Lelit make anyone do that?" Grandma's definitely watching from just inside, so I speak in a low voice. "Control them like puppets, I mean?" I can't shake the glazed look on Grandma's face; the jerky motions of Hunter's limbs as if moving against his will.

"Humans, yes," he says. "But she wouldn't be able to force her will onto another fae unless they gave her their Name." She'd said a word, one my mind refused to process.

"She took Hunter's Name? How do you take a Name from someone?"

"He *gave* it to her," Leithe corrects, as if that's different. "He's a knight in her service, hence why she can take anything she wants from him—it's all already hers."

"Then how do we get his Name back from her?"

"'We'?" Leithe scoffs. "It has nothing to do with us. It depends entirely on the circumstances of the oath between the two of them. Besides, I thought you'd be more concerned about the old woman." He shoots a glance back toward the house. "She's in danger, you know."

"But she doesn't know anything. Do any fae *actually* follow their own rules?" I run my hand through my hair in frustration and am startled to remember how short it is now.

"That *was* Lelit following the rules," he says. "Your grandmother is questioning. She's begun to see the truth, here and there. If it continues, she'll no longer be innocent, and Lelit—and any other fae—will be free to do what they wish to her."

"We need to leave. Move to Texas. Or Japan. The bottom of the ocean. Somewhere far away from here." I press my fingers to my temples. "No, what about Hunter? We can't leave him like that."

Leithe holds up Lelit's scroll. "If you want to make him whole again, this invitation will deliver its bearer straight to the palace."

I glare at the scroll like it might grow fangs and bite. "So our only option is to fall for the obvious trap?" There's no real choice here. I can't save Hunter. I can't even look Lelit in the eye.

"Lelit's making a mistake. You'll regain your strength faster if you return to the Dreaming Court. What you did, pulling that little insect out of your grandmother's dream? All fae of the Dreaming Court can do that, and the most powerful can visit dreamers no matter where in either world they are. Return to Faerie, and you could have the stuff of every dream at your fingertips—your own personal army of the worst beasts a mind can fathom; Lelit would no longer be an issue."

"We go, and then what?" I eye the scroll, but don't move to take it.

"We get rid of Lelit and anyone else in the way, then you reclaim your throne." He speaks as if laying out a grocery list.

"And then what?" I ask with more force.

"And then we do whatever we like. If you were at your full power, there would be few who'd be able to stop you." His tone becomes soft, cajoling. He almost succeeds in looking at me like he doesn't find my existence a nuisance.

"That sounds too good to be true. Too easy."

The feigned kindness vanishes the moment I fail to bite. "It *will* be that easy when your memories return."

"Mab's memories aren't coming back," I say. *Because she doesn't want them to. Because she buried them. Because she's dead.* But I don't say any of those things. It might only be his belief that those memories will come back that's keeping me alive.

Leithe watches me, eyes narrowed, intensely enough that I begin to worry he can read minds. "Fine," he eventually sighs, exasperated. "Disregarding the memories, what will you do, if not this? Hide until Lelit finds you again? Hide where? The second you set foot in another monarch's domain, they'll know, and they won't take the trespass well. Or will you stay in the mortal world until you wither away? I'm sure you're hungry, because the food this world produces wasn't made for you." He pointedly places a hand on the hood of Grandma's car. "You can't even shield yourself from iron." His hand doesn't sizzle and smoke like mine would.

"No," I admit. "I just try not to touch it." Being this close to the car makes my eyes prickle and my stomach turn. Being inside is ten times worse.

"For the ..." He rolls his eyes and grabs my hand. Immediately, my senses dull as if I'm covered in several layers of plastic wrap. Sounds are dimmer, and I can barely feel his skin where he's touching me. The acrid metal smell emanating from the car is now barely noticeable. "Go ahead."

There's no pain when I place my hand gingerly on the car door, my fingertips only tingle slightly. There's no more constant burning in my eyes as if I'm standing next to a smoking fire.

"It will burn out on its own eventually, faster if you're in direct contact with iron. And it won't help if your skin is pierced." His expression becomes reproachful. "You could have asked me to do this at any time."

"No, I couldn't have. If I'd asked you, you wouldn't have done it for free."

Leithe snorts, but doesn't seem angry. Then his expression becomes serious. "If it's what you want, I could glamour the old woman into going somewhere far away from here."

I think about accepting—just for a second, but a second too long. "In exchange for what?" I ask. "You're using her just as much as Lelit is. Just ... go away." As soon as the words leave my mouth, I'm terrified. What if he does leave? What if he leaves and Lelit comes back?

Leithe watches the emotions that must be cycling across my face with little emotion of his own. He always stands too still. I'm not sure he breathes. "When you ask me to do it, I'll tell you what I want in exchange," he says. "You've officially run out of time, so I wouldn't think about it too long."

Grandma's at the window when I go back inside, staring intently at Leithe's retreating back. "I don't like that man."

"I know," I say.

"You act like you're scared of him, Tamsin," Grandma says.

"I …" I am scared of him.

Grandma notes my non-answer. "If you don't want to tell me the story, fine. But if he comes back here, I'll make him leave. If you want me to." She sounds as if there's no doubt in her mind that she could do it.

But Leithe could make her move. I wonder if he could glamour enough people to get her in a new house in a new state overnight. Would she know, somewhere deep down, what I did to her?

Before I know it, I'm hugging her. "I'm sorry," I say. For even considering it. For still considering it.

Grandma returns the hug, though she seems taken aback. "It's alright. It's really alright." I don't know what she thinks I'm apologizing for.

The praying mantis crawls across the door, so I open it and usher the creature outside. When it spreads its wings, they catch the sun and fracture the light like stained glass. It seems to nod at me before flying off.

I could make something up, tell myself it flew in while the door was open, but I know, without a doubt, that I pulled that creature out of Grandma's dream. I *did* something. The combined joy and despair cancel themselves out and become numbness. I did something; I'm not useless. I did something; I'm not human. As if I'd been clinging to the hope this whole time that despite the burn of iron, if I couldn't use magic, nothing had changed.

The grocery store, cooking the casserole, even dinner with Zach's parents. I make it through the entire day. I make it through the movie Grandma picks out, though I don't remember what it was about.

After Grandma goes to bed, once I'm alone in my room, the emotions of the day surge out. I half let out a choked scream and my phone ricochets off the wall before I register that I threw it. I sink to my knees, press my face into my mattress, and try not to cry.

"Young Miss?" Cheeps says. I didn't hear him approach.

I rub the burgeoning tears from my eyes and sit up. "What's wrong?" I didn't think I'd see him for at least a week after Lelit's appearance.

Cheeps retrieved my phone from where it landed. There's now a crack running along the corner of the screen. "Young Miss, we're not supposed to throw things or tear things or chew things when we're sad or angry, remember?" He looks up at me sternly. "You made that rule."

He's right, I did. "I'm sorry," I say. "Won't happen again."

Cheeps climbs onto my knee and pats my leg reassuringly. "I will tell you a secret. I am scared of many many things because I am very small. But even though there are terrible scary dogs downstairs right now, I will go all the way to the pantry and get you some salmon cat food right now if it would make you feel less sad, because you are my family."

Despite everything, I smile. "That's very kind of you, Cheeps, but I think I should sleep."

"Then sleep," Cheeps says. "I will stay here the whole night so you do not have to be afraid."

# Chapter Six

"You left again," Zach says. We're lying inside a pillow fort we once built in the living room. The Zach beside me is young this time. Maybe ten years old.

"I'm sorry," I say. "I have to be awake sometimes." The cream sheet forming the roof softens and diffuses the afternoon light. We taped the sheet to the TV so we could watch movies while inside. A cartoon is playing, but there's no sound.

"Why?" Zach asks. "Aren't you a queen? Shouldn't you be able to do whatever you want?"

"The people saying that are usually also trying to tell me what to do." The fort isn't big enough for an adult. I prop up on my shoulders to look down at my ten-year-old body. I'm wearing cat-patterned pajamas Grandma cut up for dish rags years ago.

"Why are we here?" Zach asks.

"Because I don't want to be alone, so I'm talking to a figment of my imagination instead." The characters in the movie aren't doing what I think they should, but I don't remember it well enough to say for sure.

"But why here? Why like this?" he asks. "I think I know the answer. Do you?"

"I was happy here. Safe. The only responsibilities we had were to brush our teeth and do our homework. We'd never seen consequences before."

"So this is where you want to stay?"

I lay back down. "I wish I could. I'm ruining everything out there, you know. I'm scared that any step I take will lead to someone getting hurt, so all I'm doing is sitting on my ass. I know I should do *something*, but ..." My chest tightens up. I imagine Grandma, Cheeps, Hunter, even Leithe, lying in the dirt, staring glassy-eyed at the sky long after the life has bled out of them. "There's no right answer."

"Is that it?" he asks. The ground beneath us is cold. The only light now comes from the television, flickering harshly across Zach's face. My stomach twists. The words are on the tip of my tongue, but get no further.

"Young Miss!"

I'm awoken by Cheeps jumping up and down next to my pillow. It's still dark out. My old alarm clock reads just before four in the morning.

*Is that it?* Zach's voice still echoes in my skull. I shove that thought far away.

"What?" I rub my eyes. "Did I forget to put your salmon out?"

"There's someone in the yard," Cheeps says. That has me awake.

"Another faerie?" I ask. Cheeps pulls me over to the window that looks out over the front yard; a figure stands where the driveway begins to widen into a loop, their hands shoved into pockets and their face concealed by the hood of a jacket. Much too short to be Leithe. No sign of any telltale fae features from this distance; also no sign of a shotgun.

They look human. My first thought is to wake Grandma and call the police. But looking harder, the figure's outline is just the slightest bit fuzzy.

"Cheeps, that person is invisible to humans, right?" Cheeps nods frantically in response. A faerie, then.

Cheeps watches me, wide-eyed and expectant. I look around for Leithe's birds, but can't see any of them in the dark. Moving them further from the house was what I asked him to do, but now I have to admit he had a point. There's no way to contact him without getting around the person outside. I could try to sneak around the back and make my way to the Randall Place, but I don't want to give Leithe the satisfaction of crawling to him again.

"Maybe they'll just leave," I offer. But I doubt it. Whatever they're doing probably has something to do with me. Cheeps doesn't seem convinced, either.

"I will defend my family with my life," Cheeps says. "Even if I get pulled into tiny pieces and eaten up." But even as he says the words, he looks at me with huge, plaintive eyes.

"It's okay, Cheeps," I relent. "You stay inside and guard Grandma. I'll ... I'll go see what they want."

He lets out a huge sigh of relief, hugs my arm, and darts off, presumably to hide.

My hands shake as I slip my phone into my pocket. But somewhere in that fear is a kernel of curiosity. Of excitement.

Hunter is asleep on the couch, but the dogs wake up as I pass through the living room. They watch me go, tails twitching. Whatever's outside doesn't seem to bother them.

I've never seen Hunter asleep. He's propped up on the arm of the couch, as if he didn't mean to succumb. A glass of water and an array of all the painkillers we have in the house is spread across the coffee table, though it looks like he didn't take any of them.

I could wake him, I *should* wake him, if I was smart. But he's in no shape to help me even if he wanted to, and I can't ask him to risk his dogs.

The figure hasn't moved by the time I reach the front porch. I stop at the top step. "I said I'm not going to that damn party," I say. The figure says nothing. "Leithe is watching. He'll come if you try anything." I hope. "What do you want? Are you with the Dreaming Court? Do you work for Lelit?" I hope that sounds authoritative enough. I cross my arms for good measure.

The figure says nothing. Instead, they turn and take a few steps down the driveway before stopping and looking back. The hood still obscures their face. Their hands are still buried in their pockets.

They want me to follow. Realistically, I'm probably not any safer inside the house from a faerie who'd want to hurt me, and the road is closer to Leithe and farther from Grandma. So I do follow. At a distance.

"Who are you?" I ask. They ignore me. "Look. If you're not going to say anything, I'm going back inside." The figure turns and extends an arm toward me. At the end of the arm is a handgun. I put my hands up. "Okay. I get it, but this isn't necessary. We can just talk like normal people."

Instead of answering, the figure gestures with the barrel for me to walk until I'm in front of them, and then places the gun against my spine, the metal frigid through the fabric of my tank top.

We walk to the road, where a beat-up red Subaru is parked. As I cross the property boundary, a bird takes off from somewhere in the trees. Leithe's minions probably have orders to tell him if I leave, I realize. I'm simultaneously angry and relieved.

"Stop," the figure says when we're next to the car. It's a woman's voice, scratchy and gruff. "If you talk aside from answering my questions, I will shoot you. If you try to glamour me, I will shoot you. If you move a muscle—"

"You'll shoot me," I say. She doesn't shoot me. "You killed the kelpie."

"Are you a faerie?" she asks.

"You decided to start waving a gun around *before* coming to that conclusion?" Any fear I had of the gun is gone, replaced with indignation. According to Leithe, I'd just come back eventually if she killed me, anyway.

She jabs the barrel into my spine. "Answer."

"Okay. *Yes*. I'm a faerie. What are you?"

"I saw you with another fae earlier today," she says, ignoring my question. "Where is he now?"

"He's probably on the way," I say. "And you probably don't want to be pointing a gun at me when he arrives."

"A man named Zach Foster went missing last month," she says. "What happened to him?"

Zach's name yanks the bravado from me. "Who are you?" I ask.

"Answer the question before I shoot your kneecap out." The pressure from the gun barrel vanishes from my back, presumably because it's aimed lower.

"... He's dead." The words refuse to come out any louder than a whisper.

"Did the kelpie kill him?"

"A ..." What had Hunter called her? "A ... hob named Thistledown killed him."

"Where's his body?"

Buried by Hunter years ago. "I don't know."

"Where's the hob?"

"Dead." Those questions, at least, I can answer honestly. "Why are you spying on my house?"

The woman reaches around me and slams a piece of paper against the car door. It's a printout of a news article. My smiling, nine-year-old face beams at the camera next to Zach's as we both pose with muddy uniforms and shiny plastic soccer trophies. "What was the point of this?" she asks.

"Well, they gave everyone on the team a trophy so no one would feel left out." I half-expect to get shot for that. "You're threatening me because of a picture from when we were nine?"

"You knew him. You knew how he died. Are you going to try to convince me you weren't involved?"

"No." I feel a sudden weight fall off my chest as I form the words, leaving me almost giddy. "I was involved. He was trying to help me and he got killed for it. It's my fault, so shoot me if that's what you came here to do." For a moment, she says nothing. I wait for her to shoot. I would deserve it.

"Twenty-one years ago, a baby was stolen from that house," the woman says. "And you were left in its place."

"Yes, but—" And then it hits me. How this woman would recognize me from the news. How she would know where I lived, what I was. "*Skye?*"

# Chapter Seven

"Where's my son?" Skye demands. She doesn't stop me from turning around. Now, this close to her, I recognize her face as one that's stared down at me from Grandma's mantle for as long as I've been alive. She has the same belligerent jaw and dark eyes captured in her high school graduation picture, but now the face around them is more than twenty years older; her dark hair is short and choppy. The resemblance to her mother is startling. And her gun is currently pointed at my stomach.

"I don't know," I admit. "I know who took him, but she won't tell me and I don't know how to find her. This—" I point at the gun, "isn't necessary. I'm not going to try to hurt you and I'll tell you whatever you want to know."

"Do you think I'm stupid?" she asks. "Where's your friend from earlier, the one you said is on the way?"

Leithe. My adrenaline spikes for a new reason. "You need to put the gun down. Right now," I say. "I don't know what he'll do if he sees you threatening me." It was only by coincidence I'd been able to stop him from killing Hunter.

"Stop." Skye hauls me in front of her and makes a show of brandishing the gun next to my head. At first, I think she's talking to me, but then I see Leithe in the middle of the road, arms crossed. "Try to glamour me and I'll shoot."

"Wait," I say to Leithe.

He doesn't wait. "*Drop—*" The gun rattles as Skye's hand shakes with the effort to keep it raised; before he can get a second word out, she shoots him. The sound of the gunshot rings in my head and doesn't stop. I throw my head to the side and press my hands to my ears. The successive shots sound as if I'm hearing them underwater.

Leithe's body falls backward and lands on the road with a dull thud. He doesn't move, but Skye shoots at him a few more times for good measure as I stand frozen and open-mouthed.

"Is he dead?" I ask, my own voice barely audible to my ears; the gunshots echo in my head long after I realize Skye's stopped shooting. Do I want him to be dead?

Skye swears as one of Leithe's birds dives for her face. She grabs its body and slams it against the roof of the car, cracking bone, before dropping it on the ground and stomping on it.

I take a step toward where Leithe fell, as if to check if he's alright, then freeze. The shadows around his body boil upward, covering him and rising into a wave that falls somewhere between smoke and liquid. Animal and human forms weave in and out of sight from within the mass, all coming together to form a larger whole. A pair of baleful yellow eyes glares out from within the cloud, which rises higher and higher until it's as tall as the trees lining the road. Then the wave comes crashing down toward us, a stampede of bodiless wraiths. The entire thing is eerily silent.

Behind me, I hear more swearing, then a car door open and close. In a panic, I yank open the rear passenger door and climb inside. "Go!"

Skye doesn't spare me a look. The engine roars and the car lurches forward before jerking to a stop despite the screeching wheels. I fly forward from the momentum and slam my head into the back of the passenger seat. The car's body buckles and groans as if squeezed by giant hands. Shadowy tendrils quest across the vehicle until I can't see anything but darkness through the rear windshield. Cracks spiderweb across the glass. Leithe is going to flatten the entire car.

And then we break free with a metallic crunch, the car careening forward from the sudden lack of resistance and sending me rolling against the back seat. We're headed straight for a tree until Skye whips around the bend without slowing. She takes the next several turns so fast I think we're going to spin out, but we don't.

After a few short minutes of a roller-coaster ride from Hell where I barely manage to scramble into a seat and buckle, the town of Shrike Run and its few working street lights are shrinking in the rear view mirror, no sign of Leithe in the darkness behind us.

Leithe's glamour shields me from the stink and sting of being in a metal box. Instead, Skye's car smells like stale French fries, shoe shine, and cigarette smoke. Old fast food wrappers spill out of a larger plastic bag and roll around on the floor. Whatever's in the trunk is hidden by a tarp.

"Don't touch that," Skye says when I try to peek under it. A pause. "Why the fuck are you in my car?"

"Um." Why *am* I in her car? "I panicked?"

"I thought that guy was your friend."

"I'm really not sure," I say. "And what the hell is happening right now? Where have you been for the last twenty years? How do you know what faeries are?"

"If you try to glamour me, I swear to God I will shoot you before you can finish a sentence." Skye snatches up the gun she'd abandoned on the passenger seat.

"Yeah, I heard you earlier. I can't glamour my way out of a paper bag with a hole in it, if that makes you feel any better. The thing is—"

Skye cuts me off. "The guy who attacked me—does he know where my son is?"

"I doubt it. He was in a tree when your son was taken. The faerie who switched him with me—the faerie that ordered it at least, the one who actually did it is dead—I just know her as 'the witch'. She's got at least three different bodies and I have no idea how to find her. She shows up when she feels like it. Now will you answer any of my questions?"

Skye makes an annoyed sound in her throat. "Do you know *anything* useful?"

"*No,*" I snap. "I've only known I was a faerie for about a month and I'm trying to have as little to do with it as possible. You probably know more about what's going on than I do."

Skye ploughs on as if I said nothing. "This witch, is she your mother? Does she care about you?"

"No, and I don't know. But you're welcome to hang out and threaten her the next time she appears to dispense some cryptic wisdom." Skye offers nothing more than an irritated sigh, so I continue. "Where have you been?" This question is softer, more careful. "Grandma misses you."

"Don't call her that." Her tone is vicious. Her face, visible in the rearview mirror, screws up with disgust. "She's not your grandmother. She's not anything to you. She doesn't even know what you are, right?"

A lump forms in my throat. "No, but she doesn't know you're even *alive*." If I don't bite back, my only other option is to cry, and I won't cry in front of her.

"It's to protect her," Skye says. "It's harder for your kind to hurt her if she doesn't know."

"My kind," I snort. I want to be offended, but she's right. The problem *is* my kind. "Then we're in the same boat. I haven't helped her figure it out because I don't want her to get hurt."

"Then you should have stayed away. You left years ago, didn't you?" She asks. "Why did you come back? Easier to leech off some human than do whatever you do in Faerie?"

"How did you know I left?" I ask. "Have you been spying on me?" She doesn't answer.

My phone's camera flash lights up the car. Skye turns around with a snarl, but I hold the phone too far for her to grab, finger hovering over the 'send' button. "It's kind of hard to make out your face in the picture, but your own mom would probably still recognize you."

"I could still shoot you."

"Can you do it before I hit a button?" I start typing. "'Hi Grandma, guess who I just ran into? Crazy, right? Anyway, if you don't hear back from me soon, this is who I was last with, XOXO.'"

"What is wrong with you?" she says.

"What's wrong with me is I'm getting *really* tired of people who won't answer my questions, so now I get to ask one: where have you been for the last twenty years?"

For a tense moment, I think she really might just shoot me. Then she sighs in defeat and shoves the gun into the glove box, exchanging it for a pack of cigarettes. She doesn't speak until after she clamps a cigarette between her lips, lights it, and exhales a stream of smoke out the window. "First, I was looking for proof to bring to my mom to convince her I was right. After I learned she was better off not knowing, I just started trying to figure out where stolen children go."

"Why did you wait so long to come after me?" I ask.

"I didn't. This—" She grabs the collar of her jacket. "It's enchanted. When the hood's up, humans can't see me. I came back when you were, I don't know, seven or so. You couldn't see me. I didn't know what else to do, so I just left."

"I'd probably just had my Sight and memories taken away. They came back later. It's a long story. How did you get an enchanted jacket?"

"I helped an old lady cross the street," Skye says. "I came back again when you would have been a teenager. You were gone. I figured your faerie parents had come to get you and I'd lost my chance."

"Nope." For a moment, I'm reliving the hours after Zach's death—Grandma finding me on the porch, covered in blood. Hunter glamouring her to send me far away. "Boarding school."

"And then I saw your picture a few days ago in an article about Zach Foster's mysterious disappearance, so I thought it was worth another shot."

"You could have knocked on the door like a normal person and *asked*." I bristle, even though she's not wrong; I *was* involved.

"I didn't want to give you the chance to use my mother as a hostage." The words, said in a tone that implies they're simply common sense, are like shards of ice under my skin.

"Why didn't you just shoot me when I was a kid if you're so worried about what I'd do to her?" If I'm angry at her, I don't have to risk feeling anything complicated.

She's silent for so long that I don't think she's going to answer me. "I thought about it."

"Kill a lot of children over the years?"

"I found a woman in Kansas who almost died of exhaustion because the changeling that replaced her son ordered her to make cakes. She'd been doing it for days. He was six. He didn't even realize what he'd done." She taps her cigarette into the ashtray in the center console.

"And you killed him?" I ask. "He didn't know what he was doing. It was an accident. He was *six*."

"Does it matter?" Skye asks. "Accident or not, he still nearly killed her."

"That's ..." Intentional or not, I still led Zach to his death. What anger I was able to muster fades.

Skye looks at me in the rearview mirror. "I didn't kill him. I found the closest door to Faerie and tossed him through."

"Why leave me, then?"

"You didn't even have Sight. You seemed ... normal. My mom seemed normal. I heard some changelings are left behind because they're 'defective.' I thought that might be the case with you." She's silent for a long time. "He wasn't breathing. My son, I mean. But I always wondered why they'd bother taking him if he was dead, so I've thought there might be a chance."

"The witch said he was alive the last time she saw him. That's all she would tell me."

"That's something, at least." There's an edge to her voice. I can't tell what answer she was hoping for.

Before I can speak again, the car begins thudding rhythmically against the road.

"Shit," Skye says. She checks the mirrors; I follow her gaze. At this time of night, there's nothing but empty highway behind us. No horde of wraiths on our heels.

"Do you think he's chasing us?" I ask.

"I don't know." The car veers to the right as Skye pulls onto the shoulder and rolls to a stop. "But I'm not outrunning him with a flat tire." On the other side of the shoulder is a sharp decline into a ditch where many years' worth of trash has accumulated in standing water.

"This was a misunderstanding," I say. Skye gets out of the car; I follow her to the back. "We could have worked it out." The rear bumper has been ripped off and some of the body crushed inward.

Skye laughs. A sharp, angry noise. "Could we? You promise? If only what, I came out with my hands up and asked nicely?" She kneels to examine the back passenger wheel. Air hisses from more than one puncture.

"You shot him first."

"The bitch who took my kid shot first." The trunk is stuck from the damage, forcing her to pry it open. She unloads it, setting the boxes on the ground. "If I asked nicely, would that guy have been nice back?" She pulls the trunk's floor panel up and examines the spare tire. "I'll tell you what I think: I think, at best, he'd have wiped my mind and left me a drooling mess on the side of the road."

I say nothing. There's nothing *to* say. Every interaction I've ever had with Leithe has been when he needed something from me. First to release him, then as the—temporary, he hopes—occupant of his betrothed's body. I don't need to wonder how he'd treat someone with nothing to offer him.

Skye puts the jack in place and starts lifting the car, wincing, I notice, as she works. "You can leave whenever, by the way. Coming here was a waste of time."

"You're bleeding," I say. Her wrist sports three long gouges, as if from the talons of a bird.

"Parting shot from Tall and Dark, I guess. It's fine."

"Leithe might be able to help you. He might at least know where to start looking for stolen kids. He definitely knows more than me, at least. You'd just need to stay away long enough for me to explain everything."

Skye pauses her work long enough to give me a withering look. "Yeah. Sure. Just call me when you get all that worked out and I'll come right over." She starts twisting off the lug nuts.

"Look," I snap. "He's the best lead I can offer you, okay?"

Skye pulls the wheel free and pauses. "Shut up."

I cross my arms. "I'm *trying* to help."

"No." She drops the wheel. "Did you hear that?" I didn't, so I shut up and listen. Skye goes to the open trunk and digs around, and I hear it, a squelching sound coming from the ditch.

"Hello?" I say. In response, a hand—fingers proportionally longer than any human's—rises and comes to rest on the crest of the ditch. It's followed by a second. Then a third. Then a fourth.

Behind me, I hear the sound of Skye racking a shotgun.

"Wait." I step between Skye and the thing in the ditch. "Hi, we're just passing through. Didn't mean to bother you." It rises further, exposing a wormlike body the size of a horse cocooned in trash—newspapers, takeout boxes, broken furniture, and the like—woven together with white, filmy threads. The only indication of a face is the suggestion of a deep-set pair of eyes reflecting the glow from the car's brake lights. Instead of legs, the creature balances on six humanoid arms that extend at intervals down the side of its body; each one is much longer than a human's and emaciated, skin clinging tightly to the bone.

"I scented blood," the creature says. Its words are punctuated by the sharp clicks of what might be mandibles. "Prey. Already claimed by you?" Each word is sharp and clipped.

"Yep," I say. "Mine." I can feel Skye bristle behind me.

The creature clicks thoughtfully. "You fled. From the one who smells like bone-dust and shadows."

"You can smell him from all the way out here?" I ask. I didn't think Leithe smelled that bad. I'm not sure he smelled like anything at all.

"I smell him. His territory. His touch in the human-thing's blood. Waited on the outskirts for the leavings. Are you leavings?"

"'His touch' in her blood? What are you talking about?" I ask.

"Is he your lord?"

"No," I snap. "He is not."

"Shit," Skye says under her breath.

"I smell you now, dream-creature. You smell weak. Weak and unprotected." I barely have time to realize I messed up before the creature wraps a hand around my calf and pulls me off my feet, its body disappearing back below the lip of the ditch and dragging me along with it.

I do have enough sense to roll onto my chest and cover my head as Skye steps forward and shoots the creature in what is hopefully its face. The shot splinters and shreds the trash shrouding the creature's body, exposing patches of pulsing, maggot-like flesh that leaks clear fluid where it's broken. I can't tell if the hissing is coming from the creature's wounds or somewhere deep in its throat.

The creature releases me to grab at Skye. Even though she's already backing up, its arm whips forward, suddenly much longer than it appeared to be, and snares her ankle. Her second shot goes wide as the creature pulls her off her feet, only clipping the edges of its cocoon. It grabs the barrel and is thrown off balance when Skye simply releases the weapon.

When the creature recovers and rears toward her, she meets it by shoving a knife into the recess that hides its face. The faerie shrieks and convulses, grabbing at Skye's face, at her eyes. It claws at her, but she only twists the knife in deeper.

By the time I yank a machete from the mess Skye cleared from the trunk and return to help, the creature is still, its body slumped over her.

"Nasty," Skye says as she extricates her arm from beneath the creature. Blood oozes from two punctures in her sleeve. "Are you just going to stand there?" She glares up at me from the ground.

"Sorry." I try to lift the creature's sagging bulk off Skye, but she still hefts most of it, cursing all the while until she's on her feet. Her face is covered in scratches, but nothing that bleeds as heavily as her arm. "I think you need stitch-es."

Skye examines her arm. "The next time you stand be-tween me and something that wants to kill you, I'm going to let it." She digs through the stuff from her trunk until she finds a first-aid kit.

"I guess I won't be able to blame you." I kneel by the car and put the spare tire on the axle. "But I thought it was worth a shot. Not all the faeries I've met have tried to eat me."

"I can't relate," Skye says. "Stop that."

"I know how to do it. I spent half my childhood in my friend's dad's garage." I use the edge of my shirt to pick up the lug nuts and put them in place.

"If you want to help, go load the trunk back up." She nudges me out of the way with the toe of her boot. Her sleeve is rolled back, her forearm wrapped in tape and gauze.

I obey. Some of the boxes are stupidly heavy, but at least I can touch them with my bare hands without further wear-ing down the limited protection Leithe's glamour affords me. "How do you have Sight?" I ask as I work.

"There's no way I'm telling you that."

"Because it could get taken away?"

"You could probably walk home from here." She finish-es with the tire and begins lowering the jack.

"And right into another one of those." The creature shudders. I jump, expecting it to attack again, but it's sim-ply the trash settling to the ground as countless maggots wriggle out in all directions. "Ew. It turned into bugs."

"I'll drop you at a gas station or something."

"You can drop me at the hospital on your way in." Skye shoulders past me to throw the jack and the flat tire in the trunk. The gauze over her arm is already dotted with red. My stomach lurches. "You should let me drive."

"It's not that bad. My jacket caught most of it." She pauses with her good hand on the trunk door. "Can faeries get infections?"

"I ... have no idea," I say. She pulls a squeeze tube out of the first-aid kit and tosses it to me. My palm stings when I catch it. The skin on both of my hands is scraped and bloody, along with some of the right side of my face and shoulder from the creature dragging me over the road.

After slamming the trunk, Skye stomps around to the driver's side; I quickly get into the passenger seat in case she changes her mind about leaving me here.

Skye lights a cigarette as soon as she's in the car. Her hands shake so badly I almost offer to light it for her. For the first time, I notice the bags under her eyes. I pull up the directions to the nearest hospital and rattle them off.

"You're overreacting," she says.

"I'm reacting a normal amount." I can't see anything but the blood. It's on her. It's on me. Skye doesn't respond or make any move to start the car. I take a breath. "If we are not at a hospital in the next hour, I'm calling your mother."

She examines her arm again. She looks like she wants to argue, but instead she sighs. "That is the last time you are using that threat. But we need to go farther away than that. If your guy survived, I need to get as far away from here as possible."

# Chapter Eight

WE GET TO THE hospital just as the dawn casts everything in gray light. It's a little more than sixty miles from Shrike Run and as far as Skye is willing to drive on a spare tire—a town bigger than Shrike Run, but not big. After she parks, Skye limps on her own through the automatic ER doors, refusing any help from me.

When we enter the waiting room, I gasp. In addition to the few people waiting to be called back, there's a woman floating two feet in the air. She wears a long white gown, the hem of which flares out like dispersing fog several inches from the floor. Lank blond hair falls in tangled ropes to her waist. Her fingers—longer and with more joints than a human's—end in broken nails crusted with something reddish brown.

The woman had been leaning unnervingly close over a tired-looking man, but looks up in response to my alarm. Her solid black eyes leak bloody tears down her pallid face. She smiles at me—her pale, cracked lips splitting apart to reveal a mouth full of blood-stained teeth. Skye's eyes pass over the woman as if she isn't there. She's good at this.

"Good morning," I say weakly. The woman inclines her head before returning her attention to the man below her, running a finger down his cheek and leaving a trail of red he doesn't acknowledge. My curiosity gets the better of me; I leave Skye to check herself in and step closer to the fae woman, putting my phone to my ear so I can pretend to be on a call. "What are you doing to him?" I ask.

"He's going to die tonight," she says. Her voice is raw and scratchy. "He has an inkling, but no one can find anything wrong. All that can be done is to take away the pain." A man in scrubs escorts Skye through a set of double doors. Open, bleeding wounds must be high on the priority list. I offer a quick goodbye, but the woman grabs my wrist before I can leave; her skin is cold and her jagged nails dig into my arm. "The human you came in with. She's going to die soon."

"Why do you say that?" I ask.

"I know a Crawling Court death curse when I smell one." She shakes her head sadly. "Court fae can be cruel, but I could take away her pain. It would be like falling asleep."

Skye is already out of sight. "Can you fix her?"

"Could you?" She laughs. It's a hoarse, choked sound. "They're poor, fragile things, aren't they? Always dying through no fault of their own." The woman suddenly pulls me closer, nostrils flaring. "You wear a glamour made by one of the lords of the Crawling Court."

"To protect me from iron," I say impatiently. "This 'death curse': what do you mean? How do I fix it?"

The woman releases me and backs away, offering me something between a nod and a bow. "Forgive me. I didn't realize you served the court." She backs away hurriedly, eyes lowered. "Please tell your master I meant no disrespect." She drifts out the door before I can yell after her.

With nothing else to do, I follow Skye.

"You need to check in first, hon'," the receptionist says as I try to push through the double doors.

"I'm with the lady who just went back. With the ... blood."

"Are you related?"

Skye's going to hate this. "She's my mom." Legally, that's true.

"Make a name tag." She slides a sticker and a marker across the desk. I scribble something that could be a name and stick it to the front of my shirt before passing through the doors.

The back of the ER consists of a nurse's station surrounded by tiny rooms hedged off by curtains along the walls. I peek discreetly through gaps until I find Skye's. She's on a bed, expression pinched as a nurse cleans her wounds. With the blood wiped away, the jagged red lines of torn flesh are clearly visible across Skye's arm for moments before blood wells up again. Too much blood, too fast. I look away. My breath gets short.

Skye glares up at me. "Go wait outside if you can't do blood."

I don't realize until Skye says something that I've grabbed the metal curtain frame for support. I yank my hand away before I realize it doesn't prickle. It's hard to keep track of what has iron to burn me and what doesn't. "I'm ..." not fine. "I'm not looking." I stare at the curtain opposite me. It's beige. There's a stain shaped like an elephant.

The air in here stings my nose slightly when I inhale. This building might as well be a giant metal cage, even if its steel skeleton is muffled by layers of other materials.

The nurse—a tall woman with short salt and pepper hair—pricks Skye's skin with a needle. "Did you feel that?" Skye shakes her head, and the nurse removes a crescent-shaped needle from a tray and starts stitching the wounds shut, pursing her lips as she works. "Do you take any medication? Blood thinners, maybe?"

"No," Skye says. Even though she looks exhausted and gray-faced, her eyes are alert. "Why?"

"I'm concerned about the lack of clotting." Blood oozes through the stitches—slow, but showing no sign of stopping. Skye's eyes flicker to me, as if I might have answers. "Hm." The nurse tries hard to sound unconcerned as she examines her completed work. "We'll give it a little bit longer. Keep pressure on it. Someone will be in to see how you are in a little bit."

"Did you see the lady in the waiting room?" I ask as soon as the curtain falls back into place behind the departing nurse.

"The one sleeping in the corner or the one floating in the air and bleeding from her eyes?"

I ignore the question. "You don't seem surprised that she's here."

"I'm sure a lot of people fall asleep in hospital waiting rooms."

"Seriously: how often do you see faeries just … around?" I ask.

"Everywhere. Things like that woman are all over hospitals, nursing homes, places where people die often." She shifts uncomfortably and winces. "One of many reasons I don't like hospitals. They come sniffing, looking for the worst-off patients, I guess, and I have to just pretend I can't see anything."

I stare at the red already blooming through the gauze Skye holds to her wounds. "She told me you have a death curse. Leithe must have done it."

"You think?" Skye rubs her eyes and leans back against the bed. "Shit."

"How do we fix it?" I ask.

Skye rubs her eyes. "Hope modern medicine trumps faerie magic in this instance?"

"How often does modern medicine win against faerie magic, in your experience?"

"It's a crapshoot."

Whatever Leithe did, he could probably undo it.

If he's not completely homicidal after being shot.

If he doesn't demand something I can't afford to lose in exchange.

But he's Skye's best—and only—option. I can't call him, but I could call Grandma. But I can't tell her anything that would satisfy her. I settle for a text.

*I had to go out. If you see Leithe, can you let him use your phone to call me? It's important.* I write, delete, and rewrite the words *I'm sorry* at the end several times before ultimately leaving them off.

Grandma calls me not a minute later.

"Good morning," I say.

"Where the hell are you?" Grandma asks.

"Um." I think. Skye glares at me, rolls her eyes, and pointedly makes a suggestive hand gesture. "I ... went out with someone I met last night. It was a last-minute thing. Didn't want to wake you up, so I left without saying anything. Sorry."

Grandma is quiet for a moment. "Where did you even meet someone, the internet?"

"Maybe." I make the word sound sheepish.

"You could meet people in real life if you went out more," Grandma says. "It would be good for you."

"*Okay*," I say. "Did you see my text about Leithe? Is he there? I really need to talk to him."

"About what?"

"We got into a fight and I really need to clear things up with him."

"I have no idea where that man is, Tamsin. Honestly, good riddance."

"Please just go check the Randall Place."

"Why would he be at the Randall Place?"

"He doesn't have a job?"

Grandma sighs. "I don't like him."

"I know."

"And not because he's unemployed and homeless and doesn't even own a phone. Everyone has rough patches. But is he ..." The question dies in the space between us. "You've been acting so strange. You meet this disrespectful deadbeat of a man who makes you call him some made-up name and now you're sneaking around and not telling me anything." She pauses. "Is he a drug dealer?"

"He's not a drug dealer," I say. She scoffs, unconvinced. "He's *not* a drug dealer."

"You're using condoms, right?" she asks.

"There is absolutely no need to talk about this," I say.

"I don't know what you learned at that boarding school, but I never did the sex talk with you, and I should have."

"We do not need to have this conversation right now." My face must be hot enough to fry an egg on.

"Well, you can talk to me, okay? If you want to. And you don't need to sneak off for dates in the middle of the night. You can talk to me about … anything you need to."

"I promise: when there is important love-life news to share, I will tell you. But please, I really, *really* need to talk to Leithe."

She waits, and in that silence I can hear her disappointment. "Fine," she says. "I'll go see if I can find him." A pause. "Please stay safe."

"I'll do my best."

"I'll buy condoms if you need them. And we can see about getting you on the pill."

"I am being *so* careful, but I really need to go. Please have Leithe call me if you find him. It's—"

"It's important, I know." Her tone has a sharp edge to it. She's silent; I'm about to say goodbye before she speaks again. "I love you." I can't remember the last time she said that.

"… I love you too," I say. The words sound just as strained and rusty coming from my mouth as they do from hers. Speaking them is excruciating, like using a muscle that's been atrophied. I hang up the phone before anything else can be said. For a moment, the room is silent aside from the sounds of the hospital on the other side of the curtain.

"So," Skye starts.

"If you say anything about condoms, I'm just going to die right now," I say.

"Sounds like she thinks you're one tequila shot shy of repeating my mistakes." Skye gingerly lifts the pad of gauze from her arm. The dressing is splotched with red, and dark bruises surround the cuts. "What are the odds your guy will fix me after I shot him in the head?"

"He'll do it if I ask. He probably cares way more about having leverage on me than killing you," I say. "No offense."

"I don't even know you," Skye says. "Don't make a bad deal to save my life." She studies her arm. "It might wear off, anyway."

I force myself to look at the wound, to look for the signs of glamour the way Leithe taught me. As my vision relaxes, I see it: the web of pale, creeping threads of Leithe's power. They're not just knotted around Skye's cuts, but wound through her veins, her bones, twisting like choking weeds around her heart, her lungs. The threads pulse steadily, drinking the life out of her with each passing moment. It isn't just her arm. Her blood isn't clotting because her entire body is failing.

"Do I look that bad?" she asks.

I reach out and tug at a thread. It only tightens; Skye gasps in pain. "I'm sorry." I pull my hand back. I have no idea what I'm doing. I could make it worse. I could accidentally kill her. "It's ... I don't know what to do. I'm sorry."

"Then leave it." Skye settles back on the bed. "Why did the witch leave you at my house?" she asks suddenly.

"It ... was part of a larger plan, one I probably only have pieces of." I hesitate, but only briefly. "Well ..." I trail off, find the beginning, and start again. "Last month, I found out I'm an amnesiac fae queen named Mab who was—mostly—imprisoned in a magic tree along with my fiancé by my traitorous vassals right before our wedding. The witch made the prison and wanted—or needed—to give Mab an opportunity to free herself. An escape clause. That was me, I guess. Now that I've gotten us out of the tree, said fiancé wants me to retake my throne and said vassals probably very much don't want that, so one of them showed up yesterday to terrorize me into going to a party." *And it was all possibly because Mab wanted to end her life.* That, I can't bring myself to give voice to. "Questions?"

Skye listens in silence, eyes closed. "Makes as much sense as anything else I've heard in the last twenty years." She doesn't sound angry, only tired. She lifts her hand from the hospital bed and watches her fingers tremble from the effort. "That changeling boy I told you about."

"The one you left in Faerie?"

"I thought I was doing the right thing. I could tell if I was around him much longer, he'd worm his way into my head and I'd end up just as bad off as his mom was when I found her. But afterward, I couldn't sleep. I went back that night, but the door I'd put him through was gone, not that I know what I would have even done with him if I'd found him again." She closes her eyes. "I have no idea what I'm doing. I've never had a plan."

"I don't want to hear your deathbed confession," I say. "Give me your keys. I'll drive back and make Leithe undo whatever he did." But even as I say that, I doubt it would work. It would take at least an hour to get home, if the spare tire holds. Skye deteriorated so quickly that there's no guarantee she'd last long enough for me to find him, especially if I'd need to get him back here for him to undo it.

Skye thinks for a moment. "Fine." She frowns. "But if he'll help, bring him here before making any deals. You're not going to bargain for *my* life."

I nod instead of agreeing out loud. Through a tiny gap before I finish pulling the curtain closed behind me, I see Skye sink into the bed and discard the mask. She looks exhausted. She looks like death.

When I get outside, Grandma texts to tell me no one was at the Randall Place. Either Leithe isn't there or won't show himself to her.

Skye is going to die just hours after I met her. Because of me. I stop and lean heavily against the wall to wait for the panic attack to pass. Until I can get breath back in my lungs. Skye's blood. Zach's blood. It's all the same color on my hands.

"Are you alright?" someone asks. I look up. A blonde woman in hospital scrubs stands in front of me with a look of curious concern on her face.

"No," I admit. "But I don't think you can do anything about it."

"Well," she says with a shrug and a smile. "If you say so. Good luck, then." The woman turns and walks through the automatic doors. I lean against my wall for a few more moments, trying to collect myself, until my mind finally processes the fact that the woman had a tail.

# Chapter Nine

"WAIT!" PEOPLE IN THE waiting room look up in alarm as I run after the woman with the tail. She's not in there, but a door labeled 'Staff Only' swings shut, and through the small glass window, I think I see the bobbing of a blond ponytail.

I cross the room and push through the door, ignoring the receptionist telling me not to go back there.

*I'm not visible. No one can see me.* I repeat the words in my head, whisper them under my breath. Leithe said it should be easy.

The woman is nowhere to be seen. I look into any rooms with windows in the door. No sign of her.

"Ma'am!" A large man in scrubs grabs my arm and stops me short. "You can't be back here." I guess it's not easy.

"I'm allowed to be back here," I say. But I've watched Leithe do it enough times to know I failed to muster a hint of glamour.

"Do you have a work ID?" he asks.

Someone places a hand on my shoulder. "I have a work ID. She's with me." The woman I'd been chasing gives the man a dazzling smile and holds out a work badge with a picture that looks nothing like her.

"Alright. Sorry about that," the man says. He seems like he might say more for a moment, but then returns to the waiting room.

"Hi. Um," I start. She's tall and powerfully-built, with long blond hair in a tight ponytail. Her makeup—red lips, winged eyeliner—is bolder than I would ever have the nerve to wear. She looks human aside from the tail, which is long and tipped with a tuft of blond fur. But if I look closer, there's a hint of something else beneath the layer of glamour.

"That's rude," she says.

"What's rude?" I ask, startled.

"Undressing me with your eyes," she says. "I take you at face value, yeah? Whatever you're hiding beneath that glamour is none of my business." She pokes my shoulder lightly.

"I'm sorry. I hadn't even thought about it that way." I pause. "But I'm not hiding anything. I'm not glamouring myself." I lean in to whisper the last few words, looking around to make sure no one else is near.

The woman cocks her head and looks me up and down. "Why are you whispering? No one who might hear us will give our conversation a second thought." She adjusts the bag she has slung across her shoulder—a square-ish cloth cooler—and holds her hand out to me. Each of her nails is painted a different color; the middle nail is covered in glitter polish. "Eifa."

"Tamsin." I shake her offered hand. Her skin is cool, similar to Leithe's. "Humans can't see your, uh, tail, right?"

"Oh." Eifa twists to look behind her. "No. It's a few layers of perception too deep for most humans to see. But it's harder to keep track of than everything else if I'm not focused." The tail winks out of existence before my eyes. "Is that all you were chasing me down to say?"

"Are you—" I stop myself. For all I know, this question might also be rude, but I already started speaking and Eifa is staring at me expectantly. "My, um, person I know is dying. A faerie from the Crawling Court did something to her. I'm looking for someone who can help."

Eifa smiles. "I thought you said I couldn't help you."

"That was before I saw your tail and realized you were a faerie."

"You shouldn't need eyes for that. It's a different sense, recognizing one of our own." Eifa starts walking, gesturing for me to follow. "I have an errand to finish," she says. "Then I can take your person to someone who might be able to help."

Her legs are longer than mine, and I have to almost run to keep up. "What will it cost?"

She shrugs. "Something you can afford." Her expression hasn't once changed from a friendly, easy smile. "You wouldn't have had any trouble following me if you'd made yourself invisible to humans, or at least glamoured yourself to look like you belong here." She gestures to her scrubs.

"I can't make it work."

Eifa opens the door to a stairwell leading down and holds it for me as I follow. "You're a changeling?"

I nod. "Is it that easy to tell?"

"You still think like a human. You think 'I'm standing right here. Everyone should be able to see me!' and so everyone can see you. You make it so. All you have to do is stop thinking like that."

"It's not easy to just change how I think."

"I said it was simple, not easy." Eifa starts down the stairs and I follow. "It takes time and practice. And it's even harder for changelings if you've had no guidance."

"I thought I was just a screw-up."

"Whoever told you that was probably a bad teacher," Eifa says. I laugh at the thought of her saying that to Leithe's face.

I read the sign above the next set of doors Eifa leads us through. "What does your errand have to do with the morgue?"

Eifa smiles at a woman seated at a desk and flashes the badge that isn't hers. The woman nods without looking up.

The temperature plummets once we're through the next set of doors. My eyes tear up from the sudden, overwhelming burn of iron. The floor and three of the walls are tile, while stainless steel lockers dominate the far wall. My skin itches. Without Leithe's glamour, I imagine it must feel like standing in front of an inferno.

Eifa isn't bothered; she hums to herself as she crosses the room and pulls one of the lockers open using a handkerchief where she touches the metal. I take another look at the bag—cooler—she's carrying. "Are we *stealing body parts*?" I look away from the sheet-covered form on the slab Eifa pulls from the locker.

"We're taking body parts," she says. "Ones that were bought and paid for long ago. All above-board."

"*Why?*"

"Lots of reasons. Including helping your person, possibly."

I make it until she pulls a knife—slender and bone-pale—from her bag. After that, I retreat into the outer office where the woman who waved us through drinks coffee and scrolls on her phone.

Eifa is back out in a surprisingly short time. She pauses by the desk and squeezes the woman's shoulder, offering her a smile. *"His autopsy was all normal.* I know you'll do a great job with the paperwork."

"No problem," the woman says.

I follow Eifa out the double doors and back the way we came. "Aren't people going to notice if bodies are missing organs they're supposed to have?" I whisper.

Eifa shrugs. "Things get lost. No one's shown up to tell me to stop."

"What if ... what if he was murdered and you just tampered with evidence of a crime?"

"Well," Eifa says, "he wasn't murdered." She pats my head. "Now where's your person?"

Skye is gray-faced when I lead Eifa into the exam room. I must have been gone for less than half an hour, but she already looks much worse.

She looks up, groggy, and does a double-take when she sees Eifa. "This isn't your guy." Her words are carefully enunciated, as if it takes effort to form them at all.

Eifa takes a step toward Skye, nostrils flaring. Skye's hand twitches to her side, as if searching for a weapon that isn't there. "You angered someone powerful." Eifa looks impressed. "This is a bad curse. Your life is going to leak out of those cuts on your arm until you die. Human medicine won't save you."

"But I bet you're about to tell me you can," Skye says.

"I can't. But I can take you to someone who might." Eifa notes Skye's hesitation. "You could kill the one who cursed you, that might work. But if you could do that, you wouldn't be here in the first place. You could beg them for mercy instead, but you don't want to do that, either." She says the words with a smile, but not a cruel one. "Your final option is to die here, I won't judge you. It would be easiest. I could even do it quickly, if you'd like."

"And the person you can take me to, what'll they want?"

"Something you can afford to pay."

Skye glares at the other woman. "Fine." She lurches forward and swings her legs off the side of the bed. Eifa whips off her bag and shoves it into my hands. I hold it as far from my body as possible, which isn't far, because it's uncomfortably heavy.

"Shall I carry you?" Eifa asks.

"No." Skye slides off the bed and stumbles before catching herself.

"Shall I carry you when you fall over, then?"

"Skye," I warn. I have no doubt that if Skye says no, Eifa will leave her to die on the ground.

Skye glares at me. "Watch me."

"There's no shame in allowing someone to help you." Eifa keeps pace with Skye, watching her with something akin to amusement—lips quirked, one eyebrow raised, though that may just be how she watches everything.

"Oh? And how much would it cost me?" Skye asks.

"What would you charge?" Eifa asks.

"Nothing," Skye snaps through teeth gritted with the effort of walking. No one stops us as we leave the exam room block and enter the waiting room, perhaps due to Eifa's uniform, her magic, or maybe everyone is simply too busy to care.

"Do you mean the human version of nothing?" Eifa asks. "When humans say 'nothing,' what they really mean is: 'the next time I need something, I expect you to remember the time I helped you for nothing.'"

"Well, people *should* help each other," I say.

"I'm glad we agree. Oh." Eifa stops as we walk outside. "Do you have a car? Because I don't, and it's a long walk."

Before we leave, Eifa pulls the hospital badge from around her neck and drops it on the ground. She watches me watch her. "It will find its way back to Dr. Schwartz eventually, yeah? He won't remember giving it to me. He'll think he must have dropped it."

"Why couldn't you just make a badge with glamour?" I ask. "Why did you need to steal a real one?"

"It helps to have something real."

Skye barely complains about being relegated to the back seat, and for a while Eifa only speaks to give me directions. I can only stay silent for so long before the questions bubble over—questions I could never level at Leithe because I was too busy avoiding him. "So you live in the ... human world?"

"For a little while, now."

"Why here, and not Faerie?"

Eifa studies me. "You're a baby changeling, aren't you? Have you ever been to Faerie?"

"Briefly. There were doors in the woods where I grew up. It was the same as this side, but more. Bigger, more vibrant. "

"Then you didn't go very far at all," Eifa says. "You were in the thin places where court fae rarely go. If you'd kept going you would have found them eventually: the Gentry and their big courts with their countless little courts, taking and breaking each other's things because they themselves don't stay dead for long. Below them are the lesser nobles who fight over the scraps, and at the bottom the dogs who do the fighting and killing on their betters' behalf." Eifa twists her ponytail around her fingers as she speaks.

"And you came here instead," Skye says from the back seat. "So you'd be higher up on the food chain."

Eifa smiles at Skye through the rearview mirror, and even though she doesn't look particularly hostile, I'm reminded that for most animals, showing their teeth is a threat display. "I prefer to make up my own mind about who I'm killing, rather than do it at someone else's command."

"So the courts are bad," I say. "And the Gentry are bad."

"They are what they are," Eifa says.

"And you're any better?" Skye says.

Eifa twists in her seat to look at Skye directly, wrapping one arm around the seat headrest. "Being weak is a terrible feeling. Nip at me all you like if it makes you feel less afraid."

"You come to the human world where you can ignore human laws and do whatever you want. Don't try to convince me that you're a victim." Skye leans back in her seat, winded from those few sentences.

"Humans ignore human laws." Eifa twists back around to face forward.

"How do you get your blood?" Skye asks. "Also hospital morgues? Or do you find living victims for that?"

I take in Skye's words. "Are you saying she's a vampire? Vampires are real? Vampires are faeries?"

"You're either a glaistig or a baobhan sidhe, aren't you?" Skye asks Eifa, ignoring me completely. I recognize neither of those words.

"Those are human words and human categories. But you can call me a glaistig, if it makes you comfortable. When there aren't any maidens offering me their necks, I get pig's blood from a butcher," Eifa says. "Or milk. From the grocery store. Sometimes the farmer's market." She studies me for a moment. "I'm happy to answer any questions you have about me. I won't demand you do the same, but I did notice that the protection glamour you're wearing smells the same as the curse your friend bears," she points out. "An interesting combination."

"It's ... yeah." After so much time in the car and the hospital, Leithe's protection glamour is starting to crack and slough away, making my skin prickle in places. "Skye shot my fiancé, who I am not marrying, and he cursed her," I say.

"*Oh*," Eifa says. "How romantic."

"No," Skye and I say at the same time.

"Oh. Well, I'll kill him for you if you'd like. He sounds unpleasant, and the sport is its own reward."

"He would just come back." I study Eifa's face for any trace of a reaction. "He's Gentry." I wait for her to get angry, scared, to bail out of the car to get as far away from us as possible. But she just looks thoughtful.

"What name does he go by?" Eifa asks.

"Leithe," I say. "He's tall. And dark haired. And ... pretty. I guess?" For all I know, that could describe a good third of fae men, considering I've only met about three.

"I know of him," Eifa says. "The old lord of the Phantom Isles. He and my former lord disagreed often, so I faced his knights many times during my service. Some of them were strong." Leithe lived somewhere before this, has an entire history spanning a length of time I can't fathom. I have no idea who he is.

"So could you kill him?" Skye asks.

"I've always wondered if I could kill one of the Gentry," Eifa says. "It seems like you're in way over your head, baby changeling." Instead of fear, there's anticipation in her eyes; hunger in the curve of her smile. I have no idea who Eifa is, either.

I say nothing. There's nothing I can say. I can only think of Leithe's warning. It occurs to me for the first time that I might be one wrong word from getting killed.

# Chapter Ten

EIFA GUIDES US TO a dingy white Victorian with a sagging porch in a gray and aged part of town. The front door is marked with a red sign declaring the building condemned and warning trespassers away.

After I pull to a stop in the narrow dirt driveway, Eifa gets out and opens the door for Skye before she can protest. At some point during the drive, Eifa's scrubs vanished, replaced by bedazzled shorts and a crop top. As she stands in front of the house, she shakes off the rest of her glamour as well, revealing her tail again, along with a pair of curling ram's horns protruding from her temples and legs covered with a layer of blond fur that end in cloven hooves. I can't remember what color her eyes were before, but they weren't the deep red they are now.

Eifa notices me staring and smiles, showing off sharp canines. "Just inside and down the stairs." She turns to Skye. "But I'm going to have to insist you leave your weapons in the car." Skye and Eifa stare each other down. "If I wanted to do you harm, I'd just have to wait," Eifa continues. The sound of wind chimes from the porch punctuates the otherwise tense silence.

Finally, Skye grumbles something under her breath and pulls a gun from her jacket pocket—a smaller gun than the one she stowed in the glove box before we entered the hospital—and puts it back in the car.

"You can keep the knife if it makes you feel better," Eifa continues. "But if you try to use it on anyone in that house other than me, I might kill you." Her smile doesn't waver.

"You can try," Skye says. After a moment's consideration, she pulls a stainless steel water bottle from the glove box. "You banning water too?" Eifa shrugs in response, and Skye begins her struggle toward the house. Eifa only continues to smile, her tail lashing back and forth behind her.

Several sets of wind chimes hang from the porch. Only when we get closer do I realize each one is lovingly carved from bone. Some depict animals or nature scenes, others spiraling, hypnotic patterns. The smallest chimes are made from human teeth.

"Where did these bones come from?" I ask.

"Dead people," Eifa says.

"How did they die?" Skye asks.

Eifa shrugs. "Lots of different ways, I assume."

I check my phone. No calls. No texts. Maybe I should have just driven back home and begged Leithe for help, but Skye's skin hangs off her bones as if she's hollowing out. It's too late to back out now.

As we step onto the porch, the chimes increase in pitch until my ears pop. I feel a faint sensation, like passing through the membrane of a soap bubble, and look questioningly at Eifa.

"A glamour," Eifa explains. "Just a little barrier to keep away problem visitors." Within the barrier, the noises of the town sound much farther away.

"Like who?" I ask.

Eifa grimaces. "Realtors." She opens the front door for us. The house is quietly rotting, walls and ceiling sagging inward, the smell of mildew and age omnipresent. A pile of bulky black trash bags sit by the door. In one corner, away from the boarded-up windows, is a sleeping bag atop piles of old newspapers.

"Is that yours?" I ask.

"That's Brendan's. He sleeps here sometimes, but he can't see us. Come. We're going down." Eifa guides us toward the back of the house to the basement door. Stairs lead down toward a far wall of plaster-coated brick. A wall alongside the staircase keeps me from seeing anything below aside from the landing.

Eifa leads, directing Skye to follow immediately behind and for me to go last.

With each step down, the walls press further in. The temperature plummets; packed dirt gradually overtakes the bricks until there's nothing but root-riddled earth pressing in from all directions. Beetles, worms, and other burrowing creatures weave in and out of the walls.

There are more stairs than should be possible. When I look behind me, the space in the periphery of my vision warps and stretches; the door above us looks simultaneously only a few steps away and a speck of light in the distance.

"Are we in Faerie?" I ask.

"Yes. No." Eifa lets a millipede crawl across her hand before it burrows back into the wall. "We're in a place with thin walls that can't decide what it wants to be. Not quite mortalside, but not quite the domain of the courts."

Skye stumbles on the final step. Eifa—far faster than me—catches and steadies her. Skye pulls away quickly.

"My mistake." Eifa bends down, rummages around, and picks up an electric lantern. "I forgot you can't see as well." When she clicks the lantern on, her eyes reflect the sudden light. She waves the lantern to beckon us forward, shadows dancing across the uneven walls.

We turn the corner and the space yawns open into a cavern. The light illuminates a decades-old living room set in the center—two overstuffed armchairs and a sofa surrounding a coffee table, all sitting atop a patterned rug laid out over bare earth. A plastic house plant sits on the table.

A withered, pallid-skinned man in loose pants and an open terrycloth robe dominates the sofa. "Put the dying one on the table," he says. His speech is warbled. His jaws are oversized compared to the rest of his head, and they look overstuffed with sharp teeth. The flesh covering his face has receded like corpse's; the eyes in their deep-set sockets are milky white.

Next to the dead-looking man sits a white-furred rat the size of a small child in a tie and button-down. The rat taps his pink, claw-tipped fingers on the coffee table and cocks his head, nose twitching and round black eyes taking us in. Teeth braided into his fur clink together when he moves. "Where's the third?" His voice is deeper than I expect.

"It was just the two of them," Eifa says. She turns to us and gestures to the men on the couch. "Martin." She points to the one in the robe. "And Chisel." The rat.

I'm not sure what names I was expecting, but it wasn't those. "Tamsin. Skye. Nice to meet you," I say. "What do you mean, 'where's the third'?"

Martin ignores my question and frowns at a shallow dish on the table that holds four knobby ivory cubes. "Did you read them wrong?" he asks Chisel.

Chisel runs his fingers over the cubes. "No. They said there would be three. Maybe even four. Not two."

Martin grunts in annoyance before turning back to us. "Well? You're not going to die any slower by standing there. Sit on the table."

Chisel takes the dish of cubes—bones, probably, given everything else—and retreats to a different chair. He offers me a smile as he sits.

Skye only hesitates for a moment before following Martin's instructions and sitting. "Hand," he says. She places her hand in his and he unwraps the soaked bandage. Blood oozes steadily through the stitches and the veins around the wounds are an ugly red against her skin. Skye fights a losing battle to control her face when Martin presses a finger against the bloody bandage and sticks the finger in his mouth. "You were wounded by one of the Gentry of the Crawling Court. The wound is cursed to bleed out your life until you die."

"Yeah," Skye says. "We were told you could do something about it."

"I could slow it, but I can't stop it. I could, at most, give you another day instead of another hour. There would be no payment. I don't take payment for incomplete work."

"So we'll have to go find Leithe anyway," I say. "And beg him to fix it."

"It would take a token of equal or greater power for me to remove the curse," Martin says. "I might be able to heal her if you were able to bring me his hair. Maybe his blood." That wouldn't happen.

"Could it be something from anyone of equal or greater power?" I ask.

"Any Gentry that's at least as powerful as he is," Martin says. "But even if there were any you could reach, they would not help for free."

"Try it with my hair," I say. Everyone turns sharply to look at me.

Martin recovers first. "Eifa." He gestures toward me. Eifa picks a slender knife off the table. For a moment, I wonder if she's just going to stab me, but she gently cuts a few strands of my hair where it's longest and gives them to Martin. He twists the strands until they become a single long, silvery thread, which he ties to a crescent-shaped, bone needle. After examining the thread a final time and mumbling under his breath, he offers Skye a vial of something dark and murky. "Drink."

Skye glares at the vial. "What is it?"

"Necessary for your healing," he says. After a moment's hesitation, Skye drinks it. Almost immediately, she starts to lean back unsteadily; Eifa gently takes her shoulders and guides her down until she's lying on the table.

"You didn't say it would knock her out," I say.

"I did not," Martin agrees. "But rest is necessary for her healing." He delicately severs and removes the hospital stitches before replacing them with his own, working with precision despite his size.

With each pull of the needle through Skye's skin, the threads of Leithe's glamour snap and unravel into nothingness. The thread woven from my hair shimmers when it catches the dim lantern light as Martin draws it taut after each stitch. When he's done, color has returned to Skye's sleeping face, and the wounds are almost invisible aside from the slightest raised lines of flesh. "The curse is severed," he says.

My body has been a single tensed muscle since I woke up, and now I finally let myself take a breath. Skye is fine. Leithe is alive. No one died because of me. "What do we owe you?" I ask.

Martin studies me for a moment. "My price is usually the body, once its owner has no more need of it. But I'll take a lock of your hair, for the next person who angers one of the Gentry."

"I'll be bald by next week if this keeps up," I say as Eifa ties off a lock of hair and cuts it.

"You can't even tell," she says. "Besides, I think the lop-sided look is very stylish."

"You'll stay until she wakes up," Martin says. "She's still weak. She needs to rest."

"Thank you," I say. Eifa stares at me as I awkwardly fidget in my chair, air heavy with the weight of questions, the answers to which they're probably waiting for me to volunteer. Eifa doesn't have her hand on a weapon, but her fingers do hover close to a sword leaning against the wall.

It's not the only weapon. The room is littered with weapons made of bone in varying stages of construction, alongside other creations: utensils and dishes, toys, wind chimes-in-progress. In his rocking chair, Chisel carves a slender bone absentmindedly the same way another might knit. Not just carving, I realize. Under his fingers, the bone bends and warps like putty.

I expected to be interrogated, but instead, Martin unzips a corner of the insulated bag and peers inside, mumbling to himself.

"Why do you take organs?" Asking outright if he eats them seems rude.

"I eat them," he says.

"Oh," I say. "Eifa mentioned you ... bought them?"

Martin nods, removing a withered black organ from the bag. "He had a weak heart when he was a boy. He would not have reached adulthood. I loaned him mine on the condition I could take a few other things when he no longer needed them." He swallows the heart whole.

"That's something fae can just ... do?" I ask.

He nods. "Any fae can gift a piece of themselves."

"How?"

"By removing it," he says.

"Removing it via the, um, normal way?" I mime cutting open my chest. Something about the idea renders me unable to put it into words.

"Yes," Martin says. "The normal way."

"... Right," I say. The solution hangs there, in the forefront of my mind. Hunter doesn't have a heart; I do. All I need to do is cut it out. It's what I *should* do, what I owe him.

Caught in my own thoughts, it takes a while for me to realize the others seem indifferent to my presence. Martin goes back to cataloging the contents of the bag and ignoring me. Eifa stares but says nothing. Chisel hasn't looked up from his project. I finally break. "When my hair worked, I figured you would ask. Or get mad. Or ... scared," I say.

Martin zips the bag back up and looks at me. "About what?"

"That I'm Gentry? You don't like Gentry, right?"

"If you meant us harm, it would be far too late for us to do anything about it," Chisel says.

"And you seem a little sad and pathetic, honestly," Eifa adds. "But I am curious about how you can be a changeling and Gentry."

"It's …" I remember Leithe's warning. I remember Thistledown. I look at the people who helped me and Skye for hardly anything at all. And I want to trust them. "It's a long story. I'm Gentry, allegedly. My … fiancé says so. But I only remember growing up human for the last two decades. I can't do anything Gentry are supposed to be able to do. I'm powerless." I pick at the scratchy fabric of the armchair. "So, I guess I should just ask and get it out of the way: are you going to murder me and harvest my organs or something?" Eifa starts laughing.

Martin lets out a snort. "Only if you're offering."

I realize I've pulled a thread loose from the chair upholstery and ball my hand into a fist to keep from doing it again. "Can I learn to heal people like you can?" I ask him. For just a moment, I imagine an alive and smiling brown-haired man wearing an aged and faded crescent-shaped scar across his throat like a necklace.

"If it's in your Name," he says. Names, again.

"She just said she's a changeling," Chisel says. "She probably doesn't know what you're talking about."

Martin sighs. "We can all do little tricks, little suggestions—though some are far better at it than others—but all other gifts are tied to one's Name. My Name—like many who were born of the Crawling Court—is tied to flesh and bone, in fixing them, remaking them, reading them. Unless your Name is as well, you will never be able to do the things that I do, the way that I do them."

"And your Name is *Martin*?" I ask.

"That's a collection of sounds I allow others to call me, just like 'Chisel,' or 'Eifa,' or 'Tamsin.' Your *Name* isn't chosen or given. It comes from within and belongs only to you: the thing that encompasses everything you are. You have it, and no one else can even perceive it unless you give it to them."

"Then how do I know what my Name is?"

There's an awkward silence as the other fae stare at me strangely. "How do you know how to find your own feet?" Eifa finally asks.

"Eifa," Martin chides before turning back to me and pointing to his own head. "It should be there, clear to you. If you've given it away, you should feel its absence like a wound."

I squeeze my eyes shut and listen. All I hear is the white drone of anxiety. A single word that sums up everything that I am. I'm not sure that's something I would ever want to know. "There's nothing, and it doesn't feel like there *should* be anything. Do changelings have problems knowing their Names?" I ask with a flicker of hope. Maybe they can offer advice that Leithe couldn't.

"I don't know," Martin says. "I have no answer for you." Despite everything, I feel a little bit disappointed. The feeling is immediately smothered by shame. What, exactly, had I been hoping for?

"You can stay if you would like," Eifa says. "If you're running from your betrothed, we'll do what we can to hide you. If he comes after you, we'll do what we can to stop him." I stare at her and silently take in the words I don't deserve to hear.

"I don't know who I'm running from," I say. It isn't just Leithe. The specter of the Dreaming Court—of Lelit, Noctiva—looms over me. How easily could they hurt these people, just for helping me?

Eifa looks at me with an expression of pity that makes me nauseous. "Then rest here for a while, at least. Until you decide." I should rest. My body isn't tired but my mind is exhausted. It's never not exhausted.

I don't know what to do when Skye wakes up. We should go our separate ways. I should get as far away as possible from anyone else. But I worry that if she leaves now, she'll disappear forever.

# Chapter Eleven

I SET DOWN THE paper crane—blue with a golden fan pattern—next to the rest. They extend in a line that vanishes into the gloom. My hands are small and round with baby fat. Zach sits across from me, watching my hands as he folds his own crane—cream paper blotted with red that might be roses, might be bloodstains.

When we were nine, we read a book for school about a girl who wanted to fold one thousand paper cranes so they would carry her wish up to heaven. Zach and I were determined to get our own wishes heard, whatever those were back then. We folded them out of anything—newspaper, magazines, homework. We folded them until our hands were covered in paper cuts. I remember leaving a string of cranes—the ones made with the real, colorful origami paper I bought with my allowance—hanging from the Randall Place's rotting front porch railing.

I finish another crane and set it down. This one is pink with white tear drops. In some corner of my mind, I realize this isn't where I should be, were this a memory. We folded our cranes under our desks at school, in Grandma's living room, on Zach's porch. Here, the world is gray and empty save for the line of tiny paper birds.

Zach was always better than me. Grandma got me an instruction book for my birthday with many different patterns, but Zach was the one who learned them all. Flowers, turtles, butterflies, boats. His favorite was the gorilla. We hung them from strings around my room. He would never take them home. He didn't tell me why, but as the memories trickle back in, I see his father enter Grandma's house to pick Zach up and roll his eyes at the penguin taking shape in his son's hands. I remember Zach's interest waning until he finally called the whole thing stupid.

"What would you wish for?" I ask him.

He looks from my hands to my face, smiling his crooked smile. "What do you think?"

What would a dead boy wish for? "Yeah. That was a stupid question," I say.

"But we're folding these for you." He sets another one down. Jade green. Red pinwheels. "What will you wish for?" I open my mouth, but he cuts me off. "And don't say 'I would wish you back to life'. That's boring. And pointless."

We don't move, but there's always space to set down another crane, always a fresh piece of paper in my hand. "I wish I could tell Grandma the truth. I wish I could keep her safe. I wish those things weren't mutually exclusive."

Zach's nails hiss along the crease that forms the bird's wing. "I thought Hunter was the one you wanted to save."

"I'm not sure I *can* save Hunter. With Grandma, maybe there's a chance."

"So you want power." He places another crane down. Hot pink. No pattern. "Why not get strong enough to save them all?"

"No." I set a crane down. Black. Covered in a gold lattice. "I don't want to be like Leithe, or Lelit, or any of them. I just don't want anyone else to get hurt."

"I think," Zach says, "that you have no idea what you really want. Or—" In the pitch darkness, the cranes in all their vibrant colors shine like lanterns. "You don't want to admit it."

What I want.

The only sound is the whisper of fingertips against paper as we fold our cranes by muscle memory. My mind works while my hands move on their own. The words I could say bump up against a wall, regroup, press again, but each time I choke them back down before the half-formed thought can escape my throat. "I think ..." What I might have said is lost when I hear something that was until now hidden by the rustle of paper: the slightest shifting in the earth beneath us. The slither of a body through dirt. "What is that?"

Zach freezes, listening. The crane in his hands—emerald green; a shimmering fish scale pattern—only needs one more fold to be complete. My hands, I realize, are fists, the delicate blue paper crushed in my palm. In the sudden silence, both of us frozen, I hear something from below that might be words.

"Get out," Zach says. He locks eyes with me; there's fear in them. "*Now!*" He launches himself over the line of cranes and shoves me hard in the chest.

I fall. It could have been miles or inches until I land on something soft with a gasp. Skye leans over me, eyebrow raised. I'd fallen asleep twisted into a pretzel in one of Martin's armchairs. The others watch me curiously. My phone reads just after two P.M. I slept for almost eight hours.

"What's wrong?" Zach's warning echoes in my ears. I try to be discreet about wiping a line of drool from the corner of my mouth. Before Skye can say anything, a paper crane flutters through the air on stubby wings and lands on her head. "Oh."

Origami cranes fly all over the basement, filling the air with the whisper of rustling paper and the lyrical trilling of songbirds—what I thought such tiny, delicate creatures should sound like when I was a child.

"They just popped into existence," Skye says. "And we all agreed it wasn't any of us." She changed her clothes. Cargo pants and a long-sleeved shirt beneath the same jacket. A half-hearted attempt was made to clean the blood from the jacket sleeve.

"I didn't do it on purpose." But I had to have done something. I gently pluck the crane off Skye's head and cradle it in my palm. It feels warm. Familiar. Real. A tiny heart beats rapid-fire within the paper body. "Is this it? Nothing … else?" Nothing wrong? I can't shake the image of Zach in my head. It was only a dream, true, but so were these birds. Skye narrows her eyes.

"What else were you expecting?" Chisel asks, frowning between me and the dish of carved bones in front of him.

"Maybe you could tell us," Skye says. "Since you've been rolling those knucklebones like you're worried about something."

"If we wanted you dead, we wouldn't have needed to do anything," Eifa points out matter-of-factly. She holds out a finger to allow a crane to land.

"You've said so." Skye's hand rests casually close to her waistband, poised to reach the gun that must be hidden against her spine. She would have been able to get it if she went to her car for new clothes. Eifa's hand rests just as casually within reach of the sword leaning against my chair. "But maybe you were just trying to keep Tamsin happy and in one place until whoever you called could get here," Skye finishes.

"If you point the weapon you have down the back of your pants at Chisel or Martin, I will kill you before you can fire it." Eifa speaks those words with the same friendly tone with which she's spoken the entire time. It sounds less like a threat and more an observation. "They called no one."

"Did *you*?" Skye asks.

"None of us called anyone," Chisel says. "Whatever threats might find their way here are only those you brought with you."

"What did we bring?" I ask. I'm not sure when the cranes went silent, or when they froze in the air as if captured in ice. But in the newfound quiet, I hear something else. Just the suggestion of a noise.

I slide off the chair to the floor to get closer to the sound. Far beneath us, something—countless somethings, maybe—slithers and writhes against the dirt. The same noise from the dream, but louder. Closer.

The feeling of being observed starts at the back of my neck and spreads down my spine. I suddenly feel very small, held by the sheer weight of the attention of whatever is beneath like a butterfly pinned to a board. "There's something down there." The pressure chokes the air out of my lungs, making my words come out in a whisper. Skye and Eifa are too focused on each other to pay attention to me, and Martin and Chisel are more focused on Skye and Eifa. No one spares me a glance.

The sound gets louder, rising until the rumbling threatens to collapse the entire cavern. It breaks itself into a pattern that could almost be words, plucking at my mind like musical strings, the reverberations of which I feel in my teeth.

It presses and presses until it forces itself into my head like the popping of a balloon, and suddenly a storm of countless howling voices lurches into icy clarity. My voice might be one of them. As one, the cranes pop out of existence.

The voices are old. Old, and so cold. They pull and twist at me, prying me open, searching. In the impression of the mind touching mine, I see something akin to a hand reaching up. We're standing like ants in its palm and its fingers are closing.

"We need to leave!" I scream to be heard over the chaos in my head. Then Eifa and Skye are on either side of me, their conflict apparently forgotten for the moment. They look concerned, but only for me, not themselves. The cavern isn't actually shaking. Only I am. "You can't hear it?" I ask.

Martin meets my eyes. He must not like whatever he sees. "Up the stairs. Now," he says.

But the fist continues to close. Clods of dirt tremble and fall from the walls and ceiling. At first I wonder if it's still only happening in my head, but then Skye shouts as a hand—flesh sloughing off and slick with black rot—breaks through the dirt and wraps itself around my calf.

Eifa skewers the hand with a blade I didn't see her pick up and throws me toward the stairs. "Go!"

Bodies push their way out of the floor, walls, and ceiling. Some are human, but many are animals, or things that must be faeries. And they all reach for me and me alone as Skye and I make for the stairs. They grab at my ankles, my wrists, my clothes; it makes me grateful I hacked off my hair earlier.

We're almost to the top of the stairs when a gnarled, fleshless hand grabs my ankle through a gap between the steps and pulls. I fall back into Skye, who braces against me.

"Don't move," she says. Skye shoots it point-blank through the wrist; the noise reverberates off the cramped walls. The hand's grip slackens and Skye finishes her work by stomping down on its shattered bones before shoving me forward, shouting something muffled by my ringing eardrums.

I make it the last few steps and throw open the basement door, stumbling out and into the dingy sunshine able to make its way through the boarded-up windows. A vicious howl reverberates through the cavern as it collapses in earnest, ceiling and walls bowing inward as if they're about to burst from the weight of the bodies.

Skye isn't behind me; she's gone back for Chisel, grabbing him by his scruff and crushing the skeletal hand grasping at him under her boot. She pushes him ahead of her and turns back to help Martin, catching him by the collar of his robe and shoving him across the threshold just before a pair of canine jaws lunging from the wall can snap closed around his head.

Eifa is the last one. She fends off the onslaught of grasping, tearing limbs as the walls close in. Hands, talons, and claws wrap around whatever they can grab, pulling her down farther for each step she manages to take. Soon, there's no more room to maneuver, making her weapon useless.

"Hold this." Skye shoves her gun into my hands and shakes her water bottle twice before yanking the lid off. "Sorry." She flicks the bottle at Eifa, dousing her in a black slurry.

Eifa's eyes widen an instant before her skin starts to smoke and sizzle where the water contacts her open wounds. But the hands restricting her burn, too. She takes advantage of the opportunity to struggle up the last few stairs, far enough to grab Skye's outstretched hand.

Skye—other hand wrapped around the doorframe—pulls Eifa through the door and slams it behind her. Martin and Chisel clutch each other in relief. For a moment, the only noise is our labored breathing.

"It likely won't chase us into the mortal world," Martin says.

Then the knob flies off like a bullet and the door opens so violently it slams into the wall and cracks down the middle.

On the other side, an oily black substance oozes through the door frame. Bodies emerge: Grasping hands, empty eye sockets, grinning mouths. They come together to form a mockery of a human form that fills the doorway. The countless skulls speak, their voices overlapping but finally understandable.

*Mab.*

*Mab.*

*Mab.*

The skulls repeat the name over and over. Calling her. Calling me.

Eifa, ignoring her blistering skin, readies her blade and moves to cut the creature off. "Run," she says to us.

Before the creature can take a step over the threshold, the house shudders. The door frame cracks and slumps. The creature, if it had a face, might look surprised as it's suddenly forced back. For a moment, it fights. It rises another step before it flies backward and vanishes, rock and earth collapsing and filling the basement before my eyes.

I blink. The basement is normal. The walls are once again unremarkable brick.

"Who did that?" I ask.

"Me," Leithe says.

# Chapter Twelve

Leithe stands in the open front door, scowling, one shoulder leaning against the frame. The upper right side of his face is covered with cracks like broken porcelain that leak wisps of black smoke. He looks at me, then at Skye behind me, eyes narrowing.

"Don't—" Before I can finish the sentence, he extends an arm toward her. I'll never know what he planned to do, because he snaps his arm back just before the sword Eifa throws sinks into the door frame, slicing through the space his hand had just occupied.

Leithe barely pulls the sword from the wall in time to block Eifa as she barrels into him with a second sword she must've brought from the basement. They're locked together at an impasse until Eifa headbutts him, simultaneously twisting the sword out of his grip. She brings her own blade back to swing, but then something beyond the door catches her attention and she launches herself back just as the kelpie crashes through the doorway and nearly snaps its crocodilian jaws shut around her head.

The kelpie's shattered skull has been meticulously woven back together with dead branches and small animal bones. It still has most of its teeth, and those it's missing have been replaced with razors of jagged, broken bone and wood. The unbroken parts of its body still look almost alive, bone and muscle only showing through the parts of its hide shredded by Skye's gun.

Skye's gun. Skye doesn't have her gun. I do, held in front of me and pinched between as few fingers as possible to keep it from eating through what remains of Leithe's glamour too fast. My fingertips prickle where I hold it, only threatening to get worse as the glamour flakes away.

The gunshot is loud and I almost hit myself in the head with the barrel from the force of the recoil. The bullet leaves a surprisingly small hole in the ceiling, considering the noise.

"Leithe, stop!" I scream into the moment of surprised silence that follows. Leithe hesitates, and by extension so does the kelpie, pulling back mid-lunge and instead scoring the floor with its hooves while a crackling, hissing sound burbles from somewhere deep in its throat.

Eifa's hand shakes. For a moment, I think it must be from fear or pain, but then I see the naked bloodlust in her eyes and the grin on her face and realize it's from the strain of holding herself back.

"Eifa." Martin's voice is calm. Eifa takes a breath and steadies her hands, but doesn't take her eyes off Leithe and the kelpie.

"I'm confused," Leithe says, black blood dripping from his nose where Eifa headbutt him. He looks furious. "Am I not rescuing you from a kidnapping?"

"You are not," I say. "Which I tried to explain to you before you attacked Skye. And then cursed her. And then attacked her again." I pause. "Thanks for stopping the basement monster, though."

"Is that not a weapon?" He points to the gun in my hand. "A weapon that human was pointing at you hours ago?"

"It was a misunderstanding that would have been re-solved a lot faster if you *listened*," I say.

"*I'm* the one who doesn't listen?" He points at the basement door. "I suppose you don't remember that I warned you about the attention you'd attract if you stuck a single *toe* into another monarch's domain. And you did, clearly, or the Crawling King himself wouldn't have nearly dragged all of you straight down to his palace. And he would have, if I hadn't closed the door."

I falter. He did say something to that effect. And in my panic over Skye, I forgot. "Well," I say, refusing to cede any ground. "We wouldn't have come here in the first place if you hadn't cursed Skye."

"I have little interest in continuing this," he says. "But if that human attacks me again, I'm going to remove her bones and turn her into a rug."

"How's your head feeling?" Skye asks. The temperature drops. The early afternoon light dims. The shadows at Leithe's feet get agitated. But Skye meets his glare with one of her own.

"Okay, stop it!" I say to Leithe. "Do the threats and special effects make you feel tough?" He scoffs and rolls his eyes, but turns his attention to the others. Chisel and Martin kneel. Eifa, with only a hint of reluctance, follows suit.

"Who are you sworn to?" Leithe asks.

"No one, My Lord. We've been courtless for many years," Martin says.

"You don't have to kneel," I say. But Martin and Chisel don't rise until Leithe gives a slight nod. Only after they stand does Eifa shoot to her feet and begin slicking the water and iron from Skye's water bottle off her body. Her back and limbs are scored with bloody and burned claw marks.

Skye shrugs off her jacket and throws it to the other woman as a makeshift towel. "Sorry."

"That I'm alive?" Eifa smiles, picking a few burnt strands of hair off her head. "I forgive you."

"Tamsin, we need to leave," Leithe says. "It won't be hard for the Crawling King to re-open this door." He turns to the others. "And you should be well out of his way before that happens."

"We know," Martin says. Standing, he's at least six feet tall, though his robe hangs loose on his gaunt frame.

"I'm sorry," I say. "He was looking for me."

"We know," Chisel says drily. "We're already packed." He gestures to the trash bags I saw by the door on the way in.

"You expected this to happen?" I ask.

Chisel nods. "I saw that the people who would come to me for help would bring with them the loss of my home and those close to me. So far, one of those things has not come to pass. I would like to keep it that way, so we shall go."

"Then why would you help us in the first place?" Skye demands.

"Why do you think?" Martin sighs. "Omens are like tiny candles in the dark. Each one only illuminates a small bit of space around it. Trying to blindly flee a warning may simply lead you to tripping into it anyway. If I must make my decisions in the dark, I would rather make the ones I won't regret."

"What's the point, then?" I ask. "If you can't actually change anything?"

"Did we not?" Chisel asks. "I told Eifa to use the front entrance to the hospital today. And we had time to pack."

"Before you depart, there is the matter of debts to be paid," Leithe says.

"Are you seriously going to extort them?" I ask.

"Of course, My Lord. We owe you our lives," Martin says.

"No, you do not," Leithe says. "My betrothed's actions have run you out of your home and into danger." He gestures to the kelpie. "Take this creature as recompense. I don't need it." I'm too surprised by Leithe's sudden generosity to be offended.

Martin looks as perturbed at being gifted an undead horse as I would be. "I am grateful for your kindness."

"How did you find me, anyway?" I ask.

Leithe nods toward the open door. One of Hunter's dogs sits panting cheerfully in the yard. "Former Wild Hunt beasts. Probably among the greatest trackers in Faerie." He pulls a loop of long blond hair tied in a knot from his sleeve. "I did tell you that you should burn your hair so no one could use it to track you. How unsurprised I was to find that you ignored me."

I step outside. "Is Hunter here?" As if waiting for permission, the dog crosses the yard in a few strides and presses its flank against my legs.

"No," Leithe says with offense. "Though I'm sure you'll be pleased to know he would have walked all the way here to get himself killed for you if he hadn't realized how much

I would enjoy that. He and the other beast remained behind to watch the human woman."

Outside, Eifa loads the bags onto the kelpie's back—its bones rearranging themselves to keep them in place. She has new weapons: three blades of varying lengths hanging from a belt and a spear strapped across her back. When she's done with the bags, she gives Chisel and Martin a rueful smile.

Martin gives Eifa a long look. "I expected as much."

Eifa squeezes each of their hands in turn. "It was an honor."

"You're not going with them?" I ask.

"No," Eifa says. She turns to Skye. "You saved my life." Skye takes a step back when Eifa suddenly drops to a knee before her. "And I owe you a debt. Please give me a quest or allow me to accompany you until my debt has been fulfilled."

"God," Skye says. "You don't owe me anything. Please get up."

"You don't believe my life has value?" Eifa asks.

Until this moment, I haven't seen Skye look so thoroughly thrown off. "I didn't do it so you'd owe me."

"I don't care why you did it, and I know the value I place on my own life, so you can either give me a worthy task or tolerate my presence until I've done enough to repay my debt," Eifa says with a tone of finality.

"I'm not sure why this must be spelled out," Leithe says, "but you'd be insulting her by not letting her repay her debts."

Skye doesn't acknowledge Leithe. "Fine. Do whatever you want. You can decide when you feel like you've repaid me."

Eifa beams. "Excellent, My Lady."

Skye's face turns red. "Do not ever call me that again."

"I must give you something as well, for helping to save me and my husband," Chisel says. Skye looks too taken aback to argue as Chisel holds out a pale, crescent-shaped needle between two of his claw-tipped fingers.

"Thank you," she says with uncertainty as he drops it into her palm. "But you already saved my life. We can just call it even."

"Tamsin paid for the curse-breaking already," Martin says. "If you want to owe anyone, owe her."

Skye's face screws up in annoyance. "I told you not to do that," she says to me.

I shrug. "You were unconscious. Was I supposed to go through your wallet?"

"I'm considering us even for me stopping that thing with all the arms from eating you," Skye says.

"Yeah," I say. "Seems fair."

Skye holds her hand out to me. "Gun."

"Oh, right." I hand her the gun I forgot I was holding.

"Right, then." Skye checks the gun and holsters it. "Tamsin, what are you going to do now?"

The question sounds like a trap. "Go home," I say. "Grandma's probably going crazy."

"No," Skye says. "Someone already came to my mother's house looking for you, right? You can't stay with her."

"Oh." Leithe raises an eyebrow. "I see. Tamsin, you could have just said this was a matter between you and your strange, fake human family."

"I've been trying to get her to move. It's kind of hard when I can't explain *why*," I say.

"You get her to leave with you, and then what? You have an immortal chasing you who probably has an army of people like her"—Skye gestures at Eifa—"at her beck and call. How could you possibly think you could keep her safe if what's-her-name came back?"

"It'll be two armies, now," Leithe says, then turns to me. "Unless you would like to inform the Blooming Queen where you are and add a third to the mix?"

Skye reaches into her jacket pocket and scowls when she only comes up with an empty cigarette pack. She crumples the pack in her hand and shoves it back into her jacket. "Would they chase Tamsin?" she asks Leithe.

"If they didn't think there was any point in waiting for her to come back," Leithe says. "They'd have no interest in a human Tamsin abandoned."

Skye crosses her arms. "Then this is what you're going to do," she tells me. "You are going to go back to my mother's house. You are going to pack a bag. You are going to tell her you are leaving and never coming back. Then you are going to leave and never go back."

"No," I say. "She's going to think it's her fault."

"She's going to be alive," Skye snaps. "You can't have both."

She's right. Anything else would be selfish. I've only been putting off the inevitable. "Fine. I'll do it." Maybe it's for the best. Maybe I'm trying too hard to cling to something I should have never had.

"Then we should go to the Dreaming Court," Leithe says. "It's the best hope for getting your strength back. Head off Lelit by going directly to the ball. If you don't, the rest of the court will think you're scared of her."

"I *am* scared of her," I say. "I'm not going to Faerie. I'm not walking into the obvious trap." Leithe opens his mouth to argue, but Skye cuts him off.

"Lelit would be weaker in the human world, right?" Skye says.

"So am I," Leithe says. "So is Tamsin. There's more advantage to be had in us returning to Faerie."

"But guns are strong anywhere," Skye says. "She's probably never seen a gun before, and she's not going to expect a human to shoot her. So she comes after Tamsin, and shooting her should put her out long enough for you two to clean up, right?" She gestures to Eifa and Leithe. Skye doesn't need to point out that it worked well enough on Leithe. His face says that he knows that, too.

"Perhaps," Leithe says, frowning. "And what do you gain from helping?"

"I help you do whatever you're going to do to her, you and Tamsin help me find my son." She says it as if it's already been decided.

"And then what?" I ask. "Because it sounds like Lelit will be pretty pissed about that, and when she inevitably recovers—given that she's *immortal*—she's going to want revenge, right?" I turn to Leithe for confirmation.

He nods. "Yes, and we'll deal with it when it's time to deal with it."

"I don't want to spend my entire immortal life playing … revenge tag," I say.

"That sounds like a future problem," Skye says.

I realize I'm outvoted. "Fine. Then my right-now problem is that I have been walking around barefoot in pajamas that got dragged across a dirty highway," I say. "Let's just go home so I can at least put on a bra."

# Chapter Thirteen

Every single service light flickers on when Skye starts her car. After much swearing, glaring at Leithe, and crawling under the vehicle, she declares that the only place we're going is the nearest mechanic.

After the car sputters into the shop, Skye spends the next twenty minutes trying to convince the mechanic to let her do the work herself. He declines.

So we end up in the bar across the street. Chucks—no apostrophe—is dimly lit and almost empty in the not-quite-late afternoon. The bartender is a balding, middle-aged man who stares openly when we enter. Skye doesn't look out of place here, maybe Eifa as well. The bartender says nothing about my lack of shoes or real clothes.

After studying the few patrons, Leithe renders himself visible to humans between one step and the next, at the same time glamouring his clothes from a loose, floor-length black robe to a plaid button-down and jeans, all slightly different shades of black on black.

The bartender gives us a curt greeting and Skye gives an equally curt beer order. No one pays any notice to Hunter's dog as it curls up beneath our stools.

Eifa orders milk. I get water. The bartender turns to Leithe, and Leithe pulls his attention from the collection of deer heads mounted on the wall over the booths, each with a more impressive rack of antlers than the last.

"I don't have any money," I tell Leithe.

Leithe ignores me, gesturing to Skye. "What she ordered." The bartender turns away to make the drinks.

"I don't have any money," I say again. "And neither do you."

"I will," Leithe says. "Find some pebbles, buttons, something that has the shape of coins, and I'll give him more gold than he'd ever see in his life otherwise."

Skye nods toward the bartender. "What happens to him when the glamour eventually fades?"

"It'll last long enough for him to spend it," Leithe says.

"And someone down the line is going to end up with a pile of pebbles and buttons," Skye points out.

He rolls his eyes. "I thought I needed to pay *him*, not some other person."

"But someone will get in trouble," I say.

Leithe shoots an *are you hearing this* look at Eifa. In response, she removes several bills from her pocket. "Some of Martin and Chisel's customers pay cash," she says. "If you have no money, I'll pay for you. Consider it thanks for closing that door." Leithe rolls his eyes harder, but doesn't stop Eifa from placing a few bills in front of him.

Leithe turns to Skye. "I'm curious, who would you blame if your mother dies because you wouldn't let me glamour the mechanic into repairing your car faster?"

"You're not glamouring anyone," Skye says.

I turn my attention to my phone. Several texts from Grandma came in after I emerged from Martin and Chisel's basement.

*How is it going?*

*When are you coming home?*

*You can bring your friend over.*

*Are you going to be here for dinner? I just want to know how many I'm cooking for.*

The texts came in almost precisely on the hour. I want to respond, say everything's fine and I'll be home soon. But I can't, not if I want her to believe it when I tell her I'm never coming back. Maybe the best thing to do is make it bad. Make her relieved to never see me again.

But I want her to call. Even though if she calls, I might break, lose my nerve entirely. But she doesn't call. And I don't text. Nothing I could say is worth a thing, not when I'm about to disappear as completely as Skye did when she was my age.

I need to think about something else.

"Skye," I say. "Do you have a job?" It's both a question I've been wondering and a convenient way to distract myself. "Or is driving around and shooting bad faeries profitable?"

"You don't even have a job," Skye says.

"It's 'Faerie Queen.' Allegedly."

Skye snorts. For a while, I don't think she's going to answer the question, but then she says, "I'm a carnival mechanic on and off. And whatever other odd jobs I can get when I need them."

"You're a *carnie*?"

"Yeah. I guess so." She idly plays with her lighter. "I started working at the Foster's garage when I was fourteen. Then I ran off with a guy I met at the state fair right after I graduated high school, so I just fell into maintaining the equipment."

"The guy, was he ... ?" I trail off.

"The dad? Yeah." She sighs. "He was also almost thirty and a general piece of shit. But he was a way out." A long silence follows. Hunter's dog rises and rests its muzzle on Skye's leg. She jerks in surprise from the contact, but eventually rests an awkward hand on the animal's head.

"So, carnie by day, faerie hunter by night?" I ask.

"Well, it turns out faeries really like carnivals."

"I love carnivals," Eifa confirms sagely. "They always smell like sweat and sugar. And the people are always so … alive."

Skye digs a half-empty cigarette pack out of her pocket and pulls out the needle Chisel gifted her, setting it on the bar cautiously. "Alright. One of you, tell me what this does."

"It sews things," Eifa says patiently. "It's a needle."

Skye glares at it. "It doesn't turn into a sword? Or put someone to sleep if it pricks them? Is it cursed?"

Leithe picks it up and scrutinizes it. "It stitches things together, assuming you have thread." He sets it back down in front of her. "Nothing else, far as I can see." He eyes Skye curiously. "You can see us, and you're resistant to glamour. How?"

"Fuck off," Skye says perfunctorily.

"Four-leafed clovers?" he presses. "Hanging around your neck? Is that what you keep touching through your shirt, just to reassure yourself it's still there?" Skye's hand drops from her chest to rest on her thigh, as if she hadn't realized what she was doing. Hunter's dog growls softly.

"So it was, uh, nice of you to give Martin and Chisel … a zombie," I say to Leithe. A pathetic attempt to change the subject.

Leithe takes a sip of his beer and scowls at it. "No, it's just what's done," he says. "You owed them for the hardship they endured by aiding you."

"I'm surprised you care," I say.

"Of course I care," he says. "We're engaged, so if you don't pay your debts, it reflects poorly on both of us." *And I had to do it because you couldn't pay it yourself.* He doesn't need to say the last part out loud for me to hear it.

"The Crawling King did those things," Eifa says. "Not her."

"It doesn't matter," I say. "It still happened." And as much as I want to snarl at Leithe, he's right. I couldn't do anything about it.

"Yes, but you look so sad I thought I would say some nice things to make you feel better, since no one else was going to." Eifa finishes her drink and waves the bartender down for another. She looks better, the burns and scratches sustained in the basement already healing.

"Well," I say. "Thanks."

"You're welcome," Eifa says.

Leithe studies Eifa, though she pays him little attention, her focus mostly on asking questions about things Skye's killed. Several other men in the bar are looking at Eifa as well; she gives a smile to anyone she catches staring, completely at ease with the attention. Once again, I wish I wasn't wearing pajamas.

"Leithe," I say. "How do you glamour clothes?"

"The same way you glamour anything else," he says. "See it in your mind, know that it's true, and force it into reality."

I think really hard at my clothes, imagining myself in a sundress I lost years ago. What it looked like. What it felt like. "Nothing."

Leithe places his hand on my head; I almost shrug it off on reflex. Before I can ask what he's doing, a feeling like cold water travels down my limbs and I'm suddenly wearing the clothes I wore yesterday: old denim shorts and a loose, pale pink t-shirt, the hem of which I tied off with a rubber band because it was too long. If I focus, I can see both the glamour and reality at once, feel the cotton of my pajamas and the rough denim of the shorts. It quickly gives me a headache. I still don't have a bra, not that I'd ask him to glamour me one.

"Can you make me some shoes, too?" I ask

"Do it yourself. I just showed you how," Leithe removes his hand from my head and returns to judging his beer.

"You didn't show me anything." I stare at my bare feet and imagine them encased in socks, and then a pair of boots. Unsurprisingly, nothing happens. "Isn't it against the rules to do things like this where people can see?"

"Don't turn around." Eifa says. "What color is the shirt the bearded man at the table behind you is wearing?

I have no idea. "Point taken."

"Gray," Skye says, giving Eifa a half-smile over her beer.

"Is the lady in the booth wearing glasses?" I ask.

"Yes," Skye answers.

"With thick black rims," Eifa says. This turns into a game that passes some time, though Leithe doesn't participate. He only watches Eifa.

"Ask questions, if you have them," Eifa finally tells him. "Or keep staring. I don't mind."

"You were a Crawling Court knight," Leithe says. "Sworn to Nevain, I'd guess? You have his look."

Eifa sips her drink and nods.

"Who's Nevain?" I ask.

"One of the Gentry of the Crawling Court; the lord of the Blood Orchard." Leithe smiles without any warmth. "How many humans did you bring to his garden during your service?"

Eifa meets his eyes with no shame. "Many."

"I can only imagine you're in the mortal world because he exiled you," Leithe continues.

"Incorrect," Eifa says. "I'm here by choice."

"You're here, living in a shack, playing servant to a ghoul, by choice?" Leithe sounds appalled.

Eifa smiles, resting her chin in her hand. "Martin is more worthy of me than any court fae I've had the displeasure of serving."

"What could this world possibly offer you?" he asks.

"The freedom to kill or not kill by my own choice. I much prefer it."

"So this Nevain guy," I interject. "You were his knight, so he had your Name?" Eifa nods. "Then how did you get your freedom?"

"I killed enough people that Nevain offered me a boon for my service. I asked to be released from my oath," she says.

"I take it he wasn't pleased," Leithe says.

"No." Eifa finishes her second drink. "But it's been a long time; I doubt he'd bother remembering me."

Skye pushes herself off her bar stool. "I'm going to smoke."

Eifa stands as well. "And I'd rather talk to Skye."

Then it's just me and Leithe at the bar. The dog remains at our feet, watching the door Skye exited intently.

Leithe stares pensively at his nearly-empty beer. "Eifa has no real loyalties. She's unpredictable."

"It sounds like she's loyal to Skye," I say.

"Until she's not. She's no doubt taken more lives than that kelpie you so badly wanted rid of, and she probably sleeps just as easily." He finishes his beer and requests the strongest thing in stock. The bartender returns with a glass of clear liquor.

Leithe has several more drinks, none seeming to impress him; Skye comes in between smoke breaks; Eifa entertains herself by beating other patrons at darts near the back of the bar. I give up quickly on trying to glamour myself a pair of boots and pass the time by staring despondently at my phone, willing Grandma to call so I can ruin our plan before it starts. She doesn't call.

"She's rotting from the inside," Leithe says. The first words he's spoken to me in a while. He's had an alarming amount of alcohol by now, but the words aren't slurred and his eyes aren't glazed as I follow his gaze to the sallow-skinned woman sitting by herself at the far corner of the bar. "And not even from a curse, simply because left long enough, mortal bodies just stop working."

"That's normal," I say. "Dying is normal."

"Dying for a *reason* is normal," Leithe complains. "Eifa will die the day she loses the wrong fight, and she knows that. But mortals, their existences are defined by expiration. They all wither and drop dead for no reason after some random, infinitesimal amount of time, even if they did nothing to warrant it. What logic is there in that? You can do nothing wrong, offend no one, and yet you still die. I don't know how they can stomach it. I don't know how you stomached it when you still thought you were human." He sounds genuinely disturbed by the thought.

"I didn't really think about it," I say. "No one does, really, not until they're older, I guess."

"It's why you shouldn't get attached." His expression borders on sympathetic. "Not to humans, not even to low fae. The only certainty for anyone who isn't Gentry is death. You can enjoy your time with them, but if you cling too hard, those moments will be gone before you're ready. They might feel real to you now, but the longer you think like that, the more painful it will be."

"If you're trying to make me feel better, you're not." Grandma, Hunter, Cheeps, Skye, Eifa, Martin, Chisel. All of them will die eventually. And I'll still be here. With no one but Leithe for company.

"I'm not trying to make you feel better," he says. "I'm telling you the truth."

"You get chatty when you drink."

"I'm always chatty. You just don't have anything better to do at the moment than listen."

I study the sallow-skinned woman Leithe pointed out. "Could you cure her?"

He gives me a pensive look, like he knows his next words are about to start a fight. "I could cut out my own liver and give it to her. Then she'd live until something else killed her."

"But you won't."

"I won't."

"Because what, you don't feel like it?"

"You could give her yours." Leithe eyes me from over his glass. "Eifa could even do the cutting if you're squeamish.

I'm sure she's quite efficient. You'd be weaker, in pieces, but you could always come back and get it when she dies." That shuts me up. I drink the last of my water and stare at the melting ice while failing to formulate a response. I could help someone. I have no excuse not to. I should do it. It's what good people do. People like Martin. But it isn't that woman my thoughts go to. It isn't a stranger I could cut myself open to help.

Leithe watches me with narrowed eyes; I realize I've been picking apart a bar napkin. I cover the pieces with my hand. "Have you considered that Lelit may expect you to offer up your own heart to her poor knight in order to save his life?"

"Because if Hunter had it, Lelit could just order him to give it to her, and that would be bad for me," I guess. He's right.

"I don't understand you. That knight helped keep both of us imprisoned, and now you want to reward him for it."

"He was nice to me when I thought I was human."

"When he thought you were a harmless pet, you mean?"

"I would have died a long time ago if he hadn't been there."

"Or you would have broken the prison much sooner."

I stare at my cup, trying to imagine if this had all happened when I was a child. It's easy: I would have embraced it all. I wouldn't have hesitated. It would have just been the next step of the quest I'd been given. I'd probably be in Faerie right now, for good or ill.

Leithe suddenly grabs my wrist. "I get it," I snap. "You made your point." But he isn't looking at me; he's looking at the door. Hunter's dog launches to its feet and barks once.

"That took less time than I thought." He turns to me, expression grim. "Running won't do any good at this point. You are *Mab*. Do you understand? Let me talk. Act like they're all beneath your notice. No matter what they do, *do not make a scene.*"

# Chapter Fourteen

"Wh—" Before I can finish, the door swings open. Skye walks inside, looks out at the scattered patrons, draws her gun, and fires it into the ceiling.

"Get in the back, now!" Skye gestures toward the kitchen door with her weapon. The crowd is a mix—some sit frozen and wide-eyed, some scream and hide behind tables or flee toward the back as Skye ordered, and some look like they're debating the merits of playing the hero and tackling the crazy woman. But no one gets the chance.

"*Let's all calm down.*" The voice comes from behind Skye, and with it, sheer *power* floods into the room like a tsunami that would have sent me reeling into the bar if Leithe didn't grab my shoulder. It coats my tongue and throat with the coppery tang of blood mixed with the heady smell of overripe fruit, the sweetness barely failing to conceal the undercurrent of rot. The smell burrows through my head and down into my stomach, rendering me lightheaded and nauseous.

Eifa's head whips toward the door, eyes wide and nostrils flaring. Leithe sips his drink with cool disinterest.

The human customers reel as if they've had the wind knocked out of their lungs. Then they blink and smile dumbly, Skye's threat forgotten.

Skye pivots to point her gun at the door, but she moves like she's swimming through molasses, limbs shaking with the effort.

The man behind her grabs her wrist before she can point the gun at his head. He looks my age or a little younger from the bit of teenage gangliness still in his limbs, though I'm sure he's far older. Dark hair falls nearly to his shoulders. His eyes are light, maybe blue, but it's hard to tell at this distance.

Wait—why do I care about his eyes, or anything else? I try to stand, to help Skye, but Leithe pushes me back down onto the stool.

"Lay down, you fool," Leithe says to Hunter's dog as its hackles raise. "You're not saving anyone."

"Sit, please," I whisper. Hunter's dog dying here would be another thing he's lost because of me. The dog reluctantly obeys.

"That's better," the man says. "Everything is fine. *Look.*" Skye's head jerks up violently. When she meets his eyes, her body loosens; she releases her grip on the gun as her arm slumps back to her side, leaving it in his hands. He throws the gun on the ground—I flinch, expecting it to go off—and puts a companionable arm around Skye's shoulders, spinning her around to face us. A bland smile is plastered across her face. "See? We're fine. Maybe even friends."

The glamour radiating from him washes over me, filling my nose and mouth with the stench of blood and rotting fruit so strong I can feel it in my teeth. It makes me feel dizzy, almost drunk. I only realize I'm listing to the side when Leithe pulls me upright before I can fall off the stool.

The man's gaze passes blankly over Eifa, slides across Leithe and then to me. He smiles. I feel like I'm breathing through soup. The air scours its way down my throat and settles in the pit of my stomach, turning into a knot of sudden and painfully ravenous hunger. The shadows across the man's face turn the gangliness into gauntness—his skin pulled tight over muscle and tendon with no layer of water and fat in between. His eyes are the same deep scarlet as Eifa's. When I force myself to blink, just for the sake of no longer looking at him, they're blue again, but there's a hungry, predatory glint there. I almost sigh with relief when he looks back at Leithe.

"This isn't where I would have expected to find you," the man says. "You hate the mortal world, so imagine my surprise when the king sensed you here, of all places."

"This is exactly the kind of place I'd expect to find you, Nevain," Leithe sets his empty glass down on the bar. He sounds bored. Utterly unbothered. Eifa hasn't moved from her spot near the back; she keeps looking between Nevain and Leithe, expression calculating.

Nevain laughs. "I do love the mortal world. There's always something new." He gestures, and several more fae meander into the bar. Some have the same hooves and horns as Eifa; others look nearly human, save the teeth. They're dressed like magpies—wearing different centuries as layers. Petticoats beneath a leather jacket; a brocade frock-coat over a t-shirt. But they all carry themselves with languid, catlike energy. They're all beautiful in a razor-edged way, skin drawn gaunt and dehydrated over lean muscle. Some wear weapons—archaic things with slender blades—others have deadly-looking claws only when viewed from my peripheral vision. Every single one of them has blood-red eyes. Most of them take us in with lazy, lidded expressions before turning their attention to the humans.

One of the fae men absently strums a small harp. He plucks a note on the strings that hangs listless in the air, plucking a second only once the reverberations of the first fade. The sound stabs at my ears, the pause between each one just long enough to fool me into believing another might not follow. The effect is distracting, making it difficult to string two thoughts together.

A human girl—probably no older than me—trails behind Nevain. She wears a sleeveless sundress that exposes clusters of red, puckered bite marks covering the curve of her throat and the creases of her arms. Her waxy skin hangs loose from her frame, but her huge, glamour-glazed eyes follow Nevain adoringly. She rests her head against the shoulder that isn't thrown around Skye.

Other humans arrived with the fae, I realize, all bearing similar puncture marks and blitzed-out smiles. I want to shake Leithe and scream at him to make this stop, to help these people, but I remember his warning. Don't make a scene. Let him talk. I bite my tongue so hard I think I draw blood. Did he say that because he's worried about the outcome of a fight against these people, or because he doesn't want to bother?

Nevain crosses the room to the bar, arm still hanging loosely around Skye's shoulders where it could easily curl around her neck. He gets close enough to me that I have to resist the urge to lean back, the edge of the bar already digging into my spine.

"Mab," Nevain says. "*Queen* Mab, my apologies. Anyway, it's been such a long time. I'm surprised to see you outside your own court." The coppery, cloying stench of blood and rotting fruit seeps from his pores, his breath, filling my head. My body wants to relax. My mind wants to drift. He dislodges the human girl from his arm and holds out his hand for mine. The girl giggles at nothing. I almost join her.

My body almost obeys on its own before I remember myself and grip the edge of the bar instead of his hand. "I felt like a change." I look at his eyebrows, his ear, anything but his eyes.

Nevain frowns slightly when I don't acknowledge his offered hand, but quickly shifts his attention to the bartender. "We want drinks." He catches the bartender's eye and gives a disarming smile. "May we drink?"

"Yes," the bartender says, staring dumbly at Nevain. As dumbly as I was, probably. Several of Nevain's hungry-eyed faeries meander around the bar to surround the bartender; others approach various patrons.

"You can't hurt them," I say.

"Hurt them?" Nevain looks genuinely confused. "I'm not a rule-breaker. They give permission. We take what they don't miss, and all they remember is what a nice time they had." His minions have already spread around the room.

"Do they know what they're giving permission for?" I ask.

"Why wouldn't they?" He puts an affectionate hand on the girl's head, traces the scabbed-over punctures down her neck. "I think she'd say something if she minded." He turns to Skye. "You wouldn't mind giving me some blood you don't need, right?"

Skye smiles, teeth grinding together, jaw rigid. "No."

"See?" Nevain says. "This is why I love the mortal world. They're so generous here." He gives Skye a pat on the back. "I don't need you. Go." She obeys without a word.

"What would they say if they weren't glamoured?" I ask.

"What does that have to do with anything?" Nevain asks. The question sounds genuine. He has no idea.

"You're mind-controlling these people. They *have* to agree with you," I say.

"Oh," he says. "I don't think so. They could leave if they really wanted to."

"Then let them go and see what happens."

"All I'm doing is helping them be happy, Your Majesty," he says.

I try to catalog the things I could do, and they mostly come down to different objects I could throw at Nevain's head, which would be satisfying for a second and ultimately pointless.

"So the king sent you?" Leithe asks.

Nevain nods, his argument with me forgotten. "He's waiting for you. We were all concerned when you didn't return to court for your tithe, him most of all."

"Hardly my fault," Leithe says. "I was forbidden to return to the Crawling Court until my quest is complete. It's not yet complete." Quest. He'd said something about a quest, back in the dream prison.

"He must've thought highly of you to believe you'd return in time," Nevain says. "So we were even more concerned to hear you'd given up on your quest—one sworn before the whole court—and gotten yourself engaged to a different monarch." Leithe's face is stone, so Nevain turns to me. "Oh. Your new love *does* know about the quest, doesn't she?" He leans toward me conspiratorially. "See,

Leithe was given a quest by the Crawling King, to prove he was worthy of being the king's consort. He was to travel to Elsewhere, the lands beyond Faerie, and bring the king what he found there. But he never came back to us." And that was where Mab found him. That was the meeting the prison showed me.

"I know," I say.

"Oh, well," he pouts, but recovers quickly. "It's generous of you to take him in after he couldn't win his first choice." He turns back to Leithe. "It really wasn't very nice, what the king did. If he didn't want to make you his consort, he should've just said so, not given you an impossible task."

"What does the king care, Nevain?" Leithe asks. "As you said, I missed my tithe. I'm no longer—technically—his subject. And since I've clearly proven myself unworthy of him, I'd think not having to see my face at court would be a relief."

"He cares quite a bit, actually. He requested your presence—and Mab's—several times after news of the engagement reached him. But he was ignored." Nevain pauses for dramatic effect. "But then we heard the two of you had vanished entirely, and that *Lelit* was ruling the Dreaming Court in her queen's stead. Obviously, he suspected foul play. He's been threatening war—for you, isn't that romantic? The Blooming Court's still deciding on which side to stand. He'll be relieved to see you again." Something flickers in Leithe's eyes.

"Then you can pass on our intent to visit once a few remaining matters in the Dreaming Court are addressed," Leithe says.

"You can tell him so yourself, since he sent me to escort you back to his court," Nevain says. He doesn't need to say out loud that this isn't a request. "His feelings are a bit hurt after you slammed that door in his face while he was trying to talk to your new queen. Worried about your old love and your new love talking behind your back, are you?"

Leithe's expression is inscrutable for a long moment, then the corner of his mouth curls upward in a slow smile that doesn't reach his eyes. "You think I would have let him take her?" Leithe asks. "When it would have led to a few low fae getting the credit?" Leithe's hand tightens on my shoulder. "I did find something in Elsewhere, after all. What better gift could I offer the Crawling King than the queen of another court?"

# Chapter Fifteen

I SHOULD FEEL AS if the floor is falling out from under me. As if I've been betrayed. But I feel nothing. I haven't been betrayed. I've known what Leithe is from the beginning.

Nevain's eyes widen, then he laughs; the noise sounds far away.

"Skye should have run you over." I shove Leithe's hand off my shoulders. Rather, he allows me to push him away. He's much stronger than me, as is everyone else here.

"Alas," Leithe says. "Hindsight."

"Then this was all a deception to lure her somewhere she'd be vulnerable?" Nevain asks.

"Delivering her will mark the conclusion of my quest," Leithe says. "But I'm sure the king will still reward you with something suitable for escorting his future consort back to court." Leithe sounds perfectly at ease. Nevain laughs again—a little disbelieving, a little nervous. Leithe only smiles. "We can leave whenever you're ready, Nevain."

"I see no need to rush. We just arrived. My people wish to enjoy themselves," Nevain says, frowning slightly. Trying to stall until he can take control of the situation again. Even outnumbered, Leithe won. He beat both of us without the slightest bit of effort.

"I suppose there's no point in keeping this." Leithe produces Lelit's invitation from his sleeve. "It seems you're getting your wish," he says to me. "You won't be attending Lelit's ball after all." He tosses the tiny scroll onto the floor; Nevain's eyes follow it as it bounces and rolls to a stop against a table leg. Leithe leaves Nevain to his thoughts and turns back to me. "Why not order a drink? It will be your last one in the mortal world."

"I knew I shouldn't have trusted you," I say.

"Oh?" He rests his chin on his hand, looking bored. "Then why did you?" Because I was scared. Because I was clinging to whoever seemed to know what they were doing. I should have run and kept running.

"She's acting so strange." Nevain studies me curiously, like I'm a funny animal. I hate him. I hate him looking at me. It makes me want a shower. "What did you do to her?"

"Nothing," Leithe says. "Lelit decided to play a trick—a wedding present, I suppose—torture the both of us a little. I think it drove her a little mad."

"Well." The hungry glint is back in Nevain's eyes. "That's grounds for a blood debt, harming a member of another court, and if we have their queen, the Dreaming Court can't put up much of a fight."

"That would be something for the king to decide," Leithe says. "Not you."

"Of course," Nevain says defensively.

Leithe turns to me, a terrible smile working across his face. "If you'd like, perhaps we can bring the old human woman you're so fond of to keep you company."

"Don't you *dare*," I say.

"Maybe we'll just bring her anyway, to keep you in line. It wouldn't be hard to lure her into Faerie. If she thought it was you asking, she'd say yes to anything." I grab for my phone where it sits on the bar, but Nevain beats me to it.

"Interesting little things, aren't these?" he says to Leithe. "More convenient than magic, sometimes." I want to throw a bar stool at him, but it would accomplish nothing save give them another reason to laugh at me. There's nothing I can do. The glamour and the music keep scattering my thoughts each time I try to string two together. I could run for the door, but I'm sure the fae eying me lazily would get far less sedate if I tried. The glint in their eyes—in Nevain's eyes as well—marks them as predators waiting for signs of panic. They'd love it if I ran. "The Crawling Court is very nice. Our king is a gracious host. I'm sure you'll enjoy your time there."

"You trust him?" I ask Nevain, flailing desperately for anything. "He's swapping sides whenever it's convenient. How long before he changes his mind again?"

Leithe suddenly grabs my chin and forces me to look at him. His expression says I've found a nerve. "You seem like you're getting irritable. Perhaps you should go take a nap." I try to shove his hand away, but he holds on for a moment longer, just to show that he can.

No one stops me when I push off the bar and stomp into the cramped bathroom. I lock the tiny latch, not that that would stop anyone from coming in. There's no convenient window for me to squeeze out of, but with a door between me and Nevain and after splashing water on my face, I feel more sober.

But that doesn't mean a plan presents itself. Skye is out of it; I doubt Eifa can take on a dozen armed faeries by herself.

I punch the mirror in frustration; my fist bounces off the glass painfully and ineffectively. No dramatic cracks. Not even a bit of blood.

Then, as silently as I can, hands clutching the edge of the sink, I cry. I cry for a long time. And then, even though I'm no closer to a plan, I blow my nose, wipe my eyes, and leave the bathroom.

Once back in the bar, the glamour immediately begins trying to clog up my brain. I pick up a fork off one of the tables, wrapping the handle in a napkin and pressing the pad of my thumb into the tines. Whether it's the pain or the presence of iron, my thoughts stay a little sharper.

Leithe and Nevain aren't paying attention to me. Other fae cluster around most of the humans in the bar. Several watch Eifa, waiting for her to give them an excuse.

A human man holds his arm out to me. The inside of his forearm is covered in shallow, congealing cuts. He holds a pocketknife in his other hand and smiles blandly.

"Go to the hospital," I say. "Right now." Without a change in expression, he turns and walks toward the door, though he only gets halfway before one of Nevain's faeries stops him.

Another try that accomplishes nothing. I'm close to simply stabbing people with a fork when someone snarls in pain. Eifa pushes Skye behind her and drives a dagger into a fae woman's gut. Several of Nevain's soldiers stop what they were doing and circle Eifa, who watches them with an air of calm resignation. Nevain and Leithe observe with mild interest.

"Hey." I push past Nevain's minions and grab Skye's sleeve, pulling her toward the wall. She doesn't resist. Nevain glances at me, as do several other pairs of red eyes.

Even if I left Eifa to die as a distraction, I'd never get away. Nevain's soldiers dart in and out, testing Eifa's defenses. She cuts one, only for another to graze the back of her leg.

Skye's sleeve is wet with blood oozing from a bite near the crease of her elbow, but her eyes are blank. She might as well be asleep. It isn't fair. None of it's fair.

"Skye," I say. "Wake up, please." Nothing happens. Threads of Nevain's glamour weave through her head like a net. But something else pulses beneath her skin: hate, fear, rage—everything she isn't allowed to feel right now, boiling away behind a wall of consciousness. Skye's half-dream is messy and unformed, a riot of violent color and chaos.

"Did you hear me?" Leithe places a hand on my shoulder, jolting me out of Skye's head.

"What?" I still feel it, just beneath the surface. There's something there, some shape I can't make out lurking in the vortex.

"I said we can take her, too. That's what you want, isn't it? Your entire little family, reunited forever." He came to gloat, just because he can.

Something inside me snaps. For a brief moment, the shell of self-loathing in my chest falls away to a core of white-hot rage. I grab and pull with savage instinct, and the dam in Skye's head bursts. Then with a sensation like my ears popping from pressure, nightmares pour into the bar.

The screaming starts immediately.

Throughout the room, creatures erupt from the floor, walls, and ceiling. Women with long, filthy hair and too-long arms and too-long fingers tipped with jagged, broken nails drag themselves forth and wrap their claws around Nevain. Spiders rain from the ceiling. Monsters from movies grab Nevain's fae and tear into flesh. Humans all over the bar collapse to their knees.

A dark, hulking shape pulls itself up through the floor next to Skye and lunges at Leithe, sending them both barreling into a wall before Leithe has time to look surprised.

Skye gasps and jolts up from where she'd slumped against the wall. "What did you do?" She clutches her head.

"Something." I pull Skye along the wall toward the exit. "Let's go!"

After only a moment of surprise, Nevain's fae gather their wits and begin fighting back. Blades and claws flash, but the nightmares are relentless. Wounds to their bodies don't bleed, but instead form new fanged, gnashing mouths.

Nightmares swarm toward Nevain, but I lose sight of him when a woman with horns and hooves like Eifa's zeroes in on me and lunges. I lurch back, scrambling across a booth seat and banging my head on the wall, but the woman never connects. She stops short, face frozen in surprise, when the deer mounted on the wall bends and skewers her through the face and throat with its antlers. Black smoke leaks from around the deer's glass eyes. Leithe's wraiths.

Each step is harder to take than the last. My limbs and eyelids are heavy; I feel strangely empty to my core, hollow. Making these monsters real took something from me.

I slip on a streak of blood and almost slide stumbling into one of Nevain's people struggling with two nightmares. One side of her face has been chewed off, leaving her ear nothing but a few strips of bleeding flesh. I cut around her, slip and land hard on the bloody floor, and scramble to my feet. Blood from the floor wicks off me and slithers in tiny rivulets as if alive back toward the center of the room. Nevain, probably.

We've almost made it to the door when someone grabs me by the shoulder and wrenches me around. Nevain—expression murderous—grabs me by the neck, nails digging into my skin.

The fork I've been carrying is buried in his eye socket before my brain can catch up with my arm. He howls in pain, but doesn't let go. He pulls me closer, the inside of his mouth growing circles of fangs that spiral down his throat.

The girl in the sundress hits him in the back of the head with a beer bottle. He turns to her in surprise, and in that moment, every nightmare in the room abandons its current target and buries him in an onslaught of hungry bodies, tearing him off me. I watch him vanish under the wave of violence with a sense of savage satisfaction. *Good*.

Free, I stagger out into the dimming evening sunlight. Outside the bar, everything is frighteningly normal. I take a few steps and realize I have nowhere to go. My legs buckle; I can barely stand. A truck skids to a stop next to me, honking, the driver yelling. I'm in the middle of the road.

One of Nevain's fae emerges from the bar in pursuit, shaking off the grasping hands trying to pull him back. He raises a sword and stalks toward me. It suddenly seems very silly to die from getting stabbed by a faerie in broad daylight in the middle of the street. It all seems silly. I'm so tired.

There's more shouting, maybe a car door opening. Then the truck jumps the curb and slams into the fae man with a crunch, sending him flying into the wall of the bar with a second crunch. Ghostly hands drag his body back inside.

I collapse to my knees, then my face hits the pavement, exhaustion pulling me under. My eyes close.

Footsteps pounding.

Hurried arguing.

Hands lifting me, sticky with blood.

A car door slams.

Nothing.

# Chapter Sixteen

THE ALL-ENCOMPASSING RUMBLE OF Zach's dad's pick-up truck brings me back to the days he'd drive into town while we sat in the bed, waving at cars going the opposite direction. I almost fell out, once. I'd wanted to see if I could grab a leaf from a tree as we rode by. But I didn't fall. Zach pulled me back into the truck by the belt loops of my jeans. I got the leaf.

I'm lying in the bed, a scratchy blanket beneath me and the sky racing by above as Mr. Foster drives. Zach lies next to me.

"I think I might be dead," I say.

"Not yet," he says. He's a teenager. "But you kind of look like it."

"I feel so helpless," I say. "It's not fair. They do anything they want, and no one stops them. The rules might as well not exist, for all the good they do. They're too easy to snake around."

"So do something about it," Zach says. "Aren't you a queen?"

"No," I say. "I'm just a person. I thought things would be better once I knew the truth, but they would be better if this could go back to being a game in our heads. Then those people wouldn't ... and you wouldn't ..." I take a breath. "How am I supposed to accept it? What would I be if I wanted that?"

"I don't know," Zach says. "What are you?"

My head pounds. I'm lying in a bed, blankets piled around me. My limbs shake with fatigue as I curl myself up into a ball. I'm starving, but the prospect of getting up to look for food is too daunting, especially when the bed is so soft.

Instead of Zach, I dream next about blood and tearing flesh and screaming that isn't mine. I wake up again and don't feel any better. My mouth is dry and I think I might throw up. I pull a blanket over my head and wait to drift off once more, to roll the dice and hope for Zach.

"I know you're awake," someone says. It takes a moment for my sluggish thoughts to register Leithe's voice.

Leithe. Bastard.

Groaning, I force myself up on my elbows and blink in the dim light. I'm in a room bereft of furniture and covered in ragged brown carpet. Leithe sits on the floor against the far wall. He looks more tired than I've ever seen him. His hair—usually pin-straight—is even slightly frazzled.

"Is this the Crawling Court?" I ask. My jaw doesn't want to cooperate and the words come out slurred.

"No," Leithe says, sounding offended by the idea. "This is yet another half-rotten house in the mortal world. The others are out there." He gestures to the closed door. The others. Nevain and the rest, I assume.

"Thought I got away," I mumble.

"You made it outside, where you passed out in the street. I threw you into the vehicle that Skye and Eifa stole. Now we're here." He squeezes as much disdain as possible into the word *here*.

"So you switched sides again," I say. "Welcome back."

Leithe sighs and pinches the bridge of his nose. "Do you remember," he asks, "when I was still trapped in the prison tree and you said several very unkind things in order to antagonize me into unconsciously sending wraiths after you so you could escape Lelit's knight?" I stare at him. "We both know you can't do anything on purpose, so I gambled on making you angry. It worked. You're welcome."

I lay back down and pull the blanket over my head in embarrassment. "Oh." Then I jolt back up, angry again. "Was that really your plan, or are you just trying to cover for yourself?" If I hadn't been able to summon those nightmares, he could have easily continued to go along with Nevain as if that was the plan from the start. Maybe it was. Maybe coming with me was the pivot. He'd arranged things neatly so he could play both sides as needed.

"I think you have very little room to be offended that I would sell you out," Leithe says. "Have you not spent the entire time we've known each other making it clear how little you want to do with me? Tell me you wouldn't do the same thing if you had the opportunity. To save yourself? To save your humans?"

*I wouldn't.* No, that isn't true. Wouldn't I, if it was to save Grandma? I wouldn't *want* to, but would that make it any better? "I didn't ask for this," I say instead.

"Neither did I." He's silent for a moment, thinking. "That curse I placed on your human should have drained the life out of her in less than a minute. After being trapped for so long, being shot, and forcing a door closed in the Crawling King's face, I would never have been able to fight Nevain and his creatures by myself." He sounds reluctant to admit it. "The only way we could have escaped was if you managed to do something. And you did."

I sigh, breathing out a bunch of anger that suddenly has no easy place to go. "What would you have done if I hadn't been able to summon those nightmares?" I regret asking as soon as the words leave my mouth; I don't want to know the answer. Leithe looks up at me from fiddling with his hair. He looks tired.

"We would have been taken to the Crawling Court and forced to dance along to whatever tune the Crawling King chose to play. On a wider scale, taking you would be an act of war. Without you, the Dreaming Court would be weak and undefended. Lelit would be forced to capitulate to whatever the Crawling King demanded in exchange for your return, or seek help from the Blooming Court. Either way, the balance of power would shift and the damage would be enormous for everyone."

I pull myself to a sitting position and wrap my arms around my knees. "Objectively," I say, "if the Crawling King would take you back, make you his 'consort' or whatever, wouldn't that be a better deal for you as opposed to …" I gesture vaguely at myself.

Leithe frowns. "I'm not interested in groveling. Nevain's mostly an idiot, but the Crawling King isn't. He'd see that I'm coming back because I have no other choice and I'm not interested in facing that particular humiliation. I'm still a traitor, I suppose, for abandoning the quest he gave me, but at least I'm not a traitor twice over yet. No, I chose Mab, and I won't have the Crawling King or anyone else believe I'm anything but thriving because of it."

I laugh; the effort hurts my throat. "So you're ride-or-die for Mab out of *pettiness*? So your ex won't know that you're miserable?"

Leithe glares at me. "What do you want, love poetry?"

I shrug. That motion also hurts. "I think that's a better reason than whatever the Crawling King guy has going for him. I mean, you shouldn't have to pass some dangerous test for someone to love you."

"You'd marry anyone who bothered enough to ask, then?"

"No, but I also wouldn't send them to the Land of Certain Death unless I was hoping they wouldn't come back," I point out. "Why would you want to be with someone who'd ask that of you?"

"Because he's the king." Leithe says it as if it should be self-explanatory. "It was my own fault for thinking he might have enough fondness for me that he wouldn't ask for something impossible."

"Does he have a name?"

"Plenty, though 'king' serves as well as any other."

"Were you trying to get with a person or a title?"

He shrugs. "They're one and the same."

"Did you want to marry Mab for the same reason?"

"Of course." He's quiet for a moment. "She could have left me where I was. If she did, I'd probably still be wandering aimlessly in Elsewhere. No one would have ever known. But instead, she led me out, brought me to her palace, treated me as a guest, and asked for nothing in exchange. It was infuriating. We both knew what I owed her, and I asked her every day what she wanted in return.

"I stayed both to find a way to repay my debt, and because I thought Mab—the only one who could travel freely in Elsewhere—could get me something I could bring back to the Crawling King. But the second reason gradually mattered less and less to me, until I was surprised by how little I cared. Eventually—in a moment of exasperation when she again declined to say what she wanted from me—I proposed to her. I did not expect her to accept."

"So you got engaged to her because you thought you owed her?"

"It's not so unusual," he snaps.

"It doesn't sound very equal."

"Of course not," he says. "I have no idea why she accepted. I was an exile from my own court. I had nothing." He laughs. "But as much as the mystery infuriated me, it infuriated Lelit more. She was always one of Mab's closest sycophants. Didn't trust me; hated that Mab seemed to. I figure she must have been jealous, which is why she did all this before the wedding." He gestures at our surroundings, as if Lelit is personally responsible for the dust.

*She thought she was saving Mab's life.* Guilt almost brings the words out of my mouth. Maybe Lelit was wrong. Maybe she was trying to sow discord. Maybe Leithe would change his mind and drag me down to the Crawling King if I ever said the words out loud.

He's looking at me. I worry my guilt must be showing on my face. "Did Mab also give you some kind of insane test?" I ask, as much to change the subject as from curiosity.

"I didn't think so at first," he says drily. "But the longer this goes on, the more I'm inclined to think she did."

It takes me a second to realize what he means. "You think this—*I'm*—a test?"

"You act like it often enough." He leans his head against the wall and closes his eyes. "And I often wonder how Mab could have fallen for any kind of trap in the first place. I wonder if she didn't. If this is what she always intended to happen. To see what I would do."

"Maybe it had nothing to do with you in the first place." It comes out in a poorly thought-out rush. Far too close to things I don't want to say.

"Oh?" Leithe studies me through narrowed eyes, waiting for me to elaborate. I shouldn't have opened my mouth.

Footsteps approach from beyond the door, giving me a convenient way out of this conversation. Eifa pushes the door open without knocking. "You're alright?"

"No, but I'm awake," I say. "Where's Skye?"

"I'm glad you asked," Eifa says. "Come."

I stand—or try to. My legs buckle when I put weight on them, and my head spins as I try to rise.

Leithe beats Eifa to my arm. He pulls me to my feet and supports most of my weight. Even so, my legs shake.

"What happened to me?" I cling to his arm with both of mine.

"You overreached," he says. "You were already weak from the imprisonment and living in the mortal world, and you used power you didn't have." He turns to Eifa. "She needs food or drink from Faerie."

"Do you expect me to let her take a bite out of my arm?" Eifa asks. "One generally needs to go to Faerie for Faerie food." Leithe looks like he's considering it.

"No," I say. "God no. Where is Skye?"

"Downstairs." Eifa hesitates. "Just come and look. That will be easiest."

As we leave the room, Leithe gives the blankets and pillows I'd been using a dismissive gesture and they return to their original state: a ratty, moldy rug.

"Don't go all the way down the stairs," Eifa says as we walk. "Stop on the last step."

"Why?" I stop on the final step and stare at the scene before me. "Oh."

A monster dominates the small living room. Its hunched back brushes the ceiling and its spade-like claws hang just above the floor. Dark, shaggy hair covers its body, leaving its eyes nothing but two deep-set red pinpricks. Its mouth hangs open and distended, full of jagged teeth. Other than its eyes, the creature is made from layers of black on black, a sketch that hasn't been finished.

"So," I say slowly. "Is it friendly?" The nightmare growls and runs a questing hand across the floor, claws scraping against wood. It raises a severed arm and bites it in half, chewing loudly. "Whose—"

"Not Skye's," Eifa says. "One of Nevain's servants. It brought that from the bar. Look." Eifa points to where Skye sprawls asleep on a couch behind the monster, wan but unharmed. "Skye tried to drive us away, but she pulled over when she realized she was going to lose consciousness. We hid here to wait until one of you woke up, but that creature chased us. It won't let any of us get close to her." Eifa shows me a slowly-healing line of gashes on her forearm, held closed by a crooked line of stitches. "And it seems I owe Chisel for gifting Skye that needle."

The nightmare crunches through bone and uses a single claw to pick shards out from between its teeth. Texture gradually spreads over the claws—what was once as dark and smooth as an ink drawing becomes cracked and pitted as if from years of wear and violence. "It's becoming more real," I say.

"You made it, didn't you?" Leithe asks. "Control it."

"If it attacks you, we'll intervene." Eifa gives me an encouraging smile.

"Before or after I'm missing chunks?" I sigh. This was decided upon before I woke up. I push away from Leithe and take a step onto the floor, leaning heavily against the wall. The nightmare doesn't react. "Hi," I say. "Thanks for helping us with Nevain. But these guys"—I gesture to Leithe and Eifa behind me—"are cool. You don't need to attack them." At this angle, I see streaks of crusty red decorating one of the walls. A discarded leg lies nearby. "Oh. That's very ... art." The monster's eyes track me as I take another step forward. It crunches another bone between its teeth. "I'm going to walk around you to check on Skye. I'm not going to hurt her."

The monster raises its arm until its hand dominates my vision. There's a brief scuffle behind me. "Wait," Leithe hisses. The monster presses a dull claw to my forehead. It speaks but says nonsense, its mouth laboring over non-words.

"I'm sorry. I don't understand," I say. The monster trails its claw down my face, hard but not hard enough to break skin, then lowers its hand, picks up half a mangled arm, and pushes it into my chest. "Oh. Thank you." I take it and try not to look disgusted. "I think it's a baby."

"It *is* only a few hours old," Leithe says.

"I'm going to check on Skye now," I tell the monster. It loses interest in me and begins drawing on the wall, using the leg as a morbid paintbrush. "Hey." I gently shake Skye's shoulder. She groans and slaps at my hand. "Skye!" I shake her until her eyes open. She takes in the scene slowly: me, the house, the nightmare. "Hi," I say again. "Are you okay?"

"It hurt," Skye says. "What you did to me." She sits up; the effort seems to wind her. When she moves, it gets the monster's attention. It reaches for her and she instinctively throws her arms up around her head. The monster roars and flails its arms in response, catching me in the midsection with a backhand and sending me rolling across the floor back toward the stairs. Eifa pulls me the rest of the way.

"Skye." I gasp for breath. My voice won't go above a whisper. "I don't think it wants to hurt you."

"There's something missing." Skye pushes herself off the couch. "Did you know you were taking something from me?" The monster howls and throws the severed leg so hard it cracks the drywall. "There's a hole in my head. And I can feel it." She nods at the monster. "It's inside me, or I'm inside it. You gave it something from me."

"I'm sorry," I say. "I didn't know what I was doing."

"Are any of the humans still alive? Do you even know?" As Skye's voice rises, the monster takes a step toward me, snarling.

"Skye," I say carefully. "I think it's reacting to your feelings. Try to—"

"Don't tell me to calm down!" Skye yells. The monster stomps its foot, shaking the entire house.

"The nightmares attacked no humans," Eifa says. "I saw it."

"And you used to work for him," Skye says to Eifa. "Nevain."

"I did," Eifa says. Her tone holds no apology, no guilt.

Skye looks like she's about to be sick. "How do you live with yourself?" She rubs her eyes. "No, I know how. It just doesn't bother you. You got bored of it, you left, now you don't need to think about it because that was then and this is now. You're all the same. How many people did you kill? How many people did you watch him feed on until there was nothing left?" The monster lumbers closer, now focused on Eifa.

Eifa doesn't back away. "I won't deny what I did in Nevain's service. If you wish to take your shot, you're welcome to try."

"But she helps people now," I say. "She helps humans. She saved your life." The monster lunges forward, stops short, and pulls back like a dog at the end of its lead. Eifa doesn't flinch, only waits, spear in hand.

"And that *makes up for it*?" Skye snarls.

"No," Eifa says. "It doesn't." I want to beg her to stop talking.

What can I do? It was an accident, but I still did this.

Skye is aiming it. Leithe could glamour her. It seems simple. An emergency solution. Make her sleep, just until we figure out what to do.

Before I can make a decision, Leithe speaks. "Eifa swore to you," he says, frowning at Skye. "This drama is unnecessary. If you hate her so much, order her to kill herself."

Skye watches Eifa watch her, then covers her face and lets loose a sound somewhere between a scream and a sob. The monster pushes forward. "Stop," Skye says. "Stop.

Stop." She grabs fistfuls of the monster's fur, but it only drags her along as it bears down on Eifa.

Eifa raises her spear, but the creature shudders and stops short when Leithe's fingers brush its arm. Where he touches it, the monster withers. It happens fast—the creature falls to its knees and then its head hits the stairs, all the while leaking a final, wheezing breath like a balloon leaking air. And then it's dead.

"What a shame," he says. "I hoped we might be able to use it." He turns to Skye, who stands staring down at the nightmare's husk, hand clamped over her mouth. "It seems you came to a conclusion."

"Skye—" I begin.

"Go somewhere else." She falls back on the couch. "Now. All of you."

Eifa leads us through a kitchen and outside into an overgrown backyard littered with beer bottles and cigarette butts. Hunter's dog thumps its tail against the porch boards when it sees me.

Once the door is closed behind us, I turn to Eifa. "You really worked for him? Nevain?" It's one thing to hear about it, another to meet the man.

Eifa shrugs. "He's Gentry. It was a great honor to be accepted as one of his. It offered power, protection, a vantage point from which to place your heel on the necks of the unchosen. Many want little else." It's what Thistledown wanted. What Thistledown was willing to kill for. What I hated her for. Eifa's tone holds no trace of apology.

"Do you regret it?" I ask. Leithe gives a short, derisive laugh, then winces as if the action caused him pain.

Eifa smiles, resting her chin on the butt of her spear, point buried in the dirt. "What would the point be? Regret will undo nothing. Skye has a right to try her vengeance on me in the name of all those who never got the chance, if that's what she wants."

"Do you need her to grovel?" Leithe asks me. "Cry, perhaps?"

Would that make me feel less hollow? Less confused? Eifa gives me a small smile, and for a moment her expression makes her look far older. "What happened to Nevain and his people?" I ask.

"You humiliated him, so he'll be furious, but he'll also be scared. Your creatures had the upper hand in that bar full of humans. Nevain himself couldn't do anything drastic for fear of accidentally killing an innocent. He'll stay away until he comes up with a new approach, especially since now he'll be wary of you doing it again."

"*Can* you do it again?" Eifa asks.

"I shouldn't," I say. "You saw what it did to Skye. I did that to every human in that bar, didn't I?"

"Please," Leithe says. "We all lost something in that fight. Skye's losses aren't special simply for being in her head." Leithe leans against the side of the house as he speaks, arms crossed. He stands stiffer than he normally does, voice consciously measured and deliberate.

"How badly hurt are you?" I ask.

"Only a little mauled by your pets," he says. "They paid me some attention, but were more interested in Nevain. I'll heal quickly after draining that nightmare. Don't get your hopes up."

"Sorry." I focus my attention on a scrubby patch of grass.

"I knew what I was risking by antagonizing you," he says. "And Nevain got it worse." He sighs. "The nightmare would have been an effective deterrent for the next person who wants to try their luck against us, if it had been controllable."

*The next person who wants to try their luck against us.* I pick at the peeling, discolored paint on the porch railing. In the moment, I'd felt a fierce sense of joy, of *pride*, in seeing Nevain and his people fight for their lives. But that's replaced by a sense of hollow shame.

For the first time since I awoke, I realize my hands are crusted in dried, flaking blood. Maybe Nevain's from when I stabbed him. Maybe someone else's. For a moment, Zach's blood runs unimpeded through my fingers.

It's not just my hands. My feet are covered in it. My legs and arms are flecked with dried drops. Memories of the bar flood back. Slipping across the tacky, sticky floor. The taste of copper splashing across my lips as a nightmare sinks its teeth into the neck of the faerie in front of me, her expression only surprised because she didn't have time to register the fear or pain. I did that.

I lean over the railing and vomit into the grass.

"It's alright." Eifa offers me an encouraging smile and places a hand on my back. "It will get easier."

Easier.

I vomit again.

# Chapter Seventeen

SKYE HAS THE TRUCK ready to go before she lets us back into the house.

"If Nevain's looking for us, I'm not risking going back for my car," she says. "We'll take this and dump it somewhere visible when we get to Shrike Run. One of you can glamour it so it won't be noticeable, right?" Eifa nods. "Then get in. Let's go finish whatever this is." An unlit cigarette hangs from her lips as if forgotten. All evidence of the events from earlier have been wiped from her face and replaced with the same default scowl she usually wears. Hunter's dog follows at her heels as she checks over the truck again; it casts wary glances at Leithe and Eifa.

"Skye—"

She cuts me off. "Are you going to do what you need to do when we get to my mom's house?"

"Yes," I say. "I'll make it final." If it's the only way to make sure people like Lelit and Nevain stay as far away as possible from Grandma, I'll be awful enough that no one could possibly believe I'd ever come back.

After searching every inch of the house we sheltered in, it became clear I left my cell phone in the bar, meaning I have no way of knowing if Grandma has tried to call. Not that it matters, when I have nothing honest to tell her.

"Then get in," Skye says, climbing into the driver's seat. She doesn't acknowledge the others.

Leithe's hand brushes my arm as I contemplate the very-metal truck. A renewed glamour settles over my skin, frigid like I've been dumped in icy water. But it holds as I hoist myself into the cab, the metal-stench barely tickling my nose. Still, I can't help but shiver.

Hunter's dog is the only one who seems excited about the ride. It sits in the truck bed, tongue lolling. Eifa refuses to leave her spear out of reach, so it lies lengthwise down the center of the cab, cutting it in half, tip protruding through the truck's back window. A barrier between me and Leithe. We roll out of the driveway as the sun rises; the clock on the dash reads a little after six in the morning. I slept for almost twelve hours after what happened in the bar.

Skye turns on the radio just loud enough to discourage discussion. Eifa hums along to it enthusiastically off-key. Skye does nothing but glare at the road ahead.

After a long, tense silence, Leithe leans forward. "Where is the music coming from?" he asks. "Do you have a tiny musician trapped inside there?" He points at the radio.

"No, it's ..." I start, but I trail off when Skye laughs—against her own will, if the hand she clamps over her mouth is any indication.

"You sound like ... a time-traveled medieval peasant," Skye snorts.

"*Peasant*?" Leithe leans back in disgust.

"It's from waves that travel through the air. They're transmitted from a tower and the car picks them up," she says.

"So the musician is trapped in a tower," Leithe says.

Skye smothers her laugh this time, and Leithe listens intently to her more in-depth explanation. By the time she's done, the mood in the car feels much lighter.

"I was being silent out of consideration, just so you know," Eifa says, speaking up for the first time since we got underway. "Not because I have any fear or distaste for hearing the things I think you want to say."

Skye stares at the highway for a while longer. "I was mad. Didn't mean to make a giant monster attack you, though. So that's embarrassing. Getting glamoured by Nevain in the first place was embarrassing. And I get it. We're doing what we need to; I have no business throwing a fit about things you've done. Apology over."

"Accepted," Eifa says, smiling.

After that, the conversation in the front seat ebbs and flows. I wait to speak until Skye is caught up answering several questions Eifa has about her guns.

"'Is there a tiny musician in the box'?" I mimic to Leithe under my breath. "You asked me if Grandma's television was showing images projected from a different location, and you're acting like you thought for a *second* there was a tiny person in the car radio?"

"Sometimes the best solution to a problem is to think about something else," Leithe says. "And it benefits us to get along. Would you not agree?"

"I'm just shocked you're willing to look like a clown to make Skye feel better."

"I find no shame in not understanding human things. It's not as if they matter."

"There you are," I say with mock relief. "I thought we'd lost you." With the weight of silence lifted, I ask a question

I've been afraid to have answered. "What happened to the other nightmares after I passed out?"

"Nevain and his servants probably killed most of them," Leithe says. "I assume the ones that survived are running loose."

"They might hurt people," I say. "Shouldn't we do something about that?"

"Would you like to turn around and check?" Skye asks, interrupting her conversation. "Or did we have something else we were doing?" She catches my expression in the rearview mirror and sighs. "We can only do one thing at a time, Tamsin, and those nightmares aren't currently trying to kill us, so they're pretty low on my list. What about you?"

"And the people at the bar?" I ask.

"Nevain's probably already forgotten about them," Leithe says. "The glamour he put them under will fade. They'll find their ways home."

"They'll try to put their lives back together while never being able to tell their families what really happened, because they'd never be believed, all while knowing they'll never get justice," Skye says.

"There's an easy fix," Leithe says. "I could have taken their memories. I could do that for you, too, you know, but I don't know what you'd do with yourself without something to be angry about."

"As I have made clear," Skye says. "If you try to glamour me, I will shoot you. Again."

"Which *might* give you enough time to flee," Leithe says. "Again."

"Glamour doesn't work like that anyway," Eifa says softly. "Humans sometimes come to Martin to ask him to take away things they don't want to remember, but glamour can only paint over the memories, not get rid of them. They come back as nightmares or feelings one can't shake. It's never perfect."

"I always knew," Skye says, "about my son. Some part of me always knew."

"Because you're too stubborn for your own good," Leithe says. "Otherwise, you'd probably have been happier."

"I wouldn't have been me," she says.

The closer we get to Shrike Run, the sicker I feel until I'm counting clouds to distract from the nausea. I rehearse the not-truths in my head. *I can't be here anymore. I'm going where people will understand me. Don't expect to hear from me.* And then it will be over. Maybe she'll make it easy and will have already thrown what little I own out on the porch for the lies I've already allowed her to believe.

I can no longer distract myself once we pass through the town proper and curve onto the tree-flanked and meandering Butcher Road. A few miles and a single turn away from Grandma's, I can't concentrate on anything else.

"What the hell?" Skye jerks the car to a stop. "Those weren't there a few days ago." Fat red roses the size of my open hand choke out the trees on either side of Grandma's driveway, wrapping around trunks and hanging heavy off branches, dyeing the light rays coming through the trees pink.

"Well," Leithe says. "Lelit beat you back."

"No," I say. "Please, no."

Skye pops her handgun out of the glove box and slams the truck back into motion. The farther we go, the larger the roses get. The woods open up to reveal Grandma's house blanketed in roses the size of my head, ropy stalks the thickness of my forearm, and thorns like daggers. The vines tighten around the bricks, making them groan and shudder. The front door hangs wide open; more roses wend their way inside. Flowers constrict Grandma's car as well, the roof and sides already bowing in.

My hand freezes around the door handle; it's Skye and Eifa who are out of the car first.

"Mom?" Skye shouts. She's up the steps and into the house before I get the car door open.

I tumble out of the car, fighting against my throat closing and vision tunneling. "Grandma?" The air is stiflingly sweet.

"Tamsin?" Grandma's muffled voice comes from somewhere inside. Relief turns my limbs to jelly. She's here. She's alive. My bare feet slap against the wooden porch as I rush through the door. Grandma's in the kitchen, watching me quizzically. "Are you okay?" She wipes her hands on a dish towel.

"Are *you* okay?" The flowers. She must not be able to see them. No, I look around, confused. There are no flowers. Maybe they were never here, just an illusion to scare me. I cross the room. Grandma looks fine, unharmed. "We need to go. I know I've been asking a lot but someone can explain in the car."

Grandma steps around the counter to meet me. "Honey, you're talking a mile a minute." She takes my arm. "Sit down. Take a minute to breathe. Do you want me to make you a hot chocolate?"

"Wait," I say. "Skye should be behind ..." No, Skye was in front of me. She should already be inside. "Skye?" I turn back to the door. "Leithe? Eifa?" The doorway stands empty.

"They're all off in their own little worlds, right now," Lelit says. She stands in Grandma's place, nails digging into my arm. "I thought we could talk."

"Where's—where's the human woman?" I try to pull myself away, but Lelit's grip only tightens, nails threatening to pierce my skin.

"Does it matter?" Lelit asks. "I found her here, all alone." She draws out the last two words. "I just *had* to bring her back to Faerie with me. I mean, she really was pitiful. Is that a problem, Mab? You weren't here; I thought you might be done with her." Her lip curls in smug, expectant satisfaction.

Wordless terror and rage fight to drown every other thought in my head. I close my eyes and take a breath. Don't sound desperate. Don't let her know how much you care or it will just get worse. I can't cry, can't beg. "I was done with her," I say. I was going to leave her, after all. "I came back to pick up some clothes, actually. I wasn't planning on staying." That's right. Give her nothing.

Lelit's smile vanishes, just for a second. Her eyes flash with sudden fire, but she closes them, smiles, laughs it off. "You're so cruel. Sometimes I wonder if you've ever cared about anything at all."

"Are you done?" I ask. "I'm tired of this. So you want to go back to Faerie? Fine, let's go." That might be the easiest way to get her away from Grandma.

"Did you not hear me earlier?" Lelit asks. "I'm not here, and neither is the human." She gives me a knowing smile. "If you change your mind and want the human back in one piece, you should hurry and follow. You of all folk know what the Dreaming Court can do to an unprotected human mind. You know what *I* can do to a human mind."

My resolve shatters. "Please just bring her back," I beg. "Just bring her back and I'll—"

Something strikes me and sends my head reeling to the side. "Wake up!"

"Hunter?" My cheek stings. Vines and roses cover the interior of the house. Lelit is gone. In her place is a hydra-like mass of bloom-topped vines that meet in the center in a mangled knot, looming above me like a rearing serpent. A vine wraps around my arm, thorns digging into my skin where Lelit's nails were.

Hunter stands next to me, one hand pressed to his chest, the other ready to strike me again. "Are you awake?"

"Tam ... sin?" The sound comes from the rose at the center. The petals ripple as the thing speaks, revealing hooked thorns spiraling into a gullet. I try to step back, but vines wrap around my calves and wind steadily upward. Blood oozes out around thorns buried in my flesh, but there's no pain. My legs are numb.

Hunter kneels to cut away the vines at my legs; the blooms hiss and lunge at him in response, slamming him into the kitchen counter hard enough he drops his dagger. At the same time, they pull me off my feet.

I hit the ground hard, and from my new vantage point see that no one else has fared any better. Skye and Eifa are wide-eyed and frozen just out of reach, while Leithe is stock-still at the front door, vines wrapping around his hand where it rests on the frame.

"Skye!" The vines drag me toward the base of the mass. "Eifa!" A slap. A slap woke me up. I grab Hunter's fallen dagger and throw it at Eifa. It spins blade over handle until the handle bounces off her leg.

The impact is enough to jolt Eifa back to consciousness. She forces her arm free and grabs bloom lunging toward her, stopping it short in front of her face. With a snarl, she crushes the stalk with her bare hand before tossing it to the side. In a liquid motion, she sweeps up the dagger and throws it, pinning the bloom lunging at Skye to the far wall. She tears her other arm free, unbothered by the thorns leaving behind trails of blood.

Eifa quickly rips her legs free and clears the distance to Skye before slapping her across the face. Awareness returns to Skye's eyes. Eifa tears at the vines wrapped around Skye and succeeds in pulling one of her arms free.

"No," Skye says, taking stock of the situation and nudging Eifa away. "The source." She nods toward the mass, from which the rest of the vines grow.

Eifa obeys without a word, looping her arm under mine and pulling me free. I scream, though it doesn't hurt. The thorns tug painlessly at my skin even as my blood spills over the vines. Where blood lands, the mass pulses and grows, sprouting new heads. It's feeding on my blood—Gentry blood.

Several vines slam into Eifa with redoubled strength, throwing her into the dining room table and sending it skidding across the floor as Eifa goes through the living room drywall.

One by one, the blooms begin to laugh—a hollow sound, formed as if they have no idea what emotion a laugh is meant to convey. The walls groan. The living room window cracks and shatters as vines press against the exterior. They burrow through the mortar to pin Eifa against the exposed brick. They bind Skye's arms as she struggles to free herself, her gun now pressed against her side, useless. Hunter is occupied keeping the vines away from his face. His dogs bark and howl outside.

I kick at the vines around my legs; pull at them with my hands and only succeed in pricking myself on the thorns. My fingers fumble as they go numb. Skye is just out of reach. If I could reach her, maybe I could create another monster to save us, but my outstretched hand stops just short of her boot.

Skye struggles against the vines. Her gun is in her hand, but she can't aim it freely while it's pressed against her side, not while I'm between her and the center of the mass. Still, she tries to aim it, maybe as a final protest, but she can't turn it toward the bloom rearing toward her, thorny, lamprey-like maw exposed.

Skye fires. The shot echoes in my ears. The vines twist around Skye's hand until the weapon slips from her bloody grip and bounces out of my reach.

"Lelit," I say, unsure if she can hear me. "Please, I'll—"

The roses begin to wail and thrash. They abandon me, Hunter, Eifa, and Skye, instead turning their attention to Leithe as he appraises the scene disdainfully. The vine in his hand withers under his touch. Several blooms converge on his location, but he isn't there anymore—as quick as if the distance was only a single step, he's standing above me, hand wrapped around the stalk of the largest flower as if it's a neck. The petals turn gray and fall, the stalk browns.

The withering radiates out from the center of the mass and the vines sink to the ground under their own weight, weakly wriggling like worms that don't yet know they're dead.

Leithe releases the flower and it falls to the ground, the impact breaking its now-brittle form into scattered pieces.

Everything is still, the vines shriveled and dead. "Well," Leithe says. "That was utterly expected." He examines his hand—bloody and smoking, finger bones clicking back into place and flesh knitting together before my eyes—and turns to Skye. "Were you actually aiming at me, or did you just get extremely lucky?"

"You'll never know." Skye picks up her gun. Hunter's dogs bound inside and crowd their master as he sits up. Eifa climbs out of the hole in the drywall. "Where is she?" Skye asks no one in particular. "Where's my mother?"

I tug at the vines wrapping around my ankles and try to stand, but my legs don't want to work. Neither does my mouth, but I manage to force out the words. "She's gone."

# Chapter Eighteen



"Is she dead?" Skye's voice is dangerously calm.

"Lelit took her to Faerie." My head feels full of cotton, emotions out of reach—maybe an effect of whatever numbing toxin is pumping through my body from the thorns. "She's bait."

"I find it unlikely Lelit would have bothered kidnapping a human unless someone gave her information," Leithe says. "Perhaps someone trying to save their own skin?"

Hunter gestures to his chest, still leaking a token amount of blood as if to remind him what he's missing. "Does it look like I traded the woman for Lady Lelit's favor?" He waves a hand at the withered knot of vines and roots in the center of the room. "My apologies for ... this. I tried to convince her that taking a human was unnecessary. That angered her, so she plucked this from your grandmother's head and left it behind for you."

"Well," I say. It's hard to hear over the dull roaring in my ears. "Thanks for trying."

"My mother didn't know the truth," Skye says. "Lelit shouldn't have been able to take her."

Hunter studies Skye. If he's surprised by her presence, he gives no indication. "My lady returned disguised as

Tamsin. She asked your mother to come away with her and promised to tell her the truth.”

“And the woman then unwittingly gave her permission to be taken to Faerie,” Leithe finishes.

“No,” Hunter says. “She excused herself, returned with a gun, and demanded to know who Lelit was and what she’d done with Tamsin. When my lady implied Tamsin’s safety was in jeopardy, she shot her. That was enough to render her no longer innocent. My lady was free to take her.”

“But how did she know?” I ask. “I didn’t tell her.”

“You think you needed to?” Leithe snorts. “That woman was the smartest of the three of you.” Skye stares at the wall, squeezing the bridge of her nose.

One of Hunter’s dogs perks up, nose working. It trots to the fridge and paws at the door. Eifa follows with a be-mused expression and opens the fridge. Something inside screams; an egg flies out of the fridge, though Eifa catches it before it cracks against her face. She catches the next and dodges the third, which cracks on the floor.

“Please do not eat me!” Cheeps cries. “I am small and stringy and surely do not taste good!”

“Cheeps!” I call out. To my shame, I forgot about him completely until now.

“Young Miss!” he gasps, still inside the fridge. “Are you the real Young Miss, or the fake one?”

“The real one,” I say. He gasps again. I hear the scurry of little feet across the floor as he rushes into the living room, makes a cautious berth around Hunter and Leithe, and wraps both his arms around my forearm. “Oh, it is terri-ble!” Fat tears roll down his face, as well as a line of snot. “The Mistress has been taken away forever!” He squeezes into the crook of my arm so I'm shielding him from the other fae, pressing so close I can feel the rapid beating of his heart.

"Exactly how many faeries have been living in this house?" Skye asks.

Cheeps gasps. "Old Young Miss?" He sniffles and squints. "I did not recognize you because you smell very bad now. Oh! You should not be speaking to me because you are a human; you could get in trouble and he might kill you dead." Cheeps points at Leithe. "Or him." He points to Hunter. "Or her." He points to Eifa. "And if they don't kill you dead then they'll take you away like they took the Mistress," he wails. "I was so *scared*. The Fake Young Miss made a very hungry flower that wanted to *eat me* so I hid in the ..." He thinks for a moment. "The fridgerator." Tears well up in his eyes again. "I was so scared you would never ever come back and I would be so alone forever." He sobs theatrically into my arm.

"It's ..." It's okay? It's not okay. "I'm glad you're alright, Cheeps." My voice sounds far away. My whole body feels far away. Detached. Like I'm running on autopilot. I pat him gently on the head. "She was supposed to be safe," I say weakly. Maybe to the others, maybe just to myself. "That was the whole point of not telling her anything."

"I'm not sure what you expected," Leithe says. "Neither of you could bear to keep your noses out of Faerie. Are you surprised it runs in the family?" He glances at Hunter. "Without the knight, Lelit wouldn't have even known you were free. If you wanted to make sure that woman stayed safe, you would have killed him yourself." He gives Skye a meaningful look. "Without this man, your mother would be safe. He's Lelit's knight, utterly her creature—a liability to all of us."

"Do you think I work for you?" Skye asks.

"Stop it," I say. "He helped us, and that flower thing attacked him the same as the rest of us." Feeling gradually returns to my legs—an itching that quickly gives way to pain. I tug at the vine wrapped around my calf, thorns embedded in my flesh, and wince.

Hunter turns away from Leithe and kneels by my side. "Do you want me to do it?"

"I'll do it." I grab the vine and pull, but go queasy when I pull much more thorn out of my leg than I was expecting. The pain radiates up my leg and into nerves I didn't know I had, paralyzing me until it passes. There are still several more thorns. I lean back against the wall. "Okay, you can do it."

Hunter is as gentle as he can be, but I cry anyway. When he's done, blood oozes out of a spiral of widely spaced punctures and makes several small puddles on the floor.

"Will I heal as fast as you?" I ask Leithe. I wipe my face, ashamed of the tears. His hand is already whole and unbroken once more.

"On your own? Only if you eat something," Leithe says. "Or return to the Dreaming Court."

Skye looks at me like she'd forgotten I was there. "You need stitches."

Leithe frowns at my leg. "That won't kill her."

A dull roar builds in my ears as I stare at the blood leaking out of my leg. I'm back at the bar, back in the glade, hands pressed against Zach's neck. Then his face becomes Grandma's.

"Skye," I say. She doesn't look at me, her attention instead focused on the far wall. "I'm sorry. We'll go after them. I'll do whatever I have to do to get her back."

Skye takes a deep breath and exhales slowly before answering. "Go take a shower."

"What? No. We don't have time for that!" I stand and catch myself against the wall when putting weight on my legs feels like forcing brand-new thorns into the wounds.

"How much time are you going to waste arguing with me?" She snaps her fingers and points at the stairs. "Does someone need to carry you?"

I'm too stunned to do anything but obey. "No." The pain is bearable when I know it's coming with each step.

I avoid looking in the bathroom mirror as I strip and throw my pajamas on the floor. They were a Christmas gift years ago from Grandma, with their little smiling cartoon clouds and rainbows, now crusty with someone else's blood.

I don't wait for the water to get hot before I step into the shower. The water stings where it runs over the wounds in my leg.

For a few seconds, minutes, or maybe an hour, I stand under the water and struggle to breathe. The roaring in my head paralyzes all other thoughts. I'm dimly aware of a crash downstairs, but I couldn't move even if I wanted to. My limbs won't obey me. I only unfreeze when the water gets so hot that I can't stand the pain. Then I sit under the scalding water for a few moments longer before turning the temperature down.

I scrub my skin red and raw and still find flecks of blood when I look myself over. Only when I feel disgusted with myself for the time I've wasted do I turn the water off.

The ancient alarm clock on my bedside table says it's nearly eight in the morning. I dress in a fresh shirt and jeans and dig a pair of old hiking boots out of the bottom of the closet before going back downstairs. When I reach the landing, everyone gets quiet in a way that makes it obvious they were discussing me. There's a hole in the living room drywall that wasn't there before; Skye has a Band-Aid over one of her knuckles.

"You can say it to my face," I tell her. "You were right. This is all my fault. I should have left a lot sooner. Maybe you should have just killed me when I was a kid. There are people who would still be alive if you had."

"That sounds like something we'll both have to live with." Skye crosses her arms. "Now, are you done, or do you want me to get you a cross?"

"Why aren't you angry at me?" I ask.

"I'm furious," she says. "All the time. And it's exhausting. And I'm really doing my best to keep it together, because there isn't any alternative. So: first thing is to figure out a way to the Dreaming Court." She looks at Leithe expectantly.

"Lelit's invitation would have worked, but—" he starts.

"But you threw it on the floor at the bar," I finish. "How is Lelit coming and going? Shouldn't we be able to use the same door?"

"She creates temporary doors," Hunter says. "She can make them in any sleeping mind."

"Can either of you do that?" I ask. Hunter shakes his head.

"Any door I open would go through the Crawling Court," Leithe says. "And the Crawling King would know as soon as you stepped foot in his domain. There are a few natural doors in the forest around us, but they'd lead to Blooming Court land, and—"

"And the Blooming Queen would know as soon as I stepped foot in her domain," I parrot.

"But you—" Leithe begins.

"*I* should be able to open the same doors Lelit can," I finish for him. "I know. I figured. If I figure out how to do that, you'll be the first to know."

"We could just take the train," Eifa says.

"The *train*?" I ask. But then any sense of surprise or disbelief I may have had fades. "Of course there's a train. Why wouldn't there be a train? Makes as much sense as anything else. I'm a magical queen, and there's a train to fairyland." I rub my eyes. "Why not just take the airplane?"

"Well," Eifa says patiently. "There isn't an airplane."

I sigh and turn to Leithe. "Why didn't you just say there was a train?"

He looks between me and Eifa, brow furrowed. "What is a train?" After listening to the explanation, he shrugs. "So it's a thing low fae use to get around. Why would you expect me to know about it?"

"Okay, so we know where we're going and how we're getting there. Let's go," I say.

Skye looks at me with pity in her eyes, something so much worse than anger or blame. "You shouldn't go, Tamsin."

"*What*?" My voice rises to a shriek.

"A nymph in Georgia owes me a favor," Eifa says. "She'll shelter you. She's quite talented at glamour as well; she might be able to teach you."

I turn to Leithe. "You agree with this? You've been pushing for me to go to Faerie this entire time. Now you want me to go to *Georgia*?"

"What is your plan once you make it to the Dreaming Court?" he asks.

"To …" By the looks in their eyes, they all know what I'm about to say. There's no use trying to obfuscate it. "To trade myself." I give him a defiant stare. "Lelit won. Don't pretend you all don't know that. There's no fight anymore. There's no more chance to run. I'm not risking my grandmother. I have to do it."

"Yes, we know you're so desperate to perform some dazzling selfless heroics that you'd love nothing more than to climb up onto a sacrificial altar for anyone who asks," Leithe says. "And we all talked and decided that's not a good investment for any of us."

"And what would *you* even do? If you could beat Lelit on your own, Leithe, this wouldn't be an issue in the first place," I point out.

"What would *you* do? Because you're right. You're not prepared. You have no control over yourself. You don't even realize how lucky it was that the nightmares you summoned against Nevain left the humans alone. You're just as likely to be completely impotent as you are to kill Skye or Eifa with an errant thought," he says. "But if you're not there, we'll have a bargaining chip. She cares about getting you more than any of us."

"Why would you go?" I ask. "You don't care about my Grandma."

"I care that Lelit has leverage that will make you do stupid things," he says.

I turn to Skye. "Why would you even care if I traded myself? You hate me."

Skye ignores me. "Eifa wrote down the directions to her friend. You're going to take the truck there and wait for someone to come get you."

"Amaranth is very kind," Eifa says. "And a skilled witch. You'll be safe with her."

"I'm not ... I'm not a *child*," I say.

"No," Skye says. "But there's clearly something going on. It's not—" Skye sighs and fidgets with her lighter as if she can't decide whether or not she wants a cigarette. "We're trying to *help* you."

"Well ... why would you even bother going to Faerie for someone you already abandoned? And It's been two decades. Your son is either dead or might as well be." I feel sick as soon as the words leave my mouth, but it's too late. I said them.

"Tamsin—" Leithe begins.

"No one wants to hear whatever snide comment you have queued up!" I barely feel in control of my own body as I turn to him. "You're only here because you think this is a test. You think if you put up with enough of my bullshit, Mab will appear and tell you that you passed. *But maybe she just didn't want you.*" The room gets a few degrees colder, but Leithe's face remains carefully blank. "And what are you doing here?" I whirl on Eifa. "Do you think you're making up for all the things you did while working for a psychopath?" Eifa isn't smiling, but she doesn't look angry. She looks sad. Pitying.

"Are you going to do him next?" Skye gestures to Hunter, who's been watching us in silence. "Or can we move on? 'Okay, you win. We all hate you now and we don't care if you go martyr yourself.' Is that what you were hoping we'd say?" She sighs. "Grow up, Tamsin. Because if you're going to act like a child, you're going to get treated like one. Go to Eifa's friend. We'll find you when we make it back, and we'll figure out what to do next from there."

For a moment I'm fourteen again, watching Grandma drive away after dragging my bags into my boarding school dorm room, while all I want to do is scream, throw something out the window. Anything to make her stop the car and turn around. I watch the words come out of my mouth as if I'm standing next to myself, seeing it from the outside and unable to stop. "You're telling *me* to grow up, you've spent the last two decades—"

"*Tamsin*," Leithe says.

"Oh my god," Molly Foster says from the doorway. "Skye? You're *alive*?" She gapes at Skye in disbelief.

Skye stares at the other woman like a deer in headlights. "Hey, Molly."

"I *did* try to warn you," Leithe says, sounding vindicated. Molly doesn't acknowledge him.

Molly takes a tentative step inside. For a moment, she looks like she can't decide if she wants to start yelling or crying, but then she crosses the room and envelops Skye in a hug. Skye stands stock still, arms at her sides, until Molly lets her go.

"I was supposed to have coffee with Mrs. Bellamy and the door was open, so ..." Molly trails off. "God, where have you been? Why does it look like you've been burgled?" The fight with the roses overturned chairs and scattered objects from shelves and counters across the floor.

"Um—" I start, but Molly continues over me.

"Twenty years, and you only come back now? Did your mother tell you what happened to my son? Did you even know I *had* a son?" I've never seen Molly angry, but now she looks furious. "You have a lot of nerve." She turns back to me, must see something on my face. "Tamsin looks like she's about to cry. Your own daughter, Skye. What did you say to her?"

A plan comes together. An awful, awful plan. "Mrs. Foster," I sniffle pathetically. "It's not her fault."

"Oh, honey." Molly hugs me tightly.

"I'm sorry." I whisper my next words. "Please sleep." Soothing, the way Lelit said it. Is it my imagination, or do Molly's eyelids droop?

I watched Lelit do it twice. I should be able to do this. Leithe thinks I should be able to do this. "Sleep." Is she leaning harder against me?

"What are you doing?" Skye asks, stepping toward me.

I felt the ripple of the glamour when Lelit spoke. I watched it saturate Grandma's mind. Something roils in the pit of my stomach. I am a thing like Lelit. A thing that can do this. "*Sleep.*"

Molly slumps against me and we hit the floor together. Her body's much heavier than I thought it would be, but I at least keep her from hitting her head.

"Tamsin!" Skye kneels next to Molly and looks like she can't decide whether or not to hit me. Before she can, I take Molly's limp hand.

Just like that, I'm in the Fosters' kitchen, but changed. The real one doesn't have weeds pushing their way through the aged linoleum floor, nor cracks running up the walls. Only one flickering lightbulb still functions. Fog presses against the dirty windows.

"Zach?" Molly's voice comes from upstairs. I follow it into the living room, passing a couch spotted with black mold. Cobwebs spread from the corners of the ceiling and around the light fixtures. Nightmares. Molly's been having nightmares.

"Zach?" Molly comes downstairs, a red backpack in one hand. "You're going to be late for school." She spies me, and for a moment I worry she'll get mad or confused. "Tamsin's already here. You don't want her to be late too, do you?" To me, she says, "Tamsin, honey, apologize to your grandma for me. He's never like this." She wanders into another room, still calling out for her son.

"I'm sorry," I say again, too low for her to hear me. I leave her alone and go to my real target: the Fosters' front door. Just like Grandma's dream before, looking at it fills me with the sudden certainty that I'm standing at an edge, and the Fosters' front yard isn't beyond this door.

Something knocks on the other side—a light, rapid tapping. I place my hand on the knob, then step back out of the dream. I'm back in Grandma's living room. Skye looks horrified; Leithe's expression is unreadable.

The front door to the Fosters' house hovers in the air just behind Molly's head. "If you left me here, it wouldn't have mattered. I would have done this the first chance I got."

"Tamsin, wait," Skye says. The tapping comes again, more insistent. I throw open the door, revealing a passage filled with cobwebs. Threads waft out from the edges of the frame. A shape skittering across the ground retreats until it's swallowed by the webs.

"I made the door," I say. "And I'm going through it. You can follow if you want."

"Wait." Leithe takes a step forward.

Before he can stop me, I step through the door.

# Chapter Nineteen

Webs brush against my face, softer than feathers but packed so dense I can barely see my own feet. They snap and drift away as I pass through, so light they could be mistaken for heavy fog. Maybe it *is* fog.

After a few steps, I can no longer see a door behind me. No sign of the others. No sign I'm going the right way, if there *is* a right way. The ground beneath my feet has the spongy texture of wet, rotten wood.

"I think." The fog eats my words as soon as they're out of my mouth, "that this was probably very stupid." My moment of triumph at making it this far is dampened. Am I in Faerie? Trapped somewhere between Faerie and the mortal world? Maybe I'm in Molly's head, and once she wakes up I'll disappear forever.

With each step, it gets harder to breathe, the air I pull into my lungs is thick and soupy. Threads of webs catch in my nose and throat until I pull my shirt collar over the lower half of my face. The fog thickens into grit that fills my eyes and presses against the fabric of my shirt until I can't breathe. I can no longer tell what I'm walking on, if anything at all.

My throat spasms as my body fights for air. I can't turn around. My legs can no longer move. I'm pinned under a great weight. I can only push my arms forward, searching for something, anything.

Then my hands break free of the dirt and close around open air. In a frenzied rush, I clear the earth away from my face and suck in desperate lungfuls of air along with enough dirt to send me into a coughing fit.

Still hacking, I dig myself free and roll onto my stomach and elbows. When I can finally breathe, I wipe the tears from my eyes and take in my surroundings.

Without a doubt, I've made it to Faerie.

Twisted black trees tower over me, their branches crowned with spider webs instead of leaves, choking out even the hint of a sky. Curls of mist swirl in unhurried eddies from the ground. Flickering blue lights bob in the distance. The loudest noise in the vicinity is my own breathing; all other sounds sponged up by a heavy blanket of fog that carries with it the scent of damp earth and wood.

The air I pull into my lungs radiates through my chest to the tips of my fingers. My breath bubbles back out as a giggle. My body feels light, as if up until now I've been living my life in a bowl of molasses.

Home. I'm home. It's a feeling that resonates through the trees, through every grain of dirt beneath my feet. I somehow know that if I wanted to, I could mold the trees like wet clay between my fingers. I could paint the fog like a canvas. The entire world is calling out to me, begging to be commanded. It's calling a single word, over and over and over again.

*Mab.*

My throat catches. It's wrong. It's all wrong. It's not calling for me. This isn't my home. I've never been here.

*Mab.* I feel the word pressing in against me from all sides, changing with each repetition. The sounds that make it up peel away, leaving behind the shape of something else. A new word. A word that threatens to swallow me even while it dances around the fringe of my hearing, eager to tear apart the barriers between me and itself, the delineation of *me*. To unmake me.

"No no no." I press the heels of my palms into my ears. It blocks out nothing. *Go away. You've got the wrong person.* I withdraw into myself, waiting, begging it to stop. *It isn't me. It isn't me. It isn't me.* I repeat those words until they've lost all meaning, until they're just a sequence of sounds to focus on.

Deep breaths. I don't know how long it takes, but the screaming sensation eventually fades to a dull prickle at the back of my head. Present, but ignorable. Subdued, but waiting for an opening.

Calm. I'm calm. I'm alone in Faerie, but I'm calm.

No, I realize. I'm not alone. There's a spider the size of a small dog staring at me. It's covered in dark bristles and a collection of saucer-like black eyes. "Hi," I say. The spider only stares at me. "I'm looking for Lelit; I don't suppose you could give me directions?"

The spider looks around as if getting its bearings, skitters a few feet to my left, runs in a small circle, and stops again, looking at me and waving its two front legs.

"I assume that means I should follow you." I take a few steps; it keeps moving, staying a few feet ahead of me. "I'm guessing you could talk if you wanted to. Why are you helping me?" The spider doesn't answer, not that I expected it to. I run my hands through my hair in annoyance. "This is just like with the witch's cat. Why do I keep following suspicious animals?" Because I don't have any better options. Every direction looks exactly the same: trees, fog, and creepy blue lights.

A heavy creak catches my attention; I turn to see a lopsided, oblong triangular structure jutting out of the earth, clods of dirt clinging to its surface. The pitched roof of a house. The Fosters' house. As I watch, it gives a resounding shudder and sinks another several inches. The ground beneath me tilts toward the sinking building. I slip and scrabble on rivulets of loose soil until I'm free of the sinkhole; from a safe distance, I watch until the earth closes over the ridge of the roof, erasing any evidence it was ever there aside from an indent in the ground.

I don't know if I was hoping to see someone's grasping hands break through the ground, but they don't. I'm stuck in Faerie with only a spider for company.

"I should have thought this through better," I say to the spider. I might have had time to at least grab a kitchen knife, for all the good that may have done.

"Alright," I tell the spider. "I'm following. Lead on."

We only go a few dozen feet before we come across a gently-curving path made of pale stones—no, bones—embedded in the earth. As we walk, only a few small sounds filter through the fog: the snap of a branch here, what might be the flutter of wings there.

Something catches my eye: a figure in the distance, but when I turn to look, it's just fog. "Hello?" I call out. "Anyone out there?" No response. Of course there wouldn't be a response. If someone's stalking me in the haunted fog forest, they're not going to tell me so.

There's no one else here. The path sometimes branches; though there are no signs and everything around us is the same fog and trees, the spider moves like it knows where it's going. I follow it for what must be a long time, but I don't feel tired. If anything, I've felt better than I have in weeks. I'd even forgotten about my injured leg, which has healed to the point of only being a dull, ignorable throb.

Then someone screams. A drawn-out, agonized scream that terminates in a gasping sob.

It's probably bait. That thought only gives me pause for a second, because there's a chance it's not bait.

I run toward the sound, or at least where I think the sound came from. As I approach, a shape materializes out of the fog. At first it looks like a knotty mass of exposed tree roots, but then I realize it's a body.

Skye's body. She's propped against a tree, eyes blank. She looks as if she's been hollowed out; nothing but bone jutting out angrily against discolored, sagging skin, face slack.

I cover my mouth with both hands to stifle my scream. My thoughts race, scrambling over themselves to form an explanation. Her state reminds me of how she looked when Leithe's curse was sucking the life out of her. Of course he wouldn't forgive her for shooting him. He killed her as soon as he had the opportunity. As soon as he thought he could do it without me catching him. This is my fault. I can't breathe.

The prickle in the back of my head returns, rising in volume as if drawn by my panic. It seeks an opening, the pressure looking for a way to crack open my head and drown me in itself.

"Go away. Go away go away go away." I close my eyes and take ten measured breaths, only opening them again when the calling dulls. Skye's body is still there, but I'm thinking clearer. This doesn't make sense. It's too convenient—that it would be left here for me to find, that she would be dead in the exact manner I'd blame myself for the most. The spider is several feet behind me, waving its front legs insistently.

Trap. It's a trap. Has to be. But still, I can't look away. I need to know. I nudge it with the toe of my boot, hoping that if I touch it, it will melt away to nothing and prove itself a fake. But it feels like a body.

I squat down on my haunches, looking for any imperfection, anything to prove it's not real. Then Skye's blank eyes swivel to mine, enlarging until they take up most of her face. Her mouth splits open in a razor-toothed grin as she lunges forward, her form shrinking to the size of a small child. Spindly claws grotesquely long for the creature's body slash at my face as it launches past me and vanishes cackling into the fog. By the time I lose sight of it, the faerie has become a naked, hairless thing bounding on claw-tipped feet and trailing a rat-like tail.

"B-movie jump scare little shit!" I yell after it.

I sit where I fell until my breathing returns to normal, fingers pressed against my temples. When I stand, I see a flash of a distant figure in the fog.

"Hello?" I call out. "I want to talk. I have ... um." I dig around in my pockets. An empty gum wrapper. "We really don't have to do this," I say. "We can skip to either you talking to me or trying to kill me; I'd be fine with that." I take a step, but the figure steps behind a tree and out of sight.

"Tamsin!" The voice is weak but unmistakable. I follow it and find exactly what I expect: Zach lying in a pool of his own blood, reaching out to me with the last of his strength. His hand goes limp as I watch, light leaving his eyes. Even though I know it's fake, I still have to fight to stay composed.

"That's a good one." I ball my hands into fists, nails digging into my palms. "How do you know my name? How do you know what to turn into?" I force myself to look for anything to critique, to bait the creature into engaging with me, but its disguise is exactly how I remember that moment.

"Tamsin?" A different voice comes trembling through the fog. The instant I'm distracted, the creature disguised as Zach reverts to its rat-like true form and bolts.

"No!" I dive for it, my hands grazing the tip of its tail before the thing darts out of sight. I'm not even sure what I would have done if I'd caught it.

"Tamsin?" The distant voice calls again, closer.

"Grandma?" My bravado vanishes. There's a chance it could really be her. A slim, nearly nonexistent chance, but a chance. I go toward the sound until her shape materializes out of the mist. She's huddled over, arms wrapped around herself, eyes darting to follow every errant noise. They find me and widen.

"Tamsin," she says. It sounds like her. It looks like her.

"Is it you?" My voice sounds small. "Grandma?"

"Don't call me that," Grandma says. "She told me the truth about what you are." Every word I want to say catches in my throat. "You *used* me. You used my family. You *killed* my grandchild. You drove away my daughter. How *dare* you call me family." There's disdain in her eyes like I've never seen before. "We'd be so much better off if you'd never existed."

I can't help but laugh. It comes out bitter and sharp. "That's exactly what I was afraid you'd say. Exactly."

Grandma looks taken aback. "I always thought of you as a burden."

It just makes me laugh more. "I was always worried about that, too." I laugh so much that it brings tears to my eyes. Or maybe I'm just crying—out of relief that this creature isn't her, out of the pain its words caused anyway, or maybe from the absurdity of it all.

The creature wearing Grandma's face looks thoughtful for a moment. Then it begins to rot. Its skin purples and then blackens before sloughing off in pieces, revealing maggots already picking her skeleton clean. Its emptying eye sockets bore holes in me as an eyeball liquefies from rot and slides down its skinless cheek.

I want to laugh in its face, deny that it scares me. But it does scare me, far more than the parody of her rejection. Grandma is going to die. She's going to die and rot and turn to dust while in a hundred years I'll look exactly the same. Even when I thought I was human, I knew it would happen, but that was always in the distant way you'd think about death, as something that was always consigned to the distant future. But with my future a yawning black hole, the timeline I once thought I had is now bunched up at the beginning. Grandma's death might as well come tomorrow. Or it might have already happened.

The skeleton lets out a hissing cackle and lunges forward, slamming into me as Grandma's skull melts away, replaced with a wide-eyed, toothy visage. It hits me in the chest and knocks me onto my back, talon-tipped hands pressing into my shoulders.

Two more of the creatures emerge from the fog. One tears at my pant leg, and the other wrestles with the first one for its position. The first one pushes the other one away and brings its jaws to my neck. I'm about to get eaten.

My spider companion taps rhythmically on the trunk of a tree, and then the weight is gone. A spider the size of a car drags the creature on top of me into the web-choked branches. The other fae howl and flee. I barely have time to process what happened before the spider is gone, and the world around me perfectly silent.

"Thanks," I say, still lying on the ground. I lay there for a while. My spider waits next to my head, studying me with black, unreadable eyes.

My shoulders protest when I finally push myself to my feet. The rat-like faerie left punctures along my upper arms where its claws dug into my skin. Not deep, but noticeable. This is getting me nowhere.

It takes longer than before for the next figure to appear. I don't know who to expect next—Hunter, Leithe, Lelit, maybe my old therapist; the list makes me realize I don't have many friends—but it's a little girl huddling against the base of a tree.

The girl starts at the sound of my approach and turns toward me. "Daddy?" I don't know how she speaks, because her face is a featureless plane. No eyes, no nose, no mouth.

"I have no idea who this one is supposed to be," I say.

An arrow flies from the fog and sinks through the side of the girl's head, pinning it to the tree on the other side. Her body melts into another of the rat-like creatures that have been harassing me, dead. "Because it wasn't here for you," Hunter says.

# Chapter Twenty

Hunter's covered in a layer of fresh dirt.

"How do I know you're not another shapeshifting rat monster?" I think about it. "Or Lelit?"

"Boggles can't maintain false shapes for very long," Hunter says. "And I'm not, nor have I ever been, Lady Lelit."

"I'll take it," I say. "Where are we?"

Hunter surveys our surroundings with disdain. "This is Blackbower, Lady Noctiva's home."

I remember her bent-double, black-veiled form from the dream prison. And all the spiders. "Well." I look out at the fog, spider webs, and creepy, leafless trees. "That tracks. Where's everyone else?"

"I went through the door but lost you in the fog soon after. I'm not sure if the rest followed. Even if they did, it would have been easy for Lady Noctiva to separate us once we entered her domain, if she wished. It was hard enough to find you. The land here—trees, mist, everything—serves her. If the others were just out of sight, we might never know."

I survey the landscape with newfound suspicion. "Where are your dogs? Could they help track them down?"

"I left them in your grandmother's house. There's no longer anything there Lelit wants, so it's safer than here."

I turn to the spider; Hunter follows my gaze. "Do you know where the others are?" I ask. The spider scurries a few paces away and pauses, waiting for me to follow.

"Tamsin," Hunter says warily. "Spiders are Noctiva's favorite servants."

"It's been helpful so far," I say. "I think it saved me from the boggles." Still, his hands linger near his arrows. "Who was the girl? Why didn't she have a face?" An attempted distraction. It doesn't work. Hunter shoots. The arrow sinks into the dirt where the spider was as it darts into the fog.

Hunter lowers his bow, but keeps an arrow nocked. "The boggle couldn't mimic her face because I don't remember what it looked like." He studies our surroundings. "Who do you trust more, me or the spider?" He nods in the direction opposite the one the spider indicated. "Because I believe we should go that way."

"Was she your daughter?" The question is out of my mouth before I can stop it. Hunter's shoulders tense. "You just asked if I trust you," I point out.

He sighs. "It was a boggle. It took an impression from my memories. It was not my daughter."

"But you have a daughter." Or *had*. I know nothing about Hunter, I realize. Nothing about his past. I fall into step with him.

For a while, Hunter doesn't speak. "And a son."

"Does Lelit have them?" I ask. "Is she holding them hostage? Is that why you work for her?"

"No," he says. He's silent for long enough that I begin to think that's his entire answer. "I left them in your grandmother's house."

"The dogs," I realize. A knot of unease coils in the pit of my stomach. "They're ... they can shapeshift, change back and forth?"

"No," Hunter says. Again, it seems like he isn't going to elaborate. "Do you know of the Wild Hunt?"

"Leithe mentioned it, but he didn't explain."

"It's a band of fae that haunts the skies and hunts for sport. I was outside the night the Hunt passed over my home. I survived the night, but in the process killed a hunter and two hounds. Therefore, my reward was the privilege of replenishing its ranks. My son and daughter replaced the hounds." His delivery is distant, apathetic, as if he's describing something that happened to someone else. "The Hunt remade us."

The fog feels suddenly claustrophobic. "I'm sorry," I say. Two pointless, silly words.

"It doesn't matter anymore," he says.

"Can it be undone?" Though I have a feeling I know where this is going.

"Lady Lelit believes so," he says. So there it is. "I serve her until I've worked off three lives' worth of debt to her satisfaction; she finds a way to turn them back."

"'To her satisfaction'?" I ask with skepticism.

"I wasn't wise enough to negotiate terms," he says with some chagrin.

"Do you think she ever actually plans to do it?" Anger at Lelit simmers under my skin, potent only when she's not here to terrify me.

He doesn't need to think about the answer. "No. I think I'll be dead before she's satisfied with my service. But what other choice could I make?" He sighs. "They liked playing with you and Zach when you were young. That's why I stayed close over the years, though I shouldn't have."

"It would have turned out the same way no matter what you did," I say. "I was being led by the nose to the prison. The only way to stop it would have been to kill me, but I'm sure even that would have somehow been temporary."

"I know I shouldn't hate you," Hunter says. "Not for being what you are."

"I wasn't deceiving you," I say. "I didn't know the truth, either. I told you that." I feel the need like a gnawing hole in my chest: to hear he doesn't hate me, that he forgives me. I try to quash it.

"I know. You arranged things so you wouldn't have to lie; laid out your plans in advance so your memories will return when it serves you, Your Grace. And you made yourself into something I'd want to protect, knowing I wouldn't be able to kill something I thought was a child, so I waited too long. If I hadn't, the human boy would have lived."

"I know." I start walking again, though we may as well be walking on a treadmill for how little the scenery has changed. "If Lelit won't do it, I'll try to find a way to turn them back."

Hunter doesn't seem impressed by the offer. "And when your memories return?"

"I don't want them back," I say forcefully.

"Will that be 'your' choice?" Hunter stops walking and places an arm in front of me. "Someone's coming."

I'm not left in suspense. Eifa strides out of the fog, covered in dirt, a crusty, blue-ish liquid, and a spattering of dark blood from a few puncture wounds. She walks with a strange, woozy stagger.

"Eifa." I step around Hunter and toward her. "Are you—"

Eifa kicks me in the chest. I land on my back, gasping and choking. Before Hunter can drop his bow and draw a sword, she impales him through the chest with her spear.

"Where's the human?" Eifa's words slur together. She forces Hunter back against a tree. "What did you do to her?"

"Eifa, it's us." I reach for her, but her hand snaps out and wraps around my neck. I clasp my hands around her wrist. Her head is a mess, full of dark threads that pulse with her heartbeat. It clouds her eyes like a veil. Asleep, but not. "She's under some kind of glamour. I think I can—"

Eifa gasps. I pull myself out of Eifa's head in time to see Hunter twist a dagger into her chest and yank it back out.

"No!" I cry. Eifa releases her spear and sinks to her knees. Blood spills down the front of her shirt.

"She was going to kill us both," Hunter grunts, trying to dislodge the spear from his chest.

"She's under a glamour." Blood. Eifa drinks blood. Gentry blood has power. I hold my wrist in front of her face. Do I need to make a cut? Shove my arm into her mouth?

"And she'll *still* kill us both." Hunter tries to yank my hand away, but can't before Eifa's teeth sink into my arm.

It hurts. I scream. When I pull my arm away on reflex, Eifa lets go. She stands and ungently withdraws her spear from the tree and from Hunter's chest.

"My apologies," Eifa says, wiping the blood from her mouth. "I should have known better than to get caught up in a glamour. So that's my fault; I'll admit to it. But my senses are now back." She gives Hunter a smile that bares her bloody teeth. "Though I'd be happy to finish this now instead of later." Power radiates from her like a heat haze. Her chest wound is already closing.

"Eifa," I say. "We don't need to kill each other."

Eifa and Hunter share a long look. "*You* don't," she says to me. "But at least one of *us* will be dead before this is done. He's got a master to serve, and so do I."

"I'd prefer later," Hunter says.

"In case you get your heart back and think you have the advantage, you mean," Eifa takes a step back. "Please, I see no need to kill my enemies while they're compromised."

"That will be what kills you," Hunter says. "One day."

"I expect it will." Eifa steps away from Hunter and rolls her shoulders, stance relaxing as if death threats hadn't been made moments ago.

I shake my head. "How can you be so casual about it?" I ask. "Like you'd kill each other and the winner would just go on with their day."

"Yes," Eifa says. "Gentry have always fought their battles with the blood of lesser fae. This isn't any different."

"It ... shouldn't be like that." I feel lightheaded. White spots dance across my vision. Maybe it's blood loss. No, don't look at your arm. See the blood that must be gushing from your wrist and you'll be back in the glade. Look at a tree, look at one of the few things here that aren't bloodstained. "It shouldn't. But what could I change, even if I was queen like Leithe wants, whatever that actually means? This entire time, you must've been thinking the idea was ridiculous."

Eifa shrugs. "I don't think about that."

That makes me laugh. "You must be the only one who doesn't."

"It's Gentry who care about this nonsense: whoever's sitting on whichever throne, whoever has what land, what knights. Leithe and all them make a big deal about it now because they have nothing better to do, but nothing will change for me, or for him." She gestures to Hunter. "You're no exception." She says the words matter-of-factly, with no venom. "So I don't think it matters what you do."

"I didn't—" I did. I created nightmares—living things—to use as weapons against Nevain. "I didn't realize how much I was hoping you'd tell me what to do until you didn't."

Eifa thinks about it. "Alright. I think you should be happy. You, Skye, Leithe, you're all looking for things to be miserable about."

"I can't just ... *be* happy," I say. "It's hard."

"Yes," she says. "It's very hard. Now, have you seen any sign of Skye since you arrived?" I shake my head.

Hunter stares warily at her for a moment longer before turning to me. "May I see your arm?" I hold it out, forearm up. Blood wells from two jagged punctures near my wrist.

"It's already healing," I say. The blood's already slowing and clotting; the injury to my leg has healed so completely since I arrived I'd forgotten it ever existed. It feels strangely like a betrayal, my own body exposing me as inhuman. "Eifa, you don't think you're going to flip out and attack us again, do you?"

Eifa shakes her head. "That was my carelessness. The venom of Noctiva's children causes waking nightmares; allies appear as enemies, and so on. The spiders have given me no rest since I arrived and managed to bite me more than once." She examines the collection of bite marks on her body that now look weeks old. "I've fought them plenty of times before. I should have known better."

"You've been here before?" I ask.

Eifa nods. "Blackbower usually borders the Crawling Court. Nevain and Noctiva often skirmished with each other when I still served. I've killed many of her children and it seems they remember." Eifa glances up. Shapes moving through the webs above cast rippling shadows across the ground.

"What do you mean, 'usually' borders?"

"I mean 'usually'," Eifa repeats. At my confused expression, she rubs her chin and thinks. "I'm no good at explaining these things. Leithe might be able to do it better. You've seen maps of the mortal world, yeah?" I nod. "Well, Faerie isn't like that. Faerie is like ... a pudding?" She ponders. "Maybe a soup? Anyway, it's all squishy and doesn't sit still. Places like this, they're like the carrots in the soup. They're held together by whichever Gentry calls the land theirs, but if someone stirs the soup—" She makes a stirring motion with her fingers for emphasis. "Then they'll end up next to other carrots. And, let's see ... like attracts like, so the carrots want to stay near the carrots and the peas want to stay near the peas, so it tends to settle in certain ways, but Gentry can move their land if they really want to. Or force the entire place to rearrange itself so they can get to where they're going faster." She gives me an awkward smile that's begging me not to ask any more geographical questions.

"Okay," I say. "Faerie is a soup."

Hunter rolls his eyes.

The fog eats our voices and our footsteps. The silence buzzes in my ears. For a while, I concentrate on Eifa's humming, a lopsided tune that's nonetheless more pleasant to listen to than the impression of the echo of a sound prickling around the base of my skull.

"I'm sorry, by the way," I say. "For what I said at Grandma's house. I was trying to hurt you, but I didn't mean it, and I shouldn't have said it."

"I don't care what you think of me, so no harm was done." She slaps me lightly—for her—on the back. I almost fall into a tree.

A dull *pop* sounds somewhere beyond the trees, muted as if coming through layers of cloth. "Was that a gunshot?" I ask. But Eifa is already moving, grabbing my wrist and dragging me along so fast my feet risk leaving the ground entirely. A few minutes later, another goes off, then another after a similar interval.

As we near, the fog solidifies into Skye. "That's close enough," she says. Her gun is in her hand, but not yet pointed at us. "I figured gunshots would get attention. Now prove it's really you." Her eyes are wide, face covered in a sheen of sweat.

"You need to clean your car out," I say. "It smells like week-old cheeseburgers if they were also chain smokers."

Skye gives me a skeptical look. "If these goblin things can copy the appearances of people I know, why wouldn't they be able to copy memories?"

"Why did you ask if you weren't going to believe me anyway?" I ask. "I'm not a boggle. I'm Tamsin. We met…" I think. "Two days ago? Besides, these things' tricks haven't exactly been subtle."

Eifa tenses beside me and I follow her gaze up. We have an audience: spiders sit in the upper boughs of the trees, stock-still and watching. The largest could easily carry a person off. A smaller one peeks out from the base of a tree—the one I'd started thinking of as my tagalong.

"Tamsin," Hunter says. "*She* could be a boggle."

"She's holding iron," Eifa points out. One of Skye's hands is wrapped around an object hanging from a chain around her neck.

"What if it's fake iron?" I ask. "They can fake other things, like clothes." Eifa thinks about it and shrugs. Skye's gun rattles in her shaking hand. I worry that any second, she's going to start shooting. This is getting us nowhere. Instead, I nudge Eifa and whisper a request.

"Skye," I say. "I swear on my last stop of blood that I am not a boggle. That's really the best I can do, so if you aren't satisfied with that, you should just shoot us."

Skye takes a breath and rubs her eyes, releasing her grip on the necklace and revealing a heavy, antique iron key alongside a resin pendant with a four-leaf clover preserved within. "Fine, Tamsin. Only you could sound that fucking dramatic." She looks around, as if seeing her surroundings for the first time. "What happened to Leithe? Where is he?"

"Out of all of us, I'm least-worried about him," I say. "He's probably looking for us."

Skye shakes her head. "He and I came through the door together. And something .... It was like he was ripped out of space." She looks down at her hand. "There was blood."

*That's not supposed to happen,* some distant part of me thinks. He's supposed to be helping us. He's the strongest thing we have. If something happened to him, what could any of us possibly do?

The sound of a struggle unceremoniously ending brings me back. Eifa emerges from behind a tree trunk, holding the spider that's been shadowing me by the middle of its body, ignoring the creature's enraged flailing. Eifa presents the creature to me. "As requested." The other spiders watch, but don't make any moves to help it.

"Okay," I say to the spider, feeling suddenly very silly. "I know you're playing some kind of game, so you need to start talking. I'd rather you not make me turn you over to them." I gesture to Skye, Eifa, and Hunter, who all look much scarier than me.

Eifa gives the spider a shake for emphasis, and, like an unfurling length of cloth, the spider's form unfolds to become a young girl, now dangling by the collar of her dress.

The spider girl gives me a sheepish look. "Hello, Your Grace."

# Chapter Twenty-One

Hunter and Skye blanch; only Eifa seems unaffected by the spider's transformation into a girl.

The spider girl wears a frilly ivory dress edged with lace, pale against skin as dark as her spider form. Her black hair is tied back with thin pink ribbons. A tiny silver bell dangles from each braid; they chime when she turns her head. She doesn't look more than twelve. My questions get stuck in my throat. I would have preferred interrogating a spider.

"Are any of us boggles or otherwise shapeshifted monsters?" I ask her. I can hear the newfound nervousness in my voice; I'm sure everyone else can hear it, too.

The girl scrabbles at Eifa's hand, legs kicking in frustration, teeth bared as if she'd bite if she could reach skin. She finally slumps her shoulders, relenting. "No."

"Where's Leithe?" I ask.

The girl makes another effort to wiggle free, this one half-hearted. "Mother caught him."

"'Mother'?" I ask. "Noctiva?" The girl nods. Noctiva has him. I don't need anyone to tell me that's bad. "Where is he? What's she going to do to him?" Instead of answering, the girl snaps at Eifa's arm, which Eifa easily avoids.

"She's going to eat him, Tamsin," Hunter says bluntly.

Eifa nods solemnly. "Many of Nevain's knights met their ends in Noctiva's larder." It feels like it should be fake. Absurd. Being eaten by a spider woman is not a problem real people should have.

The girl looks at me with round, pleading eyes. A trick, in all likelihood. She's probably far older than Skye, at least.

"Eifa, let her down, please," I say. Eifa lowers the girl until her feet touch the ground, but doesn't let go of her.

"Is he bait?" I ask. "Are you supposed to tell me Noctiva might give him back if I go see her?"

"Mother gave me no orders, Your Grace," the girl says with a pout. "I'm not sure she knows you're in Blackbower at all. I thought you *wanted* to go to Mother's house, so I was trying to guide you there."

"Lady Noctiva may eat the rest of us if we don't go while she's distracted by Leithe," Hunter says. "If the girl guides us, we could be out of Blackbower before Lady Noctiva ever notices we were here." We could leave and go where? Back where we started in the mortal world? Forward to face Lelit without Leithe?

"Absolutely not," Skye says, crossing her arms. "I'm not leaving him to get eaten by a giant spider, or whatever Noctiva is."

"He wouldn't do the same," Hunter points out. "Not for any of you."

"This isn't about that asshole," Skye says. "This is about me. I'm not just leaving someone else behind like that. I'll go by myself if I have to." Even when she barely knew them, Skye risked her life in that basement for Chisel, Martin, and Eifa. A sudden sense of guilt washes over me. She's not saying those words because she's scared for herself.

"Tamsin," Hunter says. "This isn't a confrontation the three of us can win for you." He's nervous, more nervous than Skye or Eifa. Why doesn't he want Noctiva to know we're here? Because she's with Lelit? Against her?

I make a decision. "Then it's a good thing I'm the queen." *I'm the queen*—is this the first time I've pulled that card? The spider girl watches our exchange in silence. When she looks at me, I can see my distorted reflection in her black eyes. "What's your name?" I ask her.

"Mother calls me Daughter. My sisters call me Girl, or Little One," she says. When she opens her mouth, I catch a hint of horizontal pincers resting against the insides of her cheeks. "I haven't picked out a name of my own, yet."

I try a different tack. "What would you like me to call you?"

The girl runs her fingers over her braids. "I like bells."

"Okay, Bell-for-now: Eifa is going to take her hand off you, and then you're going to take us to your mother," I say. "Deal?" She nods, and Eifa releases her after looking to me for confirmation. Above us, the council of spiders disperses, the excitement apparently over.

Bell slips out of Eifa's reach. "I can take you to Mother's house, but she hasn't allowed anyone inside for some time, not even us, not even any of Lady Lelit's messengers. But, Your Grace, I'm sure she would open the door for you." Hunter tenses at the mention of Lelit's ignored messengers.

Bell skips a few steps down the path and stops, shuffling her feet in the dirt. "If I take you to Mother, will you get her to speak to us again?"

If she's trying to feign being a child, she's doing a good job. "I'll tell her you miss her," I say.

Bell scurries back to me and wraps her arms around my waist in an enthusiastic hug, then pulls away and beams at me, her fangs clearly visible. "I knew this was meant to happen when I found the door you made, Your Grace. Do you remember me? I was a hatchling the last time you visited Blackbower, but I still recognized your power from back then." She takes my hand and pulls, not waiting for an answer to her question. "This way. Let's go!"

The others follow with varying levels of reluctance. They're following *me*, and I'm leading them to a woman who eats people. Hunter has the same look he's worn since his return: quietly resigned to his doom. Eifa looks as she always does, at ease with a curious smile on her face. Skye, however, has a hand pressed absently to her pendant, her other hand lingering within easy reach of her gun. Her eyes dart in the direction of every snapping twig and whisper of spider silk; her face still shimmers with sweat.

"Are you okay?" I ask.

Skye fixes me with a glare. "I'm fine."

"Bell," I ask. "Is she fine?"

"Oh," Bell says, as if she'd forgotten to mention. "Mortals can get funny in Blackbower. Even outsider fae have trouble keeping their heads around Mother." She says it like it's a point of pride. "Just don't claw your eyes out or bash your head to mush against any trees, no matter how much you want to." Skye's hand tightens around the necklace and stays there.

After a while, a pair of flickering blue lights approach from farther down the path. At first, I think they might be the eyes of some horrible monster, but as they near they become two distinct creatures: twin fist-sized balls of pale blue flame held within transparent, glass-like spheres.

Extended from the sphere—the body, I realize—are six tiny legs, a bug-like head, and a set of lacy insect wings. The watery light they cast does barely any good in the fog.

"What are they?" I ask.

"Wisps," Bell says. "They're attracted to outsiders in Blackbower. Boggles and other hunters follow them in the hopes of being led to prey, and the wisps feed on the scraps left behind." She describes them with the glee of a child rattling off their favorite animal facts.

The wisps bob close to my head, like gnats attracted to breath. This close, the cold they radiate hits my face in waves. I gently touch one, its glasslike body giving just slightly from the pressure of my finger. It's so cold that it burns my fingertip. The creature makes a faint noise that sounds somewhat like a child's laughter.

"They're so cute I almost forget they're trying to get me killed," I say.

"Many people do," Bell says cheerfully. Skye smacks a wisp that gets too close to her, sending it spinning off into the fog, trailing a noise like a baby crying.

More wisps come and go, bobbing around for a while like moths on a porch light until nothing comes to kill us, then drifting off until the fog engulfs them.

Eventually, the jagged, dead trees give way to something akin to a town. Mismatched buildings rise out of the fog as we walk. Brick row houses adrift from the rest of their blocks; pieces of apartment buildings, hotels, hospitals, shopping malls, all piecemeal as if a giant tore the chunks free and dropped them on the ground at random, forming a maze connected by a looping path. They loom like monsters in the mist, but even when I'm close enough to make them out, they seem distorted, the angles sharper and crueler than what they'd be in reality.

"Why just pieces?" I ask. "Why not whole buildings?"

"These are the things that wash up from dreams. Most of it sinks after a while. Only some things stick," Bell says. "Even fewer things have stuck since Mother sequestered herself."

I catch glimpses of fae lurking in shadowed doorways and clouded windows, suggestions of shapes and faces. Some look similar to the boggles from the woods: maggot-white, naked and rat-like. Others look almost human, save for some features either exaggerated or missing altogether. Huge webs connect the upper levels of the taller buildings, upon which sit spiders ranging in size from large dog to large car. The spiders remain still as they watch us from above. No one else is on the street.

"Are they hiding from us?" I ask.

Bell nods. "From us, and from each other."

"Why do they feel like they have to hide?" But even as I ask, I catch sight of the cocooned bodies suspended in the webs.

Bell turns around to face me, walking backward, arms waving cheerily at her sides. "They all must eat."

"They don't need to eat *each other*, do they?" I ask.

"Mortals eat mortals eat mortals, do they not?" Eifa says, shrugging.

"Plants and animals, not other *humans*," I say.

"I said mortals, not humans," Eifa says, not unkindly. "What would the human monarchs do if the cows asked not to be eaten? If the trees asked not to be chopped down and burned? What would the humans eat, then?"

I study a nearby window until a boggle presses its face against the other side, needle-filled mouth split into a grin that fogs up the glass. "The same things, probably," I concede.

"Everything here is Mother's, she can't let some eat and some starve. That wouldn't be fair. But she has rules," Bell adds, "Like 'no eating in town.' She hasn't enforced them in a while, so my sisters have been keeping the peace by eating the troublemakers." She suddenly brightens. "Here we are."

The fog spits out a wrought-metal gate, its harsh lines at odds with Bell's animated declaration. The scrollwork is severe, black metal bars bent and curved like broken limbs. I'm fairly certain they shift and coil into new shapes when I'm not looking directly at them. As we approach, the gate swings open gracefully—and silently. I'm almost disappointed. A long, drawn-out creak seemed called for, given everything else.

Beyond the gate sits a garden. The jagged skeletons of spider web-wrapped hedges reach out like grasping fingers on either side of a path that expands and contracts like a twisting heartbeat, growing large enough to accommodate a sitting alcove with stone benches or a scum-choked fountain topped with a stone cherub missing half its face, strands of spider silk hanging from the stone and drifting in the slight breeze. I hear movement, legs skittering across branches, the pattering of feet on stone, but see nothing, whatever else lurking in this place determined to stay out of our way.

Cocooned shapes bulge from the hedges, some humanoid, some not. "Are those the troublemakers?" I ask.

I expect to see them move from the corner of my eye, but they never do.

"Some of them," Bell says.

Finally, the hedges open into a circular courtyard, at the center of which sits a large spiral staircase—pieces of several, rather, all held together to form a navigable path by thick robes of spider silk. The steps vanish above us, circling too high up to see the end.

Bell begins skipping up the stairs, so I follow. The steps wobble just slightly when I place my weight on them. I don't hold the railing for fear of getting my hand stuck in the silk. Fat black spiders—though none bigger than my palm—scurry out of our way and watch our passing from just out of reach.

"Are all of these your, uh, sisters?" I ask.

"Yes," Bell says. She gently picks a spider up off a step and places it out of the way.

When I can no longer see the ground, our destination begins to materialize—a lopsided behemoth of a Victorian mansion topped with a roof of pinched gables and spires held aloft on massive spider webs anchored to trees taller than redwoods. Fat cocoons hang from the web like parodies of Christmas ornaments.

"Is Leithe in one of these?" I ask.

Bell shakes her head. "No. Mother would be keeping one of the Gentry somewhere secret."

The house is in pieces, like a dollhouse broken apart on a bedroom floor, held together only by pale silk. Pieces from other houses resemble later additions, stitched onto the Victorian with more silk. Sheets of dead ivy snake up the walls.

The staircase spits us out on an aged wooden porch that bows under my weight. "Sister." Bell nods at a horse-sized spider clinging to the wall near the door, so still I don't notice it until Bell speaks. The spider returns the gesture and makes no other move.

A heavy brass door knocker hangs from the thick, warped hardwood front door, surrounded by a ring of fangs jutting from the sculpted mouth of some monstrous creature. "This is Mother's house," Bell gestures to the door knocker. "If you please, Your Grace."

I stare at the toothed maw suspiciously. "It looks like it's going to bite whatever I stick in there."

"It probably won't," Bell says helpfully. "It should know better."

"I'll do it," Eifa offers. For a moment, I consider letting her, but then sigh and reach for the brass ring myself. But I don't have to knock; as soon as my fingers brush the metal, the door swings open on silent hinges. Beyond is a dark wood foyer. A staircase sitting against one wall leads to a second floor. The chandelier has six prongs; at the end of each is a filigreed cage containing a wisp, each of them casting ghostly, bobbing light down below on the mirrors covering the walls.

Bell beams. "I knew the door would open for you, Your Grace." She gestures for me to enter, but remains outside the threshold.

"You're not coming?" I ask.

Bell shakes her head, braids bouncing against her skull. "Mother hasn't permitted me to enter, Your Grace." Of course not. "Mother will be in the attic," she continues. "It's her favorite place."

I turn to the others. "I have no idea what's in there. You don't have to come."

"Save it," Skye says. "Let's go." She steps past me and enters the house. I wish she wouldn't have. I feel so much braver when it's just my own life I'm playing with.

"At least let me go first," I say. The other two follow me, Hunter directly behind and Eifa stepping back to take the rear.

The click of the shutting door echoes as Bell pulls it closed behind us. I didn't notice the constant susurrus of crawling spiders until it's noticeably absent. There's no sound in here aside from Skye's breathing and the faint, ghostly murmuring of the caged wisps. The mirrors on the walls catch the faint wisp-light and volley it back and forth, leaving plenty of darkened corners for things to lurk. Shapes dance in the corners of my vision, but each time I turn to look, it's only someone's reflection.

Bell said Noctiva's in the attic, so we go up. Unlike the gate, the stairs creak in an appropriately foreboding way. At the top is a hallway that stretches unchanging to the left and right, walls lined with mirrors just like the foyer. It's impossible to tell what lies at either end, so I pick the right. The others don't contest my decision.

The hallway is barely too cramped for two to walk side by side. There are no doors, only mirrors that range from those encased in heavy gilt frames and reach from the floor to the ceiling to tiny hand mirrors with delicate silver or ivory handles. Most are whole, some are broken, tarnished, or warped and produce mutilated reflections.

"The hallway's too long," Skye says. "Based on what we saw of the outside, it shouldn't fit."

I open my mouth to reply, then freeze as I catch sight of something over Skye's shoulder. One of my reflections is wrong. It isn't just a distortion in the glass—the reflection's hair falls past her waist. A pair of scissors dangles from her hand. "Do you see that?" I ask.

Skye turns to look and takes a step back, though she can't go very far before she risks running into the mirrors on the opposite wall. "Do we break them?"

"I'm worried that might be the trap being set," I say. "For now, let's just keep an eye on them." When I turn to keep going, I come face to face with my younger self on the other side of the glass. She's a teenager, and her hands are covered in Zach's blood. Slowly, she presses her palms against the inside of the mirror. My pulse pounds in my ears; I can't get enough air into my lungs.

"Shit!" Skye grabs my arm. "Eifa." I pull my eyes away from the thing in the mirror and realize what Skye means: Eifa's gone.

# Chapter Twenty-Two

"Eifa?" Skye calls out. The hallway is empty aside from the three of us. I scour the mirrors for any sign Eifa might be within, but I only see us: Skye beaten bloody and clutching a wounded shoulder; Hunter with a tangle of thorns and roses sprouting from his chest; countless versions of me that look *off* in a way I can't place.

"I heard nothing," Hunter says. "She was right behind me until she wasn't."

"I'm not blaming you," I say.

"That's not what I meant," Hunter says. "I heard *nothing*. She didn't go anywhere, at least not with her feet."

"That's it," Skye says. "I'm breaking the mirrors. I'm going to break down every wall in this house." Skye raises her boot. "They never expect you to go through the walls in these goddamn magic funhouse mazes."

"*Waitwaitwait.*" I grab her arm. Hunter grabs the other. Skye could probably shove both of us off with little effort, but she brings her foot back down.

"Why?" she asks. "Do you have a better idea?"

"Well," I say. "It's bad luck to break mirrors, remember?"

Skye gives me a long-suffering look. "So we're supposed to just keep walking?"

"It's probably a puzzle," I say. "Like the dream prison I told you about? There's always a key to get out. There has to be. That's what makes it fair."

"The key could be my boot," Skye says.

"It would be best to play along," Hunter says. "If we don't perform the roles Noctiva gave us, it will anger her."

Skye gives Hunter a brief look of pity. "And what we're doing now is any better? Should we just keep walking while she picks us off one by one?"

Hunter returns her pitying glance. "We haven't had a choice in that since we arrived in Blackbower."

"We've already been given the answer," I say. "It has to be in here somewhere."

Skye looks at Hunter, then back to me, throwing her hand up in disgust. "Fine, I'm outnumbered."

I grab Skye's hand and Hunter's hand. "Just in case." We walk, and our reflections walk with us. The imprint of two bloody palms remains on the inside of the glass where my reflection touched.

I scour the mirrors, looking for patterns in the reflections. They're all us, but twisted. Then a few more steps forward, the pattern changes. Instead of any of us, Zach stands on the other side of the glass, throat cut and blood long dried. Beneath the layer of dirt, his skin is discolored and ill-fitting; he looks like he crawled out of a grave. His eyes find mine, and he raises his arm to point an accusatory finger at me.

"Is that it, Noctiva?" I ask. "I was *there*. I remember what happened."

"That's Molly's son?" Skye asks. I nod. Zach's reflected in every mirror. His blank eyes peer out from every surface. Just as many reflections point squarely at Skye as point at me; not even Hunter is excluded. "It wasn't your fault," she says. "No more than it was mine for leaving." She sounds like she believes that.

"No," Hunter says. "It was mine. And then I buried that boy where no one would find him."

Skye's gun goes off and the glass behind Hunter explodes, shattering Zach's face the moment his reflection lunged toward the glass as if to tackle Hunter. Skye stares wide-eyed at her own outstretched hand as if she's as surprised as the rest of us. "I thought it was going to climb through," she says.

The nightmare pushes against the web of shattered glass; shards flake away as the surface bows outward until a dirt-crusted hand emerges. If it couldn't get through before, it certainly can now.

Even injured, Hunter doesn't hesitate before driving his dagger through the glass and into the nightmare's chest. But the nightmare's arms wrap around Hunter's torso in a macabre embrace and pull him into the mirror as sudden and silently as a drowning. Hunter doesn't even have time to look surprised.

Skye freezes mid-step toward the spot Hunter stood a heartbeat ago. More hands emerge, questing like the fronds of an anemone, bodies pressing against the glass and each other, competing to be the first through. "Go." She shoves me away from the break. "Go!"

I run, Skye close behind me. We run until we realize the reflections of Zach are gone, Hunter's gone, and we're only running from ourselves. "I *told* you," I say. "I told you not to break the mirrors."

"I panicked." Skye clutches the key hanging from her neck so hard her knuckles go white. "It's this place. I've been jumpy since I got here. And I think I just killed him."

"No," I say. "They're not dead. Noctiva's probably just like Lelit. She doesn't want bodies, she wants bargaining chips." I hope.

"Or she's just going to eat them," Skye says. "And us." She pinches a cigarette between her lips and lights it with shaking fingers and noticeably calms. After exhaling a long line of smoke, she seems to come to a decision. "Look." She tugs the collar of her shirt down to expose the flesh of her shoulder, revealing a puckered circle of dark, knotted scar tissue—a ring of teeth. Pits in her skin mark where flesh was torn out. "2003 was the first time a faerie almost ate me." She pointedly taps ash onto the floor. "It was also the year I almost went to jail." She pulls her collar back into place. "When I left, it was originally to find something I could bring back to my mom as proof."

"You only do this when you think you're about to die," I say.

Skye starts walking and gestures with her chin for me to follow. "I might be, but you aren't. If I die here, I want you to tell my mom what happened; why I left. So, listen."

"This can be your practice session for when you tell her yourself." I won't acknowledge the possibility she's worried about.

Skye's hand runs over the pendant. "If I kept four-leaf clovers on me, I could see them. Iron helps resist glamour, but not completely. I saw little ones sometimes, but they were cautious. And fast. So I decided to set a trap. I didn't know what was true and what wasn't, so I slapped a bunch of things I'd read about together into a plan: I went to a liminal space—a graveyard—at midnight with a bowl of milk and honey at the full and new moons. Got nothing. I went back to the carnival circuit when I ran out of money.

"My first day back, I saw a woman with green skin take a little boy by the hand and walk him out of the carnival." Skye suddenly laughs. "And that wasn't it. She put something in his mother's purse. Gold. She *paid* for him. That's what she told me when I caught up with her, anyway. I grabbed her arm and shouted that that wasn't her kid. I asked whose kid he was; his own parents didn't say a thing. Everyone looked at me like I was insane, so I followed her until she left the carnival. Then I stopped her, told her I knew what she was. Told her I'd kill her if she didn't let the kid go, but all I had on me was a lighter and a pocket knife." A small set of hand mirrors reflect a copse of pines cast in shadow by the setting sun. Brightly-colored tents and carnival rides glitter in the distance.

"She just laughed at me. I hadn't seen a faerie bigger than a grade-schooler before. I didn't know the stronger ones were better at blending in if they wanted to, so I thought I was talking to a little old lady. Then she grew another five feet and arms that dragged on the ground." Skye presses her fingers against the scar on her shoulder. "She played with me. She told me the boy had a little bit of Sight, so the laws allowed her to take him. Then she told me what she was going to do to me, what she was *allowed* to do to me because of what I knew. She told me in great detail."

"But you're here," I say. "You made it."

"I ran," she says. "I lost my knife right away, so I stuck my lighter in her face. She went up like paper—some trolls do that—and that distracted her long enough for me to run. I just wanted to get away. I forgot all about the kid."

Her breath comes out in a shudder. "But she was beyond pissed. She chased me; probably could have caught me easily, but she wanted to play. Wanted me scared. I made it to a gas station, completely by accident. I doused my own coat in gasoline and threw it at her. I almost killed myself igniting it, but she died." Skye shifts awkwardly. "I also started a small forest fire. But I was able to go back and find that kid. He was waiting in the same place that thing left him. But I ran. If she hadn't decided to chase me, he would have been eaten." In the mirrors, fire licks at the rug, crawls up the walls and blackens the mirror frames.

"Even if that happened, it wouldn't have been your fault," I say. "You tried. And you *did* win." Skye doesn't respond, so I ask a question, just as much to keep her talking as to satisfy my own curiosity. "How did you almost end up in jail?"

Skye sighs. "I brought the kid to a police station. He told them over and over again that an old lady led him out of the carnival, but after he told them she turned into a giant green monster who wanted to eat him, they thought it was more likely I'd taken him and then had second thoughts. There wasn't any proof either way and he insisted it wasn't me, but I'm probably on a list somewhere."

"So you still saved him," I say.

Skye snorts. "That's not the point. That was the first time I heard about the innocence law. That's when I realized I couldn't tell mom, and that I was already tainted and the best thing I could do was stay away." Skye drops her cigarette butt and grinds it into the carpet with her boot, daring Noctiva to care. She draws and lights a second one before speaking again. "That troll woman is what the nightmare in the bar based itself on," Skye continues. "She was the scariest thing I'd ever seen. I felt so helpless; had nightmares about her for years." Skye snaps her fingers in front of my face, making me backpedal. "And Leithe killed it just like that. One of my worst nightmares, and he didn't even blink." She laughs ruefully before rubbing her eyes, her expression slipping into one of mild annoyance. "That's what I'm up against. That's why I don't expect to make it home."

"I think you're giving up a little early." They're the easiest words; the ones I'm supposed to say.

"Did I say anything about giving up?" Skye stares at a mirror beyond my shoulder. "I can't even remember what he looked like anymore." I follow Skye's gaze. The mirror reflects back a younger version of her, hands resting on her pregnant belly.

"There's nothing you could have done," I say.

"That's exactly it." She taps more ash onto the floor, her one avenue of resistance. "I've wondered for years if the storm and the power outage were part of the plan, or if it just provided the opportunity. It must be hard for a faerie to snatch a baby in a hospital. But a house in the middle of nowhere, with so much snow there was no way we'd ever get down that driveway?" Powdery snow drifts across the twin hallways behind the glass. "Did that witch have the power to make sure my son would be where she could reach him? How far back does it go? Was it my choice to run off and get knocked up? Was it my choice to go home? That abortion I remember agonizing over, was it me deciding against it, or was that choice made for me too? Did my parents really choose to buy that land? All those dominoes, lining up to make a convenient hiding place for you."

"I don't know," I say. "I don't know anything, really."

"You really don't." Skye exhales another stream of smoke. "I shouldn't have taken my own shit out on you. You were just what was in reach, what I could put a face to. I wanted you to be a monster *so* badly, something I could kill, as if that could make things right. After meeting you, I still thought you might be playing some kind of long con, but now I just think you're kind of a brat."

"A *brat*?" I stare at her, trying to decide whether or not to be offended.

"Yeah," Skye says. "A normal brat who grew up with normal brat problems. And that would have been fine, you could have gone on to live a normal brat life, except shit happened, and now you're being asked to do things you were never prepared for." She blows a stream of smoke into the face of my reflection—one with lupine eyes and a blood-rimmed mouth full of fangs. The smoke disperses against the glass. "And it sucks. I know it sucks. You didn't ask for this. But none of us asked for what we got, and now we're all here in it anyway." She sighs. "For every monster I've somehow managed to kill by the skin of my teeth, there are a hundred more. For every human I've walked out of Faerie, a thousand have been forgotten. My entire life, I've changed *nothing*."

"If you hadn't been there—if I hadn't jumped in your car that night—"

Skye waves sharply in my direction to cut me off. "I'm not done. All these assholes"—She jabs her cigarette toward the mirrors—"are fighting over you, and that's shit, but they're fighting over you because they're afraid of you. Me, my son, my mother? We're trash. We only matter to them because we matter to you. We're bait instead of food because *you* say so. That's fucking infuriating."

"But I'm *not* what they think I am," I say. "I mean, two months ago I worked at a fudge store. I was worried about rent and the easiest way to get my roommates to stop eating my food. I'm just some person, and—"

"I'm so tired of this," Skye interjects. "You're not just some person." This sounds so much like a compliment it stuns me. "And you need to get over that and grow up." That sounds more like Skye. "You have *no idea* what people would give for the opportunity you've been handed. If you think things are unfair? *Change them.* You'd really rather hide in my mother's house? The world is going to keep moving no matter what you do." Skye pauses to take a breath, and then sighs. "Personally, I'd burn the entire fucking thing down if I was in your place. But you're free to do whatever you want. Lucky you."

"Don't try to tell me I have any right to rule anything," I say. "I'm not delusional."

Skye flicks more ash onto the ground. "Did Mab have the right? Does Lelit? Noctiva? Does anyone?"

"I can't even do anything, Skye," I say. "Whatever power I'm supposed to have won't listen to me."

"You pulled a nightmare out of my head. You opened a door to Faerie. You did things that needed to be done, but now you're just ... waiting for Noctiva to do whatever she wants with us. Her name sounds like an over-the-counter insomnia medication, by the way."

I can't find it in me to laugh. "I'm jealous of who I used to be. I did more when I had nothing than now, when I'm supposed to be able to do anything. I wasn't scared of the woods when I was a kid. I wasn't scared of the fae. I went looking for the prison because it was an adventure, because it's what heroes did. I used to be brave."

"No," Skye says. "Kids just don't know any better. It's easy to be brave when you don't know what's at risk." She contemplates her dwindling cigarette. "Do you remember what you said back there at mom's house, about my son?"

"Yeah. I'm sorry. I was lashing out, but it still wasn't—"

"Stop." She puts a hand up. "People I've liked better have said worse. I was just going to say you were right. I do know that. I'm not stupid. He's probably dead or ... bad off. It's too late to 'save' him. Even if I found him alive, even if I got him away from whatever fae have him, he probably wouldn't thank me. He'd probably just go back, because he wouldn't know what else to do. I've seen it before. People who've lived in Faerie, who've had their minds taken from them, you don't just recover from that. It haunts you for the rest of your life." She stares at her reflection, one with a string of Grandma's pearls and the dazzling smile from Skye's high school graduation photo. "But I can't stop looking. I don't know who I'd be if I stopped looking, even though sometimes I don't think I actually want to find him, because then it would be real." She looks at me, sees something in my expression that makes her scowl. "Don't hug me. Or cry. Or anything weird like that."

The reflection walking beside me wears Mab's wedding dress, her hair falls until the ends become wisps of fog. "I think she wanted to die," I say. "Mab, I mean. Leithe doesn't know, but I think she planned at least part of this. And I ... If I try to do what she could do, if I try to get closer to her ... then what will I be? What will I want? I'm damned if I do, damned if I don't."

"Well," Skye says. "That's fucked up."

I can't help but laugh. "You know, while we're being honest, those things will kill you."

Skye exhales a stream of smoke. "God, I hope so. I'd love to live long enough to die of lung cancer." I laugh more. Skye even cracks a smile.

"I'm sorry," I say, "that I don't know what to do."

"You're very binary," Skye says, giving up on her nub of a cigarette. "You're either going along with what you're told or running in the opposite direction. I can't stay here and wait for Noctiva to decide what to do with us. Something needs to happen, and it's not going to happen on its own." She grinds her cigarette butt into the mirror, over the forehead of her own reflection. Smoldering cracks radiate outward.

"Skye!" I reach for her, but she yanks her necklace off and shoves it into my hands. The sudden bite of the iron sends me reeling back a step, letting the necklace fall to the floor. Before anything can emerge, Skye lowers her shoulder and forces her way through. Then, like a rewinding film, the cracks close themselves up behind her, until I'm only looking at myself.

Myself, and Skye's necklace. A key.

While I was following the path in front of me, I could delay it. I could walk forever without finding out what waited at the other end. I wouldn't need to find out that Grandma and Leithe and Eifa and Hunter and Skye are dead or eaten or worse. It wouldn't be up to me.

The metal burns when I pick the key up, but I grit my teeth and push it into the mirror. I made one door, I can make another. The glass gives; when I turn the key, there's a click. The mirror swings inward on invisible hinges; be-yond is a rickety, cobweb-covered staircase going up.

# Chapter Twenty-Three

THE STEPS CREAK AS I make my way up. Loose gossamer threads caught on whorls and nicks in the wood sway in the breeze stirred by my passage.

I take the stairs two at a time, my body bursting with nervous energy. I should be tired. The last time I slept was on the floor of an abandoned house after passing out from magic-overuse-induced exhaustion. I've been walking for what must be hours and put through mental hell, but I'm only excited. And hungry. It seems wrong.

The stairs lead to an attic. Covered mirrors line the walls and low, slanted ceiling. Bits of cloth cover the floor—pieces of intricate gowns and other garments, either unfinished and frayed or shredded to ribbons. The room is dim, lit only by what light seeps through the dirty windows. Fat, unlit candle stubs sit haphazard on tables and shelves, dripping frozen wax waterfalls.

Noctiva sits in the center of the room—a gaunt figure, so hunched her spine nearly bends in half, draped in a black gown and lace veils that only leave exposed long spindly fingers tipped with blackened nails that taper to needle-like points. She faces a standing, vertical loom, hands flowing gracefully over the threads despite her claws.

Tiny mirrors stitched into her gown catch and warp the dim light as she works.

Seeing her in person is nothing like her image in the dream prison. Just from looking at her, my vision tunnels. I feel her talons wrapping around my spine, squeezing my lungs, my throat. My pulse pounds in my ears. If I could move, I might run screaming out of the building, but I'm frozen in place. She helped imprison Mab once. It would be nothing for her to do the same to me.

It's a fight to get enough air into my lungs to speak. "Hi, Noctiva."

The loom clicks as Noctiva works. Slowly, she brings her hands down to her lap. "I was not expecting you, Your Grace, otherwise I would have had tea ready." Her voice is high and girlish. She stands and faces me, hands clasped in front of her. Even with her back bent double like an exaggerated question mark, Noctiva's veiled face is level with mine. "You cut your hair."

"Not *expecting* me?" I ask. Be commanding. That's what queens do. "It seemed like you were having fun with us while we were trying to get through your house. Where are the people who were with me when I entered?"

"The house has its own sense of humor, Your Grace. Would you hold me responsible for the fate of uninvited guests?" Noctiva doesn't make noise as she glides forward. Her movements are off, as if she must constantly remind herself how people with skeletons move. When she stops close enough to strike me with those taloned hands, I try to set aside the image of her cutting my throat with a nail the way Thistledown cut Zach's.

"Your daughter invited me," I say.

"Then she's a precocious little creature," Noctiva says. "And, importantly, a creature who does not have permission to let guests into my home, despite what she may have implied."

"Where are my friends?" I try to channel my terror into anger, though I feel both in equal measure. "What did you do with them?"

Noctiva cocks her head as if listening to something I can't hear. "They're elsewhere in the house." She circles me slowly. I clench my fists and stay still. "Alive."

"Safe?"

"So long as they behave," she says, crossing her heart with one crooked finger. "It could be dangerous for them to wander. I'll return them upon your departure."

"And Leithe."

"That Crawling Court traitor?" Noctiva reaches out and strokes a lock of my hair; even though she doesn't touch my skin, I feel the ghost of her nail across my cheek. "*That's* what you came here for?"

"Give him back." I force myself to look at her no matter how much I'd rather look at anything else.

Noctiva watches me, hands clasped before her. "You're afraid I'll say no. Terrified, really. Of *me*." She giggles, a sound completely at odds with her appearance. "What did you see in the mirrors?"

I was never going to be able to hide anything from her. "I doubt you need to ask."

Noctiva giggles again. "No, I don't." She studies me from beneath her veils. "Do you remember what you feared the last time we spoke, Your Grace? Because I remember."

"What did I fear?" I ask, though I think I already know.

I get the impression Noctiva smiles. "I cannot remember the last time I looked into your heart and saw anything at all, Your Grace. But today, you fear so many things. You fear for yourself, for others, for the future. Fear keeps you *here*, renders you present in the world. I much prefer this, don't you?"

"And that's why you and Lelit did it?" Shadows ripple behind the covered mirrors, creating leering, screaming faces pressing against the sheets in my periphery. My own reflection looks back at me a hundred-fold from the countless mirrors decorating Noctiva's gown, each no larger than my thumbnail.

"The very fact that we succeeded was a sign of the problem, Your Grace. Ages ago, we would have never been able to trick you, and we would never have been able to hold you. But over time, you became weak, distracted. You spent your time wandering Elsewhere. You shunned our company. When you brought that Crawling Court lord back and allowed him to stay by your side, Your Grace, we couldn't bear it." Noctiva leans closer—no, her neck extends—until her veils are inches from my nose.

"The Crawling Court is a place of insatiable hunger. Of taking. And you chose one of the Crawling King's favorites, one who could steal the life from you with a single touch. I worried he plotted to betray you to the Crawling King and that you were too blinded by your own thoughts to notice. Lelit, however, foresaw worse. If any knew a way to deliver true death to one of the Gentry, it would be the Crawling Court.

"Lelit believed that even if the marriage wasn't a plot against you, you intended to use Leithe's Name to order him to kill you once you were married. For what other reason would you agree to exchange Names in your vows? What need did *you* have for *his* power? We had no desire to discover if such a thing was possible, but when we begged you not to marry him, you only laughed."

"Putting us both in trees still seems a little extreme," I snap. Anger, my only defense.

Noctiva backs away, as if only now realizing how close she'd gotten to me. "Then tell me we were wrong, please." The plea sounds genuine. Pained. She waits, and I can't answer. "Do you know what desires Lelit saw the last time she looked into your heart, Your Grace?"

I have a good guess. "... Nothing."

"You were untethered. We watched the love you had for your court wear away over the years like sand against the tide. We did not know what you would do, and we did not know what would happen if the court lost you."

Something thumps against the inside of one of the mirrors, loud and angry enough that I jump. Noctiva ignores it, so I try to ignore it. "Someone else would take over," I say.

"No, Your Grace. There would be nothing left for someone else to take. If we imprisoned you in the Dreaming Court, it would have been simple for you to break free on your own, so instead we chose a thin place far from the court on the border of the mortal world. But without you here, the Dreaming Court has begun to unravel. Territories of weaker fae sink into the sands. The ocean wanders under its own whims. Stars fall from the sky with no one to hold them in place. Even my own domain crumbles at the edges.

"Imprisoning you was an ... awkward stopgap, admittedly. We had a choice between two poor decisions and a problem we did not know how to solve. We chose to delay the issue by stalling the wedding in the hopes it would give us time to decide how to proceed."

"So?" I ask. "Did you figure out a solution while I was away?"

"No," Noctiva said. "We sent the court into chaos and figured out nothing." She sighs. "But even so, you return to us tethered once more, so it seems we managed to win, regardless." She takes my hand in her own. "Thank you, my friend, for allowing me to explain why, though I know it changes nothing. Lelit may be too proud to say what she feels, so when you go to her, please know that everything she did was to keep you. Now, from the moment we acted, I have been ready for this—eager for it—because it means you are back with us: I am pleased to accept your judgment, Mab. I regret nothing."

"No," I say, suddenly angry and unsure why. "*You* didn't win. *Mab* won. She's gone. Whatever you knew her as is dead. All of her memories are gone. I'm ... something else."

Noctiva is quiet for a long time. She stands unnaturally still, but the shadows in the corners of the room twitch and coil in my peripheral vision. "What do you call yourself, then?" she finally asks, gently removing her hand from mine.

"Tamsin," I say.

"Tamsin," Noctiva repeats. "It was impossible for me to fathom an existence without Mab," she says softly. "But now it would appear I must do so while looking at someone else wearing her face." She straightens her many veils. "You truly have no interest in justice?" The concept sounds alien to her.

"What would Mab's justice have been?" I shouldn't ask. Shouldn't want to know.

"Throw us into Elsewhere, where she puts all things she wants to stay gone." Her voice betrays no emotion. "Or, if she was feeling merciful, perhaps she'd have simply turned our trick back on us: locked us in a dream that would have us questioning the veracity of our existence even after we were free, always wondering if we had ever even escaped in the first place, or if one day in the future we would awaken to discover we had never even been free at all." That's the *merciful* option?

"Perhaps Mab even sussed us out, and all of this has been a dream, and tomorrow I will awaken in chains." How would I feel if I woke up to find myself in my bed at Grandma's house, and discovered everything was just a dream? I might be able to find comfort in it—if I remembered nothing. But going back to the raging uncertainty of questioning my every perception would be pure torture.

"So she was awful," I say. Just as bad as Nevain or Lelit.

"She was a queen, dear," Noctiva says.

"Did you like her?"

"I loved her, Lelit and I both. We were the first to swear to her when she raised her palace from ashes of the old Faerie and named it the center of her Dreaming Court. I have called her my friend longer than memory. That is how long we served her, and that is why we were the only ones to notice her weakness."

Her weakness. "Did you ever just try ... talking to her?"

"What good would that have done?" Noctiva laughs. Lower. Almost sad. "What should we have said? That we thought she was weak? Unfit? No, no, no. It would have done no good at all."

*What should they have said?* I realize with a jolt and a harsh laugh what I would have said: nothing. I would have ignored it until it festered. Until it rotted away. Until I'm chasing a woman who might not even be my grandmother anymore across Faerie because I didn't just tell her the truth when I had the chance.

"We served Mab," Noctiva repeats. "And Mab or not, the Dreaming Court is now yours." To my surprise, she kneels before me. "If you have come to rule, then I gladly swear fealty to you and the Dreaming Court once again."

I step back in disgust. "I don't accept it. I'm not here to rule. You kidnapped Leithe, Lelit kidnapped my grandmother. I'm here to get them, then I'm going home. And ... your daughters wanted you to know they're worried about you."

"They worry for themselves," Noctiva says with a trace of amusement. "About what would become of them if another of the Gentry took Blackbower for their own. But it was kind of you to deliver their message, so I must return the gesture." Noctiva rises to her feet. "If a lost child is what you wish to be, dear, then I will give you the same help I give every lost child in Blackbower: a door back to the mortal world."

A child. A brat. Maybe that *is* what I am. "I'm not leaving Faerie without Leithe and my grandmother."

"That's very greedy for a lost child." Noctiva taps her nails contemplatively against a table piled with spools of wispy thread. "I could help you," she says. "What games Lelit plays now are her own, but I'll go with you to her and bring an army of my daughters with us to get this human back for you, if you do something for me." She reaches under her veil and produces an ornate but tarnished hat pin, the point of which glistens like oil. "Leithe is contained, but he still struggles. Subduing him enough to feed properly will be difficult for me, but Leithe trusts you, as he trusted Mab, no?" She holds the pin out to me. "All you'll need to do is pierce his skin."

I stare at the needle, nausea simmering in the pit of my stomach. "Why?"

"Because I won't be able to get close enough to do it myself. Not that it would matter, it's the betrayal that will make the curse work. I can't betray him; he has no love for me."

Morbid curiosity gets the better of me. I take the pin, keeping my fingers away from the point. "What will it do to him?"

"Put him to sleep, dear, so that I may eat him at my convenience."

I wonder what would happen if I drove the point of the pin through the back of the hands she holds clasped in front of her, if I would even have time. "No." I scramble for a reason. "He's helping me. I need him."

"Oh, I very much doubt both of those things," Noctiva says. "But if that is your only concern then I assure you that my help is worth far more than his. While we're in this court, in any case." It's what he would do, isn't it? It's what I would do to save Grandma. I can almost wrap my mind around the words: *I don't want to, but I don't have any other choice. I can't help it. It's not my fault.*

"But we're still engaged," I say.

"He won't be able to do anything about that for quite a while if he's eaten, if that's your concern," Noctiva counters. "Or do you intend to follow through with Mab's betrothal?" She sighs. "I would hope not. Honestly, if Mab had been merciful, she would have ransomed him back to the Crawling Court or let us take him apart when she found him. Instead, she made him love her."

"You and Lelit trapped him in his own nightmares for fun," I point out, trying anything to keep her talking, to delay this conclusion. "And now you're going to bring up mercy?"

"It needed to be personal or it wouldn't hold him. The cage could have been made of my nightmares or Lelit's fantasies, but when a prisoner expects pain, pain is what makes a prison easiest to accept as real." Noctiva waves a dismissive hand. "I merely provided the tools with which Leithe built his own prison. War, isolation, betrayal—his fears are not unique, but if one cannot control their own mind, they leave it open to someone who will do it for them."

"You chose to do it, and it was cruel," I say.

"Cruel?" Noctiva laughs. "Cruelty was Mab letting him believe she would protect him. Leithe knew the game he played. His mistake was thinking he served her as anything more than a piece on the board. He came to this court a reject and a failure. Perhaps he thought we would be too scared to move against him while he hid behind Mab's skirts, but she either failed to see the signs of our plans or she didn't care. The prison was a mercy to him, truly. If Mab had married him and used his Name to end her life, even if it had been by her own wish, the entire court would have hunted him beyond the end of reality and done far worse than lock him away for a few years. We would have had nothing left but revenge. And Mab would have known that."

"So you think he should thank you?" I ask in disbelief.

"Of course not," she says. "I'm sure he's plotting his revenge as we speak. I would expect nothing less. Now, dear, if you don't mind." Noctiva nods her head toward the pin in my hand. "I've given you what you need to solve a problem for both of us."

"It's wrong," I flounder.

"Are you sure you believe that?" Noctiva asks. "Do you think his goals are yours? Do you think his goals are kind?"

"No," I admit.

"Then why?" Noctiva studies me from beneath her veils. Her unseen gaze unravels me, pulls the threads apart for individual study. "I see."

In a whispering chorus, the sheets fall from every mirror in the room. I'm suddenly surrounded by myself but not. My reflections have long hair that falls until the ends dissolve into mist. Their white gowns look like organic extensions of themselves. They watch me with languid half-smiles, with eye sockets full of swirling fog and scattered pinpricks of light. They shimmer softly in an array of pale colors—the blues, purples, pinks, and oranges of a sunrise or sunset. And they're empty. There's nothing human inside. Every set of eyes looks at me like I'm less than a stain on a rug.

"Why does this scare you so?" Noctiva asks. None of her reflections are the same. Each one suggests a different shape lurks under her veils.

Mab doesn't want to come back. I don't need to be afraid of her. "Because ..." Because it isn't Mab I'm afraid of. Because it could be me. In a thousand years. A hundred. Or maybe tomorrow. Everything I am today, suffocated by the weight of time.

I'm afraid, so afraid, that there's no path forward for me that doesn't lead to the thing in the mirror. But I can't go backward, and the longer I stand still, the more ground falls out from under me. And I'm ashamed that I fear it in the first place, that I don't have the certainty in myself to reject the possibility outright, to say that could never be me. It's already happening. Is the thing in the mirror what I am to the people at the bar, to Molly Foster? Is it what I'll be if I sell Leithe to Noctiva?

I'm afraid because the thing in the mirror *doesn't* look afraid. And I want it, the power to not be afraid. I want to crush monsters like Nevain like bugs. I don't want to be afraid. But I am afraid, and it makes me angry. At everything. At myself. I hate the sight of my own face.

I take a slow, steadying breath. "Take me to Leithe."

Noctiva runs a fingernail over one of the mirrors; its surface becomes murky and ripples like water. "I'll reopen the door once your part of our agreement is done."

Before I can reconsider, I step into the mirror.

# Chapter Twenty-Four

THERE'S NOTHING BEYOND THE mirror—a great, suffocating nothing. I think my eyes are open, but everything is black. I can't hear anything but the pulse pounding in my ears, not even my own breathing. I have no sense of touch, whether there's a floor beneath me, whether I'm falling or floating.

I can't tell if it lasts for seconds or minutes, and then my senses are back as if a blindfold was ripped off my face. The space I'm in is covered in mirrors—walls, floor, ceiling, all suspended in a web of thick white thread. Taut threads emerge from some mirrors and exit through others, cutting the space into jagged pieces. The mirrors themselves hold glimpses of other places: the great hall, the garden hedge maze, the corner of Noctiva's attic, the edge of her gown barely visible as she returns to her loom.

"Leithe?" I call out.

"Mab?" Leithe steps into the space beside me from nowhere. I step back in surprise, and he grabs my shoulder before I brush the threads of spider silk behind me. Black hairline cracks trail down the side of his face to his collarbone before disappearing into his robe. Wisps of dark smoke ooze from the cracks like trails of blood. He scrutinizes me, frowning. "No, you're not."

I almost wonder why I came after him. "Try not to sound so disappointed."

"I thought being back in the Dreaming Court might do something for you," he says. "You have a connection to this land, after all." That incessant buzzing in the back of my head. The knowledge of the pressure that could bear back down at any moment, perched like a tsunami frozen at its apex.

"You were hoping I'd get Mab's powers and memories back as soon as I got here." I try and fail to quash a vague sense of betrayal. Of course he'd hope that. And of course he wouldn't tell me.

Threads of silk that make up the ground we stand on begin wrapping themselves lazily around my ankles. Leithe kicks at them irritably, sending a spike of his own shadow out to sever them. "Now we're both at Noctiva's mercy," he says. "So, yes. I'm disappointed. Welcome to the larder." He gestures with as much grandiosity as he can, and for the first time I notice the bones and desiccated husks hanging from the webs.

"Can't you have a wraith possess the bones?" I have to keep moving my feet in an awkward box step to keep the threads of wrapping around them.

Leithe pulls me closer so the shadows around his feet cover mine as well, cutting the threads before they can become a nuisance. "And do what?" he asks. "She's trapped us in some sealed up pocket of Blackbower. Any damage to the mirrors is reflected back. I've tried."

"And your ... teleport thing?" I ask.

"You're not Crawling Court, moving you that way would hurt you," he says. "Besides, I need to see my destination—*actually* see it, not through a mirror." He crosses his arms. "The only point in our favor is that Noctiva must come in here herself to eat us and she's wary of getting too close to me, so we have some time while she decides on a plan. Enjoy yourself," he says sardonically. "Take it all in. Don't touch the threads or they'll try to strangle you."

I hold my arms tight against my torso. Now, in front of him, I'm not sure what I wanted to say. "… I'm sorry." Leithe looks confused, then suspicious. "For what I said in Grandma's house. About Mab. I was just trying to hurt you. I was afraid of being left behind."

"I know," Leithe says. "It was very transparent. Does this seem like the time to bring it up?" He must see something in my face because he glances down at the hat pin clenched in my fist. "I see. What did she offer you, if I may ask?"

"Fealty," I say. "An army to help get Grandma back. Just to stab you with this pin so she could come in here and eat you." Very slowly, I open my hand and let the pin rest on my palm. "Here. I'm not taking the offer."

He stares at the pin. "It seems like a good deal. Perhaps you should take it." He sounds completely serious.

"After we got away from Nevain, you told me to tell you I wouldn't turn on you to save myself or my family. I couldn't say anything then, because I thought you were right. I didn't know for sure until right now, but you were wrong. I won't do it."

"It would put you in a much better position." He sounds offended, of all things.

"Do you *want* me to do it?" I ask.

"I *want* you to not treat me like a fool," he says, suddenly more incensed than I've ever seen him. "You don't like me. You don't trust me. The times you didn't push me away were the times you needed my power; now you have a better offer and you expect me to believe you're refusing it for *my* sake? Do you expect me to grovel in gratitude?"

"No," I say, voice rising in annoyance. "I'm not doing it because it's wrong. That's what I'm trying to—"

"*Wrong*?" Leithe says. He looks like he might yell, but instead, he laughs. "I've been honest with you from the beginning, but you can't do the same. You expect me to believe this … act." There's a sense of desperation to his words. "Whatever it is you want, just say it, this theater is unnecessary." He holds his arms out, gesturing to the space around us. "After all, it's not as if I could refuse right now. Or ever, Your Grace." He can't, I realize, because where else does he have to go?

"Fine," I say. "I'll be honest: the only thing I was worried about was whether or not we had a chance of getting Grandma and getting home without you. *Skye* was the one who wanted to come after you because it was the right thing to do. And I didn't realize what an asshole I was being until then. But now I do, so I'm here, okay?"

His eyes narrow in suspicion. "That's not a reason. Here." He holds his hand out in front of me, palm up. "Just use the pin. You don't need to keep doing … whatever this is."

"Do you want me to try and stab you so you can be right?" I ask. "So then you can kill me or eat me or drain the life out of me or whatever you do and feel justified about it?" He doesn't respond. For once, he looks unprepared, no sardonic reply at the ready. "It must be very lonely being you," I say. His eyes widen; he sucks in a breath to reply, but I don't let him. "Would Mab have taken Noctiva's deal?"

"She wouldn't have had to," he says.

"Use your imagination: if she had to?"

"Of course she would have. Anyone with any sense would do the same without a second thought."

Relief floods through me. I needed to hear that I did something different. "Mab wasn't a good person." It isn't a question.

Leithe laughs incredulously. "And you are?"

Yes. No. I'm taken aback. "I try to be." Even that sounds weak.

"Do you?" he asks with amusement.

"I ... do the things I'm supposed to do. I tip. I don't leave my shopping cart in the parking lot. I recycle. I stay out of everyone else's way. It's ... it's not supposed to be more than that." He listens, unimpressed.

"Good and bad are pointless concepts," he says. "Mab did what she wanted, and in doing so I'm sure did both more good and more bad—to use your words—with a flick of her wrist than you've done in your entire life."

My entire life, what have I done? "Fine," I say. "I'm a coward." I pause to take a breath; gather my thoughts. "Before I freed you, Zach—my friend, you never met him—he was killed by a faerie because ... I guess she thought he was a distraction, or she was punishing me for not trying hard enough to solve the prison. She knew I was Mab. I guess she thought I'd reward her for her 'help' once I was 'whole' again."

"And you did nothing," Leithe guesses.

"Nothing," I repeat. "Hunter killed her. But I wanted to kill her." It's my first time saying those words out loud. Maybe my first time admitting to myself that I thought them. "I hated her. But I didn't do anything. I told myself it was because I didn't have a weapon." I grip the hat pin so tightly I think I might snap it. "But even if I was the one with the bow, I don't think I could have done it, no matter how much I wanted to. I think I knew Hunter would kill her if I told him what she did. I made him do it because I couldn't—wouldn't.

"Because I'm a coward," I continue. "Even Nevain. He and his people were *awful*. But what those nightmares did, and when I stabbed him in the eye …" I take a breath. "For a second, I felt good about it. Then I felt bad for feeling good about it. I don't know how I'm supposed to feel. I don't know what I'm supposed to do."

He crosses his arms, expression neutral. "What are you hoping I'm going to tell you?"

"I'm not … I don't know," I say.

"I think you have an idea," he says. "I think you want me to tell you it's alright to hurt people you want to hurt, so then you can tell me I'm wrong for whatever reasons you've made up in your head, which will let you feel a little superior while you wallow in whatever this is. And I think you're confessing this to me because it's safe—you've already decided everything I say is wrong. Because if you heard the same from Skye or Eifa—and they *would* tell you the same, since both of those women are killers—you might have no choice but to believe it." He smiles. "So I'm not going to waste my breath. You feel how you like."

I don't realize how much I did want him to comfort me until he declines to do so. For a moment, I have no idea what to say. "… I'm sorry," I manage. "About what happened to you."

"No, you're not," he says without malice. "You could barely care less. You just don't like when it's said out loud."

He's right. I've barely thought about him at all, at least not outside of what I would do without him. "I trust you," I say. "I'm choosing to trust you. It'd be nice if you could do the same."

Leithe closes his eyes and grimaces slightly, as if in pain. "Fine," he says. "... I will choose to trust you, for all the good it does right now."

But how much am I choosing to trust him? I imagine forcing myself to say the words: *She wanted to die. She was using you. I'm just what got left behind.* But they die in my throat. Fear keeps my mouth shut. Fear of what he'd do if he knew. Hurt me, maybe. Abandon me, certainly. Or maybe he'd see it as another one of Mab's tests for him. If I trust him, it's not unconditionally. I have no right to hold it against him for feeling the same. I'm using him. No more than he's using me, but I'm still using him.

"I think ... maybe ..." *Say it.* But I don't say it. I stare at the web-wrapped bones around us and my mouth forms other words. "What's dying like for us?" The deflection makes me feel sick with shame.

Leithe regards me with something dangerously close to suspicion. Then he sighs. "It's as painful as you'd expect, but being dead is like sleeping," he says. "Peaceful, even, for a little while. And then you wake up, remember that you exist, and then it's quite painful until you drag your body back together. It could take years; it could take moments, and the whole thing is frankly unpleasant and embarrassing, especially if the pieces are scattered." He gestures to the bones all around us. "If they're eaten, then it's even worse." He pauses, staring at me. "That's what's ahead of us once Noctiva tires of waiting for you to follow through on her offer." I wonder if he's giving me an invitation, if he'd actually let me do it to save myself.

"I think I got all of us killed," I say. "Blindly running into Blackbower." I go down my list of options and find no good ones. I could beg or threaten Noctiva to let us out. I could stab Leithe with the pin and hope I figure out Step Two before Noctiva can eat him.

"Don't be so self-important," Leithe says. "Skye, Eifa, and I are all going to die firmly as a result of our own choices."

I'm not sure if I'm supposed to laugh. "That doesn't make me feel better."

"I didn't think it would." Leithe looks tired; his next words come out with some reluctance. "You've been expecting me to protect you, but it should be obvious now that I can't. I'll fight Noctiva when she comes for us, but I won't win. Draining the odd creature here and there didn't restore what I'd need to compete against another Gentry, and the land's no help—it knows I'm not Dreaming Court."

But the land knows me. Since I arrived, I've felt better than I ever have in my life. The thought sends a chill down my spine, imagining the ground, air, and trees as voyeurs, all knowing things they shouldn't. My body, deciding against my will that it belongs to this strange place.

I've been tapping my foot without realizing it. I can't stand still. It seems wrong to feel so full of energy given what's been happening around me.

Oh. "If you recovered enough, could you get us out of here?"

He studies the mirrors. "It's possible." He looks back at me. "But that would take quite a lot of power." Of course he knows what I'm thinking. He's probably been thinking it for a lot longer.

I put out my hand—the one without the pin. "Then use mine."

He doesn't move. "It would hurt."

"I remember," I say. "Don't patronize me. Get us out of here so we can help the others." The threads around us suddenly begin to thrash and vibrate, heralding the approach of something very, very big.

Leithe takes my hand, and the cold burrows up my arm, far worse than what he did at the Randall Place. It hollows out my bones, steals the breath from my lungs, siphons away the warmth that had been with me since I arrived in Faerie and leaves nothing behind save for pain that must be what death feels like.

When my legs give out, Leithe kneels with me. My head lolls against his shoulder when I'm no longer able to hold it up. He might be killing me. I might have let him kill me.

The webs around us tremble. From my immobile vantage point, all I can see are a great many black, carapace-encased legs that must belong to a creature bigger than any of the spiders we've seen so far, bigger than Noctiva's entire house. Its mad approach shakes the entire web, its shriek is like a needle driven into my eardrums.

The shadows around us boil and rise, becoming darker and more substantial. I watch until they surge past my face and blind me, then I drift away following a lullaby of shattering glass.

# Chapter Twenty-Five

ZACH'S DAD'S PHONE SITS in a plastic bowl to amplify the volume of the music. It plays nothing that came out after 1985. The car parts that usually spill from the barn have been cleaned up. Zach's parents, Grandma, and a few other distant neighbors sit in camp chairs around the fire pit, talking in a wordless susurrus of overlapping voices. The air smells like burnt marshmallows and hot dogs. The sun is setting. Soon, Mr. Foster will start lighting off fireworks.

We don't sit with them. Instead we lurk in the kitchen just inside the porch door, where we can watch for anyone coming. Zach looks twelve or thirteen. This was the year we swiped a beer and sneaked inside to share it. Zach has our prize—a silver can still dripping water from the cooler.

"I thought I'd see you again sooner," he says, examining the beer like it's a strange animal. "Have you finally forgotten about me?"

"It's been a busy day," I say.

Zach takes a sip from the can; his face screws up with distaste. "This isn't good." He offers it to me. "Why are we drinking this?"

The beer tastes as bad as I remember it. "I think you get used to it." The adults around the fire laugh uproariously in a way that suggests they're all several beers deep.

"Why?" he asks.

I shrug. "It's cheap. It's what's there. In real life, we drank that entire thing. I think neither of us wanted to admit we both hated it." I laugh. "I hated it, at least. But I didn't want to lose."

He pours the beer out onto the kitchen floor, watching curiously as the liquid runs through the labyrinth of cracks and divots in the old linoleum. "Neither of us wanted to be the first to break."

"We wanted to do what the adults were doing," I say. "So then we started acting out how we thought drunk people would act, which meant we started talking really loud and telling everyone how much we loved them." Saying it out loud helps excavate the muddy memories.

Zach gives me a strange look. "Why are we here?"

"Because it's a good memory," I say. More memories tumble forth, unspooling. "One of the last good memories without Faerie. In about a week, my Sight will come back." I parse through a jumble of thoughts, moments, images. "I'll meet Cheeps again, then Hunter. I'll start dreaming about Leithe but I won't know what it means. We'll play with the sprites; I'll get that silly crush on Hunter after he saves me from the kelpie, and Thistledown and the witch will use that to point me toward the prison. It'll be good for a while. We felt so special. So important. Our own secret adventure."

"And then?" Zach asks.

"And then you die." The music has been stuck repeating the same three notes over and over again. "And Hunter has the troll take all of those memories away."

"And this is where you'd rather be?" he asks. The beer pooling over the linoleum blooms red. "What would you have done if your Sight never returned?"

"I think about it a lot," I say. "If we'd just been normal. We talked about going to college together, or buying a van and driving around the country. But we probably would have just stayed here. You would have started working at your dad's shop. I have no idea what I would have done. Maybe we would have been each other's first kiss, first everything, or maybe not. Maybe we wouldn't have even stayed friends past high school." The sun has set. Outside, the adults have only blank ovals where their faces should be.

"Do you think that makes it up to me?" he asks. "That you can imagine a different life for us?"

"No," I say. "I don't think that makes up for anything." The fireworks have started. They burst scarlet against the night and bleed down to the ground. "I'm sorry."

"You know those words mean nothing, but you keep saying them, over and over again," he says. "Do you know where we really are?"

"In Noctiva's house?"

"No." He takes my hand. His skin is cold. Pale. Bloodless. "Let me show you." He pulls me away from the porch door, away from the celebration outside. The noise fades as we travel through the kitchen, through the living room. Zach places his hand on the front door knob, twists.

I wake up to something landing on my face. I squeal and knock it away; the spider lands on the floor and scurries back up the wall.

My heart pounds and sweat sticks my shirt to my chest and back. "You better just be a spider," I tell the spider. It doesn't respond.

"Welcome back," Skye says, suddenly leaning over me.

"Ow." My head pounds. Above me is a moth eaten, four-poster canopy. I'm in a bed, sinking into the mattress from the weight of all the blankets. Hunter stands on the side of the bed opposite Skye. Eifa sits on the foot of the mattress. Other than them, dolls cover every available surface of the room, ranging from tiny ragdolls that could sit within the confines of my palm to a human-sized man-nequin slumped against the wall.

Almost every single one of them has something off about it. One plastic baby doll smiles with a mouthful of real, child-sized teeth. Another has six fingers on each hand, each with an extra joint and no fingernails. A life-size mannequin has a face made of jagged shards of mirror embedded in the wood. And everything in this room is staring at me.

"I'm supposed to make sure you eat." Skye lifts the cover off a tray on the bedside table and produces a bowl of opaque broth.

Before I can argue, the smell hits my nose and wafts all the way down to the empty pit of my stomach. It's the best thing I've ever smelled, and I'm hungrier than I've ever been in my life. I ignore the offered spoon and tip the bowl into my mouth. I drink it so fast that by the time I'm staring at the empty bowl, I don't remember what the broth tasted like, only that it was amazing. When Skye hands me a piece of bread, I eat that too without a word, and the hunger is still an obnoxious pang.

"Is there more?" I ask. I stare at the bowl, process the room we're in. "No. We're still at Noctiva's. She *eats* people. What was in this?" Despite my suspicions, warmth spreads steadily from my stomach through the rest of my body. My headache is already fading.

"Not Leithe, if that's what you're worried about," Skye says.

"Catch me up," I say. "What happened?"

"I don't know much." Skye pointedly hands me a cloth napkin. I dap at the soup I spilled during my frenzy. "After I walked into the mirror, it spit me out into a room where Eifa and Hunter already were."

"Skye barreled through the door and almost shot the tea pot," Eifa says. "All to rescue us. It was very dashing."

"Anyway," Skye says quickly. "We were stuck there. All I can tell you is that the house started shaking like there was an earthquake—I thought the floor was going to fall out from under us. Then it stopped, and Leithe walked in a few minutes later, carrying you. You looked like you were dead." Skye hesitates for a moment before continuing. "He said he and Noctiva called a truce and we were staying until you woke up."

"Where is he?" I ask.

Skye gestures to the door. "Out there. Do you want me to get him?"

I shake my head and push the covers aside, thankful to see I'm still wearing my own clothes. My legs wobble when I stand, and all three people lunge forward to give me a hand. "I'm fine," I say, catching myself on the bedpost. "Just stood up too fast." But my reflection in the tarnished mirror in the corner is hollow-cheeked and gaunt. I look like I've lost several pounds.

Outside the bedroom is a drawing room crammed with countless glass specimen cases, skeletons, and taxidermied creatures hanging from the walls or set on shelves. The one closest to me holds a collection of butterflies, wings patterned disturbingly like eyes.

Leithe reclines on one of the two sofas crammed close to a coffee table piled with more creepy odds and ends, including a bottle of wine perched precariously on a stack of books with suspiciously skin-like bindings.

"We have a truce?" I ask.

Leithe looks up from the thick crystal goblet in his hand, frowning when he sees me. "Yes. Shelter and safe passage. Noctiva realized a fight risked more than it was worth." The cracks across his face are gone. He looks much better than he did; his skin even has the slightest amount of color.

By the time I make it to the couch opposite Leithe, my legs feel stronger; my hands stop shaking. "And you trust her after she tried to eat you?"

"I trust it's over for the moment. She had her chance and lost it," Leithe says. He hesitates; looks like he might say more.

"And *when* she changes her mind, could you take her?" Skye asks, following me from the bedroom. Eifa and Hunter trail close behind. I feel strangely disappointed we're no longer alone, as if something's been left unfinished, unsaid. But I'm not sure what it is.

Leithe doesn't seem to feel the same. He drains his wine glass and then refills it to the brim. "Take this." He holds it out to Skye, liquid threatening to spill over the sides. She accepts it with a suspicious expression. "Now, if Eifa were to try to kill you right now, how well would you fare while trying to keep all that wine inside that extremely breakable glass?"

Skye looks like she's considering upending the glass over Leithe's head. "And I'm the glass? That's what you're getting at?"

"Not just you," Leithe says. "Everything. If a real, true fight broke out here, Tamsin, Noctiva and I would be the only ones to survive. Everything else would be destroyed. You, Eifa, this little house Noctiva stitched together, all of Noctiva's children lurking around, gone. Noctiva is more powerful than me in her own domain—she would probably win, but she also has more to lose. She knows that."

Skye hands the glass back to Leithe roughly, causing liquid to slosh over the side. "Don't use me as an excuse. I'm not afraid to fight."

"You know one trick," Leithe says, frowning at the wine dripping down his hand. "Where are you going to shoot her? I guarantee that wherever you *think* her head is, you're wrong."

"You can't do that 'grab and drain the life out of her' thing?" Skye asks. "You did it to Tamsin easily enough."

Leithe's eyes harden. "Tamsin was willing. Noctiva has quite a bit of life to drain for someone who would be fighting back the entire time."

"That *is* the downside of your best trick," Noctiva says, from the doorway. I didn't hear the door open or close, but suddenly she's here. "To use it, you have to get close enough for me to bite your pretty head off." Skye jumps in surprise at Noctiva's appearance, her shoulder bumping an aquarium filled with murky water. She curses under her breath when a tentacle brushes up against the glass in response.

"My apologies," Noctiva continues. "I've been told I move rather silently." One of her arms hangs at her side, withered and useless. Bell peeks around Noctiva's gown and smiles shyly at me. "Since Tamsin is awake, I came to say farewell. There's a carriage at the gate that will take you somewhere else." She sounds like she won't be sorry to see us go.

"Then we're chasing Lelit," I say. "To the palace, right?" We've been scrambling since the moment we set foot in Blackbower; I haven't had time to think about what would come next.

"And when we get there," Hunter asks, "do you still plan to trade yourself for your grandmother?" The others are quiet, but their faces say they're all wondering the same thing.

"It's not my first choice." I look back at them, daring someone to challenge me on what was left unsaid.

"About that," Leithe says. "Tamsin, Noctiva has agreed to give you sanctuary while the rest of us go to the palace."

"What?" Skye asks in dismay. "She was just trying to eat us. Now we're leaving Tamsin here alone?"

"I was trying to eat *him*, dear," Noctiva corrects. "The girl has my protection until she leaves Blackbower, and no one in the Dreaming Court would dare come here to harm her, not even Lelit." With Noctiva in the room, the dead things lining the walls seem to move. Skulls leer from my periphery. The butterflies in their case twitch weakly against the pins that hold them.

"I'm going," I say. "We're not rehashing this."

Leithe nods toward Hunter. "Then what about him? He might as well be Lelit's puppet; he could turn on us at any time."

"Do you know your way through the city? How to get into the palace without Lady Lelit knowing?" Hunter asks. "Did you ever set foot outside the ballroom or your own chambers?" Leithe scowls, but doesn't answer, so Hunter continues, speaking to me. "I can get you into the palace under Lady Lelit's nose, and I can find your grandmother. Lady Lelit hasn't given me any orders to the contrary, and if she doesn't know we're there, she can't."

"Then it sounds like he's coming with us," I say. "He's the only advantage we have."

"That's not true," Noctiva says, "You have more of an advantage than you seem to think. Lelit needs you quite badly."

"She needs me?" I ask. "Why?"

"Lelit rules only through the illusion that Mab put her there," Noctiva says. "The entire court knows Mab viewed her favorably, so in Mab's absence, it was easy to lead the other vassals into believing any misbehavior while Mab was gone would lead to punishment upon her return. But Lelit alone doesn't have the power to put the other vassals in their place if they rebel, and Mab has been gone long enough that they're starting to circle like wolves."

Leithe watches Noctiva, chin resting contemplatively against his knuckles. "And you aren't?" he snorts.

"And *you* aren't?" Noctiva asks with a giggle.

"Okay," I interrupt before it gets any worse. "So she needs everyone to see me supporting her."

Noctiva nods, the barest ripple of her veil. "She needs you—or the threat of you—to wield as a bludgeon to keep the rest in line."

"What would the vassals do if they knew I was powerless?" I ask.

"Eat you to try and claim some of your power for themselves, bind you up with little chains and ribbons so you're safe and harmless, or perhaps turn you into a little figurehead of their own and rule the court on your behalf," Noctiva suggests. "Hence why Lelit is forcing you to meet her on a stage where you have no choice but to cooperate."

"Or the other vassals will do horrible things to both of us," I finish. "So Lelit also has to play along with the story she wrote for us, meaning she can't stop us from leaving once we find Grandma without outing both of us." There's a chance Grandma isn't even there, that Lelit is hiding her somewhere far away from the staging ground she's selected, or has even already killed her. But, I realize with a strange sense of certainty, Lelit won't work that way. It wouldn't be proper.

"I have a parting gift," Noctiva says. She nudges Bell forward, who's carrying a rectangular wooden box. "A gown for the ball. My daughter reports you were kind to her, despite her mischief, so allow me to repay you."

"Last time I wore a dress you made, I ended up trapped in a tree," I point out. Sometimes, when I'm waking up, I can still feel the fabric of Mab's wedding gown cutting into my throat. I've wondered many times if it's my own memory from the dream prison or the ghost of Mab's final moments.

"Then you know my work is excellent," she says with no hint of guilt. "Now, you'll need to try it on so I can make any final adjustments."

I allow Noctiva to bring me back to the doll room to change. Bell hands me a pile of cloth and I shoo the two of them out, but quickly regret that—the dress is made up of complicated layers of sheer white silk and I struggle to figure out how to get into it. Once I think I've got it, I still need to call Noctiva in to lace up the back after several minutes of contorting myself in front of the mirror and swearing.

"Is it acceptable?" Noctiva asks. The dress has a structured bodice beneath transparent layers of cloth thinner than paper. Countless such layers come together to form a skirt that falls to mid-calf. The layers have faint, barely-noticeable designs: fluid swirls and waves; in one place a tiny moth. The dress is white. Of course it's white. In the memories, in the nightmares, Mab's always wearing white. I want to ask Noctiva to change the color, but if I'm about to put on a play for the entire Dreaming Court, I need to wear the right costume.

"It's beautiful." I never attended a single school dance. Grandma sent me the money to buy a prom dress in my senior year, but I left the store without buying anything, unable to imagine other people seeing me in a gown. Now, for just a moment, I feel pretty. And then I remember why we're here. "It's ... more comfortable than I expected."

"Of course," Noctiva says with some amusement. "It has the typical charms woven in. It will stay in place, stay tidy, and turn away many weapons, though not all of them.

I did the best I could on short notice. Do you have other concerns?"

The tarnished mirror warps my reflection, rendering it softened and blurred. In this dress, aside from my hair, I could be Mab. I'd just need to look more confident, more above it all. Noctiva's warped reflection towers above mine, the peak of her bowed back brushing the ceiling.

"Just one concern: why are you helping me?"

"For taking care of my daughter, as I said." Noctiva tugs at the silks, adjusting how the folds settle.

"You said the other Dreaming Court vassals would be circling like wolves," I say. "So why aren't you? Why are you letting me leave? If the court's going to fight over me, wouldn't it be beneficial to keep me here?"

Noctiva straightens my shoulders and examines her work. "Because I don't care what happens, dear," she says, not harshly. "If Mab is gone, the Dreaming Court is dead, it just hasn't realized it yet. I do not regret the things I've done, but I no longer care to cling to the way things were. It's quite a lot of work, and I'm tired."

A strange sense of guilt washes over me. "You've given me more help than I asked for, even though I didn't turn Leithe over."

Noctiva only giggles. "And when has Mab ever done what I wanted?" She brushes a stray thread from my sleeve.

"... Thank you, Noctiva."

Noctiva regards me in the mirror, her face—as always—hidden. "Poor girl. Good luck."

# Chapter Twenty-Six

WHEN BELL LEADS US back down the spiral staircase and through the garden, a carriage waits for us beyond the metal gate. It's bulbous like Cinderella's pumpkin coach, covered in the ridges and valleys of aged gold detail work that's long lost its luster. There are no wheels and no horses. It rests on its stepping stools.

"Mother hopes this will hasten your journey." Bell gives a final bow and disappears back into the fog, leaving us alone.

"Are we supposed to get in and run like a hamster ball?" I ask.

Skye snorts. "Anyone volunteering to pull it?"

"There's no handles," Eifa says.

"Or something weird is going to happen ..." I step forward and reach toward the carriage door. Before I can touch it, the entire thing shudders as what I took for decorative vertical bands running the height of the carriage begin prying themselves free of the main body with a grinding screech. "... now," I finish.

Eifa and Hunter place hands on their weapons; Skye puts an arm in front of me. The bands unfold into eight slender legs upon which the carriage rises, doors swinging open. "Well," I say. "It's a spider. That makes sense."

Eifa offers a hand to the rest of us before stepping in herself. The carriage interior is dominated by twin benches upholstered in patchy black fabric. Lacy curtains with the texture of cobwebs cover the windows set into each of the two doors.

"Thanks for the ride," I say as I sit down.

"Is it alive?" Skye asks with some alarm.

"No idea, but I might as well be polite," I say.

"How else would it be moving?" Leithe says. "Noctiva isn't Crawling Court." Skye looks slightly green.

The cab is spacious enough that I'm not pressed into Leithe or the wall, and I almost have enough space to straighten my legs without hitting Skye.

Once the door latches shut behind Eifa, the carriage slips into motion. The movement is smooth, weight of the cab shifting from leg to leg with less lurch than I expect. It starts down the cobblestone road, buildings on either side appearing and disappearing back into the fog as we pass.

I lean forward and pull the curtains out of the way to watch our progress. More fae are out and about than when we passed through yesterday, though most clear the road as the carriage approaches.

It's only after the carriage leaves the town behind that questions occur to me. "Does it know where we're going?"

"It doesn't matter which way we go," Leithe says.

"How does that not matter?" I ask.

"Noctiva granted us passage out of Blackbower, so no matter what direction we go, we will leave Blackbower. And once we're out, we'll be headed toward the palace because Lelit wants us to get to the palace, you want us to get to the palace, and I want us to get to the palace. So we'll get to the palace."

"Is that really how it works?" Skye asks. "You just decide where you want to go, pick a direction, and you'll get there?"

"If you're Gentry, I suppose," Eifa says. "When you can't be bothered to ask for directions, you just move everything around and get the rest of us mixed up."

"I think we have less than a day left," I say. "Will we make it in time?"

"It's irrelevant," Leithe says, staring out the window. "We'll get there in time, if only because nothing will happen until you arrive." He's barely spoken since I changed into Noctiva's gown—barely acknowledged me at all, really. The few times he's looked at me, his face has been carefully neutral, which means he's actually trying to conceal what he's feeling.

"Does the dress help me pass as her?" I ask.

"Only to anyone who isn't really looking," Leithe says.

Blackbower's fog soon thins, as do the trees. But the most severe change comes between one step and the next. The land dips and becomes sand; the carriage shuffles to keep its footing.

"Wow," I say. Just like that, Blackbower and its fog are behind us, a line where it looks like a giant cut it away and pasted a new landscape in its place. Now, a desert stretches out ahead of us, dunes peaking against the horizon. The sand isn't white, but opalescent, shining pale blue, green, and pink where the light from the stars above strikes it; the sky—once visible only in slivers through Blackbower's choked canopy, now shines down in full force.

No star shines as bright as the sun in the mortal world, but the sheer number of them makes it seem almost as bright as day. The stars themselves sit on a canvas of bleeding watercolors as if someone had poured dusk, night, and dawn across a sheet of glass and let them run into one another; orange turns to red turns to purple turns to black and back again.

"Wow." I open the carriage door and lean out, hooking my foot around the frame and holding onto it so I don't fall out. In the distance, I can just make out a pale structure that rises in sharp contrast to the multicolored night sky. Even though the temperature is cool, the structure shimmers like a heat haze. Something wells in my chest when I look at it. "What is that?"

Leithe has to stick his head out the other door to see. "The palace," he says.

"So it's not far, then," Skye says.

"The palace is visible from anywhere in the desert," Leithe says. "That has no bearing on how long it will take to get there. We might walk for a month and it would still look as far away as it does now, or we might get there tomorrow."

I spend my time sitting on the carriage floor with my legs dangling out the door. The palace isn't the only thing that sticks out of the sand. First we pass little things that could be the remnants of a landfill—a tractor tire, a pile of books, an overturned tartan armchair. Then they steadily get stranger. A dining room table and chairs set for dinner, a garden of garishly patterned umbrellas sprouting up like flowers, a tiered wedding cake dripping with icing and tall enough to climb. In the distance, half a block of suburban houses, complete with lawns and fences.

I jump back when a flock of multicolored birds bursts from the sand in a cacophony of squawks and beating wings inches from my face. They launch themselves into the air in a ribbon of color and I watch until they're so far away they blend with the sky. The patch of sand from which the birds flew is a slow whirlpool sucking down.

"If we jumped in there, would we end up in someone's dream?" I ask, remembering how we climbed through the dirt to arrive in Blackbower.

"Probably," Leithe says. "So don't."

We pass more impossible things. The carriage dips to fit under a copse of translucent, crystalline trees, drooping boughs tinkling together as our passage disturbs them. A dune cracks open a single brilliant orange eye the size of a dinner plate and studies us lazily for a few moments before shutting it again. A swarm of butterflies meets us as they travel in the opposite direction. When I catch one on my finger, I see that its wings are mirrors. When another butterfly's wings cut my leg as it flutters by, drawing a faint line and a few drops of beaded blood, I pull myself back into the carriage until they're gone. Occasional flocks of dark-winged humanoids fly far above us. If they notice us, they give no indication.

Even though I'm not looking at him, I eventually can't ignore the sense of Leithe's eyes on me. "What?" I finally ask.

"You're smiling."

I frown. "Am I not allowed to smile?"

"I've never once seen you smile with your eyes before. But you were, when you were looking out there." He gestures toward the window. "It is wonderful, I suppose. The colors still give me a headache, but Mab would stand on her balcony and watch it for hours. It's where she seemed happy. Peaceful."

Happy. Peaceful.

I feel like I'm going to be sick.

Happy. Like Grandma isn't a hostage. Like Skye's son isn't gone. Like Zach isn't dead.

Guilt washes over me. I realize I lost track of how long we've been traveling. I caught myself enjoying this.

I can't let this place be beautiful. The dull roar in my head that had been sedate since I awoke suddenly rises with a vengeance. I feel like I've been punched in the head.

The carriage lurches and dips to the side, its legs sinking into ground that's become a wet crimson slurry as blood wells up through the sand. I lose my grip on the carriage and fall forward until hands pull me back in.

Someone says something, but the voice sounds far away, drowned out by the roaring in my ears as I stare at my hands. I can feel the blood even though they're clean. It would be sticky. Warm but quickly cooling even in the summer air of that night.

The carriage lurches again, tipping back toward the opposite side. I slam into someone and roll. More voices.

Someone grabs the sides of my face. Pries my hands from my ears. "Tamsin, look at me." I open my eyes. Skye's face is close to mine. "Breathe. Focus on, shit, I don't know, things you can touch. Or list the streets in Shrike Run."

I take a deep breath. "Main Street ... Done." She cracks a smile. I laugh back shakily. My breath comes out as steam. It's cold. The carriage is still lopsided and no longer moving. Outside, the carriage is partially sunk into a bloody but frozen pool, its surface so smooth I can see my reflection.

Skye touches me lightly on the shoulder. "The ground started bleeding and then you fell over. What happened?"

"Sorry." I force myself to look away from the blood. "I'm sorry. I think I might have done that."

"Yes," Leithe says. "That was clear. Why?" He waves a hand; with a humming sound, the blood around the carriage's legs unfolds like a crystalline flower, allowing the carriage to scrabble back onto the sand.

"Not on purpose," I say. "I just ..." Blood on my hands, seeping out from between my fingers. A copper stench so strong it coats my tongue. I feel panic rising again, and with it the buzzing in my ears.

"Think about something else," Leithe says sharply.

"Tamsin," Skye says very seriously. "You have a booger sticking out of your nose."

I gasp and cover my nose, my panic forgotten with her unexpected words. Then I see her face. "Are you lying?"

"Yes," Skye says. "I can do that."

"Not fair." All I can do is laugh weakly, my energy spent.

"Yeah, way more useful than being able to alter reality with my mind."

"Knowing I can make the ground bleed by freaking out does not make it easier to not freak out," I say. It's still there. I can feel it. Held barely at bay by deep breaths and clutching the slippery silk of my dress as a way to do something—anything—with my hands. "And why is it only bad things? Why can't I conjure teddy bears or a road straight to the palace?"

"Would you like us to guess, or are you just venting?" Eifa asks.

"Venting." I pull the carriage door shut and close the curtains. I don't want to look outside anymore. I press my hands over my eyes and see Zach's face. "Could someone talk about something, please? Something distracting?"

"You want to hear about the worst places I've caught people having sex at carnivals?" Skye asks.

"No. Yes," I say.

She tells us. I try to listen, but the roaring in my ears returns and only grows steadily louder. I have to stay normal. I have to stay normal.

"What is that noise?" Leithe interrupts something about a tilt-a-whirl and pulls the curtain aside to look out the window.

"You can hear it too?" I ask. The carriage stops.

Leithe steps outside. "Ah."

I follow him. "Oh."

Before us, down the slope of the dune we'd just crested, the sand ends and a river begins, vanishing into the distance in both directions. Where the current crests the sand, the water stays together instead of breaking and crashing, giving the impression of the undulations of a great slug, breaking the desert open to make room for its passage. The ground beneath us trembles and falls away inch by inch. Small glowing fish skim the surface, lights on their bodies blinking in and out in hypnotic patterns. The palace in the distance wavers in and out of sight as the water rises and falls.

"It's really moving?"

"Yes. Mab liked to keep the sea in one spot unless she needed it moved, but it appears it's been wandering in her absence."

"She could just order an entire sea around?"

"Yes, she could," Leithe says. Of course she could.

With a rippling shudder, the water relaxes and flattens, spreading toward us like an incoming tide. I scramble backward, slipping and falling down the dune until I land flat on my ass. The carriage follows, the others still within, slipping downhill so fast it nearly pitches forward and starts rolling. The carriage comes to a stop next to me like a dog at heel. Eifa leans out to grab and pull me inside, but that proves unnecessary.

The tide devours the dune and comes to a rest, lapping softly at my ankles. The water is suddenly serene. Serene and in no hurry to go anywhere. The ground stops shaking. The newly-calm water glitters under the starlight, a twin sky to the one above.

"It settled," Leithe says. He's standing behind me, though I didn't see him fleeing from the waves. "Going across is going to be difficult." The palace is a speck across the water. "Going around will likely take longer, but we'll get there regardless."

Meaning more time for something to happen to Grandma. The sea glitters smugly, if a body of water could be smug. Placid, as if it didn't just block me off from the palace. From Grandma. I dig my fingers into the sand and they close around something hard-edged and cold. A crystal ashtray.

"Get out of my way!" I scream. I stand and throw the ashtray into water, where it lands and sinks with an ineffectual *plink*. Nothing happens, and that just makes me angrier. "Move!"

"Tamsin." Skye takes a step forward, but Leithe puts a hand on her shoulder and stops her short with a small shake of his head. My face gets hot. Part of me is aware that I'm embarrassing myself in front of everyone. But the heat turns from humiliation to rage.

"You're supposed to listen to me, right?" I kick at the sand uselessly. "So. Fuck. Off! Get out of the way! Go!" I scream until I'm panting. And in the silence while I catch my breath, the water is uncaring. It's pointless. I can't do what Mab could. I'm not Mab. I'm useless. That should be a relief, but I feel a tang of bitterness regardless. I shouldn't feel disappointed. I shouldn't have hoped for anything.

But then water recedes, rising back into its slug-like mass. "It's moving," I say with more shock than triumph. It's listening. I feel joy. Satisfaction. And then horror. It's listening. The water rises higher until I'm viewing the stars refracted through a great wave. But it doesn't go on its way. It rears and bears down on me.

I put my hands out as if I could hold up a sea. "Stop it!" Instead of making it obey, I may have simply made it mad. "Back!" I yell it again and again. I don't move. I don't run. It could still work. I could still get it. I don't know if the roaring is coming from inside my head or out.

Then the sea crashes down over me.

# Chapter Twenty-Seven

"Welcome back," Zach says. The pillow fort again. Sunlight—diffused by the blanket that forms the ceiling—gives his face a hazy quality. He's young, missing a front tooth. My arms and fingers are pudgy with baby fat. We're lying on the floor of Grandma's living room, hedged in on all sides by couch cushions.

"Grandma hated when we did this because I never put the couch back together right," I say. "In real life, I think I might be drowning right now."

"Is that why you wanted to come here?" he asks.

"It's easier to be here than out there." The rug beneath my head is scratchy.

"It's comfortable," he says. "But you know this isn't where you really are."

"Last time, you said you were going to show me," I say. In response, he offers me his hand and I take it. We rise to our knees and crawl out of the fort, pushing our makeshift blanket-door aside.

I knew where he was going to take me as soon as he asked. I knew what would be behind that door. I know what's beyond the couch cushions and blankets.

There's no sunlight on the other side. I'm not surprised when my palms hit earth and roots instead of hardwood floor, when they come up sticky with cooling blood. The stars of the mortal world are dull above us.

My body is an adult's again, though Zach's is only a teenager. Blood sticks his shirt to the front of his chest; the slash across his throat is raw and jagged, painfully visible now that there's nothing left to spill.

"You've never really left this glade, have you?" He shouldn't be able to speak, but he does.

"No," I say. Every pretty memory of us, they've all been reminders of what would come. "Because this is where I want to be." I sit on my knees on the bloody grass. Zach sits across from me. "Because this is what feels right. Not anything out there, not waking up every day and pretending it never happened. It all just keeps moving, but I don't know how I'm supposed to leave.

"Sometimes I'll realize I'd forgotten you for a little while, then it all comes crashing back, and I hate myself more for letting myself forget. I can't leave this place because this is what I deserve. Because I should wish none of this ever happened. I should wish I'd wake up in the morning and realize it was all a dream. And then I'd go back to my life. And you'd be alive.

"But then I realize ... I realize how much I'd hate going back, because some part of me—a part that makes me sick—is happy. Some part of me still wants to see *every-thing*. Know everything. When I called those nightmares on Nevain's people, I felt *powerful* for the first time in my life. I wanted them to die and they died. I liked it."

I take a breath, trying to steady myself. But it's impossible. I'm shaking. "I want to go to the ball. I want to be ... special." I laugh bitterly. "But I *can't* want those things, because whose life paid for them? It isn't fair. It isn't fair that I'm alive and you're not. You died years ago *and no one even knew*. You'll never have a grave. Your parents will never know what happened to you. They raised a ... thing in your place for years, and then lost that too when it no longer served a purpose. That's why I can't leave this place. That's why I need to see you every time I close my eyes."

"I have an idea," Zach says. "You could forget, like Mab did. Wash yourself clean." He reaches up and brushes his thumb across my forehead. "Get rid of everything you don't want. Would that make it better?"

"I don't want to forget you."

Zach's eyes darken. "But you will one day, won't you? Does it matter that I was your friend? Your first friend? I didn't love you because you were a granddaughter. I didn't love you because you were a queen. I loved you before you were anything but you. But what about in a hundred years? A thousand?"

"I don't know," I admit. "And that's what scares me: that one day I could feel nothing."

"Do you expect me to tell you that it's okay?" Zach stands, hands in pockets. "Do you think this is how you make it up to me? By groveling?"

"I don't know how to fix it," I say. "Tell me what to do."

He kneels, taking my hands in his. His fingers are cool to the touch. "What would you give to make it up to me?"

"Anything you want. Everything I have."

His grip tightens. "Swear."

"I swear on everything that I am, I'd give you anything I have to make it right between us. But I don't think even that would be enough."

"No," he says. "But it would be a start." Our surroundings begin to fade into light. I'm waking up.

"Don't leave me," I beg.

He opens his mouth to speak, but no words come out. My hands close on nothing as he fades away. Again and again, at the end of every dream, they close on nothing.

Someone is retching. For a moment, I'm worried it's me.

I'm cold; it's a cold radiating from my bones that makes me want to claw myself inside out to get rid of it. I want to go back to sleep, back to making hollow promises to dead boys.

When I open my eyes and blink the water from them, Leithe looks down at me with calculated concern. "Are you hurt?" he asks. A single dark tear runs down his cheek. No, not a tear. Blood.

I'm covered in drying sea water, sand sticking to my body where it touches the ground, salt crusting my hair and dress. I try to speak and only cough up a mouthful of water. "Skye?" I finally choke out. "Hunter?"

"They're alive," Leithe says. I struggle to sit up, my head and stomach protesting. Leithe keeps a hand on the middle of my back as if he thinks I'm going to fall over.

Skye is on her hands and knees a short distance away, shaking and vomiting bile into the sand; Eifa holds her up. Hunter's pushing himself up on his elbows, retching.

A hundred feet away, the water stretches calmly to the horizon. "Why aren't we at the bottom of the sea?" I ask.

"I moved us," Leithe says. "The way isn't safe for anyone not Crawling Court, but it seemed better than the alternative." A line of blood trickles from Leithe's nose. "And now I'm going to bleed to death unless you release me from my vow."

The light from the stars jabs at my eyes; I press my fingers to my temples and fight the building nausea. "Why would you—" I begin. Hunter groans and wipes away blood trickling from his nose.

"The experience of being moved is unpleasant." Leithe spits a mouthful of blood into the sand. It releases lazy wisps of smoke where it lands. "Harmful, even. I'd hurry up, unless you stopped Noctiva from eating me just to have me die here."

Vow? My thoughts are still sluggish; it takes me longer than it should to remember. Harming Hunter, even accidentally, violated the wish he promised me, a wish guaranteed by Leithe's last drop of blood. But if I release him—if I even *can* release him—there won't be anything stopping him from killing Hunter like he's wanted this entire time.

Leithe watches me waver, face unreadable, and I know that he's waiting for me to let him die, to make him right, just like in Noctiva's larder.

"I take it back. I release you. Does that work?" I say. Something snaps in my chest, a pressure I didn't realize was there.

Leithe's face relaxes, whatever pain he was in gone. He stands and brushes the sand from his clothes with disdain.

"Don't hurt Hunter," I say, though I no longer have any power to enforce it. Hunter has managed to pull himself to his knees. When he catches my eye, he looks resigned, but Leithe doesn't even look in his direction.

"I saved him, didn't I?" Leithe says. "At great risk to myself, no less."

"Did you?" Hunter asks. "Or did I get dragged along because Eifa grabbed me?"

"Does it matter?" Leithe asks.

"Either way, it's my fault," I say, interrupting the argument. "I really thought something might happen at the last second. I thought maybe I could only figure it out if I really needed it."

"You're welcome to go back and start yelling at the water again, if you like," he says. "The rest of us will remain at a safe distance."

"I feel like I've been taken apart and put back together wrong," Skye groans. Her skin looks gray. "It's like I can feel each individual organ inside me."

"You were put back together *fine*," Leithe snaps.

"Christ." Skye rubs her face and sits up. "Where's the carriage?"

"Underwater, presumably," he says. "It wasn't close enough for me to bring."

"I left my backpack on it," Skye goes through her pockets. "I only have one extra magazine."

"How long will it take us to get there if we have to go around this stupid sea on foot?" I ask.

"That won't be necessary." Leithe points behind me. I turn and see the palace not as a speck in the distance, but close enough to see people the size of ants swarming around it. The palace towers over a network of smaller buildings and streets that spiral away from its base like roots, growing smaller until they vanish into the sand. Beyond the permanent structures is a rippling sea of tents and banners. The city is a tapestry of lanterns, the brightness of which challenges the stars. "I said I moved us." Leithe places his hands on my shoulders and turns me toward him. "Here. You look like you've been rolling around in the sand."

"I have," I say. A glamour like cool fog spreads over me, making my skin look clean and my hair feel silky.

"You'll look presentable until someone tries to see through it," he says. "Which would be rude, but people will do it anyway. We'll be passing through the scavenger's market and then the city proper. Don't speak to anyone; if anyone speaks to you, let me or Eifa answer."

"I'm not allowed to answer?" Skye asks.

"No, because you should act like a glamoured fool so no one pays you any attention," Leithe says.

"Why am I not allowed to talk?" I ask.

"Because none of these people will be worth talking to," he says. "If you accidentally make eye contact with anyone, force them to look away first." Leithe looks down at the sand with distaste. "It would have been better to have that carriage." He thinks for a moment, then draws a wraith out of his shadow, pulling and prodding at it until it loses its shape and resembles a thin, wispy sheet the color of smoke, then hands it to me. "On second thought, just cover your face."

"What about you?" I ask. "You're way more noticeable than me."

"No one will know my face until we get into the palace."

I pull the cloak over my shoulders and head; the rest of the fabric falls past my thighs. It has a cold, almost-damp feeling to it.

My shoes slip and sink into the sand as we trudge steadily uphill toward the city. I should get tired. My legs should be screaming, my breath short. But with each step, I only feel more energized, more excited. The exhaustion from Leithe draining me is already gone. It isn't normal.

"What's the city called?" I ask, hoping that listening to someone else talk will drown out my own thoughts.

"Mab never named the hive that built itself up at the feet of her palace," Leithe says. "It's called simply the Dreaming City."

The stars amble lazily across the sky like faraway fireflies, looping along no particular path. And like fireflies, sometimes they wink out of sight only to flare back to life later, in a completely different place. Or maybe those are different stars entirely.

"Are they supposed to move like that?" I ask.

"Mab hasn't been here to tell them how they're supposed to move," he says. "So I suppose they can move however they like." As we watch, two of the stars collide, sending one spinning until it catches speed and tumbles out of the sky. Light flares where it hits the sand somewhere far away, followed by a sound like distant thunder.

"I take it they're not supposed to do that, either," I say.

Leithe frowns at the sky. "No."

The palace grows in size as we approach—a behemoth towering over everything else. Much of it is pale stone that shines with reflected light from stars and lanterns. Spires twist off the main body like melted fingers of wax.

The sounds and smells from the scavenger's market reach us before we enter the market proper: laughter and shouting punctuated by the occasional shriek of amusement or terror. A thousand different kinds of music—each from a different stall—somehow work in concert instead of against one another. The scents of burning sugar and cooking meat compete for my attention, though both are nearly overpowered by something cloying and floral.

The outermost tents aren't much more than four-post canopies under which proprietors sit with blankets spread across the ground holding wares for sale.

Fae meander between tents, examining wares and haggling. Some almost look human, but subtly warped as if drawn by an artist who'd never seen one in real life. Others look like nightmares or fantasies put to paper by a child. One shopper I mistake for a regular fluffy white cat until it inquires in a deep, rumbling voice about the price of a tiny, ruby-colored fish captured in a hanging glass sphere.

"It's a little busier than normal," Leithe says. "But this is dull compared to when the Allmarket passes through."

"The Allmarket," I repeat. "Sounds self-explanatory."

"The unholy spawn of a pawn shop and a circus," Skye says.

"Ah," Eifa says. "You've been there."

The stalls get more elaborate as we go. Canopies become tents; blankets become tables and other displays. Merchants get more aggressive; barkers stand in front of stalls and physically intercept prospective customers. When a faerie reaches for my cloak to pull me toward a stall of spun sugar flowers and candy insects with twitching wings, Eifa calmly picks the woman up by her shoulders and sets her back down a respectful distance away from me. Barkers take one look at Leithe and choose a new target.

"My Lady," a voice calls out. "Yes, in the hood." I ignore it. It's easy to pretend I didn't hear with all the other commotion. "How much for your human?" I stop and turn in surprise. The speaker is a pale woman with a lipless mouth that cuts her face in half. She stands behind a stall full of orderly and labeled jars of viscera and organs, all marked to denote either fae or human origins; fae include a type—nix, faun, dreamling, and others—while humans are denoted with a sex and age range. The script is square-ish and neat, letters that wouldn't look out of place as a grocery list. "The tongue of a siren, perhaps?" the woman continues. "The hair of a nymph?"

I go through several emotions quickly. Shock, disgust, rage. I want to speak, make a scene, tell Eifa to stab her, stab her myself. But Leithe told me not to speak. He also told me not to break eye contact first, so I stare at the woman, sticking my chin out and looking down my nose at her in the way Leithe looks at everyone. Her irises are black and reach nearly to the corners of her eyes. I imagine I see a flicker of nervousness in her gaze.

"What," Eifa begins, her tone a deadly calm I've never heard before, even while her expression remains idyllic, "gave you the mistaken impression you had any right to address my lady?"

The merchant's gaze is uncertain now as her eyes flick to Eifa and then beyond me to Leithe. Whatever she sees makes her lower her head. "Apologies," she murmurs.

"Remember my lady's mercy today," Eifa says. I look away and continue forward, as if the woman means nothing to me.

I only speak once we're several stalls away. "They buy and sell humans here?"

"Why wouldn't they?" Skye says under her breath.

"They buy and sell everything here," Eifa says. "Their mothers, their own Names, for the right price."

"And Mab didn't care?" I ask.

"She spared no thought for what people did with their own things," Leithe says.

"People aren't things," Skye says.

Leithe waves a dismissive hand. "Everyone is a thing. Everyone but the monarchs."

"Even you?" I challenge.

"Even me." His tone is neutral. No disgust. No despair. Only fact.

Skye starts to speak and cuts off when there's a small tug on the bottom of my cloak. I turn to see a young human girl, freckled and strawberry blond. "Emotions, My Lady? Hate and love and lust and more. Mixtures made just for you." She stands in front of a stall full of tiny crystal jars containing a rainbow's worth of smokes and liquids. The proprietor is a short man that seems more bristling beard than flesh. The little girl has a pink ribbon tied around her neck that connects to a metal ring secured to one of the posts holding up the canopy.

"How much for the kid?" I ask.

If the man is surprised by that inquiry, he doesn't show it. "The child is like a daughter to me, My Lady, but I would trade her for your pretty cloak."

I bunch the hem of the cloak in my fingers as if to take it off, but pause. What would I do next, bring the kid with us to the ball? The fae man peers at me. Is there suspicion in his eyes? Recognition? Hunter watches the child in silence. If I asked him to kill this man, I think he'd do it without a second thought.

Skye jabs me in the back as subtly as she can, head shaking ever so slightly.

"I ... Never mind." I gently pull my cloak out of the child's grip and keep walking.

"We couldn't do anything," Skye says after a few moments. "Not right now."

"I know," I say. It doesn't make me feel any better. "But how do you just walk away?"

"I pick my moments," she says. "That's what people without magic powers need to do. A hunting knife and a handgun with seventeen bullets wouldn't free every human in this market."

But a queen could. I laugh under my breath, earning an odd glance from Leithe. The thought is absurd, that I could fix anything. As if it would be as easy as wanting it. I twist my fists into the cloak. If there were any loose threads, I would have unraveled the thing completely by now.

# Chapter Twenty-Eight

BEYOND THE MARKET, THE sand solidifies into winding stone streets while the tents transition to permanent buildings. They start off shacks assembled from whatever could be pulled up and transported from the desert—pieces of roofs lashed together, mismatched stone and brick walls, neat patios made from bathroom tiles.

Further inward, the buildings look like they were plucked wholesale from the mortal world. A modern, slate gray office block butts up against what looks like a witch's cottage from a storybook. The top of a chrome and glass skyscraper grows lopsided out of the ground, bisected vertically as if cut in half with a knife, the severed offices repurposed into balconies.

"Can they make anything of their own, or do they steal it all from people's heads and mash it together?" Skye asks.

"It all comes from *someone's* head, right?" I say. "Even in the mortal world." While they resemble human structures in shape, some houses tower over others, with front doors more than two stories tall. Others look like birdhouses stacked on top of each other.

The buildings are arranged in what could only be generously called lines, and the roads drawn afterward, creating a map I imagine must resemble a dropped pile of yarn from above. "So how do we get to the palace?"

"Discreetly." Hunter leads us into a narrow, coiling alley. "If Lady Lelit is aware of your arrival, her other knights may be searching for you."

Leithe looks skeptical. "And that would be bad for you?"

"I never wanted humans involved in this," Hunter says. "There are servants' entrances to the palace. They aren't guarded."

"Because who would dare use them without permission?" Skye guesses.

Hunter nods. "Lady Lelit will expect you to meet her as an equal, not sneak in. If all goes well, we could find your grandmother and leave before she notices you."

The smell of food fades once we leave the market, though the floral scent intensifies into a haze the further into the city we go.

Music, laughter, and the occasional feral shriek beckon from beyond each corner but never reveal their source. There are fewer people on the street; the ones we pass show little interest in us.

In the unchanging dusk, the streets are lit with soft white light emanating from cages containing glowing moths the size of my hand. More of the same moths dance in the air and settle on roofs the way a mortal city would have pigeons, their lights rippling across the sky in some unknown language. Several descend and flutter around me, coming close enough to land on my head, shoulders, and outstretched hands.

"Keep those things away from you," Leithe murmurs. "They're Mab's—they're going to attract unwanted attention." He flicks a moth off my head, sending it careening toward the ground until it clumsily rights itself and teeters away.

"Shoo," I say half-heartedly and wave gently with my hands. I go blind for a moment when a moth lands on my nose and stretches its wings in front of my face. After gently plucking the moth off, I give it a boost into the air. Sweeping them off only makes them follow from a distance rather than flee. I look away when we pass other fae, so I'm unsure if the moths' attention piques their interest.

While the palace looms ever present above us, the streets constantly have us looping around or doubling back. Like Noctiva's manor, Mab's palace is a strange medley of countless other buildings from different places and eras. One wing is formed of sharply-angled panes of glass. A spire growing off the opposite side has a multi-tiered roof that pitches up sharply at the edges. But no matter which street we take, the palace stays the same size.

Skye is the first to say it. "We're not getting any closer."

Hunter stares at the lopsided brick wall towering over us. "The city's moving."

"*Of course* the city's moving," I sigh. "But yelling at the ocean made things worse, so I don't think yelling at a brick wall is going to help."

Skye turns to Leithe. "Can you teleport us again—move us—whatever you did to get us away from the water?"

"If you're alright with the chance your heart won't start again," he says.

Skye still looks a little gray from the last time Leithe moved us. The fact that she doesn't insist on taking the risk must mean she's still in more pain than she appears. "Maybe Tamsin should be leading the way. Shouldn't she be able to magic our way there? Isn't that how it works?"

"If that's really where she wants to go," Leithe says.

"Fine." I transfer a loitering moth from my shoulder to my hand; softly glowing particles trail from its wings and coat my fingers. "Take us to the palace, please." I launch the moth into the air. It wavers for a few moments, as if deliberating, then flutters down an alley. "There," I say. "The bug knows the way." Even if it doesn't, following it makes just as much sense as any other direction. To my surprise, everyone follows without argument.

The alley is barely wider than my shoulders and curves sharply to fit between the haphazardly-placed buildings. The moth—at least I think it's the right moth—lands on walls periodically as if to let us catch up.

The alley disgorges us onto a wide boulevard of solid marble split down the middle by a median of trees with thin, twisting trunks and pale lavender leaves. The buildings on either side get gradually taller, one era stacked on top of another in a twisting tower as if grasping for the palace far above.

Once I step onto the street proper, it's as if a membrane burst, throwing the music and voices into sharp relief. Fae dance across the street, in thrall to musicians that weave in and out of the crowd so much so that the music seems to come from everywhere at once and nowhere at all.

The source of the floral scent—now so overwhelming I can feel it in my molars—also becomes clear once I'm out of the alley. Garlands of sugar-crusted red roses hang from buildings, running along walls and stretching across the avenue. The smallest blooms are easily the size of my fist. The dancers kick up fallen flowers and loose petals, sending sweet scarlet eddies swirling across a pale street lined with banquet tables piled heavy with sweets. Mountains of heavy frosted cakes spill onto the ground.

"Is this the ball?" I ask. The palace still looms some distance away. A pang of empty longing I can't place stabs at my chest.

"Just the common fae. Lelit must have sent gifts from the palace so everyone could celebrate your return." Leithe says, frowning at the flowers.

Eifa's nostrils flare. "Leithe," she says calmly. "I suddenly want very badly to fight you to the death, more than the normal amount. Apologies in advance should I stab you." Eifa's eyes look slightly dilated.

"What?" I say. "Why?"

"I've simply been wondering for a while now if I could win," she says.

"Maybe back in the mortal world. If I was sleeping," Leithe says drily. He picks up a rose that fell from a hanging garland and studies it for a moment before tossing it back to the ground. "Cover your nose." He turns to Skye, who looks as if she's just been punched in the face. "You too. Now." Skye covers the bottom half of her face with her sleeve while Eifa cuts strips from her tunic, tying one around her own face and gesturing for Skye to turn around so she can tie one around hers as well. Hunter does the same. "It should go without saying that no one should eat the food, either," Leithe says.

"You should be fine," Leithe tells me. "The flowers shouldn't affect either of us too strongly. It's a mild glamour. You should have no trouble blocking it out if you tried."

Skeptical, I don't lower the hands I've clamped over my mouth and nose. "A mild glamour that makes you homicidal?"

"Not exactly." He nods toward the crowd. As I watch, an embracing couple nearly bowls over several others in their haste to get to an alley, tearing at each other's clothes the whole way. Other couples are less concerned about privacy. On the other side of the crowd, peals of laughter turn to shouts as a fight breaks out, one faerie slashing knife-sharp claws across the face of another and tearing the pendant off from around his neck.

"And no one is going to stop them?" I ask. The injured man licks the blood from his face with a narrow black forked tongue and seems otherwise more annoyed than in pain.

"There is a reason," Eifa says softly, "that many fae choose to risk the iron of the mortal world."

"Lelit's power is want," Leithe says. "And she can make that lack feel all-encompassing, strip you down until there's nothing left." He gestures to the banquet tables. "Because no matter how much you eat, you'll only feel emptier."

"Why drug all these people?" I ask. "For kicks?"

He shrugs. "Maybe she sees it as a gift." Leithe surveys the scene, looking unimpressed. "Where did your moth go?"

Oops. "I wasn't looking," I point toward the thickest part of the festivities. "It flew that way," I guess.

"Well," Leithe sighs. "If we're seeing the celebration, we're closer. Eifa, if anyone touches us, use your discretion."

Eifa takes point as we wade into the crowd, tracking the ebb and flow of bodies and leading us down the twisting path of least resistance, occasionally pushing stragglers out of our way with the butt of her spear.

While most celebrants are consumed by their own activities, plenty of eyes track our progress, ranging from curious to predatory. Fingers graze my skin, beckoning. When was the last time I'd kissed someone? Less than a year ago, surely. Some guy from an app, a name that started with a 'T'. Trenton, Travis maybe. One date and then someone ghosted the other; I can't remember which one of us it was. Or even if it was a good kiss.

I'm drawn out of my head when a faerie's arms try to snake around Skye's waist. Eifa is there in a flash, picking up the woman with one hand and throwing her back into the crowd with enough force to knock several people down. It's enough of a show that the rest of the crowd remains a reasonable distance away.

"Oh," Eifa says with some genuine remorse. "I didn't mean to throw quite so hard."

Skye puts her half-drawn knife away. "I could have handled it."

"I know," Eifa says.

They stare at each other, Eifa's tail lashing the air behind her. Skye begins to speak and stops herself.

"Lords," Leithe says. "Go tear each other's clothes off and get it out of your system, if you must, but I thought we had a schedule to keep."

Even with the same mild smile on her face, Eifa looks like she really might impale Leithe, but she turns and takes the lead once more without a word.

Leithe's right. We're on a schedule. Grandma is in danger and I shouldn't be thinking about Travis or Trenton or whatever his name is or Eifa's arms or Leithe's hair. I bite into the flesh of my cheek and concentrate on the pain. This isn't the time.

"Is the actual ball going to be like this?" I ask.

"No," Leithe says. "The guests at the ball will be far more polite until they have you where they want you."

"I think that's our guy." I point to a moth resting on one of the rose garlands. It flies off when we get closer.

"They all look the same," Skye says.

"But it doesn't matter, right?" I say. "I just have to think I'm going the right way and everything else will fall into place. So we'll say that's the right bug. Let's go." My words sound hollow no matter how much confidence I want to project.

Then someone grabs my shirt collar and yanks me backward into the pulsing crowd, my heels skidding uselessly against the smooth marble road. I can't help the spike of fear that runs down my spine and into my stomach. The buzzing in my ears becomes a sudden roar, drowning out the raucous celebration. I cup my hands over my ears on instinct, though it does nothing. The buzzing becomes whispers becomes screaming. While the words are unintelligible, the feeling is not. The voices are scared, pressing in against me in sheer panic.

The hand is gone. Leithe touches my shoulder, looking annoyed. He asks a question I can't hear, unbothered by the noise. No one else can hear it. Nothing is happening. It will go away.

And then the twilight becomes cold daylight and flares brighter still. I look up in time to see the star plummeting toward us before the light drowns out everything else.

# Chapter Twenty-Nine

I'VE HEARD GUNSHOTS. I've heard thunder. Neither of those compare to a star crashing into the ground. It blasts through the barrier between sound and feeling, shaking the street, the *air*, radiating through my body, and knocking me flat on my back.

Then there's the pain. Not my pain, but the wailing in my ears is enough to knock the wind from me. It comes from the ground, the fractured marble paving the street, the mangled wood and stone and plaster of the buildings blown apart, the dying shards of the star itself. I feel it the same way I would feel a wound on my own body, as if both the fallen star and the ground it sundered are my own phantom limbs.

I shouldn't be feeling this. I'm normal. I'm normal. I push the pain away, rebuild the barrier between me and everything else. The buzzing fades back to an almost-ignorable level.

Leithe's face materializes over mine as I blink the spots and tears out of my eyes. He speaks, but the ringing in my ears drowns out his voice. I shake so badly that I can barely grip the fingers of his offered hand as he pulls me to my feet.

Everything is burning. Where there was once a building, there's now a smoldering pit crackling with white fire so bright it brings tears to my eyes and leaves an afterimage when I look away.

The corpse of the building is scattered up and down the road; beams, stones, entire pieces of walls, scorched and burning from the same white fire. Jagged shards of what look like diamonds jut from the ground, white flame smoldering from within them.

As sounds gradually come back into focus, I'm suddenly surrounded by cries of pain and the moans of the dying. "Where are the others?"

"Yes, you're welcome," Leithe says. Waves of dismal, heavy smoke crawl across the cracked street. Sometimes the suggestion of a hand or face protrudes from the mass before vanishing again. The clouds deposit themselves into the shadows at Leithe's feet.

We're farther down the street than we were when the star fell, barely beyond the jagged ring of char and destruction. He must have moved us.

"Thank you. Where are the others?" I take a step toward the wreckage.

Leithe puts a hand on my shoulder, stopping me. "We need to leave. Lelit will have noticed what you did. She'll send someone." Dark, hairline cracks spread across his exposed skin. There are deep-set shadows under his eyes and his breath comes heavily. The blast hurt him.

I study my arms, the skin unmarred. My face is untouched. I get the vague sense that this is wrong. I should be hurt. Bleeding. Burned. "I did ... what did I do?" I ask. My thoughts are still sluggish, uncomprehending.

"This." He gestures toward the burning wreckage. The celebratory mood is gone. The uninjured fae, recovering from the shock, either flee or begin searching for the injured and the dead. Smoldering rose garlands give the smoke an undercurrent of burnt sugar. Moths fall from the sky, their small bodies nothing but cinders by the time they reach the ground. "You did this."

A faerie pulls another free of a fallen wall only to find their body a pulpy mass below the waist. Another has been pierced by star shards through half her face, throat, and chest and yet still is trying to rise and speak.

"Skye?" I call out. "Eifa? Hunter?"

"They were too far away for me to move." Another wraith drags its smoky body across the ground and spills into Leithe's shadow. "They're not dead. They probably fled, like we should. We're going to the same place." With each wraith he absorbs, the cracks across his skin close. The shadows under his eyes fade.

"We need to save these people," I say. "Please."

"Why do you care?" he snaps. "They'd eat you if they could, suck the magic from your bones along with the marrow. They'd make Skye their pet until they got bored of her. Honestly." He crosses his arms. "It's like I'm the only one here with a brain."

"*Because it's my fault*," I say. This wouldn't have happened if I was better. If I was Mab. If she hadn't left me here. "I'll give you a wish, whatever you want, just save them."

Leithe opens his mouth to argue, but only sighs and turns his attention to the street. The wraiths trickling toward him reverse course, joined by a wave of other wraiths that surge outward from his shadow, darting into corpses through open wounds, gaping mouths, and sightless eyes.

The noises coming from the dead as their bodies re-arrange themselves to lash together shattered bones and knot together torn muscle and tendons are disturbingly wet. Limbs twist themselves back together and bodies rise, stumbling like grotesque newborn deer. They push wreckage aside, gripping smoldering wood with bare hands and dragging survivors free. Scorched bodies emerge from beneath the ruins and get to work as well.

The white fire burns hot, but burns itself out quickly rather than spreading to other buildings. "It's done," Leithe says. "The living are rescued. Nothing more to do here. Let's *go*." The surviving fae look warily between the two of us. With expressions ranging from resentment to resignation, they step forward and kneel to Leithe.

"My life is yours until my debt has been paid," a woman with black feathered wings—one broken and drooping—says. The same words ripple across the crowd.

"No," Leithe says. "They're hers." He points to me. "I had no interest in this from the start."

The crowd turns their eyes to me. Are the flickers of recognition my imagination? They're coated in a grime of blood, dirt, and faintly-sparkling dust.

"Um." The fae wait expectantly. I want to tell them to forget it, that they owe me nothing, but Eifa made it clear how offensive that would be. "I want you to rest and recover. I'll find you when I'm in need of your service." I resist the urge to look at Leithe to gauge how I did.

With permission given, the injured fae slip away into buildings and alleys, celebration forgotten. Many of the uninjured must have left much earlier, either immediately after the impact or once they'd saved who they were trying to save.

"They didn't seem happy about the help," I say.

"Why would they be?" Leithe says. "Now they have to pay a life debt to a noble. Now, have we wasted enough time here?" He quiets, listening to something. "Ah. It doesn't matter anymore."

Hooves batter the marble road as a company on horseback approaches from the direction of the palace. The horses are alien things—swanlike and slender with fat white roses twined through their manes and tails. There's at least twenty riders, all dressed in gleaming armor crusted with jewels and trailing emerald cloaks. A glittering green serpent wrapped around a rose curls around the neck of each knight; it's impossible to tell if it's a piece of jewelry or a living creature.

The lead rider—an auburn haired girl with no obvious inhuman features—stops some distance away. The other riders form a line alongside her, blocking the street completely. The girl—she looks like she can't be more than sixteen, armor-clad with flowers winding through her hair—surveys the burning street, including Leithe's small horde of zombies.

"Your Grace," the girl begins.

"Good," I cut her off, heart in my throat. "You're here. Get someone to help these people and clean this up." I point to the ruined street. The girl stares at me. How much has Lelit told her? Would she refuse my orders in front of a crowd? I resist the urge to look at Leithe for guidance, or to silently beg him to take over. I cross my arms.

The girl smiles. "It would be my pleasure, Your Grace. Shall I escort you to the palace while the rest of the company renders aid?"

I could say no. We could fight, and maybe we would win. But I wonder if this girl shares Hunter's story, if all of these other knights do. "Yes," I say. "You shall." There's nothing else to do but hope: hope that Hunter can sneak Skye and Eifa into the palace, hope that they can find Grandma while Lelit is distracted with me, hope they can escape. "It's about time. Lead on." I pull the cloak from my head. There's no use trying to hide anything now.

A sigh ripples through the dead as Leithe's wraiths release their bodies and dart back into his shadow. The abandoned corpses drop like puppets with severed strings.

The girl nods to the other riders; they obediently disperse through the crowd. "Do you want a horse, Your Grace?"

"I'll walk." The kelpie soured me on riding for the rest of my life.

The girl dismounts and hands her horse's reins to someone else. "Then we'll go on foot. Please." The girl is supernaturally graceful, each step she takes somehow its own dance.

We turn a corner and come out onto a larger street formed from an unbroken sheet of marble shot through with softly glittering veins. Here, the street celebration continues in full force. The smell of charred wood and burning meat is gone; it doesn't even cling to our clothes; maybe it's another of their enchantments.

The celebrants trip over themselves to get out of our way. I look straight ahead and try to ignore the weight of curious eyes.

"What'll it be, then?" I ask Leithe as we walk. "Your wish?"

"What wish?" Leithe asks. "We swore no oath."

We didn't, I realize. There's no debt settled like a hook in my chest. "I'm still going to pay you back, even if I'm not under the threat of death. So: a wish. Pick something."

He looks like he might argue, but then seems to realize it's no use. "I think I'll leave you in suspense."

The road leads us directly to a gold-accented, pale marble gate at least twenty feet tall that spans the street. The design mimics the sky, with glittering diamonds glowing with an inner light embedded in the center of golden starbursts. From what I've seen, the stones may well be real stars—or whatever stars are in Faerie. Walls continue straight out from the gate on each side until they vanish into the mess of the city. The wall is a patchwork, changing from carved marble like the gate, blocks of gray stone, twisted metal bars, even a thick hedge maze.

The gate opens slowly but with no scrapes or groans of protest. Beyond, the Dreaming Palace sits at the far end of a massive manicured garden. Even so far away, the structure towers over everything. It must be large enough to house a small city. It must *be* a small city in and of itself.

"Welcome back, Your Grace." Our guide bows and excuses herself, slipping gracefully away as the gate swings shut behind us.

The gardens that surround the palace stretch so far to the left and right that I can't see where they end. Each section—divided neatly by paths of glittering white stones—holds something different. Some are winding, alien flowerbeds, some hold arrays of statues, and the contents of others are completely hidden by tall hedges.

The center marble lane, wide as a highway, splits down the middle to accommodate a rectangular pond that runs most of the length to the palace. Water sprays out in gravity-defying fountains that dance in the air before returning to the pond. Sometimes a small glittering fish is caught in the fountain and thrown into the air, where it swims as easily as if it were water.

Glowing moths swarm even thicker here than the rest of the city, casting flickering light over the gardens and serving as living lanterns where they perch on the bone-white, skeletal trees lining the lane.

Music floats through the gardens from musicians perched on plinths growing from flower beds. Strikingly-dressed fae stroll the gardens in pairs or small groups.

It's so much that I don't immediately notice Hunter waiting for us on the other side. Alone.

# Chapter Thirty

LEITHE STARTS LAUGHING. THE stained bandages that had been wrapped around Hunter's chest are gone, the bare skin beneath unbroken and marked only by a line of pale crescents down his breastbone—the memory of Lelit's nails. There's a shallow cut across the side of his neck. He carries a sword, now, along with his bow.

"Did you kill them, then?" Leithe's voice is muddled by the white noise in my ears.

"I helped them escape the fire, I snuck them into the palace, and then I delivered them to Lady Lelit," Hunter says tonelessly. "Skye lost her will immediately, but Eifa fought back for a few moments."

"You said—" He said Lelit hadn't given him any orders not to let us into the palace. And I'm sure she hadn't. "What does she want in exchange for them?" I ask. I should have known. I should have seen it.

"You don't have anything worth bargaining for," Hunter says. "But my lady is generous and offers you this: she'll return your choice of one of the three she's taken un-harmed, and the other two she'll throw into Elsewhere."

There's only one answer that makes sense. *Give me Grandma*. Get her out, then come back for Skye and Eifa. If they were here, it's what they'd tell me to do. It's why we came. And if that's what I did, Grandma would never forgive me. "And if I don't choose, she'll throw all of them into Elsewhere?"

"If you don't choose, they'll stay where they are." Hunter holds his arm out, gesturing to the gardens, the palace. "Here, enjoying the ball. But not together. And I don't know where, specifically, to save you the time of torturing me. If you don't wish to accept my lady's offer, you may want to find them soon. This place can be dangerous for humans who don't know better. And Eifa won't fare any better; those of the Crawling Court have no friends here."

"Why?" I demand. "I'm here. Lelit doesn't need to do this."

"She is aware." His eyes are focused on a point over my shoulder.

"I want to talk to Lelit. Now," I say. "Where is she?"

"Your throne, Your Grace," Hunter says. "If my lady's message has been received. I'll go."

"I ... It's been received," I say. As much as I want to scream, there's nothing to be gained from him.

Hunter turns, takes a few steps, stops. The movements are stilted, rehearsed. "One more thing," he says. "If this is the last time we speak, you should know that Lady Lelit was true to her word. None of my actions after she left me at your grandmother's house until now were due to her orders. I chose to do it all."

"And she ordered you to tell me that," I say, *because she knew how much it would hurt.* He nods. "I'm sorry I couldn't help you, Hunter. I hope Lelit eventually decides to help your kids."

My acceptance seems to hurt him more than my hate ever could, though it gives me no satisfaction.

"Do you want me to kill him?" Leithe asks. Hunter waits, as if giving me permission.

"No," I say, "Just let him go."

Hunter lingers a few more moments, as if expecting me to change my mind, then turns down a small path in the hedges and vanishes from view. It's only then that I realize other fae are blatantly watching at a distance. When they notice me noticing them, they quickly pretend to find something interesting on a side path out of my view.

"Well." Leithe places his hand on my shoulder and pulls me into the shadow of a hedge, speaking close to my ear. To any observers, we might be enjoying an intimate moment. I assume that's his intent. "Assume we're being watched. By Lelit, by every single guest, all looking for an opening to take from you. I've put a bit of glamour around us. Stay close and speak softly and no one else will hear you."

"Is this fun for her?" I must be vibrating with the effort it takes not to collapse into a pile.

"Stop panicking. It's not going to help," Leithe says. "You're playing into her hands. She wants you scared and desperate enough to agree to anything to get them back."

I take a breath; try to calm down. Think. I need to think. "She wants me to look because she doesn't think I'm going to find them all before I break." Leithe doesn't comment. "I need to go straight to her. I'll threaten to tell everyone the truth." *And ruin both of us.* "She won't have a choice. Noctiva said that everything Lelit has done has been to keep me." To keep *Mab*. I look to Leithe for confirmation, but he isn't looking at me; his attention is on the garden around us, on each shadow and flickering light. He looks distracted enough that I'm unconvinced he heard anything I said. "Right?"

After several seconds, he looks at me as if he just registered my words, then he closes his eyes and sighs. "Yes. Let's go." He offers me his arm, and I loop mine around it and rest my hand on his forearm, mimicking the other couples wandering the garden.

We start down the center path and soon the hedges open into a garden of brightly-colored blown glass bulbs. The fae we pass stop to bow to me with a demurely murmured "Your Grace" before politely putting as much distance between us as fast as possible. Most of them look almost human. Most often, the telling feature is the eyes: sometimes they're a solid color, sometimes animalistic, sometimes there aren't two.

The outfits of the other guests run the gamut of time and place. A woman wearing what looks like an entire vintage thrift store stands hand in hand with a woman wearing a tall French colonial wig decorated with jewel-colored beetles that gleam when their skittering bodies catch the starlight. A man is dressed in nothing but feathers that—on second glance—might just be part of his body. I look away quickly, and instead come face to face with a woman wearing a white porcelain mask painted with dark eyes and scarlet lips. On her arm is a middle-aged human woman, tall and rail-thin, cheeks sunken and bones prominent beneath sagging, paper-thin skin. The muscles at the corners of her mouth spasm with the effort to hold her smile in place. Her adoring gaze is fixated on her masked companion.

Leithe places a hand on mine. A warning. I bite the inside of my cheek.

"Your Grace. An honor to see you once more." The fae woman curtseys, gown rustling. The human woman stumbles and almost falls over until the faerie straightens and supports her once more. The fae woman's gown is black and leaves her arms bare past the shoulder, revealing an intricate, colorful collage of what I initially take as tattoos before realizing is embroidery stitched directly into her skin, traveling up her arms and across her collarbones. "My lord the Dollmaker is eager to speak with you." The Dollmaker—is that a name I should know? Another of Mab's vassals, I assume.

"That woman is starving to death," I say. Leithe's hand tightens. I ignore it. "You need to let her go. Send her home." I might be about to find out the exact limits of the power these people are pretending I have.

"'Let her go'?" The masked woman cocks her head. "She isn't my prisoner." She places a protective, almost caring hand on the human woman's shoulder. "She asked me to make her happy. Her husband died; her children died, but she doesn't care about those things anymore. If I released her from the glamour, I'd be violating the deal I made with her. I will not break my word, so do what you must, Your Grace."

I listen, dumbstruck. I had no plan for if she said no.

The fae woman studies me from behind her cheerfully smiling mask—or maybe it really is her face. "Please forgive my impudence, but are you well, Your Grace? Would you like me to pass a message to my lord?" I stare at the mask's flat black eyes. Is she offering help? Is she looking for a weakness? Both?

"The queen will *consider* forgiving your impudence," Leithe cuts in, "so long as you get that human food from the mortal world."

"Of course." The fae woman turns back to me. "Your Grace." She curtseys again and leads her companion away.

"Shall we?" Leithe asks with a show of levity, pulling me gently along. I want to cover my face with my hands and scream, but people are watching. "Don't make demands unless you're willing to deliver the consequences of refusal," he murmurs. "Remember that all of these fae belong to someone else. If I had killed that woman for you, the Dollmaker would have sought restitution."

"She didn't even feed her," is all I say.

"She probably feeds the human quite well, in her opinion," Leithe says. "But Faerie food is as useless for humans as mortal food and air is for us. And that isn't something many bother to remember."

I laugh in disbelief and press my knuckles over my mouth to smother it. "So that woman is going to die because of *carelessness*, not malice." Not a cackling murderer, a toddler forgetting to feed her goldfish.

We pass a plinth, one of many lining the central walk. This one contains the statue of a man half-reclined, sleeping head resting on an arm, one leg dangling off the side. This close, it looks too real.

"No," is all I can say when I press my hand against his calf and the warm skin gives under pressure. "This is ... insane. *Insane.*" Tears of frustration prick at my eyes.

"Come," Leithe says. He guides me into a sheltered section of the garden dominated by willow trees with branches laden with tiny bell-shaped flowers that chime softly in the breeze. Flickering shadows dance across the branches and our bodies from countless small and moving light sources.

I squeeze my eyes shut to keep from crying, but it doesn't work. I choke a silent sob against my fist.

A burst of manic shrieks and laughter comes from somewhere farther into the garden, sending me backpedaling in surprise straight into Leithe, who places a careful hand on my shoulder to steady me.

I don't pull away. "It's exhausting, being this scared of everyone else." The words spill out with surprising ease.

"You'll learn with time," Leithe says. He doesn't pull away, either.

I let myself lean against him before I realize what I'm doing. "I don't want to learn. I don't want to get used to it." I want to run. Toward the palace. Away from the palace. It doesn't matter. But there's nowhere to go—no outlet—so I freeze instead. I want to curl up where no one will find me.

"I know." He leaves off the unsaid, *But you will.* Instead, to my surprise, he strokes my hair. I hate how nice it feels. Hate that I want him to keep doing it. This comfort is stolen from Mab.

I hate it enough that I pull away. "Why are you being nice to me?"

He crosses his arms, staring at me as if he can't decide if he should be confused or irritated. "Because I thought that's what you wanted?"

"It's ..." *Weird. Wrong. Only making things more diffi-cult.* "You don't have to be here," I say. "You can go. You're not going to be able to get what you want out of me. I think you know that."

"I can't leave any more than you can," he says. Because he needs me at least as much as I need him. An exile from his court; despised in Mab's court. Mab is his lifeline. Without his hope that she'll come back, he'd have nothing. We're both trapped.

When I look at him, an unwanted thought worms its way to the forefront of my mind: he'd only need to lean down a little to kiss me. I can't tell if I want him to, if that has anything to do with my racing pulse or stomach twisting into a knot. But that's what you do, isn't it, when you're too stubborn or too scared to cut the threads choking the both of you?

I don't know what he sees in my eyes. I don't know if I rise up on my toes first, or if he leans, one arm rising to circle my waist. It doesn't feel right. It doesn't feel safe. I'm not even sure either of us want this, but it feels like the only thing I have.

"I'm sorry." I step away, disentangling myself from his arm. I wait for him to resist, to get angry, that would make it easier, but he doesn't.

"Don't be," he says, not looking at me. "Take another moment; collect yourself. I'll make sure no one gets too curious." He takes a step back toward the main thoroughfare.

I don't move, unable to fight the waves of guilt in the face of this strange and sudden kindness. "I have a question for you."

He stops and half-turns back. "You don't need my permission to ask."

"After I got you out of the prison, what would you have done if I'd actually been human?" I pick at my sleeve, but Noctiva's handiwork doesn't unravel. "You didn't like my attitude, didn't like that I extorted a wish out of you, so would you have killed me? Destroyed my mind?"

Leithe's yellow eyes momentarily reflect the faint light radiated by a passing moth. "Killed you?" he sounds genuinely surprised. "No. You were irritating, but you fulfilled your end of our bargain. Which, to be honest, I didn't expect you to do. I would have given you whatever you asked for and never thought about you again." He studies my expression. "You look like you were hoping I'd say I would have fed your liver to that kelpie and kept your skull on my mantle as a souvenir."

"I was." It would have made it easier to say nothing. "I need to tell you something." I take a breath. I can't do it anymore. I won't do it. "I didn't say it before because I'm scared—scared of you, and scared of losing you, because then I'd really be alone." I feel almost giddy, with fear, relief that the lying is almost over, maybe both. "You're using me, and I've told myself that should make it okay for me to use you, but it doesn't.

"You thought Lelit and Noctiva stopped the wedding and locked you and Mab up because they were jealous, but that's not true. They did it because they thought Mab planned to use your Name to force you to kill her after the wedding. Noctiva confirmed it while we were in Blackbower." Leithe is silent, his face carefully blank. "And the witch, I don't know the specifics, but she told me that Mab made a deal with her when she guessed what Noctiva and Lelit were planning. Mab didn't want her memories to escape the prison because she didn't want to come back. She wanted to die, and this is how she did it."

"Why?" Leithe's voice is very quiet, his tone indiscernible. It's terrifying.

"I don't know," I say. "I can't speak for Mab."

"No," Leithe says. "Why are you telling me this now?"

"I know. I should have told you sooner, but—"

"*No.*" He pinches the bridge of his nose and speaks his next words slowly. "Why are you telling me *at all*?"

"Because ... because it's right, isn't it? You should know. Would you rather I kept my mouth shut?"

"Were you hoping I would thank you?" he asks. "Had you said nothing, you could have used me for a lot longer."

"I know. But I've already used you for too long." To protect me. To do the things I'm too much of a coward to do. To make me feel human by contrast.

"And I've used you for too long." He stares straight through me for a while before sighing. "If what you've said is true, I pity you. You, Tamsin, not Mab. You're a piece in a game that started long before you were born. You were never told the rules but you were created too entrenched to escape. If Mab did this on purpose—created you and left you at the mercy of her friends and enemies—then it was cruel."

"If she did it on purpose, it was cruel to you too," I say.

He looks at me, gaze suddenly intense. "What I told Nevain in that human bar was the truth. Lelit was almost right. I intended to trick Mab into entering the Crawling Court and present her to the king to fulfill the conditions of his quest." As he speaks, I become keenly aware there's no longer anything stopping him from doing that, no expectation that Mab would take him back at the end of this road. "At least, that was my plan for a short while after Mab brought me to her palace, but I changed my mind, and I confessed it all to her." He looks away, studying the bloom-covered willow boughs. "You wish to end this betrothal?"

"Yes." It's the right thing to do; it always has been.

"Then let it be over." As he speaks, it's as if something within my chest *snaps*, a sound that resonates through my ribcage.

"That's it?" I ask. "It's done?"

"It's done." He runs a hand through his hair, smoothing it out. "Well, then. I suppose I no longer have a reason to bother you further. I think I'll go get drunk."

"Why not leave?"

"And go where?" Leithe asks. "The mortal world? Perhaps try my luck with a monarch I haven't yet attempted to woo? I suppose the Blooming Queen is always taking new consorts." He laughs. "No. I might as well stay. At least something interesting might happen here." He laughs again. "Their effort was wasted, by the way. If there's a way to kill one of the Gentry, I don't know it."

"I'm sor—" I begin, but he puts a finger up to stop me.

"Don't. There's no need, and no use." He looks at me, a complicated expression crossing his face. "What will happen tonight will happen whether or not you're here. I suspect there will be a point during the evening where even the guards will be too distracted to prevent you from leaving."

"Well." I pause, unsure if I should be saying anything at all. "Thank you for all of your advice. I probably should have listened to some of it."

He snorts. "Good luck, Tamsin."

Leithe doesn't look back. I watch him as he turns and exits the enclosed garden and vanishes beyond the hedge wall, then stare at the empty air.

# Chapter Thirty-One

I AM ALONE. I take a breath, smooth my dress, comb my fingers through my hair, and push the willow boughs aside as I depart the small garden, leaving a trail of tinkling bells in my wake.

Leithe is nowhere to be seen when I return to the main path. I shouldn't feel as empty as I do. I shouldn't want to scream until my throat collapses. I had no right to hope he might stay, despite everything. This is how it should be.

The only thing left to do is find Lelit and make the only threat I have, so I walk straight toward the palace, ignoring every side path. It takes longer than I expect to make progress; the palace grows steadily larger until I can't see the top even when I crane my neck. Wings and other offshoots from the main structure grow with little rhyme or reason, giving the entire thing the impression of being alive since no normal building I've ever seen has such a lack of symmetry or logic. Yet still, it manages to be somehow, if not beautiful, at least striking. And completely unashamed.

Guests stare and whisper as I walk by, though none of them address me unless they accidentally make eye contact, after which they bow and offer the same murmured "Your Grace" and other generic obsequiousness and well-wishes as everyone else who's spoken to me since I arrived.

I ignore them, focusing instead on the rectangular fountain that splits the path in two. The sides are marble and come up to my knee. Gleaming white lotuses drift on the surface, while gem-colored fish swim lazily around, occasionally stopping to nibble on a flower. The bottom of the fountain is covered in a layer of shining coins ranging from freshly-minted pennies to ancient, irregularly-pressed ovals.

I'm stuck for a moment, wondering how many eras lay together at the bottom of this fountain, until a guest shoots out a long barbed tongue and spears a golden fish, swallowing it whole before turning back to giggle at something her companion says. I need to stop getting distracted.

The path widens into a large square near what must be the midpoint, though it's impossible to tell since both the palace and garden seem far larger than they have any right to be. Two heaping banquet tables run the length of the square, swarming with laughing and chattering fae. The food is, of course, both excessively lavish and deeply horrifying. Bouquets of rose-shaped chocolates—edges of the petals dipped in gold—sit next to a cage full of small poetry-reciting birds that guests eat alive.

Without thinking, I walk over to the table, shove a man out of the way, and wrench the birdcage open wide, grabbing each bird and releasing them into the sky. But instead of flying away, they perch on trees and hedges, ignorant of the danger. One gets snatched out of the air right away by a calico cat the size of a horse reclining near the far end of the table. The cat licks her lips and yawns, eyeing me as if daring me to argue.

The man I shoved grabs a handful of my hair and twists it painfully. His skin looks real, but his eyes and teeth are metallic. "You think you can just—" His voice is like the scrape of metal against metal.

Before he can finish his sentence, there's a flash of a blade from the side and his hand bounces off my shoulder and hits the ground with a dull clang. Steam hisses from the bone-colored pipes jutting from the stump.

"Mind who you speak to," a dark-skinned fae man says as he returns his sword to his hip. "Or are you so stupid that you don't recognize the queen herself?"

The metallic man's eyes widen, the mechanisms within whirring. He takes a knee. "Your Grace, please forgive me." What fear I had of this man gives way to anger.

"Whoever gets him to the dungeon first can see Lelit about a reward," I say. I don't know if there's a dungeon. I don't know what Lelit will do when approached for a reward, but I don't care. Several fae begin fighting over him, snatching at his limbs and pulling him back and forth as he begs me to reconsider, but doesn't dare fight back.

My savior assesses me with bright-green, slit-pupiled eyes. He bows sharply at the waist, and the young human man hovering behind him quickly does the same.

"Your Grace," the fae man says. "I would not expect you to remember me. I am Sylas, one of the King of Cats' sworn knights. I hope you aren't offended that I took liberties with that fool."

"Not at all," I say. I stare hard at the human man: he looks healthy, alert, no signs he's under a glamour. At my scrutiny, he takes a half-step behind Sylas, eyes on the ground.

Sylas places his hand on the human's shoulder and gently guides him forward so he isn't hiding. "My lover, Jeremy," he says by way of introduction. "Jeremy, this is the queen to whom we are here to pay our respects." Sylas' hand hovers on Jeremy's shoulder protectively, as if *I* was a threat. The shadow Sylas casts by the light of the flitting moths shifts between that of a man and a great cat.

Jeremy's face reddens at the word *lover*. "Your Grace." He sounds unused to using the words, and his eyes remain firmly on the ground.

"It's nice to meet you, Jeremy," I say.

"Likewise, Your Grace. The party is really cool," he says in a nervous rush.

"We wouldn't dare keep you, Your Grace. You must have far more important people to see." Sylas bows again before quickly but gracefully getting himself and Jeremy as far away as possible from me. As they leave, I catch broken bits of Jeremy begging the faerie to use *boyfriend* instead of *lover*.

I examine a tray of pastries, wondering if they're going to start singing or begging for their lives. The rest of the fae who'd been attacking the banquet tables now keep a respectful distance, all eyes on me.

"Enjoy the party," I say to no one in particular as I push away from the table and return to the path.

One foot in front of the other; a straight line, just like Noctiva's hall of mirrors. And just like the hall, I'm following obediently. What reason do I have to think Lelit isn't prepared to counter exactly what I have planned? After all, she's trounced me every other time we've interacted.

Search for the hostages, or find Lelit. Those were the options given to me and I've been acting like they're the only ones. Skye was right—I don't think; I freeze, or I pick a direction and run.

*Think*. I'm alone, aside from any ambiguously helpful strangers like Sylas. When was the last time I was really alone? Even in Blackbower, Noctiva's children kept an unseen eye on me. Even when I thought I was human, I had the false Zach leading me along; I had the witch waiting to offer advice when she felt the need to give me a shove.

No, I've never been alone, and there's the answer.

I wait until the perfect guest passes by: a hulking creature shaped like the suggestion of a bear on two legs made of a patchwork of animal skins stitched together with thick thread. Tiny black button-eyes peer out from a heavy brow. Her pink gown is the size of a small tent and matches the bow around her ear; her claws could eviscerate me with a single swipe.

And the important part is that she doesn't avert her eyes or bow her head; she either doesn't recognize me or doesn't care.

I stomp up to her and pull my arm back to slap her across the face, but before I can, someone grabs my other arm and yanks me roughly onto a side path.

"Are you hoping to get ripped to shreds?" the witch asks as she releases my arm. It's her middle-aged body; the young and the old ones are nowhere to be seen. Her hair is spun into twin braids and threaded with gold, falling nearly to her knees. Her floor-length green gown is simply cut.

"You didn't exactly leave a phone number, but I figured you might be moved to action if your investment was under attack," I say. We're alone in a private garden full of softly humming flowers, the main path nowhere in sight.

The witch looks unimpressed. "The next time you do that, I'll leave you to your fate." She turns to go, but I grab her sleeve.

"You already know what's going on," I say. She doesn't contradict me. "Lelit has hostages. Unless you want to risk me turning myself over to her, you'll help me get them back."

"Will I, now?" The witch sips from a glass of wine, looking, at best, vaguely amused by my demands. "Why assume this matters to me?"

"I'm not assuming. You came to stop me from making an ass out of myself. Whatever you need from me, you won't be able to get it if I'm Lelit's puppet queen."

"Need?" The witch peels my hand from her sleeve and loops our arms together as if we're friends, leading me down a hedge-lined path. "It's your mistake to assume I *need* you to do anything."

"Then just tell me what you want from me. The last time we met, you made a big deal about how I owe you for what Mab asked you to do, then just disappeared. You wanted me to escape the prison. I know there's a reason."

"Yes," she says. "Curiosity: I wanted to see if I'd succeeded in granting Mab's wish. But now I've seen, and now I'm bored. You have nothing to offer me; I have no use for a human girl's things. I made a deal with a queen and will collect from a queen, or no one."

"If I have nothing to offer you, you wouldn't have come. Do you want something of Mab's? Something she wouldn't give you when she was queen, but you think I will?"

The witch purses her lips and ignores my question. "If I were to help you find your lost companions, what would you do next?"

"Get the hell out of here," I say immediately.

"And then?"

"I don't know. I just ..." Want to go home? Keep my family safe? "I want to feel safe again. I want the most stressful thing about my life to be that I have no idea how to do taxes."

"I suspect Lelit would be happy to give you that, if you asked her," the witch says. "So if that's what you want, go throw yourself at the regent queen's feet. I suspect you'll feel safe, happy, and never be troubled with another choice after that. Your family, as well." She studies my horrified face with a knowing expression, then sighs. "You had curiosity, once, even just a short time ago. You were so determined to know for the sake of knowing."

"Was I?" I ask. "Was that curiosity? Were those really my thoughts? Or was that something you put there to make sure I performed my function?" The witch says nothing. "Choosing to run seems like the only choice I know is really mine."

"Contrary for the sake of being contrary." The witch sips her wine. "As I said: boring." The hedges open up to reveal a small, secluded garden. "Ah, here," she says, stopping at the edge. The garden is full of flowers that ripple in the breeze. Not a breeze, I realize. They're moving on their own. The blooms quiver, shifting and pulling against their stems. Their forms shift, petals becoming wings, legs, hands, tendrils, eyes, mouths that whimper and whine. Some droop half-melted like molten glass.

One succeeds in breaking free, its petals becoming the wings of a butterfly, but it only makes it a few feet before it falls apart entirely, the wings losing form and dissolving into sludge when they hit the ground. The buzzing in my head grows in intensity, but doesn't become overwhelming.

The witch stares down at the struggling flowers. "Without her, Mab's realm is losing its form. One day, the entire Dreaming Court will be like this."

"Why does it need her? Why does everything fall apart without her?" As if to emphasize my question, another star veers off violently toward the horizon and vanishes from sight, perhaps falling to the ground somewhere far away.

"In the Dreaming Court, everything from the ground we walk on to the air we breathe receives its form and purpose from Mab. It's all tied to her Name. Without her, not even the vassals can hold the court together forever. Their authority is only whatever she deigned to give them." The witch kneels to free a wriggling flower stem from where it's planted, after which it inches away like a worm. "It's only small things so far. A sea not staying where it should, stars falling here and there, flowers that don't remember how to be flowers. I find it fascinating. A monarch has never completely abandoned their realm before, you see, so this gradual unraveling is a new process." She speaks with the morbid enthusiasm of an observer set apart from the chaos. "Soon, I imagine the fae that live here will have to seek refuge in a different court, or perhaps the mortal world."

"But *why*?" I repeat. "Who set it up like that in the first place? Did Mab do it on purpose? Why can't someone else just take it?"

The witch smiles ruefully. "Why, indeed? If you were Mab, would you not close off any loopholes that would allow another to steal what you've claimed?"

"But there's always an escape clause. You and Lelit had to write one into the prison. Mab had to have left one, or it wouldn't work."

The witch shrugs. "Mab took that knowledge with her."

"The other monarchs? If they did the same thing she did, they'd have to know how to undo it."

"And a vested interest in making sure no one else learns how." The witch stands and brushes off specks of invisible dirt from her dress. "But I suppose that isn't your problem, is it?"

"I can't do anything about it," I say. "I can't."

"No," the witch says. "Because you won't use your Name to bring it in line."

"I don't know Mab's Name." There's a pleading whine in my voice.

The witch eyes me pointedly. "If you won't hear it, that's by choice."

"Of course I don't want to hear it." Mab's Name. My Name. Everything that I am, contained in a single word. That's not something I ever want to know. It terrifies me, and the fact that I'm terrified shames me. The cycle repeats over and over again in my head. "It's hers, not mine. Hers. And I don't... I should stay away from everything of hers." I don't know if Mab is anywhere I can reach, and I'm too afraid to look. Too afraid of being swallowed up by her, of becoming nothing but a fleeting moment in her life.

"If that is how you feel, then this will be the last time we see each other." The witch closes her eyes for a moment. "It took time to arrange. After Mab came to me with her wish, I had to find the right opportunity. If she foresaw it, she might unconsciously interfere. Lelit and Noctiva took time to convince that they needed to imprison her, and that the prison must be built by someone outside the Dreaming Court. But they were so worried about Leithe's plan, they never saw mine. Everything went perfectly." She finishes the dregs of her wine. "So much effort, so many moving pieces, but not so many that I can't start over another time. Perhaps the mistake was hiding you with a human family; perhaps the next one I'll raise myself."

"'The next one'?" I take a step away from her.

"Why not?" she asks. "Do you think you'll last longer than Mab?"

"There's a gun pointed at your head," Skye says. "Do you know what a gun is?" Skye steps into view from behind the hedges lining the path, gun aimed at the base of the witch's skull. She looks angry but unharmed.

"... Yes," the witch says.

"There's two more of her around here somewhere," I say, biting back the many questions I have for Skye.

Skye gives me a quick glance before returning her attention to the witch, who hasn't moved. "Is this the one who took my son?"

"Yes," the witch says before I can answer.

"Where is he?" Skye asks.

"Somewhere else," the witch says.

"Turn around," Skye says.

The witch obeys, her expression almost amused. "Girl, what are you go—"

Skye shoots, the bullet flying into the hedges to the right of the witch's ear. "Answer the fucking question."

The witch looks closely at Skye, apparently fascinated by whatever she sees. "Do you not remember? Your child was born with his umbilical cord around his neck. He would have died before he lived had he not been brought to me, but a bit of breath for an infant is nothing to one of the Gentry. And in exchange for a dead son, I gave you a living daughter. It was your choice not to love her." Despite the words, her tone holds no bite.

Skye goes rigid with rage, so tense her hands shake. "It wasn't your right."

The witch almost appears sympathetic. "I'll take you to your son, if that's what you want." She glances at me. "You as well. Your whole troupe. Meet me at the palace gate and ask me there, and I'll take you wherever you want to go."

"Why?" I can't help but ask.

"My giving nature," the witch says. "That's my offer. You may take it or leave it."

Skye stares at the witch, wide-eyed, and then punches her in the mouth. The witch takes a step back, one hand clutching her face. When she pulls her hand away, she seems surprised to see blood.

Skye looks as surprised as the witch. Then she looks angry again. "That's *it*? You ruined my life, and it means so little to you can just give him back, just like that? Just because you feel like it now?"

The witch spits red into the dirt. "Yes," she says. "The palace gates. Strike me again and the offer is gone." Skye doesn't stop the witch from leaving the garden—she looks like she doesn't trust herself to move. As soon as the witch turns the corner, I don't need to look to know she won't be there if I try to follow.

Once the witch is gone, Skye deflates. Her shoulders slump; she rubs her eyes and laughs to herself. "Trap," she says. "If she actually wanted to help us, she could have just taken us now." She finally looks at me. "You okay?"

The question almost makes me cry with relief. Instead, I nod. "I thought you were stuck in a glamour somewhere."

She nods. "Hunter sold us out. After that building exploded, he told us we had to run before the guards arrived and said we'd look for you later. When he brought us through a side entrance to the palace, a woman who must've been Lelit was waiting. By the time I kicked the glamour she put me in, I was in this maze." She looks around. "Leithe?"

"Gone." I quickly catch her up. "How did you escape the glamour?"

"My gut. It just didn't feel right. That, and I have a lot more iron and clovers on me than that necklace you never gave back," she says wryly. "Still, this place is huge. Can't believe I found you as quickly as I did. Or at all." She stares at me, frowning.

"You're not still in a glamour," I say. "I swear." Though it *is* strange. "Maybe I brought you here. I wanted to find you, and Eifa told me how Gentry can alter their surroundings."

"Then can you bring Eifa and my mom here, too?"

"I'll try, but I don't—"

Skye cuts me off with a sharp gesture, and I catch the clatter of running feet on the path. She tries to wave me behind her as Eifa skids to a stop in front of the arch leading into our garden.

"Well," Skye says. "Good job, Tamsin."

"I did it?" Of the three of us, I seem the most surprised.

Eifa looks between the two of us. "Did what?"

"I brought you here," I say, awe in my voice.

Eifa seems confused. "An old woman told me I'd find you two down here."

Realization dawns. "Long hair, green dress?" Eifa nods. "The witch sent her to us."

"Why?" Skye asks. "I refuse to believe she's actually helping, so how does this screw us?"

"She gave up on me," I say. Some of the flowers have started wailing like infants. "She's letting us go." Skye looks unconvinced.

Eifa's nostrils flare; her head whips around to one of the other paths leading into this garden. She positions herself between the path and me and Skye, but I put a hand on her arm.

"Wait," I say, the unspoken details of the witch's offer laying themselves out. "I know who it is." At least I think I know who it is. I'll look very silly if I'm wrong.

But I'm not wrong. With a rustling of fabric against the dirt, Grandma steps into the garden.

# Chapter Thirty-Two

"Grandma." It's the only word I can manage. A thousand different things compete to get spoken and choke each other out in my throat. Skye looks the same, wearing a strangled expression.

Grandma walks into the garden, unharmed and strangely calm as she takes in her surroundings. Her gaze is alert, not muddled with glamour. She's wearing a pale pink gown with puffy capped sleeves and a full, bell-shaped skirt that brushes against the hedges on either side of the path.

Grandma looks between me and Skye and crosses her arms. If she's surprised to see Skye, she doesn't show it. "Explain." Her voice is very calm. The voice she'd use in public that meant my life would end the moment we got home. "Everything. Now."

"What ha—"

"No." She cuts me off. "I will not say another word until you"—She points at me—"and you"—She points at Skye—"tell me what in the *hell* is happening."

I start to speak, but Skye cuts me off. "Is she real?" Her question is directed at Eifa.

"She smells human," Eifa says. "Doesn't appear glamoured."

"Then let's go to the palace gate," I say. "Grandma, we can explain once we're home. There's someone willing to send us back to the mortal world; we just have to go meet her."

Part of me wonders why the witch would make us meet her at the gate if she planned to bring us all here. A knot of anxiety forms in the pit of my stomach. What's going to happen on the way to the gate? Is this just a joke? Dangling an escape in front of me before snatching it away?

"Explain fast, then." Grandma plants her feet and crosses her arms.

"Fine. Let's just get all of this out in the open now." Skye steps forward. "You want to know what's happening? *I told you years ago.*" Skye's voice is brittle. "I told you over and over again. All of it was true."

"I'm sorry," Grandma says. Skye looks like she's been punched in the gut. "If you're willing to tell me again, I'm ready to hear it."

Skye deflates for a moment, banishing the energy she'd been coiling up in preparation for a fight. Without the anger, face to face with Grandma, she looks so much younger.

In stilted words, Skye sums up twenty years in five minutes, covering in broad terms her search to find her son. Grandma's expression remains neutral as Skye explains what I am. It doesn't change when I take over and confirm, explaining what the witch did, about the prison, Leithe and Hunter, Mab's secrets. My voice breaks when I describe Zach's death and the existence of the fetch. Grandma raises her hands as if to cover her mouth as she listens, but forces them back down instead.

"I'm sorry," I say after I finish. "I've known I wasn't ... known I'd replaced ..." I can't find the words. "... known I was a changeling for a month now. But once we get out of here, once we find Skye's son, if he's still—" I cut that thought off. "Then I can go."

"You visited me at the hospital after I fell last month," Grandma says. I nod. "I thought it was a dream from the painkillers. That night, I dredged up memories I hadn't let myself think about for years." She looks at Skye, regret in her eyes. "I noticed the babies were different. Of course I noticed. How could I not? I knew you were right. But there was no explanation that made sense. I needed the thing that made sense to be real, and it was easier to think I'd been wrong and the thing in front of me now was right. And that hurt you."

Grandma turns back to me. "But, Tamsin, I remembered that conversation. I was waiting for you to be ready to bring it up on your own, but then you disappear in the middle of the night with—pardon me—bullshit excuses." She scowls. "I'm disappointed," she continues. I wilt. "In myself. That I made you think you couldn't tell me."

"It wasn't just that I was scared of what you might say." I say. "While you didn't know, other fae weren't supposed to be able to hurt you. We both thought telling you would put you in more danger."

"For all the good that did," Grandma says. "But did you—both of you—really think I'd rather be at home watching TV, no idea what's going on, when you're here, dealing with all this?"

"That was my impression," Skye says.

"I'd rather be here," Grandma says. "I'd rather know, even if it puts me in danger. I'm sorry I made you feel alone." She turns back to Skye, who is staring aggressively at the hedge over Grandma's shoulder. "That goes for you too. I'm sorry."

"Congratulations on being enlightened now. Should we hug?" Skye asks. "I'm gay, too, by the way, since we're sharing."

"That one," Grandma begins carefully, "I did have a feeling about. But thank you for telling me."

Skye digs through her pockets and makes a disgusted noise when she doesn't find any cigarettes. "You told me to be normal or leave, remember? That was the last conversation we had. I'm done talking about this. I can compartmentalize for another few hours. We have other things to worry about."

"Like what happened to you," I say.

"Well," Grandma says, "after you disappeared and wouldn't tell me what was going on, I waited. Then you came home. At least, I thought she was you at first. She looked like you. But there was something off. I had a bad feeling." Grandma frowns to herself. "My memory skips. I only have flashes. I was with the thing that looked like you, then I was in a room and a bunch of people with wings or other nonsense were doing my hair and putting me in this ridiculous dress. Then I was at this party. I wasn't fully in my right mind again until a little girl took my hand." Grandma hesitates before continuing. "She said she could either send me home right now, where I'd wake up in my bed and think this was a dream, or I could go down this path." The last of the witch's bodies.

"Did she tell you what you'd find down here?"

"No," Grandma says. "But I wanted to know, and I'm glad I did."

"Then ..." I look from Grandma to Skye, surprised to feel a sinking sensation in my chest. "Then we can go. We have what we came here for." Skye looks askance at me.

The garden path seems to twist and coil like a snake as if it doesn't want to let us go. There are more turns than I remember, enough dead-ends that I wonder if this is the trick, if the witch never intended for us to get out. But we do get out. The winding path spits us out onto the main avenue through the garden; to the right is the palace, and the left the gate. Ambient music and conversation floats through the air.

Nothing hinders us as we put our backs to the palace and make our way toward the gate. No traps. No ambushes. And still, I can't shake the feeling of walking toward my own execution instead of away from it.

I should go, but I stop in my tracks. *Just one more step, then another*, I tell myself. *This doesn't need to be hard.*

"Tamsin?" Grandma asks. Everyone has paused a few steps behind me, looking concerned.

"There's no other option," I say to myself more than anyone else. "This is the smart choice. I can go home, live my life. There's nothing I can do here. I can't fix anything." But I still feel sick.

"Then what's wrong?" Grandma asks.

"This is my out. The witch is giving us everything we came for." Grandma says nothing, only continues staring at me in a way I don't like. "I should be relieved. I should be happy. But I'm not. She got rid of my excuses. I don't need to keep going for anyone else's sake. But I still don't want to go." I look plaintively between Skye and Grandma. "But the wanting—it's not right. Because ..." I turn back to the palace gleaming stark against the twilight. "Is this what I bought with Zach's life? I can't want this."

"Tamsin," Grandma says, "it's not for anyone else to tell you what to do. But you can always come home, no matter what." She hesitates. "Well, maybe we'll need to find a different place to live, but we can do that." And I believe her. I could go home. I could leave now, we could run from Lelit and the Crawling King and anyone else forever, and she wouldn't judge me. Wouldn't hate me.

But I would hate myself. I'd find a reason to hate myself for going just as easily as staying because the hate is addictive, festering. Because neither path from this point will undo Zach's death.

"If I don't stay, things are going to keep falling apart," I say. "Like the ocean; like the stars falling out of the sky."

"And?" Skye asks. "What do you want me to say about it?"

"The fae that live here will go somewhere else," Eifa says with a shrug.

I don't need to stay. There's no excuse to hide behind. I *want* to stay. I want to see it finished. I'm just as bound to this as I was when my vow to Leithe threatened to kill me if I turned back.

"Go," I finally say. "All of you. The witch will be good to her word and send you wherever you want to go. I'm going to talk to Lelit. I'll catch up."

Skye glares at the palace gates, still a tiny line in the distance, something on her face that's almost fear, almost grief. "It's just another trick, anyway." She turns back to me. "I'm not leaving in the middle. We're going together or not at all." It's Martin's basement over again, Blackbower over again: it didn't matter who or what they were, Skye would have gone back until everyone was out or she was dead.

"Right now, we're all in Faerieland," Grandma says with no small amount of wonder, almost to the point of laughing at herself. "But I keep wondering if, the next time I wake up, I'll be alone in my house, and you never actually came back from Boston, and that these last few months have all been a dream."

"I wondered that for a long time. I still wonder that." Where would I be if I'd never gotten that call from Grandma, or if I'd chosen not to come? Still working at that fudge store? Or would I have moved on to the next in a string of jobs that blend together in my head as a blur with no beginning or end. All that to barely break even. All that to stay in one place.

For a moment, I can't even remember why I'd chosen Boston. It was far away; it let me run away from school, because staying was like trying to answer a question I hadn't even yet been able to ask myself: what did I want? Why was I here?

"It might be simpler," I say. "We'd all be safer."

"I might also be dead," Grandma says. "I was in the early stages of ALS. Or am, I guess. The prognosis was less than two years." She pauses, frowning. "ALS isn't supposed to get better. But since last month, I've felt stronger than I have in decades. My doctor thinks I've just been lucky so far, and worsening is inevitable. But I know you did something—something you wouldn't have been able to do without us ending up right here." I don't need to confirm it. She already told me she remembers that night in the hospital. "I'm not leaving you alone," Grandma finishes. "Either of you."

"It's dangerous," I argue. "You can all die. I can't, not really."

"We're all in danger anyway," Skye says. "Neither of us are innocent anymore, so the fae don't even need to find an excuse to hurt us. It's open season."

"Seems like we've all made up our minds, then," Grandma says.

"I … thank you." It's not enough, yet there's nothing else to say. The witch didn't need to place any obstacles in our path. This was the trap, the point of making me retrace my steps: to give me time to regret it. The petty urge rises in me to leave simply to spite her, but this time I recognize that feeling for what it is: a reflex to avoid looking inward.

"So," Grandma says. "What's the plan?"

"I'm going to talk to Lelit," I repeat.

"Is talking a euphemism for something else?" Grandma asks, confused. "Are we fighting her?"

I shake my head. "She lost her friend, didn't she? At the bare minimum, she deserves to hear what happened."

Skye frowns. "Tamsin, who gives a shit? She locked Leithe in a tree. And you. And kidnapped my mother. And tried to kill us with a giant plant."

I have no counter, aside from a feeling in my gut. "I said you don't have to come."

"Fine," Skye says. "Lead on."

For better or worse, I lead the way toward the palace. Eventually, I notice we've gained a following—other partygoers trail us at a cautious distance, scuttling off elsewhere if they notice me looking.

No one obstructs our way, and soon we're crossing an expansive courtyard sprawling out before a grand marble staircase, the massive twin doors to the palace yawning open at the top.

Roses grow violently from a flower bed in the middle of the courtyard, choking out the other plants and spilling vines like grasping fingers over the lip of the bed and across the pale marble. Another symbol Lelit left for me to see.

The stairs are just too wide for a single step. By the time I reach the top, the garden seems even farther away than it should be.

The doors frame an entrance hall containing two snake-like staircases that curve up to join at a balcony on the level above. A chandelier of crystal-encased candles casts dancing light over the hall; a mosaic of tiny, angled mirrors covering the dome-shaped ceiling amplifies the light and casts back fractured reflections of the people below.

Others funnel in alongside us, mostly couples locked arm in arm. With each step, the sounds of music, conversation, and laughter grow louder, accompanied by the swishing of fabric and clinking of glassware. Most keep their distance; those that do get too close are politely but firmly blocked by Eifa.

The guests pass beneath the double staircase and into the chamber beyond, so we follow. That takes us to a staircase down into a massive ballroom, ceiling open to the stars. Skinny, humanoid things with bat-like wings perch along the edges of the open ceiling, watching the festivities below and sometimes swooping down to snatch food off a table.

Most of the room is an open dance floor populated with spinning couples. Other guests gather in clusters around the edges, drinking from crystal goblets and laughing amongst themselves. The long edges of the room are barely walls, only a series of arches that lead to other dimly-lit, flower-filled courtyards. The effect is like being in the skeleton of a room. It makes me feel uncomfortably exposed.

Lelit sits on a throne at the far end of the room upon a raised dais—too far for me to see clearly, yet somehow perfectly visible. The throne is a lopsided monstrosity grown of white marble and dripping like melted wax; tendrils of Lelit's roses curl possessively around it. A pale clock face—blank save for a '12' etched in gold at the top—is set into the throne's high back, which arches and looms forebodingly over the seat like a great barn owl. The hands read just past eleven. Lelit's head snaps to attention when I enter. She glances at the others beside me and gives me an enigmatic smile.

When I reach the bottom of the stairs, I travel as close to the wall as I can get, ignoring other guests until one blocks our path. The red-haired man doesn't lower his gaze when I look at him. His eyes are slit-pupiled and fiery orange-brown and his suit is a century-and-a-half out of date in the mortal world. On the surface, he appears human, but his reflection in the wineglass in his hand has the head of a pumpkin-colored cat. As the glass shifts in his grasp, for a split-second the reflection becomes a cat taller than me at the shoulder, and then back to a nearly-human-looking man. He's enormous; not as tall as Leithe but wider at the shoulders.

The man barely glances at Eifa as she moves to intercept him, and I become keenly aware of two things: he could kill her with hardly any effort, and though she probably knows that, she'll defend me anyway.

"Eifa," I say. "It's fine." She hangs back, wary.

"Your Grace." The man's voice is a baritone with a hint of a growl. Almost too appropriate for a cat. In other circumstances I could giggle at the thought. He bows—the motion more cursory than the others—and meets my eyes with no fear, only curiosity. He holds his hand out for mine and when I place my hand over his he brings it to the air just below his lips and holds it just too long to be comfortable. Claws press into my palm through his white gloves. "It's been far too long." The fabric of his suit doesn't hide the powerful muscle beneath. Even in a human form, he gives the impression of a feline resting low on his haunches, intent and ready to pounce.

"Far too long," I echo. "In fact, who are you again?"

To my disappointment, he only laughs. "Have some mercy, I beg you. I would have visited had I been able to pry your location from Lelit's lips." He doesn't use Lelit's title. I can't imagine anyone who wasn't Gentry would approach me with this much confidence. This must be the King of Cats. "Please humor me long enough for a dance." He hasn't let go of my hand, and I feel like I'd be losing a competition if I pulled it away.

An idea. I glance at Lelit, whose smile is frozen on her face, eyes burning a hole into the back of the King of Cats' head. Making her think I have other allies might keep me safer. "Why not?" I turn to the others. "I'll meet you after."

He leads me onto the dance floor and places his other hand around my waist. I lose sight of Grandma and the others when the space around us becomes a blur of colors and bodies.

# Chapter Thirty-Three

THE MOMENT I TAKE my first step on the dance floor, the music takes over, guiding each movement as if it's a pair of hands on my shoulders, fixing the angle of my arm here, nudging my foot a little to the left there. I wonder if anyone out here actually knows the moves.

"Are you enjoying the ball?" I ask. I can't see Lelit, but given Noctiva's suspicions, I doubt she'll want me talking to any of Mab's other vassals.

"Immensely," the King of Cats says. The music creates a bubble, making it easy to speak without being overheard. Despite that, he leans down to speak into my ear, pulling me closer to him than I'd like to be. "Forgive me for asking, but what reason could your betrothed possibly have for leaving you alone at a ball in your honor?"

I fight the urge to roll my eyes. "Do you think I need him?" I try to keep the words light, flippant, but I can't help but feel a spike of anxiety. Maybe this wasn't worth making a point to Lelit.

"I'd never say such a thing, Your Grace." His mouth forms the words like it's closing around the spine of some small animal; immediately, I realize that my expression or tone must have given something away. "But it's a matter of respect, is it not?"

"Whose respect?" I ask. "Yours?"

"Apologies if I've offended you." He sounds appropriately contrite, but doesn't answer the question. "I've never known Your Grace to need anyone. Though I know it's presumptuous for me to even suggest, I only wanted to say that if there's any assistance I could possibly offer you ..."

"What is there that I could possibly want assistance with?" I ask innocently.

"There've been rumors, though probably of no worth to you," he says. "But my servants are adept at traveling unnoticed. They've heard things."

"Oh?" I try to sound uninterested even though I want to shake him by the scruff and tell him to just spit it out.

"Well, Your Grace." He pauses, apparently relishing the anticipation. "As outlandish as it sounds, some have been whispering that the 'sabbatical' as Lelit claimed you and your betrothed were taking may not have been ... voluntary. Even more outrageously, some dare suggest that Lelit might be resistant to giving you back your throne." He leaves the most dangerous questions unsaid but obvious. *Are you weak? Are you broken?*

"And what do you think?"

"I've heard that—"

"What do *you* think?" I repeat with greater force.

He frowns, my directness temporarily throwing off his vaguely smug expression. Apparently, the expression isn't unique to Leithe. "I think, whether or not there's any truth to these rumors, I would consider it an honor to aid Your Grace should you have the need or inclination."

"And in exchange, you'd just want one little favor?" I ask. The current song ends with a trilling flourish and a new one begins, this one faster paced.

"No," He seems to grow comfortable, adjusting to the new pace of our exchange. "I want quite a big favor. The regent queen has had over a century on your throne to cement her power while you've been gone. Removing her would be a challenge for anyone less than Your Grace, though of course it would be beneath you to squabble with your own vassal in such a manner."

"Of course," I repeat with little enthusiasm.

"And forgive me if I'm wrong," he continues. "But I suspect your betrothal to the Crawling Court traitor has ended, and I think if you were able to tell me that's untrue, you'd do so now, so you don't need to say anything."

"If it has?" The words come out more biting than I intend, only emphasizing how cornered I suddenly feel.

"If it has, then I would like to put myself forward as consort instead. All I ask is that you announce our engagement tonight. The final details of our vows can be left for a later time. I heard you intended to exchange Names with the Crawling Court exile, but I would not demand that." He smiles magnanimously, clearly impressed with his own offer.

"... I'll think about it." Something tells me not to refuse him outright.

"Of course. If you make no announcement, I'll assume you neither need nor want any aid," he says. A chill prickles my spine. He knows—or at least suspects enough to risk this conversation. And given how cautious Mab's subjects seem to be of her, that's quite a risk indeed.

"Yeah," I say. "I—" *I get it.*

"Pardon me, Your Grace." Hunter steps into our path, interrupting our dance. Pulling myself out of step is a sensation like peeling myself off a strip of flypaper as I fight the call of the music.

The King of Cats bears his teeth; they're more slender than a human's, and sharper. I push away and position myself between him and Hunter. "I'll think about your offer," I say, just as much for his benefit as Hunter's—and Lelit's by extension. I turn away from the King of Cats, hoping he gets the message that he's been dismissed. "What does Lelit want?"

"To speak with you, Your Grace," Hunter says.

I have to remind myself that this is what I wanted. "Lead the way."

I don't look back to see if the King of Cats is watching us go. My attention is on the rest of the crowd as they scramble to get out of my way while preserving their dignity. I don't catch sight of Grandma and the others until Skye pushes another guest to the side and grabs my sleeve.

"Tamsin," she says. "Don't look her in the eye." Then she steps back, melting back into the crowd.

"Does Lelit have a problem with me talking to the other guests?" I ask Hunter.

"You already know." He opens his mouth; closes it again. "You found what you were looking for. You could have left."

"And then what?" I ask. It's an echo of a conversation I think I once had with Leithe.

Hunter doesn't have an answer.

"Where is Leithe?" he asks.

"You mean you haven't been watching?" I ask. "The King of Cats has, apparently. Leithe is gone. I cut him loose." There are many things I could say to Hunter, things I know will hurt him but change nothing. I bury that impulse, but the memory of Noctiva's hall of mirrors rises to the surface instead. I don't know if we'll ever get the chance to speak again.

"I didn't know you blamed yourself for Zach," I say.

He takes a moment to speak. "How could I not? It was my choice not to chase the two of you away when I should have; my choice to set my oath aside."

"I don't think it was ever up to either of us," I say. And as I say it, I realize I believe it. However much I've blamed myself—relived that night over and over again, dreaming of what I'd say to a boy I can only remember in flashes—Hunter's been carrying for years what I've carried for a month. Only when it's the blame someone else chooses to bear do I see what a useless weight it is.

"I can't apologize to you," Hunter says. "We're here because I ignored my duty—to Lady Lelit, to my children. I won't make the same mistake again."

I catch the gaze of a guest with a rose growing from one of her eye sockets and stare her down until she retreats out of our path. "Do you want me to tell you 'it's okay, I understand'?" I ask Hunter. "Because it's okay, I understand. You never lied to me. You can't. I just wanted to believe there was a way to save us both. It's a habit. I've been trying to save you for years. That's why I went into the prison the second time. Did you know that?"

"Yes," Hunter says. "That's why I hoped you would never come back. But ... thank you." The crowd this close to the throne is denser, but the other fae go out of their way to avoid us like a school of fish around a barracuda. "Do you remember the first time we met?"

"You saved me and Zach from a horde of zombie sprites?"

"No," he says. "Before that. You must have only recently started walking. I found you alone in the woods. I thought I'd been tracking another faerie—probably whatever had led you out there that then fled. The dogs followed your trail back to your grandmother's home. She'd fallen asleep on a porch chair—also planned, I suspect. When she woke, she had no idea you'd been gone. After that, I found myself closer to your home more often than I should have."

"You were there in the places Grandma couldn't be," I say. "When I was younger, I didn't understand what my feelings were. I've had time to figure it out." I don't say the words. He knows what they are. Instead I say, "You saved me so many times. I just wanted to pay you back."

"I never wanted you to do that," Hunter says.

I can't help but laugh. "I know."

We halt before the throne, where Lelit sits, tapping her nails against the marble. As if on cue, the music swells, approaching a crescendo, then cuts off unceremoniously, bathing the ballroom in sudden silence. Conversations continue for a few more moments, but even those peter off as guests look around in confusion and curiosity.

"Her Grace, Queen Mab," Hunter says, voice resonating in the newfound silence. He bows to Lelit before melting into the crowd. It feels like a final goodbye, and I feel strangely at peace; I have no anger for him. What choice would I have made in his place?

Lelit as she appeared in the mortal world might as well have been a washed-out photograph. Her hair looks like spun gold; the serpent resting across her shoulders shimmers as if cut from gemstones. Sheer power radiates from her skin, from her gaze, a pressure in the air so heavy I struggle to comprehend why everyone in the room isn't already on their knees. Her eyes bore into me, the green growing deeper and darker the longer I look, until I become aware of a gnawing hole in my chest. It hurts so bad that I can barely breathe.

*Don't look her in the eye.* Skye's warning to me.

I drag my eyes away; it's so painful I almost whimper. The weight of the glamour Lelit exudes lightens but doesn't go away entirely. My chest still feels empty, like I'm missing something I never had.

The entire ballroom room has become a bubble of tension as the gathered fae look between me and Lelit—at me on the ground and Lelit on my throne. No one is dancing; everyone is pressing closer until a semicircular wall of bodies encloses us, near-palpable anticipation radiating from the mass. This is what they came to witness. And not a single one of them, I realize, wants this to end cleanly.

Lelit reclines on the throne with one leg crossed over the other, spine at a slight, condescending slouch. The emerald serpent draped across her shoulders ripples with muscle as it turns its head to regard me. Instead of looking at Lelit, I look at the far wall to the left of the throne, but I can tell she's looking at me with the full force of her gaze, calling me to meet it.

That emptiness I felt when I first looked at her—that undefinable need—only intensifies, chewing away at my insides, with each step I take. But I take another step, and another, until I'm standing at the base of the tiered stone dais.

Lelit rests her chin in her hand, head tilted back to be sure it's obvious to everyone that she's looking down on me, expression a mix of mild amusement and self-satisfaction. The room holds its breath, leaving the only sound the ceaseless ticking of the clock peering down from the back of the throne.

This close, I can't avoid looking at her. But instead of looking her in the eye, I focus on the gold cuffs around her ears. She's barely wearing any clothes, just a translucent wrap around her hips. Her chest is bare save for a necklace of several loops of crystalized roses that intertwine and fall between her breasts before wrapping around her waist. More flowers twine through her hair.

"Welcome home, Your Grace," Lelit says.

"We need to talk," I say.

Instead of answering, Lelit rises from the throne and stalks down the dais until she's standing on the first step, making her a little taller than me. She takes my face in her hands—her skin is searing hot against mine. Her eyes catch mine despite my best efforts; at first, they're as deep a green as the scales of her snake, then they grow darker and darker, until they're bottomless, empty voids. They take everything, including the urge I'd had to pull Lelit's hands off me. The room might as well be empty save for us.

Before I can say another word, she kisses me and I'm thrown off my feet and falling, my vision tunneling until her eyes are the only thing I can see. Her lips burn—with either cold or heat, I can't tell. They burn away everything, leaving behind only cold tear trails down my cheeks.

# Chapter Thirty-Four

MORNING SUNLIGHT STREAMS THROUGH my bedroom window, dappled into softness by the shadows of tree branches. Remnants of my dream scatter in the light, leaving behind only a vague sense of unease.

It would be nice to sleep longer, even though it's a work day and my alarm will go off any second. Instead of waiting for the inevitable screeching, I get up and pad down the stairs. When I catch sight of my rainbow cloud pajamas in the bedroom mirror, for a second I wonder why they're not covered in dirt and blood. My hair falls evenly to my shoulders. For a long, strange moment, I imagine it shorter.

Grandma is on the couch, watching TV and sipping her coffee. "You're not even dressed yet?" she asks. "You're going to be late."

It takes me until I finish pouring myself a cup of coffee to remember. "For my job."

"What else?" Grandma asks. "You have any dates lined up you haven't told me about?" Instead of waiting for an answer, she continues. "Your mother's coming over for dinner tonight. We're in charge of the food, because I'm not letting that girl bring over another bucket of gas station fried chicken and call it a meal." Skye. My mother.

Those two things don't want to go together in my head. I mull the thought over, turning it this way and that like a puzzle piece that refuses to fit.

All the while, Grandma studies me. "Are you okay?"

My head throbs. Memories fight to reassert themselves. The events of the past month. I moved back here from Boston because Grandma was sick. And then ... what?

Grandma is suddenly standing in front of me, pressing her hand to my forehead. "Do you need to call in sick?"

"No," I say quickly. "I mean—is this real?"

"Wait here." Grandma leaves and returns with an orange prescription pill bottle and holds it out to me. "Did you take your meds today?"

"No." I take it numbly, unscrewing the lid and dumping two little white ovals into my palm. How did I get here? "The ball," I say with uncertainty. "Do you remember the ball?"

"No, honey." The question seems to sadden her. "Do you want to tell me about it?" she asks, as if indulging a child. What was I doing before I was here?

This must be a trick. A trick by ... the name won't come. Names scatter the more I try to focus on them. "Leithe," I say, recollection returning as soon as I say the name out loud. "Eifa. Do you remember them?"

Grandma looks scared now. Not of me, but for me. "Do you want me to see if Doctor Webster has anything open today?" It pains me more than I thought it would, to think we'd finally bridged a gap, only to find it firmly back in place.

In a burst of desperate energy, I throw my coffee cup on the floor. Instead of shattering dramatically, it only breaks into a few large pieces. Coffee splatters against my bare feet and calves. I don't know what I expected. Proof?

Grandma backs away, hands up in a placating gesture. "Tamsin, why don't we sit down. I'll pour you something to drink and you can take your pills."

My pills. I look down at the bottle in my hand. The label is blank. "Grandma," I ask slowly. "Where do I work?"

Grandma cocks her head, her fear discarded. "Wherever you'd like, I suppose."

"It's not real," I say, now with an overwhelming sense of relief. "It's Lelit's trick." The name springs back into my mind like a rubber band returning to shape. I need to get out of here. I cross the room to the front door and throw it open, hoping to see a way out of this false world, but instead I see Zach, the way his fetch looked as an adult, arm raised and about to knock.

He offers me a crooked smile as he steps inside, forcing me to take a step back. "You could just take the pills," he says. "That would be giving your consent. Then you could start over, wake up again, and live whatever dream you like." I imagine it: sitting on the couch under a blanket while Grandma sits in her armchair, watching rom-coms and listening to her vehemently lecture me about such films setting unrealistic expectations for relationships. The memory of some silly weekend morning floods my senses and I feel my eyes get wet.

I drop the pills on the ground. "No." Grandma crumbles into white rose petals that disintegrate to dust before they touch the floor.

Zach takes another step forward. "I can bring the humans in here with you. Even my hunter, if you like. Your bodies can slumber safely in the Dreaming Court where no one can touch them. Whatever life you want, you can have. Did you want this boy to love you? Marry you?"

"I think I lost the chance to ever figure that out, Lelit," I say. The room changes, becomes strangely flat, bereft of substance.

Lelit smiles with Zach's mouth. "This is a pretty little dream, and it would have held you if it were really what you wanted, or thought you deserved."

"And what do I want?" I ask.

"Many things. Conflicting things," she says. "Wants you haven't even been able to name. You're so ... different. I didn't think it would be true until I saw you in the flesh. It's your body, yes, but you really are like an entirely different person." There's a pause as she studies me, her smile becoming a frown that creates a slight crease between her brows. "It's been so long. Do you have nothing to say to me?"

"I know who you are," I point out. "I've seen the trick. You don't need to still look like Zach."

"Why not?" she asks. "I thought it might make you more comfortable to see something familiar. This is, after all, how I've looked almost every other time we've spoken."

"What are you talking about?" I ask. Dread sets in—a collection of horrible puzzle pieces I'm on the cusp of fitting together.

Lelit watches me; her sneer on Zach's face makes me want to vomit. She waits, expectant, and in her silence, the final pieces click into place.

"No," I say. "That's ... You can't ..." She can't have gotten into my head, into my dreams? Isn't that where we are right now?

"When you didn't return to us after you freed yourself from the prison, I looked for you from here, through your dreams. When I finally found the right door, I thought you'd want to see me." Lelit studies her reflection in the window. "But you didn't. You wanted to see this." She presses her hand against her chest, Zach's chest. "So this is the form I took. And you told me everything. All your secrets, your wants, your fears. You told me you wished for the human you call grandmother to be safe, so I brought her to Faerie. You don't want to rule, so I'll do it for you."

"You used Zach's face to torment me," I say.

"The dead are the perfect tools of self-delusion," Lelit says. "You pretend to hear their voices in your dreams, in your heart, but their words are your words; their wants, your wants. I used this face to give you what you desired at your core: to feel punished. To pretend there was a purpose to your pain." Her expression suddenly turns pitying. "And wasn't that a mercy? Because no matter how hard you *want*, you'll never wring absolution from the dead. They have nothing to give you." I accepted everything she'd ever said to me with Zach's face because it's what I thought I deserved. Because the pain meant he was still there.

For a moment I want to throttle her, shake her until she abandons Zach's form. But instead I take a breath and exhale slowly. Plotting out the words I've been mulling over since I arrived. "I've been terrified of you." Something flashes in Lelit's stolen eyes. Pride. Displeasure. I can't tell. "Leithe told me about all the terrible things you'd do to me. He hasn't been wrong that often, but I wanted to talk to you anyway, because he didn't know everything. I didn't tell him the truth about Mab until a little while ago. So I wanted to say that I'm sorry you lost your friend."

Lelit waits as if expecting me to continue, then frowns. "You're ... 'sorry'?"

"Yes," I say. "You must feel like she left you here. I lost a friend, too. You already know that. You already know how much it hurt me. I know that pain isn't going to just go away, but taking it out on other people—or on yourself—isn't going to change things that have already happened." The words are so much easier to say to someone else than to myself.

Lelit raises an eyebrow. "So what?"

"So I'm saying I have no interest in getting back at you. Leithe said you wouldn't leave me alone because you'll always consider me a threat, but you can keep the throne for all I care. I'll tell everyone you're ruling with my blessing. That will give you the legitimacy that you need. And in exchange, you leave me alone. Give me guards if you're concerned about something happening to me, but otherwise don't interfere with my life."

Lelit taps her nails against the kitchen counter in contemplation. They click like talons. "That's ... it?"

"That's it. We can both get what we want. You can win. I can leave," I say.

"Leave," Lelit echoes dully.

"Isn't that what you want?"

"*What I want?*" Lelit's sudden shriek tears through the glamour that makes up this space. Zach's face splinters and sloughs away, revealing Lelit's form beneath. The kitchen counter splits where she drives her nails through the laminate, sending cracks spiderwebbing through the floor and up the walls. "You think *that* is what I want?" She takes a step toward me, face contorted and eyes burning with sudden rage; I take a step back.

"What *do* you want?" I ask.

"Anything!" My confusion only seems to enrage Lelit more. Her hand snaps out and snatches my wrist. "This is not about what *I* want. This has always—always—been about what you want. I betrayed you on the eve of your wedding, imprisoned you, and spent the last century sitting on your throne while your vassals fought like dogs and the court fell apart around their ears. I took your humans hostage and tormented you with the memory of your dead friend. I let my hunter betray you of his own free will. What else do I need to take from you? I'll accept anything from you, save apathy. I've had enough of it. Hate me. Punish me. But feel something. *Do* something." Her expression is furious. And desperate.

"You did all of this just to make her angry?" I yank my arm out of her grip.

"To make *you* angry," Lelit snarls. "I had to do something that would force you to come back to us, even—especially—if it would enrage you. Damn the memories. I know the feel of your mind, and it's no different than when you sat on that throne."

"No," I say, getting some sense of perverse enjoyment at the dark rage in her eyes. "I'm not going to play. I'm going home. And you're going to let me, because if you don't, I'll blow us both up. You only have the throne because the other vassals think you're holding it for me. Stop me from leaving, and I'll tell everyone here that whoever kills you first gets the throne. You can tell them I'm powerless if you want, but that won't stop them coming for you, too. It'll be a bloodbath."

A cold smile forms on Lelit's lips. "You're forgetting the promise that you made me."

"I didn't make you a—" But the memory comes back of a promise made in a dream to what I thought was a figment of my imagination. "That wasn't real."

"You should know that's not true. You should mind your words more carefully." The promise tugs like a fish-hook buried in my chest. I know she's not wrong. "You promised me anything and swore on everything you have." Lelit's rage is gone as quickly as it came, replaced by something almost kind. "So when the clock strikes twelve, you will give me your Name before the entire court. You will stay here where you'll be safe from both the other courts and your own vassals, and I will rule on your behalf. I love you. Everyone in the court loves you, but I loved you before the Dreaming Court was even born. And you loved this court once. And that is why I won't let you cast aside what you've built, why I will hold your Name for you.

"I'll even give you this." She gestures to the space around us. The cracks in the walls and floor begin knitting themselves together. "Or whatever other illusion you want. I'll give you your humans. Even my hunter, if you'd like him to keep you company. But I won't let *anyone* else have the court. I'll keep it for you. I don't care what I have to do—it will stay Mab's. You will know nothing but happiness, more than you thought you deserve, no?"

I suddenly feel giddy, so much that I laugh out loud.

Lelit's passion becomes confusion, with a hint of wariness. "You find this amusing?"

"Yes," I say. "Because you lost. You lost and Mab won, and you just haven't realized it. She and the witch tricked you. I don't have my Name," I say with a laugh. "I don't know it, so I can't give it to you. You wasted your promise. So my original offer stands. You're going to let me leave. If you don't, I'll make sure everyone knows how far Mab's fallen. How much do you care about protecting her legacy?"

The house shakes. For a moment, I think Lelit might strike me. She looks angry enough to kill. "Do you want to gamble?" she asks. "How much do you want to protect your humans? When I'm through with them, they won't even remember their own names, but they'll know you're to blame for their fates."

I force myself to look unbothered by the threat. "You didn't answer the question."

Lelit is quiet for a moment, then she smirks. There's an angry desperation in the expression. "The illusion of your power is the only thing protecting your humans—not from me, but from everyone else in the palace. That illusion is, at the moment, quite delicate. Enjoy the ball, Your Grace. You have a bit more time to reconsider my offer."

The walls of Grandma's house suddenly shatter outward like broken glass, leaving us back in the ballroom. Lelit's hands still cup my face and her own face is only a few inches from mine. Our entire conversation took place in the span of a few moments after she kissed me.

Lelit takes a step back and claps her hands. "Music!" Immediately, the music picks up where it left off. Our audience returns to their own conversations. Lelit climbs the dais and seats herself on the throne, our conversation over.

*Tick*, goes the clock.

# Chapter Thirty-Five

"I thought you wanted to talk to her," Skye says when I retreat from the throne. The onlookers watch and murmur to themselves, not bothering to hide the disappointment on their faces.

"I did," I say, feeling numb aside from dull, pointless anger that has nowhere to go. "We should go. She won't stop us from leaving." I hope.

She doesn't stop us from leaving. As we cross the ballroom, no one stops us.

One step, then another. And then we're out of the ballroom, through the entrance hall, and at the exit, standing on the lip of the staircase leading down into the garden. From there, it's a straight line to the gate where the witch waits.

I have what I came here for. The hard part is over. All that's left is to go home. To wake up tomorrow morning in a place so far removed from all of this I'll wonder if any of it really happened. And should be happy that it's over, I remind myself. Happy to be done. No matter that each step away makes me feel emptier than the last, this is what needs to happen. There's nothing for me here. Nothing I should want.

The palace gate seems farther away than it was moments ago.

If everything goes right, I'll never see this again, so I can't help but turn back, take one last look. And when I do, I see Leithe standing before the throne, a number of other fae gathering around him—the King of Cats and others I don't recognize. Lelit glares down at him in annoyance, Hunter alert by her side. I can't hear what he's saying, but judging by his audiences' wary and even predatory expressions, it isn't pleasant.

"What is he doing?" I ask, more to myself than anyone else. Even at this distance, I can tell Lelit's eyes are burning the way they do moments before she erupts. She leans forward, nails digging into the arm of the throne. "I think they're going to kill him." A rumble goes through the crowd gathering to watch, punctuated by laughs and a few eager shouts.

I remember the words I said to him. I'm not sure who abandoned whom first. I don't know where the score sits. But it doesn't matter. If I leave now, I'll have nightmares about this moment for the rest of my life. "You should leave," I say to Skye. I know what the answer would be even before Skye speaks, but saying the words is a reflex.

"Fuck off with that," Skye says curtly, her hand lingering near her gun, eyes on Leithe. From her expression, she's just as reluctant to leave him. Grandma looks just as resolute. Either all of us leave, or none of us.

We creep around the crowd and along the wall, close enough to catch what's being said. The crowd is too preoccupied with the show to notice me.

"... bit ... colorful, don't you think?" Leithe picks a goblet off the tray of a mesmerized servant and makes a show of judging the contents. "But then again, I wouldn't expect the Dreaming Court to value taste over spectacle." He glances at one of the onlookers—a woman with eight dark eyes and a dress of cobwebs. "Don't you agree?" The woman looks to Lelit for guidance. What is he *doing*?

Lelit tenses like a cat about to strike, her nails clicking harsh and staccato against the marble throne. Hunter looks to her for orders, but she closes her eyes; the violence gone when they reopen. Instead, she smiles indulgently. "If you're not enjoying yourself, you're welcome to leave." She leans back against the throne, at ease once more. "Perhaps someone *else* would volunteer to listen to your complaints somewhere far away from here?"

The King of Cats takes a step forward. Leithe notes it and smiles. "Fine, fine. I can tell when I'm not wanted." He half-turns to leave, placing the untouched goblet in the King of Cats' unexpecting hands. "I just thought you'd find it funny. I know I did." He smiles wider, his eyes on the King of Cats and the others surrounding him, but his words for Lelit. "You see, the entire time Mab's been gone, the entire time Lelit's been on that throne, ruling in the queen's name—"

Leithe's voice cuts off as Lelit's hand curls around his throat. She moves faster than I can track, clearing the dais and the rest of the space between herself and Leithe in a blur. Beads of dark blood well up where her nails dig into his skin. The snake around her shoulders travels down her outstretched arm, stopping dangerously close to Leithe's face. Leithe returns her snarl with a smile, looking as smug as he ever has.

"You're not Dreaming Court; you've been banished from the Crawling Court. You might as well be courtless." Lelit looks out over the crowd, raising her voice. "Yet you have the audacity to show your face here, drink our wine, eat from our tables, and throw insults at our queen. There's a debt that must be paid." With a smile, Lelit pauses to allow the crowd to work itself up. "And it will be taken in blood. The Dreaming Court demands no less. Shall I take your obnoxious tongue first?" By the frenetic energy rippling through the room, something like this is exactly what the guests were hoping to see. They'll accept any excuse Lelit gives them to proceed with this show. All except the King of Cats, who frowns quizzically at Lelit's display, wondering, no doubt, why she's so desperate to keep Leithe from speaking.

Leithe can't speak, so he only stares at Lelit with cool defiance. He doesn't seem worried, but then again, he'd never show it if he was.

"He's a guest," I say, pushing forward until I clear the crowd. "And this isn't very hospitable, Lelit."

Leithe's eyes widen in surprise when they fall on me, then they narrow. He gives me the slightest shake of his head. Whatever his plan is, that was the wrong move, but now the crowd's eyes are on me.

"I see no invitation, Your Grace," Lelit says. "Please don't trouble yourself with this trespasser. I am happy to deal with it." *Don't challenge me*, she means. *Don't you dare shatter the illusion.* Skye and Grandma are behind me; Lelit already made clear what would happen to them if the truth got out.

"Let him go," I say. "Now." And the gauntlet is thrown. It's done. If she refuses, the illusion of my authority is gone.

Lelit stares at me, the tempestuous rage behind her eyes threatening to bubble over. But before she can give her answer, a wave of commotion radiates toward us from the entrance. Shouts and other, more inhuman sounds of alarm and violence get louder as partygoers retreat from the entrance hall into the ballroom, some with weapons drawn or bodies partially transformed to reveal teeth, claws, or other, stranger features. The crowd around us turns to watch, suddenly still and eerily silent, eyes trained toward the entrance like bloodhounds scenting prey. Or another predator.

The temperature of the ballroom plummets as the agitated crowd reluctantly parts to let a procession through, at the head of which walks Nevain. He offers a taunting smile to the room. His eyes narrow only slightly when they fall on me, and he quickly shifts his gaze to Lelit, still with her hand around Leithe's throat.

"I see you couldn't wait to start spilling Crawling Court blood, Lelit," Nevain says. "I mean, it's not even midnight." Leithe, out of everyone, looks the least surprised. He knew Nevain was coming.

The fae behind Nevain share his hard-edges and hungry eyes. Some are the solid, vampiric creatures that were with him in that bar in the mortal world, while others are hazy at the edges, hair floating as if underwater. Some, given their icy calm demeanors, may even be other Gentry. My throat gets dry. On this knife's edge, I realize how naive my blustering challenge to Lelit just minutes ago really was.

"You and the Crawling Court were not invited to this ball, Lord Nevain," Lelit says.

"Oh?" Nevain says, looking unsurprised. "But I have my invitation here." He brandishes the little scroll of paper

Leithe casually discarded on the floor of the bar days ago as he saunters down the middle of the room, a path clearing for him as if the other fae are afraid to be within his reach. "Not that it matters." He throws the invitation over his shoulder. "You people are all so violent, so now instead of enjoying the party, I have to work." Nevain smiles at me as if we're sharing a secret. Anger simmers in the pit of my stomach. This close, I can see a milky knot of unhealed tissue near the edge of his iris where I stabbed him with a fork. "Queen Mab, on behalf of my king, I demand restitution. Your court took and damaged one of his." His gaze falls on Leithe, mouth curling in distaste. "The Crawling King wants Leithe returned, and he wants one of you turned over to him. Either the one who spilled the blood, or you, Your Grace, for allowing it. My king leaves the choice to you." It finally comes together in my head. This is what Leithe was setting up.

Lelit laughs. "This man is a traitor and an exile. Your king banished him."

"And it's my king's right to welcome him back when he pleases," Nevain says.

*Take Lelit*. The words would be easy. And would leave me nowhere but with a different pack of monsters breathing down my neck.

But Lelit makes no move to comply. "If your king wants restitution, he can come here and demand it himself," she says. "Instead, he insults us by sending you. This is the court of Mab. The Crawling Court has no claim to this domain, and that makes you less than nothing here." Whatever animosity Lelit has for me is firmly on the back-burner.

"'The court of Mab'?" Nevain asks, tone mocking. "I've heard a rumor that Mab's authority is wearing a little thin these days." He signals with barely a twitch of his fingers; one of the fae in his entourage lunges toward me, blade drawn. I barely have time to gasp and backpedal before Eifa skewers her through the throat while I trip on my own feet and fall flat on my ass. The dying faerie coughs once, sending a spatter of blood across my face, then Eifa drops the woman to the ground, plants a hoof on her chest, and withdraws her spear with a sucking noise.

For a moment, the room is dead silent aside from the twitching and sputtering of the faerie on the ground. Dreaming Court, Crawling Court—everyone is watching me look like a fool, realization dawning on their faces. Realization that Nevain is right: I have no power here.

Like a burst dam, the barrier keeping the bloodshed at bay crumbles. Dreaming Court and Crawling Court fae clash with savage intensity, all semblances of civility abandoned. It takes no time at all for the ballroom to become a battlefield of blades, claws, and teeth. The Crawling Court forces might be fewer in number, but the Dreaming Court turns against itself immediately, each vassal's forces an island out for themselves. Some lunge for me, only to get intercepted by others.

Lelit tries to rip her hand free of Leithe, but he grabs her wrist and holds it in place, pinning the snake's head against her arm before it can strike him. In response, she leans close and snarls something imperceptible to him; whatever it is makes him falter for a moment—long enough for a horde of uniformed guards to surround him, cutting him off from view.

I start toward them, but Eifa puts a hand on my shoulder and says, "Stay behind me." She hands me her dagger, for all the good that will do, and clears a path between us and the tangle of guards where Leithe was, using her spear to keep other foes at arm's length. Skye and Grandma follow close behind.

Before Eifa can reach Leithe, she jerks to a stop as an arrow flies past her face and vanishes into the melee around us. Without giving her a chance to recover, Hunter discards his bow and lunges under her guard, sword drawn.

Hunter pushes Eifa back a step as they trade blows too sharp and fast for me to follow. Skye watches, gun drawn, but she has no chance of a clean shot.

But the fight ends as quickly as it began, before anyone has the chance to intervene. Eifa uses the pretense of blocking Hunter's strike to catch his ankle with the butt of her spear and sweep his legs out from under him. She flips her spear and drives the point toward his throat before his back even hits the floor.

"Don't!" I cry out. Eifa freezes, tip of her spear pressed into Hunter's neck, blood welling up around the barely-broken skin. "He's just doing his job. He doesn't have a choice." Hunter looks at Eifa, looks at me, his expression not scared, only tired.

"And he'll be doing his job the next time he tries to kill us," Eifa says. "This is simply disrespectful." I worry she's going to stab him anyway, but she withdraws her spear and takes a step back. But before I can feel any sense of relief, she drives her spear into the flesh above Hunter's knee and twists at an angle. He screams. Something in his leg pops. At my expression, she only shrugs. "He'll live."

"I'm sorry," I say uselessly. Hunter only groans in pain.

Leithe is still engulfed in a sea of guards. Dreaming Court guards. *My* guards. "Stand down!" I shout. To my relief, they pause, conflicted, eyes darting from Leithe to me. Lelit's gone, vanished somewhere in the chaos, therefore unable to countermand me.

"Your Grace," one of the guards says—a man with black feathered wings. Before he can say more, a blade protrudes through the back of his open mouth and twists to the side, tearing through the corner of his mouth and exiting through the side of his head. He crumples to the ground, revealing a staggering wraith-possessed corpse oozing gray smoke behind him.

Another guard stumbles forward when Skye shoots her through the cheek. Leithe catches her by the back of her neck; she only has time to widen her eyes before the life drains out of her, limbs spasming, locking, then going limp before she falls to the floor in a withered heap.

Wraiths dart out of Leithe's shadow, hissing across the floor and vanishing into the melee. He surveys the violence around him with a sense of calm satisfaction. Wraiths slip into dead fae and they rise to defend us, forming a small bulwark that gives us some space from the rest of the fighting.

"You. *Asshole*," I say, free to be angry now that he's not under immediate attack. "How long have you been planning this?"

Instead of answering, Leithe nods to Eifa, and she and the zombies guide us toward the wall. For the moment, we're ignored. I nearly trip over a face-down, half-savaged body, too damaged for Leithe's power to make any use of. I can't tell to which court it once belonged. The horror is distant, as if I'm watching this on a television screen. It doesn't feel real the same way it did at the bar, just a few days ago, as if I'm already used to it.

Leithe retrieves a blade from a dead guard as we pass by. "I thought you left. I *told* you to leave. I told you not to come in the first place."

I stare at him, more and more unsure of why I wanted to save him in the first place. "Since we ran into Nevain? Before that?"

"Not the time," Skye says, pushing us toward the exit.

"Since you made it clear you weren't going to the ball," Leithe continues as if Skye didn't speak. "You accidentally getting the Crawling Court's attention created an opportunity to have our problems get rid of each other. You're welcome." Which was why he changed tactics and started trying to convince me *not* to go after Grandma had been taken. This had already been set into motion.

I should be angry, but I just feel numb. "Why didn't you tell me?"

"Because I thought you were incapable of keeping a secret." A pause. "Though apparently I was wrong. There are some secrets you *can* keep," he adds drily. "And I knew you'd whine about people dying, so I thought I'd save you the heartache."

"You mean you knew I'd disagree," I say.

"Because you can't help stabbing yourself in the foot and complaining it hurts to walk," he snaps. "But now both courts will be far too distracted recovering from this to go looking for you anytime soon. So, if you don't mind, I'm leaving before Lelit finds her second wind. Come if you wish." He continues toward the exit, ambivalent to the chaos around us.

"Oh, so you did it all for me?" I ask with indignation, but following close to his side. "Should I be grateful?"

"No," he says. "I did this for me. I hope they slaughter each other and spend the next century dragging themselves back together, one thread of muscle at a time."

"These are *people*," I say.

"What does it matter?" he asks. "They're not your people anymore, or mine."

He's right enough for the moment. Grandma and Skye are my people, and we need to leave.

We almost make it to the stairs—Leithe or Eifa dealing with anyone who gets too close—when the power of Lelit's voice freezes us in our tracks. "*Stop.*" For a heartbeat, every person in the room is utterly still, staggered by her rage. In the focal point of the glamour, I can't move my legs. Even Leithe grits his teeth and struggles to react as Lelit throws his zombies out of her path and wraps her hand around my neck, spitting words through gritted teeth. "You are not. Leaving. Again."

# Chapter Thirty-Six

Lelit's body pulses, whatever's beneath shifting as if unmoored from her skin and bones. "Not again," she repeats with a snarl. Her eyes, still a brilliant green, now look more like a reptile's than a human's. A burst of her power almost brings me to my knees, a cacophony of violent emotion ringing against the inside of my skull. Behind me, Grandma gasps as if the air has been crushed out of her lungs. Tears stream down my face.

Eifa's knees only buckle for a moment before she launches herself at Lelit. Without looking, Lelit catches the point of the spear in her free hand. Time seems to slow, flowing over the three of us like oil.

Lelit's eyes slide to Eifa's. "I see your wish," Lelit says softly. "The one you don't think you deserve to have, after denying it to so many others. But don't worry. In this, you've succeeded in choosing your own death, after all."

Time speeds back up. Lelit releases her hold on Eifa's spear as it warps and bends, becoming an ivory-colored serpent that arcs back and lunges toward its wielder. As the serpent's fangs sink into her throat, Eifa only looks resigned.

When I blink, the serpent reverts back into a spear, the point driven through Eifa's neck as if she'd done it herself. The bite marks are still there, leaking a liquid akin to reddish, molten gold along with Eifa's dark blood, venom being carried through the rest of her body by the final beats of her heart. Even as she's falling, Eifa's hand reaches for the sword at her side, but she's still by the time her body hits the marble.

After everything, she died in the span of a few heartbeats. Lelit forgets Eifa exists before she even stops moving, turning her attention back to me.

It isn't fair. With a weak, pathetic snarl, I slash at Lelit with the dagger Eifa gave me, only for Lelit to catch my hand and twist until the dagger clatters to the ground.

"This is truly the best you can do?" she asks with disgust. "If you can't or won't protect your court, then let us hope your old power is locked somewhere within your flesh. By consuming it, I'll be able to carry on performing your duty, as I have been." Her gaze slides to Leithe, who hasn't moved. "You have a chance to escape right now. Once I'm done with her, that chance will be gone."

"What do you think you can do before I reach you?" he asks. They stand, frozen, each one daring the other to move.

"Mab was your friend," I say, verbally flailing for anything. "Do you really think she'd want you to do this?"

Lelit stares at me, her skin tightening as if something within is trying to force its way free. Her expression is almost sad. "It shouldn't have come to this."

Skye's gun rings out; Lelit's head tilts to the side from the force of the shot, gold-tinged blood spattering across the both of us. But she doesn't fall. She turns to face Skye, the side of her face now a shattered ruin, but there's no meat or bone within. Instead, thorns and glinting scales catch the light as countless *things* slither over each other beneath her torn flesh. "I see your—"

Skye shoots her again. She empties her handgun into Lelit's head, shooting until Lelit sways on her feet, blood spilling freely down her body as a mass of hissing, thorn-covered snakes fight with each other to emerge from the wounds. And still she doesn't let go. She opens her mouth and tries to speak, spitting out a mouthful of blood. "You—"

Then an orange cat—shoulders taller than mine—materializes from the throng around us and pounces. Lelit shoves me away as the King of Cats sinks his teeth into her neck and shoulder, claws tearing into her torso. The King of Cats' eyes meet mine for just a moment, letting me see the smirk in them. He discards Lelit's howling form and prepares to lunge at me again just as Leithe shoulders in front of me and sweeps his blade out in an arc.

The King of Cats recoils, blood welling up from a cut on the tip of his nose. The flesh around the wound shrivels and wastes, and the great cat retreats back into the chaos around us, moment of surprise lost. By then, Lelit is already gone.

Skye shoves her gun into Grandma's hands and kneels next to Eifa. "Shit," she says. "Shit shit shit." She reaches to remove the spear from Eifa's neck, but hesitates, unsure. Eifa lies unmoving, eyes empty. It's not fair.

Leithe stands over the two of them, frowning. He bends abruptly and yanks the spear free, throwing it to the side. Skye grabs his wrist with a snarl, but he ignores her, instead grabbing the front of Eifa's shirt. When he touches her, a nebulous outline becomes visible—a spirit, a soul, a wraith—peeling gradually away from its flesh.

Leithe places his palm on the wraith's head and shoves it unceremoniously back into Eifa's body. "Get up." Leithe's voice is firm. When I exhale, ice crystals form in my breath. Eifa coughs, arms twitching as she instinctively tries to press them against the wound on her neck. Leithe lets go. "She needs blood and the wound needs to be closed; I can't hold her together forever."

Skye shoulders him out of the way, cutting her own arm with her utility knife. When Eifa—half feral—sinks her teeth into Skye's arm, Skye swallows a scream and squeezes her free hand around her knee. "Mom." Skye pulls her spare magazine out of her jacket, drops it at her side, then withdraws a crumpled cigarette pack. "There's a needle in this. Stitch her neck." The needle Chisel gifted her. Did he see that this is what it would be needed for?

The sounds of violence dwindle. In the middle of the throne room, Lelit and Nevain grapple. The rest of the fae have backed away and watch the two of them warily. Nevain is a mess, barely holding himself together. His skin is purple and bloated, looking like it might burst at the seams like an overripe fruit. Where he's wounded, he doesn't bleed. Instead, fat black leeches fall from the wounds, landing wetly on the ground.

Lelit looks no better. An arm and half of her head are now nothing but a mass of snakes. Her intact hand is wrapped around the bottom of Nevain's face, forcing him to look at her.

"I have you," she says, her remaining eye an empty pit. Even from here, I can feel its pull. Nevain sways on his feet. Whatever glamour she's caught him in, only they know. "I'll send you back to your king in pieces."

Something tickles my face. A trickle of someone's blood—maybe Lelit's, maybe someone whose name I'll never know—crawls across my skin and falls to the floor, where it flows toward the center of the ballroom, joined by countless rivulets—red, gold-tinged, black—flowing together in the same direction: toward Nevain.

"What's happening?" I ask. Leithe looks at me, then to the ground.

"Nevain's been waiting for enough blood to spill," Leithe says. "He's—"

Whip-like blades of blood scythe out from the center of the room, biting into flesh and bone. Fae fall all around us, both Crawling and Dreaming Court. There are few still standing. Any who can still move have probably long since retreated. Bodies litter the floor, some still groaning or whimpering.

Behind me, Grandma lets out a strangled cry. Skye clutches the side of her head and falls to an elbow, blood flowing freely between her fingers. Nevain's attack cut through the side of her face from nose to temple, leaving her eye socket a mess of blood and milky fluid. Grandma calls her name, cradling her, but Skye is unresponsive, from shock or worse. Her remaining eye is unfocused.

Nevain shakes his head, dislodging Lelit's glamour like water from an ear, then smiles at the carnage around him.

"Your creatures are dead, and our creatures are dead," Lelit says. Thorns and roses grow from new gashes across her body, but she hasn't backed away. "You know you'll never escape the Dreaming Court with the queen. Slither away back to your master." For a moment I imagine him turning and walking away. Eifa's dying, Skye's dying, both for nothing.

Nevain grins, his teeth sharp and bloody. "Who would stop me, really?" He raises his voice to address the room. "Who would like to incur the wrath of the Crawling King to protect someone who should be protecting *you*? None of you would dare, not when you have no queen to hide behind." He spits a glob of black blood in Lelit's direction; the leeches within wriggle away across the floor. "What would you do? You're half-dead already from your own court turning on you."

Surviving party guests peek back into the room from wherever they fled to, watching the exchange between Gentry with morbid interest. Even Nevain's remaining Crawling Court soldiers simply watch. Some brave fae sneak to the surviving banquet tables, as if 'time out' has been called and they weren't fighting for their lives moments ago. Even many of the fae I'd written off as dead struggle to their feet, their injuries already knitting back together. None of them object to Nevain's words. None of them step forward to prove him wrong.

Nevain turns his attention to me with a victorious sneer. He lunges with surprising speed, clearing the space between us in moments. His mouth opens in a snarl, tearing at the edges to become wider than humanly possible, needle-like teeth spiraling down his throat.

Several people shout at once, from the onlookers yelling in surprise to Leithe and Lelit calling out commands to stop.

I barely have time to raise my arms—little protection they would have been—before a series of gunshots cracks through the air and Nevain lurches to a stop. Something cold and wet splashes across my face and arms.

Wisps of smoke rise from his bloody flesh where bullets are lodged in Nevain's body. He collapses to his knees, screaming and howling and tearing at what remains of his head. Behind me, Grandma very calmly drops Skye's gun, picks up Eifa's spear—still shining with golden poison—and drives it with vicious force through his chest. Nevain's final howl peters out into a choked gurgle before he grows quiet, slumping backward and remaining in a half-kneeling position only by the spear through his chest propping him up.

Lelit, half in a lunge toward Nevain, stops short, staring wide-eyed at Nevain's body. After the initial shock abates, the partygoers start to cautiously laugh and chatter. The band—down a few instruments—plays a few hesitant notes.

"You killed him," Leithe says. "I didn't think you'd kill him."

"I killed him," Grandma says matter-of-factly.

"It wasn't supposed to be you," he says quietly. "You should run."

"I'm god damned tired of everyone telling me to god damn run," Grandma snaps. She turns to Lelit. "My daughter needs a doctor, and if you have any sense of *hospitality* whatsoever, you will get her one right now. Do you understand me?" Lelit, her eyes still on Nevain, looks so genuinely thrown off that I half-expect her to simply obey.

"Leithe," I say slowly. "What do you mean? Why wasn't *she* supposed to do that?"

"Too late to worry about now," Leithe says with a resigned sigh.

# Chapter Thirty-Seven

NEVAIN'S CORPSE TWITCHES. SOMETHING between a cough and a gurgle escapes from his throat, along with a stream of viscous black ichor. The heat gets sucked out of the room, along with the air in my lungs. More ichor spills from the broken remains of Nevain's head; oozes around the spear in his chest. It pools on the floor around him, sucking at my shoes until I take a step back. An empty-eyed skull bobs to the dark surface, partially submerged even though the pool *should* have the depth of a puddle. I've seen this before.

Nevain suddenly rises jerkily to his feet like a puppet on strings. His face knits itself clumsily back together until his mouth is mostly intact; one eye socket holds a milky white orb, the other is shattered and empty, leaking the same black ooze that's collecting on the floor.

"Should I stab him again?" Grandma asks with uncertainty.

Nevain turns to survey the people gathered around with eyes that can't possibly function, passing over Lelit, Leithe, me. "Who killed one of mine?" The words come from Nevain's mouth, but his voice is overlaid with countless others, with undertones of the howls, roars, and snarls of animals. It's the voice I heard in Martin and Chisel's basement, now constrained by a mouth instead of trying to crack open my head. The black mud on the floor ripples when he speaks as countless somethings shift just under the surface, occasionally close enough that the outline of a hand, face, or some inhuman body part nearly breaks through the surface tension.

"This isn't your court," Lelit says. But her tone is wary. Scared. "And you were not invited here."

"Death is always an invitation, and I bring my court with me wherever I go," the Crawling King says. "I ask again: who takes responsibility for killing Nevain?" His dead, borrowed face is impossible to read. When the king's gaze slides across Leithe, he seems to shrink beneath it. Leithe doesn't speak, doesn't look at me.

"I do." I almost can't get the words out at all. The Crawling King turns to me. The weight of his gaze makes me feel small, as if I'm balanced in his palm and the slightest movement from him could send me plummeting into an abyss. His power runs deeper than Noctiva's, deeper than Lelit's.

"Mab," he says. The word echoes in the air. *Mab Mab Mab*. "You take one of my vassals for your own and kill another. Are you trying to make a fool of me?"

"Nevain attacked us," I say. "We were defending ourselves."

"I have no interest in excuses. I expect this debt paid in blood. If you claim responsibility, I will take yours, unless you'd prefer a war."

"I killed him. Not her." Grandma's voice only shakes a little as she faces the Crawling King.

The king studies her impassively. "Are you offering yourself, then?"

"Yes," Grandma says. "If you leave Tam—Mab—alone."

"No," I say. "No she isn't." Grandma looks like she's about to speak, to argue, so I press on, if only to make a point. "But for the sake of argument: if I handed her over, would you go on your way and leave everyone else in peace?"

The muscles in Nevain's face contort in a lifeless facsimile of a smile, which tells me the answer will be exactly what I expect. *There's no point*, I wish I could will her to understand. *There's no sacrifice for you to make here. Nothing that will save me. He made the decision before he arrived.*

"I will take her as recompense for Nevain." He pauses, as if savoring the moment. "However, the slaying of one vassal is a small matter compared to the theft of another. Were you afraid I wouldn't grant my blessing for your engagement, or did you consider it beneath you to ask?"

"Your Grace," Lelit takes a cautious step toward the Crawling King. "No disrespect was meant. Let us make it up to you. Stay, enjoy the Dreaming Court's hospitality. We have kept your wayward vassal secure for you and he can be returned—"

Lelit's words cut off with a shriek as ribbons of rot climb up her legs, turning her flesh bruise-purple then black before it liquefies entirely. Exposed bones turn to dust before my eyes. The pool of ichor spreads beneath her, and hands break the surface, pulling her rapidly decaying body under piece by piece. Her body finally collapses into a tangled nest of snakes, some managing to slither desperately off into the stunned crowd. Leithe steps on a snake that tries to escape past him, the first thing he's done since the Crawling King arrived.

The king never turns his attention from me. Half of Nevain's mouth tilts down, as if the rest no longer works. "Or were you afraid to admit what you did?" He picks our conversation back up as if what he did to Lelit was nothing. "For the past century, my *polite* requests to speak with *my* vassal were met with silence or excuses. When I felt you on the edges of my realm just a few days ago, you fled rather than speak with me. How long did you think my patience would last, Mab?"

"I'm ... sorry?" It's almost funny. He's come not because Nevain is dead, but because I was *rude*. I swallow the urge to laugh before I offend him even more. "I've been on vacation. My messages weren't forwarded." After the ease with which he dealt with Lelit, I'm conscious of Grandma standing next to me, almost close enough for him to touch. "But you've already melted one of my vassals. I think that makes us even."

The Crawling King cocks his head. "Does it?" He turns to Leithe, addressing him for the first time. "The quest I gave you. Did you succeed?"

Leithe's gaze is unreadable, but he seems to contemplate before answering. "I went to the land beyond Faerie and returned with nothing I can give you."

"Very well," the Crawling King says. "Leithe. I have it in me to be understanding, so I'll give you a second chance to complete your quest. Carve out the heart of the Dreaming Queen and present it to me, and I'll make you my consort tomorrow."

Leithe looks at me. I look at him. There's nothing to say. This is what he wanted in the first place, even before

Mab. "Your offer is beyond generous, even in the face of my failure," he tells the king, even though his eyes are still on me.

"Don't you *dare*," Grandma says, moving to stand between me and Leithe.

"Grandma." I put my arms around her. "Stop." I look at Leithe over Grandma's shoulder. "Let them go home, at least. Please."

Leithe rolls his eyes in response. "You're both so disgustingly saccharine." He turns to the Crawling King. "Before I do this, I have a question for you."

"Oh?" the king asks.

"What will the next test be?"

The king tilts his head in confusion. "The next test?"

"Yes. The next time you get bored, will you have me steal the Blooming Queen's undergarments?" Leithe scoffs. "My answer is no, with all due respect. You and Mab can both hang."

I can't help but laugh. From relief, maybe. But it brings the king's attention back to me. "What did you do to him?" he asks. "What is your game?"

"I'm not playing a game," I say.

"Of course we are. That's all we've ever done." He studies me as I try not to cower, still half-heartedly trying to tug Grandma behind me. "I don't understand what play you're making now, though. Does it still amuse you to be so opaque to everyone around you?"

"She's just a girl," Leithe says. "And you know that. She can't possibly hurt you, so let her leave and do what you will with the Dreaming Court. Hurting her will only demean you."

"If you would defend her, then step forward and do so," the Crawling King says. I look at Leithe, but he's looking down at Skye and Eifa, and I realize he's standing between them and the king. He looks up at me with a slight shrug. I get the meaning well enough. He can't help me and protect them, and he knows which I'd want him to do.

I hope he's willing to help a little more. "I love you," I say to Grandma. And I shove her as hard as I can. She's strong—annoyingly so—but I still send her far enough for Leithe to snatch her arm and drag her from between me and the Crawling King. The king watches the exchange with mild interest.

"Aren't you tired of this?" I ask. Behind Leithe, I catch a glimpse of Eifa, a bloody swatch of fabric torn from someone's gown pressed to her throat, drag herself to Skye and pull the other woman's unresponsive form onto her lap.

"You asked me the same question the last time we spoke." He steps forward, and I can't help backing away. "Now you're acting like a fool." He studies me, looking for something. "What did you do, Mab?" He takes another step forward. "Or is this your trick?" he continues. "Have you already won this round? Trapped me in an illusion? Am I talking to a wall while your court laughs at me?"

"No," I say. "Like I said, I'm tired. I'm not tricking you."

"Is that so?" he asks. "Then when your rotten flesh melts off your bones, will your answer be the same?" The Crawling King's hand wraps around my neck, the flesh strangely giving against my skin, as if there's no bone beneath. He lifts me until the tips of my shoes barely scrape across the ground. "I don't understand."

A blade squelches halfway through the Crawling King's neck. Hunter tries to wrench his blade free, but it remains stuck in the ichor oozing from the wound. Rust blossoms across the blade, spreading down the metal. Hunter releases the sword, but it's too late. Rot stains his fingers, devouring flesh and bone. It moves up his arm, his shoulder, his neck. Strands of hair fall free and drift to the ground. Black fingers spread across his face, and he's screaming.

No, I'm screaming. I thought I might be brave, might go quietly, but *the pain the pain the pain*. Black spots blossom across my skin where I try to pry the king's fingers from me. The pain is so great that I lose control of my hands. The flesh drips away from my fingertips, revealing white bone. I taste the rot spreading from the back of my throat.

Hunter's on his hands and knees, then his hands and knees are gone. It's not fair.

The screams get farther away until I can't hear them at all, can't hear anything. Spots spread across my vision until I lose that, too. Then it's only pain. Soon, it's not even that.

I deserve this. Seven years ago, it should have been me. The scales are being balanced. I don't deserve to be alive. Don't deserve to be here—an endlessly repeating string of words. The shame is comfortable. Familiar. And I can chase the source of that shame to the truth: that despite the words constantly hammering into my head, I want to live.

I want to live.

I want to go home.

No, that isn't quite right.

Where there was nothing, I can suddenly hear the words that have been pressing against my head since I arrived in

Faerie. Even with no ears, I hear it. Even with no body, I feel it.

It's not fair. I shouldn't want it. Shouldn't let myself step over even one body to reach for it.

But I want it. All of it. I know why I didn't leave when the witch offered me a way out.

I want to win.

*I want to win.*

The pressure threatens to crush the shield I've clung to between myself and everything else. It becomes the roaring of waves, the hiss of sand over sand, the rumble of mountains.

The voice of the Dreaming Court digs its claws into my skull, looking for purchase. And instead of shutting it out, I reach for it, shredding the shields I built up. When I meet it, it slams into me with the force of a falling star. Like the popping of a bubble, the word—the single word I've been hearing this entire time—comes into violent clarity, striking the edges of my mind and faceting in countless directions.

My Name.

# Chapter Thirty-Eight

I DON'T KNOW HOW long it takes me to remember that I exist.

Then I remember me. Tamsin. Mab. I remember my Name, a word branded into the very air of this place. A word that somehow holds everything that I am. Every shame, of which there are many. Every triumph, of which there are few. But it's mine.

At first, I'm nowhere. Then I'm everywhere. I am every atom of the Dreaming Court, all at once. I feel life pulsing through the land, a tangle of veins and arteries made of the fae that reside here.

I'm in Blackbower, watching Noctiva weave in the dark on a loom made of bone.

I'm far above the desert watching a group of mounted hunters glowing from within pursue a silver-furred rabbit between blinding crystalline stars.

I'm at the bottom of an ocean, watching a procession of fae with eel-like tails and fingers as long and thin as strands of seaweed, bathed in the eerie light of their lanterns, which each hold a single glowing pearl.

A city of cats where a family sits down to a meal of live mice at a stately oak dining table.

A living mansion breathing steam and pumping oil through metal arteries.

At the edges of the court, countless human dreams rise and fall through the sands, endlessly made and unmade. A cacophony of sights and sounds and smells screaming in my head without end.

I don't know how long I wander—fascinated by the pattern of the starlight on water or the bustling activity of the market—before I remember the ballroom. And everyone inside it.

It must take years to find my body—the slabs of disintegrating rot the Crawling King made me into, still held in his hand, trapped in a moment. I pull them back together, mote by mote, then realize I don't know how to make a body. How many bones are in a human skeleton: two-hundred and six? How big are they? Where do the muscles go? Do I even have bones under my skin anymore, or snakes, leeches, or mud? Panic begins to set in.

The power stutters, mirroring my feelings. So I calm myself, let it go, and it flows into form like water filling a mold from memory. It already knows what it's supposed to be.

And then once again I have eyes, a nose, a mouth. I'm in my body but not apart from the noise. I'm still everywhere else that I was: in the market, between the stars, beneath the ocean. Hearing, seeing, feeling every inch of the Dreaming Court at once. It takes great effort to winnow the distractions away until I can focus on the scene in front of me: the Crawling King, hand still around my neck. I can feel his presence in a way I couldn't before: a rotten, moth-eaten hole in the court, a place he's torn from me. He draws power from it. From the death. But I draw power from everything else.

I want him gone. All I do is think the words and the power responds. It overflows, as if I'm a bowl filled to the brim and every movement threatens to make me spill over. I want him gone, and he's gone, along with the entire palace. There is no courtyard, no garden. Just rubble. The only thing still even partially standing is the throne, a large crack running from the base all the way through the face of the still-ticking clock. The ripples of what I did spread through the court. Elsewhere, the ground shakes; the stars flare.

Then I remember everyone else. Raw power ripples as my horror builds. More cracks appear; the ground buckles and sinks a few inches. I swallow those feelings. I don't have time to panic. I don't have time to think about how many people I just killed, that my family was likely among them. Instead, I force myself to go numb.

The Crawling King is still here. I can feel his presence like the sucking absence left by a missing tooth. I walk through the ruins that I made, toward where what remains of Nevain's ruined body is being pulled back into shape by the Crawling King's power. With each step, each movement of my limbs, power spills out. White moths flutter into existence and fly off from the air disturbed by my passage.

Far beneath my feet, I can sense the roiling ocean of mortal dreams rising and falling. The slightest tug on my part could pull them to the surface, could give them form. He's standing in the palm of my hand.

"I knew you cared for your court less than I did mine, but I didn't think you'd destroy your own palace, and with it all those creatures that looked to you for protection." The Crawling King laughs—a wet, choking sound coming from Nevain's ruined throat. "Mab, are you—"

I close my hand. It isn't hard to find a nightmare about bugs. They come when I call, exploding out from under Nevain's skin as his body collapses in on itself, suddenly nothing more than a pile of scuttling insects. The Crawling King fights me, but his will is far away. The piece of himself he's sent here to meet me isn't strong enough.

For good measure, I nudge a star, sending it spinning out of the sky and crashing into the spot the Crawling King stood. Then it's over.

I sit down and watch the remains of the star burn out with my knees pulled to my chest. A moth settles on my shoulder; others dance above the scattered flames. Elsewhere in the Dreaming Court, other battles are fought. A faerie child buys a tiny frosted cake from a market stall; a boggle in Blackbower wriggles desperately to escape from a spider's web. Each scene flows into the next, coming and going in flashes of sensation. I wonder if Mab could filter the deluge, or if this is how she felt all the time.

"It seems you figured out your Name," Leithe says. I didn't notice him approach, my mind in many other places at once. It takes several seconds to process what he said.

"Is this what it was like for Mab?" I ask. "It's all in my head at once. Everything that's happening in the court. I have to be conscious of every movement, every thought, every breath. One wrong move and I'll ..." I trail off, turning to look at the space where the palace once stood.

"I don't know," he admits. "She never said." No, she wouldn't have.

"Are you ... okay?" I ask.

"What an interesting question," Leithe says. I wait, but he doesn't offer anything else.

"Is he dead?" I gesture at the spot where the Crawling King stood.

"Nevain? It will take him a long time to come back from that," Leithe says. "The king? He never left the Crawling Court. This was an ... avatar. A tendril, however you'd like to think of it."

"Are Grandma and the others dead?" I ask bluntly. My emotions still feel far away. Like someone else's. Maybe I'm in shock. I can't make myself move, as if I can't remember how.

"Eifa, Skye, and your grandmother are alive," he says.

"How—" I turn to face him in surprise, cutting myself off before I can ask how they're possibly alive. Leithe's skin is covered in tiny cracks, some of which ooze wisps of smoke. I did that, I'm sure.

"With great difficulty," he says.

"And Hunter?"

Leithe is quiet for a moment. "Dead. Dust." I couldn't save him. He had to know he couldn't have saved me. What brought him to do it, whether at the end he thought he was making his own choice, I don't want to know.

I take in the ruin surrounding us. "Did the Crawling King kill him, or did I?" Leithe doesn't answer. "Or did you, by getting Nevain to come here?"

"Or did Mab, by setting up the pieces in the first place?" Leithe asks. "If you want to blame me, buck up and plot revenge like everyone else," he says. "Because I'm not *apologizing*." He says it like it's a dirty word. "I thought out of everyone in that room, Lelit would be the one to land the killing blow on Nevain," he admits with chagrin. "Not an old human woman. But by all means, if you're angry, you've got plenty more stars to throw."

"Do you think I would?" I wait, suddenly desperate for an answer. If he says yes, I think I might crumble into dust.

"Would you?" he asks.

*No. Never. I'm not a monster.* "The crater where Nevain used to be says 'yes,'" I say morosely. "I guess I would." I sigh. "Why didn't you take the Crawling King's offer?"

"I already gave my reasons."

"Why'd you help me? My family, I mean. You could have just left."

For a moment, he's quiet. "Because I wanted to. And I'm fond of all three of them, honestly." He sighs. "And I'd like to think whatever debt I owed Mab is now repaid."

"That's up to you," I say. "The dead can't give you anything."

"How very profound," he says drily.

"Lelit said that." I wrinkle my nose. "But I think she's right." I stand, my movements slow, deliberate. Even so, my power ripples and threatens to spill over. "I have to stay here, don't I?"

"Which answer are you hoping to hear?" he snorts. "Would you feel less guilty for wanting to if I said yes? Would you feel like a martyr if I said no? You have one of the most powerful Names in Faerie. I don't think you *have* to do anything anymore. But I suppose I'm courtless now, so what does it matter what I think?" I could go home. With the power I have now, I wouldn't have to worry about anyone coming after me. Go home and let the Dreaming Court realize it's dead.

Back in the ruined ballroom, a clock chimes. One, two, twelve strokes, each one a more insistent stab to my chest.

By the tenth, I remember. This still isn't over. "Shit," I say. "I promised to give Lelit my Name at midnight. If this had happened a few minutes later, I would have gotten out of it." Something in my chest tugs me toward the throne room. Toward Lelit, presumably, so I can make good on my promise. It's a strange feeling to be disappointed to find out someone *isn't* dead. "She tricked me. It's a long story."

"Then I should make myself scarce," Leithe says. "The fun is over. There's nothing I can do and I have little desire to see what she's going to do with your power."

"What does it mean to swear on everything I have?" I ask. "What will happen if I don't follow through?"

"You'll lose your body, your mind, your Name—all of them scattered to the wind. You'll be a powerless, withered husk at best. But for us, everything is inevitable; you would regain those things with time." He gives me an almost-sympathetic look. "There must be a loophole. Think."

For a moment, I'm quiet. Then I laugh. "I know what the loophole is. Stay. If you stay here, she's not going to win." He gives me a questioning look. "Trust me." I'd ask him to get my family out if it all goes sideways, but I think he'd do it whether I asked or not.

I return to the place that was once a throne room, pulled along by what feels like a white-hot tether threatening to pull my ribcage inside out. A bedraggled emerald snake the length of my arm sits on the arm of the throne, maybe the same one that used to rest on Lelit's shoulders. Surviving fae congregate here. Some bow; all keep a respectful, wary distance. A few of the musicians have even resumed playing a cautiously optimistic tune.

"Is that what you really look like?" I ask the snake.

Lelit's eyes glitter. "I always look like myself, as do we all." The snake's mouth moves unnervingly in order to form human words. "Did you have something to announce, Your Grace?" She must know by what I've done that I've found my Name, which means her deal is on.

"As a matter of fact, yes." I speak loudly, making sure our audience can hear. Lelit wanted it to be seen, after all. "I have something I'd like to say." I've never felt the silent, rapt attention of so many people on me before. Grandma, Skye, and Eifa are a ways away, Eifa and Grandma standing, Skye conscious and leaning against a mound of rubble. I look away. I can't think about them right now. Leithe hovers nearby but slightly apart. Hunter is gone, not a trace of him left.

I smile up at Lelit as guilelessly and pleasantly as I can manage, and I look out over the faces of our audience, the most powerful fae of the Dreaming Court. "Lelit has worked so hard in her duties as my regent while I've been away. Can we give her a round of applause?" I clap. For a moment, it's just me as the assembled fae look on curiously, then Grandma joins me. The rest of the room quickly follows, no one wanting to be the last one to obey. Lelit cocks her head, studying me with reptilian eyes.

"Great," I continue. "Lelit, as a reward for all your hard work, I'm giving you a break. You are no longer my regent. I'm going to return to my throne." My chest burns. The promise I'm breaking will tear me apart. I climb the final few steps and sit down on the throne to hide the sudden shaking in my limbs. "Though that means I'll need a new regent, in the event I'm too preoccupied to rule. And I think the person I could trust most with the position would naturally be a spouse, consort—whatever—which leads me to my next announcement."

The crowd is dead silent for a moment, then furious whispers spread in waves through the room, stopping immediately when I hold up a hand.

"Leithe, will you marry me?" His face is devoid of emotion as my question hangs in the air. But he can't say no. Not here, in front of everyone. We both know that.

Leithe's mouth twitches, but he inclines his head. "Of course, Your Grace."

"*So*," I continue. "If I go on another vacation and *anyone* makes things difficult for my future husband, I'll turn them inside out. I expect you all to obey him the same as you'd obey me." My message to Lelit, I hope, is clear: if anything happens to me, I leave Leithe in charge. *After everything you did, you lose Mab and the court anyway.*

I feel as if my organs must be unraveling, my body shaking with the effort to keep together as the shards of my broken promise dig and twist me apart. I might explode. I might melt. I might drift away like bits of dandelion fluff. I swore on everything I had, and I'll lose everything, but Lelit will lose, too. This was never what she wanted. And eventually, I'll be back. After all, I have forever ahead of me.

Anger burns in Lelit's eyes. "Of course, Your Grace." The snake's head dips close to my ear. "I release you." The words come out like a curse, but the pain in my chest vanishes. I fight the urge to cry from sheer relief. "Well?" Lelit continues at a whisper only we can hear. "You've won. What is to be my fate?"

I could crush her. Do a thousand times worse than she did to me. "Start organizing a relief effort. Clear the rubble. Find survivors." A few Dreaming Court fae grab an injured Crawling Court survivor as he tries to slip away and begin playing with him like cats with a mouse. "And ..." I hesitate, unsure. "And stop them from doing things like that."

"Of course," Lelit says. She looks at me suspiciously, as if waiting for the trick.

"Then you can do what you promised Hunter," I continue.

"... Of course," she repeats. She slithers off quickly, then pauses, head swiveling back to face me. "And congratulations."

"Well." I turn my attention to the crowd. "That's all I had to say. Thanks for coming. Enjoy whatever's left of the ball." With my permission given, the spell is broken, and the people return to what remains of their amusements. Soon, soldiers wearing Lelit's livery begin combing through the ruins, breaking up fights, freeing survivors, and piling the dead. Many of the dead—Crawling Court and Dreaming Court alike—are already being scavenged by the living. A harpist pauses playing long enough to ask for sinews for new strings.

"Quite a show, Your Grace," someone says in passing. It opens the floodgates, and suddenly people are crowding me, asking what I'll rebuild the palace into, when my wedding will be, where I've been for the last hundred years.

"Move, please." Eifa places a hand on the shoulders of two fae desperately complimenting my dress, points them in the opposite direction, and gives them each a firm pat on the back to send them on their way. "Thank you."

I slide off the throne and meet the three of them below. "Your eye," I say to Skye before I can stop myself. In place of the eye Nevain destroyed is one with a deep scarlet iris. The slash across her face has been stitched closed.

"Eifa and I are even," Skye says. Eifa has a bloody strip of cloth wrapped around the left side of her face.

"My life is worth more than an eye," Eifa argues.

"*Even*," Skye repeats. "I wouldn't have let you do this if I was conscious."

Eifa shrugs. "Consider it a loan. I'll retrieve it when you die." She turns and slaps me hard on the back. One of the nearby partygoers gasps; a few watch with interest, as if I might smite Eifa on the spot. "Good job."

It doesn't feel like it. "Thanks," is all I say.

"So you're staying here, then?" Grandma asks.

"I think I am," I say. "I don't know what's going to happen now, but I'm sure I can find someone to get you and Skye home."

"And what if we want to stay?" Grandma asks. I imagine building an exact copy of Grandma's house where the palace once stood, of continuing on as if nothing has changed.

"You can't," I say. "This place isn't made for humans. You'll starve, eventually."

"Well," Grandma says. "I suppose this is the same as any other job. You should get holidays and vacations. Nothing's stopping you from visiting on the weekends, is it? And I expect to see you for the Fourth of July. The Fosters aren't doing their cookout because ..." Her face falters before she catches herself. "So the rest of the neighbors are putting something together for them."

"I'm not sure I'll be able to—"

"And Thanksgiving and Christmas, at least. And Easter," Grandma continues unabated. "And your birthday, unless you have other things you'd rather be doing, I suppose. You can spare the time. I don't want to hear any excuses. You're not too busy." She pauses, thinking. "And give yourself plenty of days off. Two weeks—no, three. I didn't take enough days to myself when I was younger. Don't make that mistake."

"I ... okay." Weekends and holidays in the mortal world. "I'm the queen, I guess I can give myself as many days off as I want."

Skye lights a cigarette that produces red smoke that smells sharply of cinnamon, then crinkles her nose. "I don't know why I expected this to be anything like tobacco."

"Then why are you still smoking it?" I ask.

"Desperate," she says, studying me with her mismatched gaze. "Do you need us to stay?"

"No," I answer truthfully. In the distance, the palace gate still stands. I can see the witch there, waiting, just like I can see everything else. "I'll see you at home."

I watch them until they're gone, first with my eyes, then with whatever new sense this is. I'm there when the witch pushes open the palace gate to reveal a sliver of the mortal world beyond. The tear she makes in the Dreaming Court when she opens this door might as well be on my own body. After the witch ushers the others through the door, she looks back, and I know she's looking at me.

"Did it not cross your mind to warn me ahead of time?" Leithe asks, pulling me back to myself. The witch is gone; the door closed.

"Did it cross your mind to warn me about Nevain?" I ask. "If you're mad, then buck up and plot revenge about it like everyone else," I echo. "It had the intended effect.

Lelit released me. We can break off the engagement again. You don't have to stay."

"Does your generosity know no bounds?" He scoffs. "No, we won't be breaking the engagement a second time. If you're going to use me to your advantage, I'm going to use you to mine. And you still owe me a wish, unless you've changed your mind."

A challenge. A test. "I haven't changed my mind. Use it if you want. Hold onto it if it makes you feel better."

"It has infinitely more value unused." He crosses his arms and stares out over what used to be the palace. "Why did you let Lelit go unpunished, after everything?"

I'm quiet for a moment, searching for the right answer. "Because I wanted to."

"Well," Leithe says with a small laugh. "Now you sound like a queen."

We sit in quiet, but not uncomfortable silence and listen to the musicians play. Couples dance over rubble. Moths alight on the bloodstained ground, probosci unfurling to feed on the blood of the dead. All over the Dreaming Court, life continues. Terrible, beautiful life. And I am there for all of it.

# Epilogue

Skye's son's name is Kyle.

After Thistledown brought her the baby, the witch left him with a very confused nurse at a hospital near Washington D.C., where he was quickly adopted by an overjoyed Maryland couple and experienced an extraordinarily lucky childhood, only one state away from where he was born. He stopped believing in his imaginary friend at around the age of eight, but his parents still enjoy telling the story of how their son used to play with the ghost of a little red-haired girl.

After a private conversation with the witch—the details of which Skye declined to share, the witch took Skye and Grandma home, but left Skye with a story, a place, and a time.

Skye came here several times on her own. Now, she, Grandma, and I sit on a whitewashed concrete bench in the middle of the hospital's red brick plaza. Pockets of manicured greenery and cream pavers divide the space. Pink and red azaleas frame the bench, drooping in the humid July heat of the evening. Here, I breathe freely for the first time in weeks. In the mortal world, my connection to the Dreaming Court is dimmed. I'm not in a million places at once, only here.

Skye sits stock-still, staring at the brick-and-glass building's automatic doors, arms crossed, spine rigid, jaw clenched so tight I'm worried it's going to crack. "I wrote a new letter each time I came," she says, clutching a crumpled envelope in her hands. "But none of them seem right." She reaches for her lighter, then puts it back. "I thought I needed to save him, and the entire time, he's been here ... playing lacrosse and eating pizza." She laughs softly. "It's surreal, I guess. The one thing I thought I could give him, he never needed. This entire time, he's been living a better life than I ever could have provided."

"That isn't true at all," Grandma says. She starts to say more but Skye cuts her off with a hand.

"Maybe," Skye says. "But we'll never know, so just let me believe this was all for the best." She thinks, frowning. "The witch told me that putting him here was what she owed to both me and him. If I find out there's *anything* wrong. I'll hunt down all three of her."

Kyle is extremely punctual. At seven-fifteen, Monday through Friday, he finishes his shift at his pre-med summer internship at the same children's hospital the witch left him. The hospital doors slide open and a young man exits the building. He shares the solid build and strong jaw that both Skye and Grandma have, but his hair is a lighter chestnut brown to Skye's almost-black and he's got a few freckles across his face and arms.

The three of us fall silent as he approaches down the path. His eyes are on his phone as he walks. He looks completely normal, dressed in khakis and a white button-down with the sleeves rolled up to the elbows. He looks tired from work, but as he walks by, something on his phone makes his face light up and a chuckle escape his lips as he hurriedly types out a response.

And then he's walking away from us. Nothing magical happens. He doesn't look at Skye, there's no spark of recognition, no "Excuse me, could you be . . . ?" Not even the chance for the almost-smile given when one accidentally makes eye-contact with a stranger. He doesn't stop and turn back after he passes us as if he's had a last-second realization. The music doesn't swell. He just keeps walking. And Skye doesn't suddenly jump up and run after him. She stays where she is, watching as he waits at the bus stop.

I gesture to the letter. "Are you going to do it this time?"

Skye turns the envelope over in her hands, thinking. "No." She crushes the letter in a fist and shoves it into the pocket of the leather jacket I've never seen her remove, not even in the middle of summer. "These letters, I wrote them for me. I don't know how to tell him the truth, and I don't want a relationship built on a lie."

"People can surprise you," Grandma says.

"I don't want to turn his life upside down. He seems like he's doing alright. That's enough."

"One day, he's going to start looking, if he hasn't already," I point out. "It's the same as you. He'll always wonder."

"One day, maybe I'll have the right letter," Skye says, not taking her eyes off the boy's black backpack. I still think she might change her mind and go after him until he disappears onto the bus and it drives away.

"He looked happy," I offer.

"He looked normal," Skye says.

"Maybe next week, then?" I say.

Skye watches the bus until it vanishes behind a building. "Maybe next week."

# Acknowledgements

Wow. It took a bit longer than I originally planned, but we made it. That's another book down, and another to go. I'm officially more than halfway through my original vision for the Dreams of Faerie series, and I would not have gotten to this point without a truly incredible amount of support.

Thank you to everyone who volunteered their time to making this story better, whether it was by reading the manuscript during the revising process (in some cases, multiple times), or simply by listening to me work out my ideas out loud. Thank you for tolerating with grace and good humor my countless questions on whether a sentence read better with the comma *here* or *there*, and every other minor quibble that passed through my head.

Special thanks to Ryan, Jonas, and Sarah, without whom this book would probably be much worse.

# About the author

Grace Carlisle lives in Maryland. She prefers writing about fictional people rather than herself. Sometimes she posts on social media.

Subscribe to her Substack or visit gracecarlisleauthor.com to stay on top of book news and see the occasional animal picture.

# Also by Grace Carlisle

The Forest of Forgotten Vows